"REA[...]CE YOU'LL NEVER FORGET, MR. MacDONALD?"

"It's only a bronze," Sean said as he circled the dimly lit showroom close to the wall, enjoying every intimate detail, every muscle in the metal—soft, sensuous, alive—more like flesh than bronze.

"Oh shit," he gasped, when he stopped in front of the statue. The face of the man—raked with light—was burning with pain, his mouth twisted open in agony. His chest had been sliced to ribbons. His belly and gut gored open, bowels unfolding. Flesh hung loose, tethered to bone by sinewy strands of tendon. His loins, his thighs, his genitals had been brutally clawed, as if attacked by a wild beast. "I don't believe it," Sean muttered.

"Fantastic, isn't it?" Skip asked, sounding perversely delighted with Sean's startled response. He moved away from the doorway toward the bronze, but stopped well short of walking around and looking at it. "It's titled *Man's Fate*."

Other *Leisure* books by Donald Beman:
THE TAKING

AVATAR

DONALD BEMAN

LEISURE BOOKS NEW YORK CITY

For my children:
my son, Christopher, for his amazing courage;
and my daughter, Tracy, for her undying tenacity.
Thank you.

A LEISURE BOOK®

April 1998

Published by

Dorchester Publishing Co., Inc.
276 Fifth Avenue
New York, NY 10001

ISBN 0-8439-4376-9

With affection, I would like to thank . . .

My editor, Don D'Auria—for his faith and guidance: he has shown me that writers really can fly with the help of gentle words beneath their wings.

The Spoth Family/Donald Spoth Farm—mother Rose, and sons Don, Dan, and Mike—for the peace and quiet which allows me to write; Ruth Robson—English teacher, and self professed 'schoolmarm,' for her willingness to read and critique my work with candor; and Linda Lavid-for her 'scenic' passion.

Dr. Edward J. Spangenthal, M.D., and his associates at Buffalo Cardiology—for their persistence, saintly patience with my endless questions, and their amazing nuclear medicine team, all of whom have seen to it I will have many more years to tell my curious tales; my friend, Gerry Marmillo—for his uncanny recasting of a New York City cab driver; Jenny Wegrzyn—Interpretive Naturalist with The Buffalo Zoo, for her primer on birds of prey; and Susan and Chuck Reedy—for their genuine encouragement.

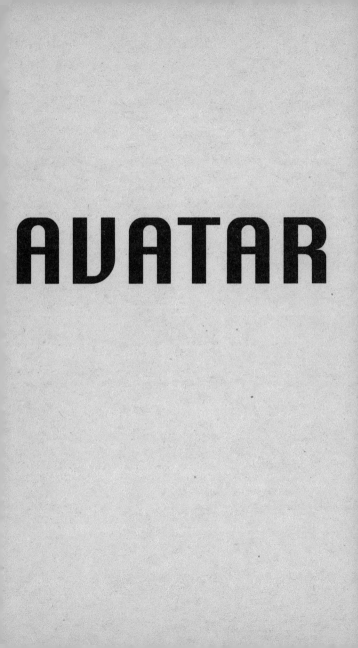

AVATAR

Chapter One

Driven by a sudden nor'east wind blowing in off Long Island Sound, the drenching rain succeeded in scrubbing the streets and sidewalks of Manhattan clean. The passing squalls accomplished in a few short hours what an army of broom pushers and a battalion of armored street sweepers would have needed a week to do. The tail end of those same on-again, off-again April showers—now only a steamy memory under the glaring late-afternoon sun—had chased Dr. Sean MacDonald in and out of doorways and sent him scurrying for safety beneath storefront awnings as he reluctantly made his way through Greenwich Village to the New York Academy of Fine Arts.

When the light changed, Sean just stood at the curb, staring down at a pond-size puddle choking the gutter, watching a candy wrapper drowning in a whirlpool of cigarette butts and Styrofoam cups. The irony didn't escape him. He asked himself again—for the umpteenth time—if he really wanted to go through with the assignment that had brought him into New York. His head immediately said yes: *You made a deal, MacDonald, you have no choice.* But his heart said no; that side of him wanted to be back in his study, working on his next book. To make things worse, something just didn't feel right, and he'd learned the hard way not to ignore his intuition. "It's your female side," his therapist had repeatedly told him. "Listen to it, it's more you than you think." *That's a lot easier said than done*, Sean thought.

He needed a moment or two to sort things out before it was too late. "Before you can't turn back," he muttered to himself, and inched back from the curb. But his train of thought was broken when everyone standing behind him bustled past, noisily chattering in Chinese as they skirted the huge puddle and shuffled across the narrow cobblestone street. Their unseen sandals, hidden by long silken pants, clicked and clacked over the rounded blocks of shiny wet granite, calling up unwanted images of the rapid-fire slap of ivory tiles on mahogany tables from heated games of mahjongg in smoke-filled back rooms.

Completing the distraction was the swirl of mysterious smells left behind in the still, damp air by the curious strangers. Sean felt a pang of hunger, reminding him he'd forgotten to eat lunch. Swallowing it away, he tried placing the elusive smells, but couldn't separate one from another. A lopsided smile tugged at the corner of his mouth, that awkward smile he'd been self-conscious about as far back as he could remember—had even been teased about it as a kid. He sniffed again, ever so gently. *Ginger? Coriander? Garlic?* he wondered. Nothing stood out alone, one hiding behind the other. *You're losing it, MacDonald,* he thought. *There was a time when you could pick out the sick lambs from the healthy ones just by their smell. Not even wily old Doc Peters could do that.*

He laughed. "Maybe it's not true after all, maybe you really can take the country out of the boy."

As those long-forgotten memories slowly played themselves out, Sean gave in to his smile. His deep-set hazel eyes wrinkled half shut, hinting at the age his athletic six-foot frame—the build of a runner—and boyish face hid so well. With a shake of his head, he pulled himself back to reality and slipped the letter from Bradley Johnson out of his coat pocket to read one more time. "Just make sure that you haven't forgotten something," he told himself.

Dear Sean:

Well, old friend, welcome aboard *Entasis* as one of our contributing editors. And let me thank you again for taking time away from your next book—Mr. Big-shot novelist. Seriously though, Sean, congratulations on your recent success: I'm sure it wasn't easy walking away from your position at the college. I know I sure as hell couldn't have done it.

"You didn't have to," Sean growled, a note of bitter irony in his voice. "You were forced to resign—and almost got me fired in the process—or have you conveniently forgotten, 'old friend'?"

With regards to the project you've graciously agreed to take over that was left unfinished when poor Bruce was murdered, I'm looking for a series of six or seven in-depth articles focusing on two parallel themes: Monique Gerard the artist; and Monique Gerard the woman. No one knows much—if anything—about Gerard's private life, in spite of the fact she's one of the hottest, if not *the* hottest, contemporary sculptor today.

Gerard's work has been characterized by one critic as a synthesis of Michelangelo and Rodin. At the same time, she's been labeled a "fraud and master copyist" by one of her less-than-kind critics, Allan Stern, who seems to have dropped off the face of the earth lately.

Your first interview with her has been set up at the New York Academy of Fine Arts in the Village. It's for 6:00, Friday, April 25th, an hour before the annual members' show is scheduled to open. I know it's awkward timing, but we had no say whatsoever in the matter. The guard will be alerted to your early arrival.

Let me warn you, however, that based upon Gerard's track record with reporters and reviewers the last few years—anyone who even smells like a critic—this assignment is not a slam dunk. I wouldn't be at all surprised if you didn't get past this first interview. Bruce was the only exception, for some unknown reason.

I want the first article to appear in the December issue—which is my annual review of sculpture—so have the drafts on my desk the week after Labor Day. This will give us enough time for any rewrites, which I fully expect will be required since this type of writing is new to you. Can't do it all, Dr. MacDonald.

"Don't push your luck, Bradley. I'm doing this because of Bruce, not you. And it sure as hell isn't for the money, although my agent did get you to cough up a nice fat fee. But then, from what I've heard, you can easily afford it."

Of course, if you have questions—or just want to talk about old times—call me. We can do lunch.

Regards,

Bradley R. Johnson
Publisher

Don't count on it, Sean thought as he tucked Brad's letter back into his pocket and glanced at his watch. It was five minutes to six. He squared his tie, buttoned his coat, and absentmindedly patted his pants pockets. Hesitating, wondering why he'd done that, Sean smiled when he remembered why. *Looking for a stick of gum,* he thought. Juicy Fruit, of course. This was one of the many old habits from his youth that had slowly crept back into Sean's life after he resigned three years before as professor of American literature at Hart College in upstate New York to write full-time.

Writing—not as a hobby—was something Sean had always wanted to do, but he had lacked the courage to listen to his heart, to heed a timid voice inside him telling him to pack his bags that summer after high school and chase his dreams. "I don't want to go to college, I want to go to Paris and write," he'd naively told his father. It never happened,

12

of course—those things rarely do, when we ask instead of take—but that voice was never silenced.

Sean had taken to the life of a writer like a duck to water. The stories he'd been writing and rewriting in his head for years, jotting down in notebooks still yet to be found—and telling to anyone who would sit still long enough and listen—were there for the taking. His compulsive nature saw to it that he was up before the sun, and at the keyboard, hammering away. He doggedly stayed at it until early afternoon, when—drained, dizzy, or both—he went running in order to untie the knots he'd twisted his brain into. "It's also when I do my editing," he'd told one interviewer.

On the downside, Sean could be blind to reality, unable—or unwilling, as his friend and colleague Dr. Oliver Shore had often said—to see the darker side of man's nature, even though it was a recurrent theme in his fanciful tales of horror, stories that had earned him his early success as a writer. It was as if he was unconsciously drawn to the darker side, the way a moth is drawn to the beautiful and hypnotic—yet deadly—flicker of a candle's flame.

When the light changed, Sean checked his watch again and shook his head. *It's too late to get out of this now,* he told himself, *and you know it. So stop whining and do what you agreed to do. It'll be over before you know it.* So, hurdling the puddle, he started across the street, still chewing on what Bradley Johnson had written in his letter. *Egotistical jerk.* The deafening blast of an air horn sent him dashing for the safety of the NO PARKING TODAY signs lining the other side of the street. Jumping onto the sidewalk, he started to raise his fist—toss the bird—at the driver in the truck barreling down the street, running the red light. Instead, he just shook his head, slapped the air, and turned around, coming face-to-face with a five-story brick building recently sandblasted back to life. The old Haverstraw brick, once red as wine and smooth as glass, was now porous and pockmarked, its mortared seams a thumb deep, waiting to be repointed. The cast-iron frieze over the converted storefront, now stripped bare of decades of old paint and rust, stood waiting for a shiny new coat of color. The setting sun, slicing between the buildings behind him—casting his shadow across the sidewalk and up against the building—added its own restorative touch, firing the powdery brick to the color of ancient cinnabar.

Stepping back, his hands stuffed into his pockets, Sean scanned the old building from sidewalk to roof. After peeking over the short, wrought-iron railing needlessly guarding the roof—starting, then stopping himself from counting each of the truncated spikes of the black iron crown—his inquisitive gaze bounced down the face of the building from window box to window box, yellow daffodils in some, lipstick-red tulips in others, and excited bursts of early red and white impatiens peeking out of the weathered wooden boxes beneath the row of open windows on the second floor.

Sean checked his watch again. *You're nervous, aren't you?*

"Yup," he said, licking the tips of his fingers and brushing the hair off his forehead. The soft orange sunlight turned the streaks of gray in his sandy brown hair to tarnished silver.

He took aim at the door on his left, but promptly swerved to his right when he saw the words DELIVERIES ONLY boldly stenciled onto the heavy, wood-planked door. He drummed his fingers over the words "New York Academy of Fine Arts" gilded in foot-high Romanesque letters on the inside of the blackened storefront window spanning the entire wall between the matching pair of deep-set doorways.

He tried the handle. The door was locked. He knocked, and waited a moment. No one answered. He tried again. Still nothing. He looked around for a doorbell. Not finding one, he jiggled the harp-shaped brass handle just to double-check. It wouldn't budge. About to knock again, this time with the heel of his fist, Sean was startled by the stuttering screech of tires behind him, flashing red lights bouncing off the building. He spun around.

"Where is she?" a towheaded young police officer asked as he threw the passenger-side door open and jumped out of the patrol car. His partner sitting behind the wheel, a man the size of a linebacker, was barking into a microphone buried in his meaty hand.

His hands raised in front of him, Sean shook his head. "I don't—"

The door behind him flew open, slamming against the building. A woman screamed, "Keep your fucking hands off me," as she stumbled through the doorway out onto the sidewalk, as if pushed. Blood was spattered around her nose and mouth. One eye was almost swollen shut. Her frosted brown hair was a rat's nest. Her black silk blouse was ripped off her shoulder, exposing the top of a breast. Her skirt was twisted and hiked up, stockings covered with runs, knees scratched and bleeding.

Pointing an accusing finger back into the empty doorway, she yelled, "It's him!"

To Sean's surprise, the young officer grabbed her, yanked her arms behind her back, drove his knee into her buttocks—standing her upright—and handcuffed her, ignoring her cries of pain.

Beside himself, Sean stepped forward. "What the hell are you doing? Can't you see someone's hurt her? Back off, for chrissake!"

The patrolman's burly partner exploded out of the police car and charged Sean like an angry rhino, blocking his path. "Stay out of this," he ordered, his chest heaving, face red, eyes bulging.

Chapter Two

A man—black, wiry, in his fifties, wearing a tailored three-piece, pin-striped suit—stepped into the doorway and said to the mountainous police officer, "She was in the showroom this time, Rocky, making a real fuss. I thought for sure she was going to damage something. She refused to leave when I asked. Got real nasty, too, swinging at me and swearing like a drunken sailor."

"You're lying," the woman cried out, and broke free of the young officer's hold. Head down, arms handcuffed behind her, she charged the open doorway.

With a powerful sweep of his massive arm, Rocky knocked her back into his partner's arms. She doubled over, gasping for air.

All Sean could think was, *What the hell are you fucking idiots doing!* He started toward her, his hand out. "Are you all right?" he asked. "Is there anything I can—"

The beefy policeman grabbed Sean's arm. "I said, stay of out it, mister." He turned to his partner. "Put her in the car, Kelly. And this time, try not to let the *little* woman get away from you." He turned to the black man in the doorway.

"You'll have to come down and sign a complaint this time, Dr. White. It's the only way I can guarantee we'll be able to hold her until your show is over. Even if she gets an attorney, she won't be—"

"I'm not going to stop until I see her, so you might as well lock me up and throw the—"

"Shut the fuck up, lady" the big man snarled, and raised his hand as if he was going to hit her.

Sean was now furious at what he saw happening. Ignoring the younger officer's wide-eyed shaking of his head—apparently asking him to stay out of it and not say anything—Sean was in Rocky's face. "Are you blind or just stupid?" he growled. "Can't you see *she's* the one who's been hurt, you fucking asshole?"

The big cop snapped to attention, his neck thick as a tree trunk, his mouth wired shut with the sinewy muscles in his huge, square jaw. Leaning his chest into Sean, he growled, "You can kiss my ass." Spinning away, fuming, he circled the car and stuffed himself in behind the steering wheel. "Move it, Kelly," he barked to his partner, and started the car with an angry slap of his foot on the accelerator. The fan belt squealed in protest, trying to keep up with the racing engine.

The hint of a smile appeared on the woman's bloodied face as she nodded appreciatively to Sean, just before her head was pushed down and she was unceremoniously shoved into the backseat of the patrol car. Slamming the door, Kelly hopped in beside his partner. The car lurched forward, tires skipping and chirping over the rounded cobblestones as it made a screeching U-turn, barely missing an orderly line of silk-clad cyclists pedaling curbside.

The black man stepped outside. "You Dr. MacDonald?" he asked.

Still unsettled, Sean nodded. "Yes, I'm here to see—"

"I know—Monique Gerard. We're expecting you." The man held his hand out. "I'm George White," he said with a winning smile, his face relaxed, as if nothing at all had happened. "I wear two hats here. I teach sculpture during the day, and—as I'm afraid you've just seen—I also play

17

security guard." He added with a sarcastic bite to his words, "Our director seems to think people will listen to a black man, and being the only one around here, I got 'volunteered' for the job."

Sean took George White's hand. "Everyone, that is, but women who weigh all of a hundred pounds soaking wet, right?" he asked, taking on George's innocent-looking gaze, challenging him.

Not responding to the comment, George bowed and invited Sean inside with a gracious but slightly stiff sweep of his hand, then followed. "If it was a man, I would have had him out without a fuss. But when it's a woman—and she outright refuses to do what you ask—I've learned it's best to back off and let the police handle things. Besides, she really wasn't about to hurt anything, so it didn't matter anyway."

What? All Sean could think was, *You son of a bitch, you lied to that cop?* Feeling himself getting angry all over again, Sean had to tell himself, *Calm down, MacDonald, it's none of your business. Just do what you've come here for, and stay out of it.*

He took a steadying breath. "From what you said, I got the impression she was here once already. Was she?" he asked. "And why was she so determined to come back?"

"Excuse me," George mumbled as he scooted around Sean and took the lead, once again ignoring Sean's questions.

Sean felt himself disliking George White more with every step he took as he followed him into a small lobby, the walls plastered with posters, notices for concerts, pleas for apartments and rides home, and the predictable adolescent protests about having to grow up. Sidetracked for a moment by the familiar images, Sean smiled to himself, enjoying the flashback into his own past.

"Ever meet her?" George asked just before turning and slipping into a darkened hallway.

"Meet who?" Sean asked. He almost missed the doorway, and had to grab the jamb and swing himself around the corner into the narrow hall.

"Gerard."

"No."

George patted the top of his head. "Keep down, the pipes in here are low. Give you quite a goose egg—and one hell of a nasty headache! I know only too well."

Sean dutifully did what he was told, going one step further and covering his head with both hands just to be safe, since he was a few inches taller than George.

"Know much about her?" George asked, sounding less than friendly.

Sean ducked to miss a sprinkler head. "Only what my publisher has told me, and what little I've been able to read about her."

"This is for *Entasis,* isn't it?" George asked.

"Yes, I'm taking over a project a former colleague of—"

George laughed. "I hope they're paying you a lot for this."

George held his hand up and waved it back and forth, as if to erase what he'd just said. "I was only kidding."

No you weren't, Sean thought, and asked, "Why did you want to know if they were paying me a lot?"

"Ask me that again after you meet her. That's if she'll even talk to you." George's laugh settled down to a smug chortle.

"But she's already agreed to the interviews," Sean said with confidence, which he realized was not echoed by his own feelings.

"Interviews?" George asked. "As in more than one?"

Before Sean could pin George down to what he meant by that, George came to an abrupt stop at the end of the long corridor. He braced his hand on a galvanized steel door painted with bright psychedelic colors. Smiling, he said softly, as if trying not to disturb someone, "She's in the showroom. The lights are out, so watch your step. And your head. Good luck," he said, making it sound like Sean was going to need it as he pushed the door open.

Sean nodded his thanks to George and stepped past him into the dimly lit exhibition hall, asking himself, *Johnson, what the hell did you get me into here?*

The only light in the enormous room was from a row of small, frosted windows circling the room two stories up, close to the beamed ceiling. Spanning the hall end-to-end, notched into the towering brick walls on either side, was a massive steel I-beam bracing rows of splintered wooden joists, sagging with age. The air was still, damp and musty. Statues, some realistic, others surreal, one or two unimaginable, cast eerie shadows onto the recently polished hardwood floor.

Cautiously, Sean walked past one sculpture, a monstrous skeleton of welded scrap metal, arms of pitted stainless steel reaching for the sky, twisted iron fingers tipped with rusted sickles clawing at the imaginary face of the sun. He ducked beneath another, a bizarre mechanical bird, hammered tin and feathered wings spread wide, suspended from the ceiling by shiny wire cables. In the center of the hall—surrounded by a mismatched assortment of metal and marble creations— was a larger-than-life-size bronze statue of a naked woman standing atop a massive rock, her arm outstretched. She was holding something in her hand, but whatever it was was blocked from Sean's view by the twisted metal arms of another hideous sculpture.

Ducking down, he moved closer to get a better look. "Jesus Christ," he gasped when he saw that she was holding the head of a man, ripped—not severed cleanly—from his body, his eyes filled with horror, mouth cast open in a silent scream that echoed through Sean's head, grabbed hold of his heart. The man's hair—vaporous strands of molten bronze cooled in midair—slithered through the fingers of the woman's clenched fist and coiled around her wrist and forearm.

Unable to move, Sean whispered, "I don't believe it."

"Do you like it?" a woman asked, her voice strong, confident, yet at the same time strangely feminine, almost seductive.

Momentarily startled, then soothed by her voice, Sean replied, "Hello?" as he traced the sound of her voice to a figure standing in the shadows at the foot of the bronze, facing away from him. She was short, her arms too long for

20

her body. *Gerard?* Sean wondered as he gathered his thoughts, which had been scattered by the unsettling sight of the bronze. Before he could say anything more, introduce himself, ask her if she was Monique Gerard, the woman raised her arm as if to command him to stop.

Obeying, Sean squinted into the dark, trying to see her better. Her raised hand was easily twice the size of Sean's, her fingers twisted and crooked, as if once broken, never set, and left to heal that way. Beneath a loose-fitting black smock, which had a silky, iridescent sheen, was a small but noticeable hump on her back, twisting her body into a permanent shrug. She pointed to the bronze figure towering above her.

Telling himself, *Don't stare,* Sean followed her point, first to the exquisite body of the woman, her face—that of a goddess—then along her outstretched arm to the man's severed head. "What do you think of my bronze, Dr. MacDonald?" She sounded provocative, sensuous, nothing at all like the diminutive misshapen creature standing before him. "Do you like it?" she asked before Sean could answer.

It must be her, Sean told himself, and said without thinking, "I love it and hate it at the same time, but I don't know why."

Monique Gerard laughed, a deep, throaty, womanly laugh. "Are you sure that it doesn't repulse you?" She clumsily shifted her weight to one foot and propped her hands on her hips. "As I do?"

Sean took a few steps closer, vacillating between staring at Monique Gerard, who was still turned away from him, and the mesmerizing bronze sculpture commanding his attention. A painful but somehow pleasing smile had been cast into the face of the would-be goddess. Sean let his gaze fall down over her perfect Greek form, only to be startled when he saw the headless carcass of a man lying at her feet, his arms wrapped around her legs as if trying to pull her down. *Or beg for mercy,* Sean thought with a chilling shudder. About to glance away, he was surprised to see that the man was circumcised. *That's unusual for a neoclassical sculpture like this,* he thought. *I wonder why she did it?*

21

Monique Gerard tipped her head to one side. "Love *and* hate?" she asked as if musing aloud. "Can that be? What do you think?" Her questions made it sound like a test of some sort.

Sean thought he saw her about to turn around, and waited to answer her. When she didn't move, he said in a matter-of-fact tone of voice, "What I see makes me feel—not think. I *feel* hate."

There was a long pause before Gerard asked, sounding thoughtful, "Are you sure it isn't fear that you feel? Fear of the fate that befell this wretched creature you see before you, a man like yourself."

Creature? Sean asked himself as he examined the head and withered carcass of the man all over again, then the body and face of the woman. "I know what I see," he finally said in a firm and confident voice. "And I know what I feel. Right or wrong."

"Oh? Really?" Gerard asked doubtfully. "Then tell me, Dr. MacDonald, what do you feel now?" She abruptly turned around and limped out of the shadow of the bronze. Her eyes were cauldrons of molten metal—instantly seizing Sean's gaze—her face a twisted lump of clay. Her nose was flat, nostrils wide, lips thick, cheekbones large and protuberant. Her long auburn hair, soft and silky—falling off her shoulders and cascading down her back—was a striking contrast to this cruel caricature of a woman.

She smiled awkwardly. "Well? Is it love or hate you now see, Dr. MacDonald?"

His gaze held captive by hers, his mind suddenly blank, Sean stepped forward, his hand held out, blindly groping at the air. "I'm honored to meet you, Mademoiselle Gerard." For some reason, Sean glanced at the bronze goddess above her, thinking for an instant he saw a resemblance. He just as quickly rejected that thought and looked back, falling even deeper into Monique Gerard's waiting gaze as she slipped her gnarled fingers around his outstretched hand. Her touch was surprisingly soft, gentle, but at the same time frighteningly powerful. Out of habit, something a man does, Sean tightened his grip, only to feel his hand being swallowed up in hers. She held firm when he relaxed his hold, adding to his growing sense of insecurity. She finally gave Sean his freedom; he certainly couldn't have taken it.

"Bruce was right," she said in a knowing whisper, as if talking to herself. "I *can* trust you."

Sean was surprised to hear Bruce Fanning's name mentioned, and in such a personal vein. "Bruce told you about me?" he asked.

Gerard looked away, giving Sean his sight back. In that instant, he saw for the first time what he'd been blinded to. He took a sudden breath and held on to it, steadying himself. She turned back, recapturing him with her hypnotic gaze, erasing those fleeting images from his memory. "We were dear friends, as I understand you two were. Bruce spoke fondly of you, Dr. MacDonald. It was as if you two were—"

Anticipating what Monique was about to say—what everyone had thought and many had come right out and said, presuming that because he and Bruce had been so close for so many years that Sean must have been gay, too—he said with a terse shake of his head, "Well, we weren't. We were colleagues, and very close friends, nothing more."

"You say that like you hadn't known he was gay. Did you?" she asked warily, and turned around to face the bronze—as if his answer didn't matter—her head tipped back, gazing up into the face of the severed head.

"I didn't find out until after his death, when the newspapers had a heyday with it. It was quite a surpr—"

Wait, Sean thought, *I'm supposed to be interviewing you.* He cleared his throat. "What in the world was that woman doing here?" he asked as he stepped closer to examine the bronze. When he did, he accidentally brushed up against Gerard. For a moment, he felt her—as cold as he was warm—before she recoiled from his touch.

"What woman?" she asked.

Sean gestured behind him. "That woman the police took away, the one who was all bent out of shape about not being able to talk with someone." He also wanted say, *The same woman that son of bitch beat up,* but thought better of it.

Gerard replied with a casual shrug of her shoulders, "I

didn't see her.'' It was a gesture that appeared painful for her to do. ''I only heard someone arguing with George when I was coming down from my studio upstairs. She seemed very unhappy about something.''

Seeing that woman all over again—battered and bleeding, clothes torn, convinced George had hit her—Sean's anger nearly got away from him before he reined it in. ''What's the title of this work?'' he asked, reaching up to touch the face of the man with the tips of his fingers. ''It reminds me of Medusa, only with a different twist.'' Sean absentmindedly ran his fingers down the leg of the woman, only to jerk his hand back when he brushed the arm of the man, then shivered at the sight of the open cavity where the man's head had been violently ripped from his shoulders.

The bubble of distant laughter made him jump and step back. He squinted at his watch in the dark. *Damn,* he thought. *People are already starting to show up.* He turned to face Gerard, whom he found watching him intently. Embarrassed, for a moment chilled, he smiled and asked, ''Would you mind if—''

''Not at all,'' she said without hesitation. It was as if she'd read his thoughts. ''George will give you directions to my studio upstate, where I do most of my work.'' She held her hand up. ''But you are not to give them out to anyone, not even your publisher. I'll see you next Friday evening, at eight. Please be on time,'' she said with a curt nod, and turned to leave, her exit slowed by a barely noticeable limp, as if one leg was shorter than the other.

Unaccustomed to being spoken to like that, Sean had to muster every ounce of self-control to keep from saluting as he watched Monique Gerard slowly walk away. He found himself struggling with conflicting feelings of compassion, repulsion, and unbridled curiosity. He smiled, but not because of what he saw or what he felt. *I know now why you wanted me to do this series, Bradley, and not someone else,* he thought. *And it had nothing to do with what you told me when you called.* Sean smiled as he watched Gerard disappear into the shadows. ''She wouldn't talk with anyone else, would she, Mr. Big-shot Publisher?''

An hour earlier, Sean wasn't certain he wanted to do this—take time away from his writing, chase down and interview some eccentric sculptor, stroke her ego, suck up, learn about her work, and, if he was lucky, write something meaningful about both of them. *Or make it up!* But now, with a hundred questions swirling around inside his head, each one begging to be asked first—the elusive image of Monique Gerard, coupled with the frightening images of her breathtaking bronze sculpture, fanning the flames of his already overactive imagination—Sean MacDonald knew there was no way in hell anyone could tear him loose from this project.

He glanced up. "Unlike your head," he said, resting his hand on the base of the bronze, only to pull it back when he felt a strangely familiar shape pressing into his palm.

"Oh, shit." He laughed, but awkwardly, when he looked down and saw in the shadows a tongue cast in bronze, undoubtedly ripped from the mouth of this wretched man, whose face was now etched forever into Sean's memory, like it or not. Unlike the face of Monique Gerard, who, no matter how hard he tried, Sean could not picture in his mind: He was left with only a feeling, one he realized that he liked, felt a kinship for, but couldn't explain why.

Chapter Three

The north-facing wall of the huge second-floor dining room in the Park Lane Hotel was plate glass, floor to ceiling, corner to corner. A single boxed-in column in the center split the panoramic view of Central Park into a sunlit diptych: Central Park West on the left, and Fifth Avenue running down the right side. Sean had remembered the column when he called to reserve a table for lunch, telling Max, the little Austrian maitre d' he'd gotten to know over the years, "I want a window seat, a deuce, away from the column and near the banquettes in the corner."

Staying at the Park Lane on Fifty-ninth Street—Central Park South to those who own pricy condominiums and co-ops on that exclusive strip of Manhattan real estate—had been prohibitive for Sean, given his modest salary when he was teaching. He only got to stay here when he came into the City with Bruce Fanning, and Bruce picked up the tab because he was billing one of his clients, more often than not a prominent dealer or wealthy collector. But thanks to Sean's recent success, the price of a good hotel room in New York, lunch or dinner at a halfway decent restaurant, and a reasonably good bottle of wine were no longer cause for concern.

Pulled back to either side of the wall of windows, tucked neatly behind the burgundy leather banquettes, were heavy, smoke-blue drapes falling from the ceiling to the floor. Below the chair rail circling the interior walls was a hand-painted flame-print pattern, flickering violet and orange. The fiery colors warmed the cool, slate-gray wallpaper, embossed with tiny yellow pineapples, rising from the chair rail to the cornice, a toothy dentil molding painted two shades darker. Floating on the ceiling like flowery clouds were white plaster rosettes, their centers, where monstrous crystal chandeliers once hung, now fitted with recessed spotlights. This elegant charade was exposed by tattered linen tablecloths, graying with age, pitted flatware, crazed china, and the harsh whispered exchanges between the short, well-dressed, gray-haired European waiters and the much younger, sharp-tongued Cuban busboys who refused to shut up long enough to learn anything.

When the hansom cab Sean was tracking through Central Park with his sleepy-eyed gaze disappeared behind a long row of cherry trees in late bloom, he blinked away and glanced at his watch, and muttered, "You were always late for your classes, too, Brad." He then absentmindedly flicked the rim of a crystal goblet with his fingernail, making it ring.

"I beg your pardon, Dr. MacDonald?"

Sean sat back and looked up. Embarrassed to find his waiter standing beside the table, Sean gestured to the nearly empty glass he'd just rung. "I'll have another Lillet, please, Anton—on the rocks this time, with a slice of orange instead of a lemon twist."

Anton nodded obediently. "Do you wish to order now, Dr. MacDonald?" he asked, his studied English failing to hide his lyrical Alsatian tongue.

Sean gave Anton's question a moment's thought, then shook his head. "No," he replied less than convincingly. "I'll wait for Mr. Johnson. He shouldn't be too much longer. He's probably stuck in traffic somewhere."

Anton bowed graciously, clicked his heels ever so subtly,

and spun away. Sean watched as the sturdy little man strode away, shoulders back, head held high—proud but not arrogant. No sooner had he pushed his way through the swinging doors leading back into the kitchen than a man appeared at the captain's station just inside the entrance to the dining room. He was tall, a bit gangly looking, with curly red hair, ruddy complexion, and eyes green enough to see from across the room. Middle age had spread its way onto his waist, straining his shirt, giving him the look of a pear with legs. Bradley Johnson scanned the dining room as he straightened his tie. When he passed over Sean, Sean scooped his napkin off his lap and stood up. Brad backspaced and zeroed in on Sean. His face lit up. "MacDonald!" he called out, waving his hand over his head.

Before he could take a step, Max, the maître d'—hands clasped in front of him—discreetly but deliberately blocked Brad's path. Once Max had Brad under his stern control, he led him through the dining room to Sean's table. His mincing stride forced Brad, easily a foot taller than Max, to take what amounted to baby steps.

Mutt and Jeff, Sean thought, doing his best to hide an amused smile as he held his hand out. "It's good to see you, Bradley. It's been a long time."

"Same here, Mac," Brad said gruffly, and reached in front of Max, brushing him back, to shake Sean's hand with manly exuberance.

Saying nothing, his disapproving frown speaking volumes, Max turned to leave. Before he could get away, Brad asked, "Maxie, be a good fellow and get me an extra-dry Beefeater martini on the rocks, would you?" He raised his hand. "Make it a double."

Without breaking stride, Max nodded and said as politely as anyone possibly could, "Certainly, Mr. Johnson."

Brad slipped into the upholstered armchair across the table from Sean. "Goddamned Huns," he growled under his breath. "Ought to send the whole lot of immigrants back where they came from."

Sean was about to ask, *Along with the drunken Irish?* but

he kept his thought to himself, not wanting to get off on the wrong foot with Brad Johnson. *After all,* he told himself, *you are working for the man, MacDonald. Show some respect.*

Brad shook his head. "Sorry I'm late, old man. I had to approve the cover shot and comps for the July issue so we could make it to press on time. Always some last-minute changes," he said, throwing his hands up as if exasperated, yet looking anything but annoyed.

Sean smiled. "No problem. I understand."

Grinning, Brad gestured to Sean's nearly empty glass. "I see you're still drinking that faggoty French aperitif. You never could handle a *real* man's drink, could you, MacDonald?"

Sean told himself not to say it—tried not to—but did anyway. "And I see you're still homophobic." As if in protest to Brad, Sean snatched up the glass and drained what little there was left of the Lillet. He then eased back in his chair, took a slow, deep breath, and said calmly, "I didn't get to interview Gerard last week." Expecting Brad to be upset, he deliberately waited for what he'd said to sink in. When Brad sat up, wired, he went on. "There was a problem with some woman who'd broken into the academy and caused a fuss. What with the police, Gerard asking me all sorts of questions—then people arriving early—there wasn't enough time to get much of anything done. So I'm afraid I—"

Brad slumped back in his chair. "Shit! I knew something like that was going to happen. It always does with that woman. Damn!"

Sean let Brad stew. He then played the rest of his hand. "So I'm going to her studio this Friday evening to get things off the ground. She wants me there at eight o'clock; told me not to be late."

Brad's face was suddenly alive with curiosity. He leaned forward and asked, half whispering, "Are you serious? She actually *invited* you to her studio?" He sat back, his head cocked to one side, doubt all over his face. "This is a joke, right?"

Sean did his best to feign ignorance. "Did I do something wrong? Are you upset with me? Should I call and cancel?"

Brad still didn't look convinced when he said, "Nobody has ever been to that woman's studio. *Nobody*. No one even knows where it is!" He eyed Sean suspiciously. "Where is it?" he asked, as if testing Sean to see if he really knew—if he really was going to Monique's studio.

Anton appeared out of nowhere and set Sean's drink down in front of him. Brad turned and asked impatiently, "And where is my martini?"

Anton nodded. "I'll bring it momentarily, Mr. Johnson. In light of your complaint last week, I asked the bartender to open a fresh bottle of Beefeater for you. Please forgive the delay, he had to send one of the busboys downstairs for it."

The moment Anton was out of earshot, Sean asked, "*Fresh* bottle of Beefeater? You could piss in that gin and it wouldn't make any difference." He laughed. "It might even taste better."

Brad struggled to suppress a smile. "You fucking Scots are all alike. You think anything the English make is shit, don't you?"

"No," Sean said, grinning. "Piss."

Sean's reply appeared to turn Brad's ire up a notch. "You think you're better than everyone else, too. But you're nothing but a wild bunch of sex-crazed Neanderthals, running around the fucking highlands in skirts, chasing hairy-assed highland cattle."

Sean's uninhibited laughter, which startled Brad, settled down to an amused chortle as he took aim at his onetime friend, and said with a smile, "At least *we* don't chase men, my Irish friend."

It was evident by the look on Brad's face, the cast of his body, his squared jaw, that he didn't appreciate Sean's comment one bit.

After a moment of silence, a truce of sorts, Sean asked in a solicitous manner, "Who represents Gerard here in the City?"

Brad wasn't immediately forthcoming with his reply. He sat for a moment, looking at Sean, his face filled with everything but an answer. "She's got a few dealers," he finally said. "But Skip Vanderbilt, down on West Broadway—although he's relatively new—is probably doing the best job for her right now."

Anton reappeared and set Brad's martini down in front of him. Brad practically dove into the glass, draining half of it. When he came up for air, he said with a sigh of relief, "Jesus, I needed that. What a crazy fucking morning this was. I'm glad it's over."

As much as he wanted to, Sean forced himself not to ask Brad about his drinking, knowing it would probably set him off and he'd order another—perhaps two more—simply out of spite, like he used to. He watched as Brad took another sip, then asked, "How long has this Vanderbilt represented her?"

"A little over a year now." Brad stirred his drink with his finger. "He's probably Gerard's tenth major dealer here in New York since I started *Entasis*." Smiling, Brad raised his glass in a mock toast. "Twelve years ago this month, as a matter of fact." Emptying his glass, Brad hailed Anton with a wave of the glass in the air above his head, jiggling the ice cubes.

Sean waited for Brad to turn back. "Does her work sell well?"

Brad noisily sipped what few drops there were left in his glass. "*Well?*" he asked. "Are you kidding? Snap your fingers, and they're gone," he said, and did just that.

Sean's first reaction was surprise bordering on disbelief. But then he reconsidered, looking at the quality of her work, setting aside the subject matter. "Are all of her pieces as good, artistically speaking, as the one I saw at the show?" he asked, still struggling with his initial reaction.

Brad nodded, nursing his empty glass. "It seems to be sort of a theme she's been developing over the last few years."

"What kind of prices does she command? On the average?"

Brad appeared thoughtful. "Nothing near what they're worth, that's for sure."

"Why not?" Brad didn't answer. "Do you know what the

one I saw in the show last week sold for, that's if it's been sold?"

"From what I understand, it did. And yes, I do know. It went for fifty thousand."

From what you understand? Sean thought. *From whom?* It was now Sean's turn to be skeptical. "*Fifty* thousand? That's all? That's insane. It must cost at least that just to cast it. What was her dealer asking for it?"

"A hundred and fifty."

"Who stole it?" Sean wanted to know.

It was as if a switch had been turned off inside Brad. He sat back, dead serious, his eyes more copper than green. "I'm paying you to write a series of articles about Monique Gerard, not a goddamned book on the art business. You're as bad as Fanning. You ask too many questions. Always did. What difference does it make who bought it? It sold, that's all that matters as far as you're concerned."

Hmm—touchy subject, Sean thought, and found himself thinking, *I wonder why?* Although he wanted to pursue this line, he knew all too well from once having worked with Brad that this was his way of giving an order. "Just curious," he said quietly.

Anton walked up, put Brad's martini down in front of him without saying a word, scooped up the empty glass, and made a beeline for the kitchen doors.

"Pompous ass," Brad snarled as he grabbed his drink, spilling it when he jerked it up off the table. "Shit."

Sean was struggling to keep a smug grin from getting out of hand.

"What's so fucking funny?" Brad asked.

This time Sean didn't give his intended comment a second thought. "I can't help thinking that maybe my grandmother was right after all."

"Right about what?" Brad asked, and took a hurried sip of his martini.

"She told me the reason God invented liquor was to keep the Irish from ruling the world." Sean finally gave license to his smile. "And ruining it."

Brad sat up, his weak chin melting into his neck as he

stared back at Sean over the rim of his glass for the longest time. When he put the glass down, his face was suddenly relaxed, matching the cast of his slumped shoulders. "You're never going to forgive me, are you?" He sounded more hurt than angry. "I made a stupid mistake once, Sean, which I paid dearly for. And in more ways than one. It was a long time ago. I'm sorry I got you involved. I was desperate, I made a bad decision." He raised his hand. "No, I made a *stupid* decision. I was the one who resigned, remember? After that, I couldn't get a position anywhere—not even as a goddamn tutor in high school!—or have you forgotten? What do you want me to do, kiss your fucking ass in Macy's window?"

Sean was surprised to hear Brad say this, to come right out and admit what he'd done, not twist things all around as he had in the past and make it sound like it was everyone else's fault, not his. The rift between them had occurred after Brad implicated Sean in an affair that Brad had with a student, which subsequently was revealed to have been one of many liaisons for Brad with students at the college. While Sean was exonerated, it was not until after Brad allowed him to be dragged before the Faculty Ethics Council, then the Board of Trustees, after Dean Potter had seen the shadowy figure of a naked woman in Sean's office late one night and, understandably, presumed the unclothed man with her was Sean. As it turned out, Brad had been using Sean's large two-room office in Merrywood Hall for his middle-of-the-night trysts with a number of all-too-willing senior girls, who were smitten by the dashing young Irishman from Dublin with a then thick brogue, which was now hardly noticeable. Even though the whole sordid affair had long since been buried under reams of lurid newspaper articles, along with as many private and public apologies by Dr. Bradley R. Johnson, it was something Sean still hadn't forgiven Brad for.

Putting his glass down, Sean folded his arms and sat looking at Brad, who didn't avoid his gaze for a second; he didn't even blink. "Why did you want me for this assignment instead of some journalist?" Sean asked, his question laced with skepticism. "We both know it would have been a hell of a lot cheaper for you to take that route, than what my agent—God bless her soul—got your managing editor to agree to pay me, I'm sure with your imprimatur."

Brad was chewing on his lip, his mouth twisting and untwisting itself. With a sigh, he finally said, "Gerard wouldn't talk with anyone else—not even me—after Bruce died. I don't know why—or how she knew about you—but she actually asked for you by name. You could have blown me away when she did. Does that make you feel better?"

Sean sat back, surprised that his hunch was right. Even more so, he was surprised to hear Brad admit it. *Have you changed?* he wondered. Before he could sort that thought out, Sean found himself wondering why Monique had specifically asked for him, and by name. Knowing about him because of something Bruce might have said in passing was one thing, but requesting him by name, and only him, to complete the series of articles was an entirely different matter as far as Sean was concerned. This prompted him to want to know more, and he asked before Brad could say anything, "Why is this Gerard woman so important to you? Why didn't you just drop the whole thing when Bruce was killed, and do a series on someone else? There must be hundreds of desperate artists in the art world for you squeeze the life out of. And a few extra dollars."

Brad fired back, "She's hot—that's why. Which means lots of people want to know about her. And they buy my magazine to find out about her, and about lots of other things going on in the market. That allows me to charge other people exorbitant rates to advertise in my magazine. And I like that money. It not only pays the bills, but it buys me lots of nice things." Hesitating, Brad asked sarcastically, "Is there anything else you want to know that doesn't concern you, *Doctor* MacDonald?"

Sean was surprised to hear Brad admit the truth a second time, and with such unabashed sincerity. He couldn't help asking himself if Brad had miraculously changed from the person he'd known years before, but that thought didn't last very long. Instead, he told himself, *Give the poor bastard the benefit of the doubt.*

He refolded his arms over his chest. "So tell me, who bought that bronze?" he asked, changing the subject. "You?"

Brad sucked an ice cube out of his glass and started chewing on it with his mouth open. "Me?" he mumbled, his mouth full of cracked ice. "I wish. Richard Hunt bought it."

"Who's Richard Hunt?" Sean asked, his curiosity piqued anew.

Brad snorted, as if jealous. "He's a semiretired business type who earned a fortune in some kind of plastics business on Long Island. Rumor has it he's got more money than God. But he's always claiming poverty. I do know for a fact, however, he gives a lot of it away. Some to museums, and some to fund exhibitions for new artists. That's how he came to find out about Gerard's work, from some purchase prize he sponsored. Had to be at least ten years ago—maybe even longer—before anyone knew about her."

Sean didn't try sorting that all out, he just filed it away for later. "Did Vanderbilt sell it to this Richard Hunt person?"

Brad swallowed the ice in a single gulp. "Nope."

"Then who did?"

"Anderson Galleries."

"Where can I find them?"

Brad shook his head. "Can't. Out of business." Sean sat nursing his drink, eyeing Brad. Brad finally gave in to Sean's doubtful gaze. "From what I understand, Anderson sold it before it was even cast. He made the deal from a Polaroid of the full-size clay model. He told me himself he got a fifty-thousand advance from Hunt."

"I thought you said the price was fifty—"

Brad held his hand up. "Let me explain. The *original* price was a hundred and fifty. Anderson got the advance, but apparently never gave a penny of it to Gerard. When Gerard wouldn't cast the bronze—because she hadn't been paid anything—Hunt was furious. However, he calmed down long enough to convince her to let him pay the foundry costs—

which would have been somewhere around twenty-five thousand—and also have it cast in a foundry of his choosing. After it was done, and he had the piece in his possession, Hunt turned around and gave Gerard ten thousand, cash, and told her that's all he was going to pay her.''

Sean thought for a second. "That only comes to eighty-five thousand, including the fifty Anderson stole. Aside from the issue of a commission, how could this Hunt person do that?" Sean asked. "It's unconscionable."

Brad grinned. "In this business, old friend, when you have the bucks, you make and break the rules." He shrugged his shoulders, his grin twisting itself into a sly smirk. *"Noblesse oblige."*

"Where can I find this Anderson?" Sean asked, suddenly feeling himself growing angry. He was surprised by his reaction, but didn't want to bother trying to figure out what, exactly, had brought on the feeling. He blew it off with a sigh. "Where is he?" Sean asked again, gently, but intentionally rapping his knuckles on the table.

"Nobody knows where Mark Anderson is. Not even his wife," Brad said with a wide-eyed innocent smile. "With all of the nosy questions you ask, maybe *you* can find him." Pausing, Brad added in a threatening tone of voice, "Just make sure that whatever you do isn't on my time, and doesn't interfere with what you've agreed to do for me." Brad stuck his finger into the table, then jabbed once more for effect. "This series must begin in December. It can't be late—there's too much riding on it—do you understand?"

Sean sat back, wanting to tell Brad he could go fuck himself, but something stopped him. Instead he bit his tongue, thinking, *You really haven't changed, have you?* He took a sip of Lillet. *And you still don't know me, either. Because if you did, you wouldn't talk to me that way—"old friend."*

Anton materialized out of nowhere. "Ready to order, gentlemen?" he asked, clasping his hands together in front of him.

Glancing at his watch, Sean shook his head, feigning a disappointed frown. "I'm afraid I can't," he said, tossing his head back and draining his glass. "I've got too much work to do, and really should get started.'' Smiling at Brad, Sean nodded curtly and stood up. ''I don't want to be late, especially now that I know how important it is to you,'' he said, buttoning his jacket.

I just don't know why. But something tells me I'm going to find out—call it intuition—with or without your help. Your lies have always caught up with you, my Irish friend.

Chapter Four

With the telephone receiver wedged into her neck, half hidden by her long orange hair, the woman seated behind the receptionist's desk in the makeshift lobby of the New York Academy of Fine Arts looked up at Sean, smiled, and mouthed the words. "One moment please." She then went back to writing down the lengthy message from whoever it was on the other end of the line squawking at her.

Sean resumed his count of the earrings in her right ear, peeking through her silky soft hair. In addition to a large diamond stud in her earlobe, which surprised him because it wasn't something he thought a student would have, there were six sterling-silver beads, arranged in descending order of size, curling up her ear. To this total he added the small, round-cut, emerald-green stud in the left side of her nose. Wondering if she had anything stuck in her other ear, Sean checked discreetly, but her ear was buried beneath her hair, along with the telephone.

Recalling the photographs in the window of the body-piercing shop he'd passed on the way to the academy, which he'd taken the time to stop and look at—gawk in amazement would be a more accurate description—he lowered his gaze. While it might have been his overactive imagination, he was certain he could see a circular shadow the size of a nickel pushing up the fabric of her snug-fitting turquoise sweater at the very end of her left breast, ever so slightly off center. At that moment, the thought of having his own nipple pierced made Sean wince and unconsciously grab his chest.

The orange-haired woman looked up, a question on her face, making him feel like she'd read his thoughts. Embarrassed, he turned away from her inquisitive gaze and began nonchalantly reading the posters on the walls around him. The name Allen Ginsberg—printed in bold black, fuzzy letters—jumped out at him. His first thought was, *Just like the old beatnik poet himself,* as he read a two-year-old poster announcing a poetry reading at a local coffeehouse, no doubt left up in memory of Ginsberg. Although he tried, Sean couldn't recall the first stanza from *Howl,* Ginsburg's signature poem that rocked America in the fifties with its angry, in-your-face admission of Ginsberg's homosexuality. Suddenly, the images of his mother's horrified reaction the afternoon she caught him—"hiding in the barn like a common criminal"—reading a contraband copy of Ginsberg's poems, was all too crisp and clear for Sean. "My own son—reading such trash—and at your age!" she'd cried. Sean smiled affectionately to himself at the memory of his mother storming out of the barn, waving the copy of *Howl* over her head as if it were a battle flag as she leveled the threat "Wait until your father comes home."

"May I help you?" the woman asked, her lilting voice— unlike that of his distraught mother—pulled Sean back from that unforgettable Saturday afternoon. He turned to face the woman at the desk, and said with a relaxed smile left over from his thoughts, "I have an appointment with George White."

The young woman sat up and drew her arms behind the back of the chair. "And you are?" she asked, tilting her head to one side.

With the sweater pulled taut over her breasts, Sean had all he could do to keep from replying, "Wondering if your nipple is pierced.'' His smile broadened. ''I'm Sean MacDonald.''

The woman's sapphire-blue eyes sparkled, adding another touch of precious color to her face. ''Oh yes, Dr. White's expecting you.'' Glancing down, she pecked at a button on the phone with one of her metallic-green fingernails. After a beep, she quickly hit three more, no doubt entering some sort of code.

She stood up, surprising Sean when she rose to his eye level. ''The machine will pick up now,'' she said with a confident nod and perfect smile. Then, sounding more like an executive than a secretary, she asked cautiously, ''You're the one doing the series on Monique Gerard for *Entasis*. It's *Doctor* MacDonald, am I right?''

''In person,'' Sean replied with a courteous bow of his head.

She gave Sean the once-over, even appeared to try peeking behind his back, then asked in rapid-fire succession, ''No briefcase? No tape recorder? No notepad?''

Sean didn't want to get into a discussion of why he didn't take notes, hadn't even taken them in college. ''Just pay attention and listen to what's being said,'' his father had told him. ''You'll remember more that way.'' He waited a few moments to let her questions fade. ''George *is* here, isn't he, Miss . . .''

The expression on her face, a skeptical one—but not the least bit irritated—told Sean she knew he was deliberately ignoring her questions. ''Eagleston,'' she said politely, just short of being cool. ''Pamela Eagleston. And yes, George *is* here.''

Pamela gestured for Sean to follow her as she started down the same hallway George had led him down the first time he was here. Only, she didn't duck into the narrow spur George had taken to the exhibition hall, the one with the pipes hanging down from the ceiling, and the garish psychedelic door.

''All of us do double duty here, Dr. MacDonald. George plays security guard when he's not teaching sculpture. Larry Anders, our art historian, who's on loan from Yale, handles the publicity and advertising for the academy. Jeannette

Brown, our ceramicist, takes care of maintenance, believe it or not. And Roberta Peterson keeps the books and bills in order between her drawing classes."

"And what's left for the director to do?"

As if responding to the dubious tenor of Sean's question, Pamela said sweetly, but nonetheless seriously, "I assure you, Dr. MacDonald, Dr. Howard is kept quite busy wining and dining people with deep pockets and a love of art."

For some reason, Sean felt unusually argumentative this morning and didn't know why. *Put a lid on it,* he told himself. "And your second job is receptionist, right?"

When Pamela shook her head, her hair flew out, revealing that her other ear wasn't pierced after all. "We've got a full-time secretary, thank goodness. Hilary had to go to the bank to make a deposit—we can't have checks bouncing, now can we?—so I covered for her. My usual part-time gig, when I'm not teaching painting and drawing, is modeling for the life study classes. Mostly for Roberta, but occasionally I fill in for George, when his regular model can't make it. However, she's here today, as you'll see."

In the blink of an eye, Sean had Pamela's turquoise sweater and tailored black slacks peeled off her tall, trim body. "I see" was the only thing Sean could think of saying without getting himself into some sort of trouble.

Pamela said with a lighthearted laugh, "You might say I challenge the students' creative imaginations." Before Sean could ask why that was, Pamela took a sudden left turn and started up a steep flight of oak-stained stairs, taking two steps at a time.

Sean had to do the same to keep up with her, only he didn't feel as graceful as Pamela looked. " 'Challenge' their imagination?" he finally asked. "How so?"

Upon reaching the landing for the second floor, Pamela turned around, hands planted on her hips, colorfully painted fingers drumming playfully over her pockets. "Now tell me, Dr. MacDonald, do I look like one of Fragonard's pink marshmallow ladies?" She locked onto Sean's gaze as if to keep him from checking to see.

Don't say it, MacDonald flashed inside Sean's head like

a stop sign, but he ignored the warning and drove right through. "You look pretty good to me," he said, and instantly wished he'd heeded his own advice when Pamela shook her head, a disapproving but at the same time amused smile fighting its way onto her face.

"So is it Doctor Eagleston?" he asked, trying to change the subject once again.

"Almost." Pamela started up the next flight of stairs, only now it was one step at a time. "I just completed my dissertation. The coronation is in August."

Sean had never heard that expression before, but he decided it rang true when he thought about how some of his former classmates acted once they were "crowned" with a Ph.D. "In fine art?" he asked, matching Pamela step for step.

"Art history," she said with a throaty chuckle. "That's my real love. I suppose that I'm what you might call a late bloomer. Like you, perhaps."

This one caught Sean off guard, and it showed. "Me?"

Pamela patted Sean on the arm, her touch a pleasant surprise. "I took a break after graduate school—ages ago"— she sighed—"and traveled around Europe. Actually, I painted my way from Glasgow to Rome, stopping here and there to study with some of the best contemporary European painters at such places as the Academie des Beaux Arts in Paris. I even made the foolish mistake of falling in love with a handsome young French painter, and getting—"

Pamela caught herself with a quick breath. "So that's why this thirty-nine-year-old woman is only just now taking her doctorate. But then, I'm sure you could tell I wasn't one of the students here."

Sean came to an abrupt stop. "Thirty-nine? You're kidding, right?" he asked, and resumed his climb up the stairs.

Pamela made an X over her left breast. "Cross my heart."

Sean looked at her in a whole new light, head to toe, and still didn't believe her. "No, I couldn't tell," he said with a subtle shake of his head. "As a matter of fact, I thought you were one of the students."

Pamela smiled, more to herself than for Sean's benefit. "It must have been my hair." She combed her fingers through her pumpkin-colored hair. "And this." She tapped the emerald in her nose. "I guess they're part of a second childhood. One just didn't do these things in Old Greenwich when I was growing up. Especially not with *my* father."

Sean hesitated, debating whether or not he should continue down this path of conversation. *Why not,* he decided. "As a matter of fact, it wasn't your hair or your earrings—or whatever it is you call that emerald thing in your nose—it was you."

Pamela was quiet for a moment. "You're sweet."

Sean chortled. "Sweet? Me? That's not something I can recall anyone ever saying about me." He half laughed. "Give it time." Sean's pace immediately slowed when he realized what he'd just said, and how it could be interpreted.

"Is that a threat or a promise?" Pamela asked, confirming his own fears. "Should I—"

Interrupting her—not wanting to hear what he thought she was going to say—Sean asked, "What did you mean a moment ago when you said you were a late bloomer—like me?"

Pamela said with a certain spunk, "I read your recent book, *The Strawberry Moon.*"

Sean was caught off guard yet again. "Really?" he asked in a surprised, high-pitched squeak, which only added to his growing uneasiness with this woman.

Pamela mimicked his response. "Yes, *really!*"

"Did you like it?" Sean asked eagerly, his voice under control but his reaction still unguarded.

Pamela stopped and leaned up against the wall, her hands locked onto the brass railing behind her. "Yes, I did, as a matter of fact." She waited for Sean to stop and look at her. "Mind if I ask the first-time author a few questions?"

Brace yourself—here it comes, Sean thought. "I suppose that comes with the price of admission." He slipped his hands into his back pockets and stepped back. "Fire at will."

Cocking her head, an eyebrow raised, she asked, "Why did you make the Devil a woman?"

Sean's boyish smile tried creeping onto his face. "Did that bother you?"

Pamela folded her arms over her chest. "Do you see all women as devils?"

His hazel eyes sparkling with amusement, Sean turned and resumed his steady pace up the stairs. Once Pamela was alongside him, he said quietly but ever so firmly, "Not to be evasive, but quite honestly, I thought the answers were there for the taking."

For the remaining two flights of stairs, Sean and Pamela went back and forth: she asking the questions, he tendering the answers, some direct, others evasive, occasionally qualifying what he'd already said. They took one step at time, slowly, side by side, without once looking at each other. The old oaken treads creaked in protest under the weight of their matched steps.

On the top-floor landing, the sunlight pouring down through the skylight overhead set Pamela's orange hair on fire. The harsh daylight also added age to her face, but it was still a decade shy of thirty-nine years. Pamela extended her hand and looked at Sean, her gaze slipping past his, deep inside him, before he could raise his guard. Uncomfortable, he was about to look away, but stopped himself. "Thank you, Ms. Eagleston," he said as he shook her hand.

"Please," she asked, refusing to let go of Sean's hand, or his gaze, "call me Pamela."

Sean nodded and said in a studied voice, "Pamela."

She turned slightly and glanced over her shoulder. "Tell me, Sean, have you ever seen a sculpture class at work?"

His gaze followed hers. "No. Why do you ask?"

Pamela gestured to the arch-topped door in front of her, which was slightly ajar. "Then you're in for a real treat."

Before Sean could ask what she meant—something inside him made him want to hold on to her for a few seconds longer—Pamela walked over to the head of the steps, sat sidesaddle on the polished brass handrail, and slid down the flight of stairs, toying with an impish smile.

When Sean raised his hand to say something, a chorus of laughter erupted on the other side of the door behind him, breaking his train of thought. He watched Pamela walk gracefully down the next flight of stairs and out of sight, as the muted sound of George White's voice filled his head and called up thoughts of his first visit to the academy, a rude reminder of what he'd come here for.

All he could think of was *Let's see what this woman-beater is like with his students.* Sean started, but stepped back from the door. *Wait—this is no way to go into an interview,* he told himself. But try as he might, Sean was unable to put the thoughts of that poor woman out of his head—her face bloodied, clothes torn, hair twisted into knots. What etched the unsettling images even deeper into his psyche was George's indifferent attitude, as if the woman were nothing. The thought of George lying to the police only made Sean that much angrier, then upset about feeling that way.

"Just forget it—let it go," he growled under his breath, and took a moment or two to let himself calm down. "Like it or not, MacDonald, you need his help. So make the best of it."

Chapter Five

Sean accidentally bumped into a battered metal coatrack standing just inside the door of the enormous loft studio. The empty wire hangers rattled like cheap tin chimes in a March wind. Heads turned, laughter died down to a murmur. Sean pressed himself up against the wall, wishing he could melt into it, and said with an embarrassed shrug of his shoulders, "Sorry."

From somewhere inside the sprawling loft—the walls, doors, and ceiling painted bone white, the hardwood floor divided into sunlit quarters by four skylights glazed with frosted, wire-filled glass—George White called out, "Come in, come in, Dr. MacDonald. We're just finishing up. I'll be with you in a few minutes."

Seated on a white marble bench atop a small, elevated wooden stage in the center of the studio was a woman, naked, black as coal. Her sumptuous flesh appeared to devour the pristine white marble of the bench. She was much older than someone Sean expected to see modeling, but nonetheless strikingly beautiful. *Delicious* is what came to mind as he couldn't help staring.

In a semicircle around the makeshift stage were a dozen young men and women standing behind single-legged pedestal platforms—some chest-, others waist-high—topped with miniature versions of the model, but in shiny wet clay. Surrounding the students, set a few feet back, were seven objects each as tall as a man, draped in dirty linen shrouds. Faceless ghosts on wooden palettes rising up out of the floor. Rope was tied around the bases of all but one of the figures, snugging the shrouds closed.

A movement in one corner of the loft caught Sean's eye. He turned to see George White carrying a yellow terry-cloth robe, slipping through the phalanx of shrouded figures, and winding his way around empty wooden stools, barren pedestals, and students busily putting this or that finishing touch to their version of an African goddess.

Stepping up onto the stage, George spread the robe out, his back to the students but not Sean. The woman nodded appreciatively and stood up. Sean felt a sudden rush of heat course through his body, his loins, when she reached behind her back and leaned forward to slip her arms into the sleeves of the robe, and her breasts fell free of her body, full, heavy. *Life's little pleasures,* he thought as she wrapped herself up in the belted robe, gracefully stepped off the stage, and padded barefoot toward the far corner of the studio, aiming for a small door marked "Office." Opening it, she slipped inside, leaving the door slightly ajar.

Turning to face the students, George clapped his hands, once and hard. "Okay, my children. That's it for today. Spray down, but don't cover up. I want to check everyone's work. See you all tomorrow."

In unison the students reached underneath their long-legged pedestal platforms, grabbed a plastic bottle dangling from a hook, and carefully sprayed their glistening creations with water, head to toe, all around.

George glanced over at Sean and stuck his hands on his hips. "Ready for a lesson?" he asked, the hint of a tease in his voice.

"Not this klutz," Sean said with a throaty laugh as he stepped aside to let the students file past out into the hall.

One of them, a short, stocky man with kinky black hair and a stubbly red beard—younger looking than the others—stopped and gave Sean the once-over, head to toe. "Want to model?" he asked, dead serious.

Sean leaned back. "I beg your pardon?"

The scruffy young man repeated his question, more slowly, and slightly louder, as if Sean were hard of hearing. "Do you want to model for us?" He sounded impatient now. "You look like you're in pretty good shape for a man your age."

Fuck you, you little shit rang inside Sean's head. "Really?"

"We want a man for our sculpture club's next project, but not some hairless beefcake. We want an older man, but one with life in his body, know what I mean? Someone who's in pretty good shape, not soft or pudgy—or wrinkly—like a lot of older men get."

He surveyed Sean once more as two of his cohorts gathered around, eyeing Sean like he was a piece of meat. "Well?" he asked.

Sean could hear George muffling a laugh. "When?" Sean asked defiantly, surprising himself. But apparently not as much as George, whose laugh abruptly turned into a nagging cough.

The young man held his hand out, looking mature beyond his years. "I'm David Rosenberg. I'll meet you here next Tuesday—six-thirty—to let you in. Okay with you?"

"Fine," Sean said confidently. "And the going rate?"

David Rosenberg grinned. "Immortality," he quipped as he turned and hurried out of the studio, the other students trailing behind him.

The moment Rosenberg was gone, Sean turned toward the sound of George's renewed laughter and said with a shake of his head, "I can't believe I just did that. What in the world got into me?"

George laughed. "Ego—and a touch of vanity. It happens to the best of us. But don't feel too bad, Rosenberg is a master at it. He can size a body up just like that," George said with a snap of his fingers. "One of my students told me he's only struck out once, and that was with a woman who, she said, had to have been at least eighty. Apparently, she'd agreed to model, but backed out at the last minute when her boyfriend had a fit of jealousy.''

Laughing even harder, George waved Sean over. "Ever model?" he asked.

Sean ambled across the studio, intentionally circling around the back of the man-size objects, looking for a break in the shrouds in the hope he could see what was underneath. "No," he said quietly. "But I guess there's always a first time for everything. Anyway, what's the big deal about taking your clothes off in front of a few artists?" Sean gestured with a toss of his head in the direction of the door the model had disappeared through. "If that luscious woman who was just out here can do it, and she's no spring chicken, I suppose I can. What do you think?" Sean stopped directly in front of one of the shrouded figures, the one without a rope around the base, his curiosity prodding him to lift the canvas and see what was underneath.

George slowly walked around one of the students' unfinished sculptures, nodded, slipped a section of old sheet over it, and sprayed it down. He went to another, shook his head, covered the clay, and soaked it like he was trying to drown it. At the third, he stopped, his gaze—his whole body—focused on the delicate clay creation. With the loving care of a parent, he gently put this one to sleep, wetting down the small cotton sheet with meticulous strokes of the spray bottle. Looking up at Sean, he gestured toward the office door in the corner. "By the way," he said, a broad smile spreading across his face, "*that* woman is a professional model who donates her time to the school between assignments." He paused and said quietly, "She's also my fiancée."

Shit. "George, listen, I didn't mean to—"

Apparently enjoying Sean's predicament, George raised his hand. "Don't give it a second thought. I took what you said as a compliment." He beamed. "She *is* luscious, though, isn't she?"

Sean stood in abject silence, hoping this would all pass. George went from pedestal to pedestal, approving one sculpture with a nod, rejecting another with a distasteful frown or shake of his head, until every piece had been put to bed.

A door creaked. The two men turned in unison. The woman, no longer a naked goddess, walked out wearing a sheer, white cotton blouse and ankle-length print skirt covered with purple crocuses and yellow daffodils growing on a background of cerulean blue. From the gentle movement inside her blouse it was obvious she wasn't wearing anything underneath. George looked at Sean and gestured to the woman. "Sean, I'd like you to meet my fiancée, Latitia Morrison," he said, and began grinning like the Cheshire cat.

Latitia walked up to Sean, toying with a smile of her own. "I couldn't help overhearing you offer to model." She glanced at George. "What do you think, sweetheart, should I sit in on his first class next week and give the beginner some pointers?"

Sean stuttered, "I—I didn't realize—"

Latitia patted him reassuringly on the arm. "No charge, of course," she said slyly. "Professional courtesy. From one spring chicken to another."

Sean laughed. "Touché," he said, and bowed graciously at the waist.

Latitia walked over to George and gave him a more-than-affectionate kiss. She then said in a throaty whisper, "George, dear, now don't forget to tell Dr. MacDonald how cool it gets in here at night, and what usually happens to the male models."

George gave Latitia a playful swat on her broad backside. "You better get going. You know how prissy Giancarlo gets when a model is late. You've only got forty-five minutes to get uptown." He pointed Latitia toward the door and gave a her gentle two-handed pat on the rump. "I'll meet you at the Polo Club at seven. Okay?"

Polo Club? Sean thought. *Which one of you has the money?*

Latitia nodded. Then she winked and smiled at Sean—warming him all over again—and left. Her fragrance trying to turn his head, Sean refused to let his gaze follow her out of the studio, regardless of how much he wanted to. Instead, he gave in to his curiosity and lifted the soiled linen sheet covering the faceless figure beside him. Before he could raise it above the waist, he was startled into dropping the cloth when George clapped his hands, but not before Sean caught a glimpse of the base of the massive sculpture—raw clay exquisitely worked into what appeared to be thick folds of heavy cloth, burlap, and the large, well-traveled bare feet of a man.

When Sean looked up, George had a disapproving frown on his face. "So. What is it you want to know about Mademoiselle Gerard?" he asked, and began rubbing his hands together as he paced about the studio, his shoulders, his whole body, no longer relaxed. For the first time, Sean noticed how large his hands were: wide and thick, as if hammered into shape, fingers bent, arthritic looking. *It must go with the territory,* he thought, before asking, "Are any of these Gerard's?" He pointed to one, then all of the cloth-covered figures. George hesitated, then shook his head. "Got any photographs of her work? A portfolio? Even Polaroids. Anything that'll help me get a better idea of the scope and range of her work, and save me from having to chase down everyone who's purchased one." He paused, thought for moment, and said, "Which might not be a bad idea, now that I think about it."

"That I can help you with," George said. "Be right back." He skipped into a lazy jog toward the office. He slipped inside, and popped back out carrying a black three-ring binder under his arm. It was thick, with sheets of plastic squeezing out the sides like an overstuffed pumpernickel sandwich. Walking over, he handed it to Sean. "These are photos of pretty much everything Monique has done since she came here. Most of the shots are of the finished bronzes; however, some are photographs of the clay models taken in her studio. The ones that look a little off as far as color are either plaster casts with a painted bronze finish, or bonded bronze, which is a composite of resin and bronze powder made to look like bronze. It weighs a lot less, and costs a hell of a lot less, too. There are also a number of plaster casts in there, which were commissioned works Monique never

51

had cast into bronze. I'm told the client, or clients, currently have them. They're Hollywood types, as I'm sure you'll recognize from the images."

George led Sean to the stage and sat him down on the marble bench. "Take your time," he said with a pat of the binder. "I've got a few phone calls to make. I'll be back in ten or fifteen minutes." As George started to leave, he said with a chortle, "When you finish, you can practice your poses for next week."

Sean sat watching George walk out of the studio. He realized he was coming to like the man, which upset him in light of what he was convinced George had done. *Why didn't she tell the cops what happened?* he wondered. Sean was suddenly struck with a thought he wasn't prepared for, one he couldn't answer without overturning his conviction of George White. *What if he's covering for Monique, and she's the one who roughed that woman up?*

He shook his head. *That doesn't make sense,* he told himself as he opened the binder and just as quickly shut it, unprepared for what he saw.

Chapter Six

George could be heard coming back up the stairs, humming to himself. His deep voice resonated melodically in the cavernous stairwell. His slow, metered pace, accompanied by the creak of each tired wooden tread, created an eerie sound a beat faster than a dirge. When he reached the landing outside the studio, he changed his tune, giving it a jazzy, upbeat bounce as he glided into the loft, head down, fingers snapping, as if in another world.

When he looked up, he stumbled to a stop. "What the hell?"

The previously hidden sculptures—all seven—had been defrocked, their soiled linen garments tossed over unused sculpting pedestals standing nearby. Stuck into the folds of fabric on one pedestal was a large black-and-white photograph positioned so that it was facing the stage, where Sean was sitting on the marble bench. His gaze was bouncing back and forth between a cluster of photos in his free hand, fanned out like giant playing cards, and the imposing figures surrounding him, each one garbed in heavy, floor-length robes delicately crafted from clay. Braided ropes circled their thick waists, the frayed ends hanging down at their sides. Hoods were pulled up over the heads of three of them, but failed to hide their hideous faces. The other four were bare-headed, their faces just as frightening.

Sean glanced at George, who appeared anything but pleased. "Look what I found," Sean said. He gestured toward the sculptures glowering back at him, and waited for George to say something. But George just stood there, hands stuffed deep into the pockets of his clay-smudged jeans, hiding behind an all-too-convenient scowl.

Ignoring him, Sean slapped the photographs down onto the binder lying open on the bench beside him, stood up, and marched toward one of the sculptures, the second one from the left. He stopped a few feet away, arm outstretched, and turned to face George. "My guess is this one's titled *Lust.*" Without waiting for George to comment, he stepped to the next one, the third masterful creation in the regimented row of tall, medieval-looking figures. "And this one is titled *Envy.*" He pointed to the next sculpture, the most frightening of the group, its oversized head covered with a hood, eyes raging, stone jaw locked into a fierce growl. It looked like Sean didn't want to get too close to it. "And that one would be titled *Anger.*"

Snatching the photograph off the pedestal beside him, Sean waved it at George, as if taunting him. Although his words were soft-spoken, they honed with a razor sharp cynical edge. "Unless I'm blind—and stupid—I'd say that the same person who sculpted this piece—" He shook his hand, causing the sheet of stiff photographic paper to make a wobbling sound, and held it up to the sculpted face beside him. "Also created this one."

Sean walked backward toward the stage, his arm held out, photo in hand. Using it as a pointer, he took aim at the first sculpture and said with a decisive snap of his wrist, "That's *Pride.*" He then went down the line, pausing at each figure only long enough to stab the air with the photo and say accusingly, *"Covetousness. Gluttony.* And finally *Sloth.*"

He turned and hopped up onto the stage, arms spread, head cocked to one side. "I'd say that we've got an example of the seven deadly sins, Dr. White, wouldn't you agree? And from the looks of it, I'd also say they were created by the gifted hands of Mademoiselle Monique Gerard. What do you think?'' Sean made it sound like he really didn't need, or even care if he got, an answer to his question.

George stood staring at the ominous, warlike figures. ''They're fantastic, aren't they?'' he finally said, his gaze drifting slowly, admiringly, from one piece to the next. ''When I saw the first one the morning after she'd finished it, I couldn't help thinking I was looking at a Rodin, only better.'' George appeared to shiver. ''The woman touches the earth and creates life. Only God has done that.''

In silence, with Sean watching, George set about carefully covering up the towering clay sculptures, all of them a head taller than he. His task completed, he moved quietly over to the stage. There, he sat beside Sean and leaned back, his hands braced on the edge of the marble bench. He crossed his legs, a thoughtful look on his face. ''It'll be ten years this August since this little misshapen, dwarflike creature walked into my studio one morning, out of the blue. Hobbled is more like it. Her head was down, her face hidden by an explosion of hair so soft and silky I was tempted to run my fingers through it to see if it was real.'' George's gaze was now somewhere off in the distance. ''At first, I thought it was one of my students playing a joke on me.'' He shook his head. ''Thankfully, I didn't say anything. I think Monique might have run away if I had. She was carrying something in a gunny sack. It was obviously heavy by the way the sack pulled at the straps. She asked if I would look at it and tell her what I thought of her work. When I saw her hand, just before she reached into that sack—before I even saw what she had in there—I knew that instant she was in great pain, and something told me she was genius.''

George paused, gave up a subtle shiver, and went on with his story. ''She pulled this head out—fired clay, unglazed— and my heart stopped. It was the head of Christ, unbearable pain sculpted into every crease and crevice of his face. The crown of thorns was so lifelike, so sharp, the wounds so real, my head hurt just looking at it. His eyes were filled with love. It took my breath away. I almost cried. I probably would have, had she not slipped it back into the sack.''

George finally looked at Sean. "It was as if she knew, as if she'd read my mind, felt my pain. Then she looked at me and—''

George took what appeared to be a much needed breath, then another, before continuing his tale of that first meeting with Monique Gerard a decade ago. His reactions, his recollections, his feelings, were as real as if the encounter had taken place only an hour ago. Leaning back, Sean gave himself up to George's apparently spontaneous tale. His eyes tracked George's every gesture, his ears tuned to every soft-spoken word. He followed every twist and turn in what became a turbulent journey spanning ten years, but sounded like a lifetime. George spoke of Monique more like a stranger than a colleague, and never like a friend. This left Sean confused at first, then skeptical when it began to sound rehearsed.

Much to Sean's irritation, which he had to work hard at hiding, not once did George respond to any of his questions about how Monique came to choose the subjects of her work, beginning with the seven deadly sins, which George revealed Monique had titled *The Seven Cardinal Sins*. Sean asked about other works selected at random from the extensive portfolio, only to be stonewalled on these, too, with the excuse, "She never told me, she said it was unimportant.''

When, out of frustration, Sean asked to borrow the portfolio until his articles were written, George adamantly refused. But he quickly reconsidered when Sean made his case that the portfolio would ensure a comprehensive review of her entire body of work.

Sean soon realized, in spite of all George had to say, that George never once revealed anything of substance about Monique Gerard, whether it was her personal likes and dislikes, her academic training, who she worked with in her early years, how long she'd been sculpting, or even something simple, like how old she was. After two hours, other than knowing of George's devotion to her, as well as his awe of her as an artist—perhaps even his fear of her, if Sean was reading him right—Sean knew little more about Monique Gerard the artist—and the woman—than he had when he first arrived.

He now knew it was Monique he must talk with; therefore, what George had to say was no longer of any interest to him. Or value. Making up an excuse to leave, Sean parted on friendly, even affectionate, terms with George, the bulky portfolio tucked safely under his arm.

As he walked slowly down the five flights of stairs, Sean found himself looking forward with mixed feelings to his meeting with Monique Gerard: the excitement of discovery, something new, tempered by the nagging doubt of uncertainty. Nonetheless, he began ordering and reordering the dozens of questions he knew he wanted to ask her, while struggling to keep the ominous images inside the black binder from clouding his thoughts.

Whatever shreds of ambivalence Sean harbored about this assignment were now completely forgotten. Except for one thing: his desire to know what really had happened to that woman, whose words for some reason he couldn't—perhaps didn't want to—forget. He recalled what she'd yelled at George—*It's him*—as he walked through the lobby, was disappointed not to find Pamela there, and slipped outside.

Struggling with his newfound feelings about George, with what he'd thought about him before today, Sean began talking to himself as he walked to the curb. "You just don't dress the way that woman did, like a lady, and act like anything but a lady. Something happened, and it it's not what George said happened."

Sean began to cross the cobblestone street, but stopped and looked both ways, the memory of being chased by a truck all too vivid. *Who was she?* he wondered as he darted across the street and onto the sidewalk. *And what the hell had she really been doing here in the first place?*

Chapter Seven

The cabby was a bull-necked little Italian barely tall enough to see over the steering wheel. His fingers were thick, stubby, and leathery, like a pair of old baseball mitts. He shook his head slowly. Each time he turned, the late-afternoon sun streaming in through the grimy passenger-side window bounced off the top of his oily bald head, making it glow: on then off, on then off. He finally looked up into the rear-view mirror, his dark brown Mediterranean eyes filled with curiosity. "Was it Jimmy Stewart?"

Sean slid over and wedged himself into the corner of the backseat, as if trying to dodge the question, and thought, *You never should have answered him the first time. When are you going to learn?* He glanced at the license posted on the back of the seat in front of him, and read the driver's name to himself. *Giuseppe Antonio Marmillo. What is it about Italians and westerns?* Sean wondered, hoping Giuseppe would take a cue from his silence and drop the whole thing.

But Giuseppe wasn't about to play by Sean's rules. "What about Henry Fonda?" He sounded excited. Eager. "He's tall and skinny, too."

Realizing there was no way out, that he had to play—*You started it*, he told himself—Sean shook his head and said decisively, "No. Fonda starred in *Grapes of Wrath*. He was really good in it, too. For my money, he carried the movie. But it wasn't as good as the book. Movies never are. *Grapes of Wrath* was a great book, a true masterpiece of American literature."

Giuseppe sat glancing back and forth between the rearview mirror and the traffic snaking its way through Central Park toward Fifty-ninth Street. Frowning, he asked with a degree of cautious optimism, "You teach college, don't you?"

Caught off guard, Sean hesitated—thought about lying—then smiled and nodded. "I did. Not anymore. How could you tell?" he asked.

Giuseppe appeared pleased with himself. "Not many people I get in here would know about *The Grapes of Wrath*—especially the book—let alone call it a masterpiece of American literature." He nodded. "Steinbeck was a genius. But my favorite story of his was *Travels with Charlie*. You know, the one he wrote about him driving around California with a big old lovable poodle, revisiting the places from his childhood. That book showed me a side to the man I didn't know existed."

Sean was more than just a little surprised. He couldn't hide his smile. "I suppose I could say the same about cabdrivers. Not many would know about John Steinbeck, and most certainly not about *Travels with Charlie*." Sean was now hooked, and he knew it. He sat back. "I really liked it, too. I've always looked at it as Steinbeck's version of Hemingway's *A Moveable Feast*, a coming-out-of-the-closet novel for both writers at the end of their careers."

Sean looked at the license again and read "Giuseppe Antonio Marmillo" with a renewed sense of respect. "Where in the world did you—"

"I know!" Giuseppe gave the steering wheel a two-handed slap. "It was Gary Cooper." When he clapped his hands, the car swerved, almost hitting a hansom cab trotting lazily through the park, a pair of lovers in the carriage. With the skill of a race driver, Giuseppe brought the car under control. He then started drumming, thumping, his chunky fingers on the large black steering wheel.

"How could I forget," he said with another whack of the wheel, this time with only one hand.

Sean still hadn't caught his breath. He was certain they were going to hit the sway-back horse pulling the carriage. "As a matter of fact, Cooper won the Academy Award for Best Actor in 1952 for his role in *High Noon*. For my money, it was one of his best performances. Maybe *the* best."

The tenacious little Italian hesitated, his olive-skinned forehead wrinkling into deep furrows. "You really like it? I mean, it wasn't a movie made from a great book or anything. I don't even think there was a book, was there?"

Sean was staring out the window, off in the distance. "I loved it," he said quietly, not answering Giuseppe's question directly. There was the faint hint of whimsy in his voice. "I'll never forget that clock on the wall in the jail. Big as life." He appeared to relax. "*High Noon* was one of my favorite westerns. Black and white, too. The only way to go with a real western. Like coffee, no cream or sugar to junk up the taste. Black."

Sean smiled, but to himself. It was that lopsided smile of his again. "For weeks after I saw the movie, I would stare at the big white clock on the wall over the door in fifth grade, watching the minute hand creep up to twelve. God, it took forever. When the bell rang for lunch, I'd sit and wait for everyone else to rush out. Then I'd stand up, one hand on my hip, the other on my imaginary gun—eyes riveted to that telltale clock—wondering what my destiny was on the other side of the door."

He shook his head, a gleam in his hazel eyes. "I must have done that for weeks, until the teacher finally called and told my parents. The poor woman probably thought I was going crazy."

Giuseppe suddenly gave the steering wheel a sharp, back-and-forth jerk, zigzagging his way through the intersection where Central Park Drive emptied out onto Fifty-ninth Street. Nodding almost apologetically, he blinked away from the mirror and focused his attention on jockeying for position with the other cabs as he fought his way down Broadway through lunch-hour traffic.

Feeling stuffy, Sean cranked the window down but stopped halfway when Giuseppe shook his head and laughed—a deep, throaty chortle—a laugh big enough for someone a foot taller than he.

"I guess I didn't get it all out, did I?" he asked.

Sean couldn't resist asking, "Get what out?"

Giuseppe's large terra-cotta eyes were filled with mischief. "Tossed her cookies, she did."

Without thinking, Sean checked the bottom of his shoes, one at a time.

Smiling, Giuseppe shook his shiny bald head again. "There wasn't any on the floor. It was mostly on the seat. Right about where you're sitting, as a matter of fact. And all over the door. Window, too. A real mess."

Sean raised his arms and arched his back. He looked like he was trying to levitate off the rear seat of the cab. *How could you have missed that smell?* he thought. *You* are *losing it, MacDonald.*

"After I scooped the big stuff out, you know, the chunks, I used some bleach mixed with that toilet bowl cleaner stuff. Even sprinkled some of my son's cologne back there. Thought I got it all. Guess I didn't. Sorry." He nodded decisively. "Most of it got on the guy she was with anyway. Served him right."

Sean finally took on the reflection in the mirror, eye to eye. "Why did it serve him right?"

Giuseppe sat up and leaned forward, close to the mirror, as if trying to get closer to Sean. "He was one of those snooty lawyer types. Mister Big Shot. Too important to talk to anybody like me. Had him a few times before. Always took him to the same spot, that French hotel on Fifty-ninth, the Saint Moritz."

Sean winced, but affectionately, upon hearing Giuseppe crucify the name of the hotel with his Brooklynese, twisting "Saint" into "Sant," and substituting a double *e* for the *i* in Moritz.

Giuseppe went on. "Anyway, this young lady he was

with—he didn't even know her full name—told him she felt sick, and asked him to please let her out. I pulled right over —after all, it's my cab. That's when this guy tells me he's paying me, and to keep going. Well, I look in the mirror, see the poor girl's face, and stop anyway. Screw him. When the lady tries to get out, he grabs her and pulls her back, and tells her to sit still and shut up. A real *gavonne,* know what I mean?''

Giuseppe laughed. ''That's when the girl leans over and tosses her cookies all over him. She was real ladylike about it, didn't even make a sound. Well, he jumps out, gagging and yelling, arms spread out like a friggin' scarecrow. Jesus, Mary, and Joseph, what a mess! Then she gets out, not a spot on her pretty red dress, and just walks away. A real lady.''

The cab suddenly swerved to miss a cyclist, one of those couriers, weaving his way through Times Square. The movement threw Sean onto his side. His face slapped into the seat. The leftover smells—fanned by his imagination—vividly repainted the scene Giuseppe had just sketched for him. ''Shit,'' he muttered.

''You okay, mister?''

Sean sat up. ''Nothing a shower won't cure.''

''Beg pardon?''

As if they'd hit a wall, the cab slammed to a stop for a fast red light at Broadway and Thirty-ninth, throwing Sean forward. When he grabbed hold of the padded door handle to pull himself back, his fingers dug into something soft, mushy. *Oh, no.* He couldn't look.

Giuseppe asked, ''You in a hurry? Want me to cut across town and take the East River Drive the rest of the way down to the Village? It might save you some time.'' He waited, eyes wide open.

''Just slow down, okay?''

Looking chagrined, Giuseppe nodded and sat back, his arms out straight, his stubby fingers hooked over the wheel. He eased the cab forward ever so slowly as the cars on either side peeled out.

Sean finally looked down at his hand. *Chewing gum?*

* * *

As Giuseppe pulled away from the curb, Sean gave the rear fender of the cab a playful slap. Giuseppe answered with a double honk of the horn before skittering around the corner. Sean shook his head, remnants of a smile on his face. "Hope we meet again, my friend." When he turned around, he saw his own reflection in the window, broken up by the letters for Vanderbilt Galleries, hand-painted in black and outlined in gold leaf. The huge storefront window wrapped around the corner of the building and continued down the side street shooting off West Broadway. He stepped up to the glass to straighten his tie, but hesitated when he saw someone peering down at him from the other side of the glass, his face framed by the huge letter *V*—bushy black eyebrows, full lips, and dark empty eyes pasted onto a small oval head. His hair, boot black and shoulder length, was blown dry. A paunch was masterfully but not completely hidden by the vest and perfectly tailored jacket of his gray pin-striped suit. His arms were drawn behind his back, shoulders narrow and rounded.

Nosferatu, Sean thought as he nodded politely, fighting back a grin. *Count Orlock, in person.*

The man in the window smiled without parting his lips. Then he looked up, over Sean's head, his gaze drifting out of focus.

He still hadn't moved, his head back, angled to one side as if deep in thought, by the time Sean had walked to the corner and through the open door, which was unusual for an art gallery, especially in SoHo. Sean began looking around, his hands behind his back, unconsciously mimicking the mannequin in the window.

"If you have any questions," the man said without moving, "please don't hesitate to ask."

Sean turned and said as casually as he possibly could, "I'm looking for something by an artist named Gerard." He paused, telling himself, *Make it good.* "I don't know his first name."

As if a switch had been flipped, the man in the window came to life. He turned around, wearing a new mask, smiling warmly. He was in front of Sean in three graceful strides, rubbing his hands as if to warm them up before touching Sean. "I'm Seymour Vanderbilt," he said, offering Sean his hand. "Call me Skip."

Skip? You can't be serious. Uneasy—why, he wasn't sure—Sean hesitated for a moment, then decided not to use his own name. "Bruce Peters," he said. He'd unwittingly stolen Bruce Fanning's given name and his mother's maiden name. *Freud would have fun with that one,* he thought. *So would Sharon,* thinking of his therapist.

"I presume this would be your first Gerard, am I right?" Skip asked.

Having used Bruce's name, Sean's head was now filled with dozens of colorful images, fond memories, of his times with Bruce Fanning in Manhattan, gallery hopping. "Yes, it would be," he replied. "I want to balance my other pieces." He said this to strengthen his position. "It's a smoke screen," Bruce had told him, a tactic Sean had learned from watching Bruce playacting as a collector, checking out a dealer's inventory. And prices.

Skip clasped his hands, held the prayerful pose for a moment, then threaded his fingers together. "I see." He motioned toward the rear of the showroom. "Mademoiselle Gerard's work is in the back, Mr. Peters, in one of our private viewing rooms. We only have one piece left. However, her work is not for the fainthearted," he said somewhat smugly.

Walking over, Skip closed the front door, checked to make certain it was locked, then turned to face Sean. "Why don't you come with me," he suggested, and led the way without waiting to see if Sean would follow. "I think you'll be quite surprised."

The room was dark, the ceiling beyond reach. There were no windows on the walls, just a skylight overhead, but it was painted over black. What little light there was crept in from the dimly lit hallway winding its way back to the main showroom. The walls were gray, possessing the look of silk. Heavy oak benches without backs were pushed against the walls. Marble columns stood on either side of the archway just inside the door. In the center of the room was a towering bronze figure, a man, facing away. He was tall, Herculean, his head thrown back as if looking up. His powerful arms were outstretched, hands bursting open, fingers curling up.

"What do you do, Mr. Peters?" Skip asked as he reached for a row of small round dials on the wall beside the doorway.

Sean thought, *Don't you really want to ask me how much money I have before you waste too much of your valuable time?* "I retired three years ago."

Skip's reply was laced with envy. "Nice gig if you can get it."

Gig? Must be the in word. He smiled. *Thirties language revival. Thank you, Cab Calloway.* "It has its good points."

Skip tapped one of the dimmer switches and slowly began dialing up a solitary spotlight hidden in the ceiling above the sculpture. The narrow beam of white light rippled down over the muscles in the shoulders, arms, back, and buttocks of the bronze god. His powerful thighs and calves appeared to flex with each twist of the dimmer, raising the level of light. Skip stopped well short of the limit, the sculpture still a shadowy hulk, half-light, half-dark.

"Ready for an experience you'll never forget, Mr. Peters?"

"It's only a bronze," Sean said as he circled the room close to the wall, enjoying every intimate detail, every muscle in the metal—soft, sensuous, alive—more like flesh than bronze.

"Oh shit," he gasped when he stepped in front of the statue. The face of the man—raked with light—was burning with pain, his mouth twisted open in agony. His chest had been sliced to ribbons, his belly and gut gored open, bowels unfolding. Flesh hung loose, tethered to bone by sinewy strands of tendon. His loins, his thighs, his genitals had been brutally clawed, as if attacked by a wild beast. "I don't believe it," Sean muttered.

"Fantastic, isn't it?" Skip asked, sounding perversely delighted with Sean's startled response. He moved away from the doorway toward the bronze, but stopped well short of walking around and looking at it. "It's titled *Man's Fate.* It's after—"

"André Malraux," Sean said, barely above a whisper.

"Yes. That's right. How did you know?"

Sean blinked, breaking the hold Monique's sculpture had over him. He looked at Skip Vanderbilt. "Lucky guess," he said with a wry twist to his words. He then took a steadying breath—he needed one—and moved closer. When he did, Skip moved back and off to one side, still refusing to walk around and face the bronze.

Recalling *The Seven Cardinal Sins*, Sean glanced down and saw that the feet were not as finely detailed as was the rest of the body. He found it curious, and made a mental note to ask Monique about it when he met with her. He slowly raised his head, his gaze feeling its way up the viciously mauled body—once a god, now mortal, seconds from certain death, but kept alive forever.

Knowing the literary works of André Malraux all too well, certain there had to be more to the metaphor, Sean tipped up onto his toes, but still he wasn't tall enough. Before Skip could object, he had dragged one of the wooden benches away from the wall and set it directly in front of the bronze. He nodded at Skip—assuring him it would be all right—kicked his loafers off, and stepped up onto the bench. "I thought so," he said as he peered into the mouth of the man.

"What?" Skip pushed himself off the wall and moved closer, but still wouldn't step in front of Monique's frightening creation.

"His tongue has been ripped out." Sean laughed. It was a forced laugh. "Not cut out—*ripped* right out of his head." He hopped down. "See for yourself." He gestured for Skip to come over and look.

His eyes wide open, Skip shook his head. "I'll take your word for it."

Sean began pushing the bench back. Skip helped. While Skip played with the bench, moving it to one side, then the other as if there was some magic spot for it, Sean slowly circled the bronze again. He went around once more, this time within arm's length, feeling with the tips of his fingers the open wounds. He smiled, realizing that he expected it to be warm, only to feel the cold metal under his touch. Out of the corner of his eye Sean saw Skip watching him, tracking him: predator and would-be prey. He stepped back against the wall, hands behind his back. "How much are you asking for it?"

Skip said with ease, "Two-fifty," making it sound like two dollars and fifty cents.

Sean hid a smile. "One-off?" he asked.

Skip sounded indignant when he replied, "Of course."

Sean gave in and looked at him. "And the pattern?" he asked, pursing his face into a doubtful frown. "Destroyed?"

"It was cast lost wax. There is no pattern."

Sean debated taking Skip to task, but chose instead to ask, "Is the foundry here in the East, or on the West Coast?" He nodded and thought, *Thank you, Bruce, for all you taught me.*

Skip fielded Sean's question by letting it go unanswered. "Where shall I have it shipped?" he asked, walking to the doorway and turning the light off. "At our expense, of course."

Sean's immediate thought was *You cocky son of a bitch.* He was tempted to say just that, to see Skip's reaction. But instead he said sternly, "I want to meet the artist first." Skip turned around, a look of concern on his face, visible even in the low light. Knowing he couldn't be seen in the dark, Sean grinned and said just as firmly, "And I want to see his studio."

Skip folded his arms into a knot over his chest. His small potbelly pushed out through his open suit coat, straining the buttons on his vest. "*Her* studio," he said, sounding irritated. "And that's not possible. She doesn't allow it." Skip stood fast, threading his arms even tighter. "I haven't even seen it. I don't think anyone has."

Sean strode across the darkened room and out into the hall. He started for the main showroom. "You want a quarter of a million dollars from me for a work by some woman artist, and you say I can't even see her studio?" He laughed out loud. "I said I was retired, Mr. Vanderbilt, not brain-dead." Upon saying that, Sean thought, *This is fun,* as he sauntered into the front gallery and quickly shut his eyes to the bright sunlight filling the room.

Skip hurried to catch up. "Where can I reach you?"

Nice try, Sean thought. "I'll call you. When I do, just tell me where to meet you, and what time."

"But—"

"In the meantime, let me have a transparency of the piece to take with me. I want to see how I feel about it in the morning."

Disappointed, Skip shook his head. "Can't do that either, I'm afraid. The artist won't allow her work to be photographed by anyone, it's part of the representation agreement. That's one of the reasons I keep it in the back room. If she finds out someone has photographed—"

A woman's voice squawked out of nowhere. "Mr. Vanderbilt, you have a call on line one. It's Mr. Hunt."

Hunt? Sean thought. *Richard Hunt?* He turned around, looking for the source of the sound. *Brad's Richard Hunt?*

Skip was glowering at a phone on the wall near the hallway entrance. "Not now," he growled. "Tell him I'll call him back."

There was a crisp electronic click. Before Skip could say anything, even take a step, the invisible woman's voice was in the air again. "Mr. Vanderbilt, I think you should take the call."

Skip hesitated, his anxious gaze fixed on Sean, his body leaning in another direction. "Call me tomorrow, after three. Okay?" he asked, and started toward a flight of stairs in the far corner of the gallery. Halfway there, he turned back, his jaw set, a scowl on his face. "You are serious, Mr. Peters, aren't you?"

Sean cocked his head to one side. "I beg your pardon?"

"Stop!" Sean said with a slap of his hand on the back of the driver's seat. "That's the Metropolitan Museum of Art." The cabbie yanked the wheel and swerved right. The car bumped up onto the sidewalk, sending a wide-eyed Asian couple scurrying for the false safety of a small dogwood tree, one of dozens struggling to survive along Fifth Avenue.

"Don't they give you guys some sort of test before they let you drive in New York?" Sean tossed a twenty over the seat. "Keep the change," he said, hopping out, happy just to be in one piece.

When he looked, he was sure he saw the little man grinning. *You little prick, you did it on purpose, didn't you?*

Looking up into the sky, his arms spread, Sean called out, "Giuseppe, where are you!" Laughing, he broke into a lazy jog down the walkway to the parking garage behind the museum, wondering if he would be able to get back in time to go running before dark, as he skirted the toll gate arm and darted up the ramp to the second floor. At the top, ignoring the fact he had a suit on, he turned on a dime—took aim at the garage entrance to the museum in the far corner, near the elevator—and started running. A woman getting out of her burgundy Volvo station wagon squealed and clutched her purse to her chest, and jumped back into her car. She locked the door with a frantic slap of her hand.

Sean stopped, bent down, and peered into her rear window. "Sorry," he said with a friendly smile and a wave of his hand.

The frizzy-haired blonde nodded her head but wouldn't budge.

Sean began walking away but found it impossible to just walk, so he started jogging again, which is when he realized he was wound up tight as a spring. Before he could ask himself why, he knew. *The man was right. You won't ever forget it.*

He came to a wavering stop behind his car, a dark green Austin Healy roadster—his love—its chrome-plated spoked wire wheels sparkling like sterling silver even in the low light of the garage. She was nestled safely between two of her stately cousins: a white Rolls Royce Corniche on the left, and a fire-engine-red Jaguar XKE roadster on the right, its soft top up. Sean decided, *There must be a trustees meeting today,* as he started digging through his pockets for his car key. He thought of the bronze again. *You hated it, but you loved it at the same time, didn't you? Just like the other one. What is it about that woman's work?* he wondered.

Fishing the key out of his back pocket, Sean stepped to the driver's-side door. He glanced at his watch. It was four o'clock. He realized it would be at least seven—maybe later, depending on traffic—before he got back. *By the time you go running and take a shower, it'll be too late to eat.*

He eyed the entrance to the museum, looked at his watch again, then slipped his key back into his pocket. "Let's see what we can find," he muttered as he headed for the door. "A little refresher course in sculpture. Start with the Greek and Roman antiquities on the first floor. Move over to the Renaissance." He shuddered. "Yuck. Then work your way through Europe up to those wonderful French bronzes you've been addicted to ever since Bruce gave you one." Raising his hand, Sean snapped his fingers. "And, of course, take a look at what the Met has of Rodin. Then walk over to the American Wing for dessert."

Sean rubbed his hands together. "Dinner is going to be on you tonight, Mr. Johnson. And a room, too, since I think I'm going to enjoy a bottle of wine, all at your expense."

The sound of tires squealing behind him sent Sean dashing for the safety of the sidewalk in front of the elevator doors. Another screech a few feet behind him was followed by the sound of a newly familiar voice asking, "Dr. MacDonald?"

Sean turned to find Pamela Eagleston sitting behind the wood-rimmed steering wheel of a Maserati roadster, with the top down. The car was pearl white with dove-gray leather interior. Her long orange hair, windblown into a swirl of color, softened the hard iridescent lacquer and crisp leather background. Sean put his hands on his hips. "What are *you* doing here?"

"No fair." Pamela laughed. "That's my question."

Pleased at seeing her, letting it show, Sean stepped to the passenger-side door. "Where did you get this fantastic Ghibli?" Stepping back, he gave the car a once-over, bumper to bumper. "Nineteen seventy?" he asked, taking another look at the car.

"I'm impressed." Pamela patted the empty bucket seat beside her. "Hop in. I have to check with security for a place to park. Someone's in my regular spot, wedged between David Andreason and Donald Beaumont, two of the trustees who practically camp out here. They usually save it for me. I'll forgive whoever it was—this time—but only because they're driving a 'sixty-six Healy in mint condition. Twenty bucks says he's short, bald, pudgy, and over sixty.''

''I'll take that bet,'' Sean said as got in.

The smell of saddle soap, old leather, and the delicious scent of Pamela's perfume filled his head. Sean took a secretive sniff.

''Shalimar?'' he asked.

''A girl's got no secrets,'' she said, peeling out.

Chapter Eight

Sean and Pamela sat back simultaneously as their entrées were set in front of them by the waiter. The small table for two in the upstairs dining room of Le Moal, an unpretentious little Bretegne restaurant on Third Avenue, left little room for anything other than the allotted dinner plates, butter plates, two pairs of long-stemmed goblets—one for water, the other wine—a sparse offering of well-worn flatware, and a basket filled with oven-fresh rolls.

The tables were draped with a combination of pink and white linen tablecloths, creating a peppermint swirl repeating itself around the room. Lace café curtains covered the windows, while tarnished brass chandeliers, fitted with an assortment of miniature shades, lighted the small dining room. If there was any doubt the restaurant was French, it was erased by the waiters in their Eisenhower-style jackets, complete with braided epaulets and brass buttons, a curious postwar French fashion statement.

Pamela glanced down at her plate, then over at Sean's. "You tell the waiter to just feed us, and I get sweetbreads, while you get Dover sole." Pamela scrunched her face into a skeptical frown. "You've eaten here before, haven't you?"

Sean gave her a wide-eyed grin. "When in doubt, ask a Frenchman to feed you his best," he said, answering Pamela's question in an oblique sort of way.

The waiter smiled as he removed the basket of rolls from the table in order to make room for the two plates he was holding, filled with golden brown *pommes soufflé*—strips of moist potato dropped into hot oil so they burst into puffy light fingers—real French fries. "Will there be anything else, Monsieur MacDonald?" he asked in his best English, and stood waiting for a reply, his hands drawn casually behind his back, relaxed, like everything else about Le Moal.

Sean glanced at the nearly empty wineglasses. "Yes, would you please bring another bottle of wine." He waved his hand. "Whatever you think will go with both entrées."

The waiter nodded approvingly and left, balancing the basket of rolls in the palm of his outstretched hand like a circus juggler as he headed for the stairs, and the wine cellar in the basement.

Sean broke off a piece of the sole with his fork, stabbed a slice of truffle, and brought the combination to his nose. "It's got to be one of the best marriages in France." He sniffed one more time and slipped the tender morsels of fish and mushroom into his mouth.

"Sole and truffles?" she asked after finding a perfect piece of sweetbread and chunk of truffle, and doing the same thing.

"No, the garlic and the shallots. It's a marriage made in heaven. Or was it Provence?" he wondered aloud, smiling.

Before Pamela could pose the question that appeared to have worked its way onto her face, Sean said quietly, "I want to thank you again for taking me through the Met and giving me a graduate course in sculpture. I was really impressed with what you know. How did you learn so much about sculpture? Weren't you trained as a painter in undergraduate school?"

Pamela picked up her wineglass and sat back. "I didn't learn it in any fine arts program here in the States, that's for sure. In most undergraduate, and even graduate-level programs, you get one, maybe two art-in-the-dark slide courses in art history. And they're usually survey courses. I guess you might say I was self-taught. That's until I embarked upon my doctoral program in art history. But the real credit is due my father, who was a compulsive collector of both paintings and sculpture. Daddy took me with him wherever he went—gallery exhibitions, auction previews, and just about every major museum from the MFA in Boston to the Getty in California, with the occasional side trip to Toronto and Montreal. Of course, living in Connecticut and being so close to the City, we spent hours getting lost in the Met. I know it like my own house.

"And you," she asked in the same breath, "where did you learn so much about art—especially about painting?"

"I suppose in much the same way you did. For years, I tagged along with someone whose entire life was consumed by art and art history. He was an expert on American painting and sculpture. As for me, my personal passion is the Ashcan School and the other early-twentieth-century Modernists. I went just about everywhere he did, much like you did with your father. Except when he had business meetings with his clients, and then he dumped me at some place like the Met, the Whitney, or the New York Historical Society, and asked one of his curator friends to baby-sit me until he got back."

"Sounds like an exceptional friend."

Sean paused and smiled, but more with his eyes. "He was, as it seems your father was for you—in addition to obviously having been a good father, based upon what his daughter is like."

With a casual shrug of her shoulders, Pamela blushed and traded her now-empty glass for her fork, and another sampling of sweetbreads. Sean watched her graceful, well-schooled moves, which hadn't once faltered. "I was surprised—but maybe I shouldn't have been—to hear you refer to your father as Daddy. You don't often hear a woman referring to her father that way anymore. It's nice."

Pamela appeared to stiffen for a moment, then relax. "I may be a woman, but I'm still his daughter. I always called him Daddy. I can't think of any reason not to."

"You speak of him as if he's still living. Is he?"

Looking away, Pamela shook her head and drew quiet. Sean waited for her to explain, say something, but she didn't. She simply continued eating her dinner in silence, avoiding his inquisitive gaze. Sensing there was something still too tender to talk about, Sean resolved not to bring up the subject again, and went back to his Dover sole.

Pamela, however, apparently had other thoughts, and said in a quiet voice, "Daddy disappeared three years ago." She took a shallow breath. "After a year, and no sign of him, I was named executor of his estate, which is when I came back to the States. I really didn't have much choice in the matter. His will also provided for me to take over as chairman of the two trusts he set up years ago to hold certain portions of his art collection." She finally looked up. "And that, my dear Sean, should answer—in a roundabout way—the barrage of personal questions you threw at me as we walked through the Met."

Pamela chuckled to herself. " 'Where did you get that Maserati? Why were you at the Met? How was it the guard gave you special parking privileges? And how was it the director knew who you were? And why,' you were so quick to ask, 'did the little man dance around like a monkey with a tin cup when he saw you in the sculpture garden in the American wing?' " Pamela patted the table as if to emphasize her point. "Well, I'll tell you why, Dr. MacDonald, that little man probably thought—prayed!—I was looking for someplace for one of Daddy's sculptures, that's why."

She shook her head. "I spend too much of my spare time these days listening to this or that trustee—and not just from the Met, either—trying to convince me their museum is the place for my father's fifty-million-dollar collection of art. They're vultures, every last one of them. The curators are the worst. Close your eyes for so much as a second, and they'll take a chunk of flesh out of you before you know what's happened."

When Sean lowered his hand, his fork clanked against the edge of his plate. "Did you say *fifty* million?"

"You heard the lady right," Pamela replied flippantly.

"And that doesn't include what Daddy left Mother and me." She zeroed in on Sean's incredulous gaze. "If I didn't love that man so much, I'd think he did this to get back at me for something I did."

Grinning, Sean glanced at Pamela's long orange hair, peeked at her ear—decorated with silver and diamonds— then stared at the emerald in her nose. "Did you ever think—"

"Don't even ask," she snapped, shaking her finger at Sean menacingly. "I know what you're thinking."

Blithely ignoring the implied threat, Sean said with a caring, yet serious tone, "Daddy's little girl had to grow up pretty fast, didn't she? Come back from Europe. Finish her doctorate. Dress up like the big kids? However, it looks like we're still fighting it a little. Are we?" he asked, a broad grin on his face

The waiter appeared carrying a bottle of wine. Without making a fuss, he opened it and offered Sean the cork to smell. Sean declined. Sean did the same after the waiter poured a smidgeon of wine into his glass and stood back, waiting for him to taste it. The moment the waiter was gone, Sean raised his glass and offered a toast. "Here's to a woman—"

"No," Pamela said, holding up her hand. "Enough about me. You've peppered me with questions for the last four hours. It's my turn."

Tendering no resistance, Sean sat back, sipping his wine. "Have your way with me," he said, peering at her over the rim of his glass.

"Who are you?" she asked, wrinkling her face into a playful scowl. "And don't give me a replay of that silly bio on the back of your book, that some teeny-bopper editorial assistant wrote."

Sean sat up and threw his shoulders back. "MacDonald, Sean. Serial number 090-43-1775. Rank—"

Pamela kicked him under the table. "Don't be a smartass, it won't work with me. Besides, it's not you, regardless of what you may want people to think." Sean was surprised to hear her say this. Seeing his reaction, apparently pleased with it, Pamela posed another toast, a silent one, motioning for Sean to go on. She then took a long sip of wine.

Still taken aback by her comments, Sean sat quiet for a moment, giving what she'd said time to work its way through his thoughts. "I taught literature—my first love is American literature—at a little school overlooking the Hudson in upstate New York."

Pamela chimed in, "Hart College—all-girls school—right?"

Amused, Sean nodded. "I resigned three years ago to write full-time. It was something I'd always wanted to do but never had the courage to pursue. Not even after my wife and son—" Sean paused, wondering if he really wanted to get into that part of his life.

"It's all right," Pamela said softly. "You don't have to explain, I know about them. Bruce Fanning told me a little here and there."

Sean sat up, stiff as a board. "How did you know Bruce?"

The look on Pamela's face said she'd slipped. There was a long silence, which Sean was not about to break. "Bruce worked with Daddy a lot. As a matter of fact, most of my father's best paintings were acquired with Bruce's help. They were very close, but not what I would call friends. Daddy said Bruce didn't let people get close to him."

Sean cocked his head to one side ever so slightly. "Then you probably already know all about me, don't you? Bruce must have told you, if he told you about my family."

Pamela reached across the table and put her hand on Sean's. She held firm when he tried slipping her touch. "Bruce never really said a lot about his private life or those close to him. He mentioned things more as an aside. He was always the consummate professional—and a true gentleman—which is one of the things I admired in him. In addition to his vast knowledge and fantastic eye when it came to art." She patted, then rubbed Sean's hand. "Please, go on. I won't interrupt again."

Sean turned to look for the waiter, who arrived table-side before he could wave him over. It was one of the benefits of a small dining room, which was now empty except for

Sean, Pamela, and their waiter. Without having to be asked, the waiter freshened both wineglasses and gathered up the dinner plates, the food only half eaten, balancing both plates in one hand.

"Dessert?" he asked, looking at Sean, Pamela, then back to Sean. "We have *crème brûlée* this evening, Dr. MacDonald. Maurice made it after you called for reservations. The maple syrup is from Vermont. Maurice brought it back with him the last weekend he went skiing. He's cooked it down to where it's almost like a maple *framboise*." The waiter stepped back to give Sean and Pamela time to decide.

Pamela didn't need a moment longer. "That sounds delicious to me. I'll try it, along with a cup of espresso."

"Make that two," Sean announced. "And if you have any in the cellar, see that Maurice gets a split of Chateau Y'Quem with my compliments. Put it on my bill."

Andre stood wide-eyed for a moment. "Certainly," he said, and made his way through the empty dining room to the leather-covered kitchen doors.

"Chateau Y'Quem?" Pamela asked, appearing miffed. "We're feeling rather generous tonight, aren't we?"

"Why not share the spoils," Sean said with a renewed sense of good humor. "I couldn't hope to repay Maurice for all he's given me with his compliments over the years, when I couldn't afford to pay my own way and he knew it. Bruce was always the man with the money. At any rate, hold off final judgment until you taste the man's custard."

Pamela sat back, her head tipped to one side, a wry smile working its way onto her face. "You're an interesting man, Sean MacDonald. Now, do I get to hear the rest of your story, beyond the few little tidbits Bruce Fanning accidentally dropped here and there about some crazy colleague of his, but never once said his name?" Pamela leveled her gaze at Sean. "Who I now know was you."

The waiter suddenly reappeared, busily flitted about—bussing the table and topping up the wine—then disappeared, all without making a sound. Sean and Pamela exchanged amused glances as they eased back in their chairs, each with a wineglass in hand, she to listen, Sean to talk.

"I never really wanted to go to college, even though I'd applied to and gotten accepted at a number of good schools. All I really wanted to do was go to Paris and write." Sean saw Pamela smile but chose to ignore it. "I wanted to get drunk at the Crazy Horse Saloon. Get in a fight with a wild Spaniard. Argue with Gertrude Stein! And walk the streets of Paris at night with the ghost of Scott Fitzgerald, a lovely lady on my arm. You know, pursue all of those adolescent, sophomoric daydreams we indulge in as would-be adults. But it never happened. I got a scholarship, complete with room and board. Unfortunately, the letter was sent to my house, and my father read it before I got to it. I'm sure I would have thrown it out. So off I went to the University of Buffalo, doing exactly what a good son is supposed to do."

Pamela interjected, "Just for the record, daughters get caught up in the same guilt trip."

Sean nodded. "So I see." He took a deep breath, held it for a moment, then exhaled slowly. "So, after a roundabout journey, I came to realize I wasn't happy. My penchant for storytelling was getting me in trouble. And I had become difficult to work with—I was quite literally an argument away from insanity. If all that wasn't enough—according to my doctor—I was looking down the barrel of a heart attack waiting to happen. And to make things worse, my love life was a big fat zero." Pamela appeared surprised to hear Sean admit this. "Since I had no one to worry about, I set about planning my escape. First, I started running again to get my health back." He knocked on the table. "Which I now have, thank God. And when no one was looking, I went over the wall."

Sean made a show of dusting himself off. "So here I am, trim, healthy, and doing what I love, writing. And I'm getting paid for it, too. The only thing missing is—"

"A woman," Pamela said with a hearty laugh as the waiter approached the table carrying a large saucer in each hand with a thick round of yellow custard shaped like a drum—topped with a dark caramel glaze—floating in a pool of thick maple syrup. He set them down, one in front of Pamela, the other in front of Sean. Instead of leaving, he stood there, looking hesitant. "Excuse me, Monsieur Mac-Donald, but we'll be closing in fifteen minutes. Do you expect to want anything more from the kitchen?"

Sean looked at his watch. "Damn. I've got to get my car out of the garage before it closes." He looked over to Pamela. "So do you."

Unfazed, Pamela just smiled at the waiter. "This will be all, thank you. Just bring the espresso, please."

Sean reached over and took Pamela's hand. "I'm really sorry, I didn't realize what time it was. We'll grab a cab as soon as we finish, and get over to the Met. We might just make it."

Pamela graciously slipped Sean's touch and took a spoonful of the custard. "This is heavenly," she said with a throaty moan. "Send the man another bottle of wine."

As if he'd just lost his appetite, Sean played with his dessert. "I don't think it's smart for me to drive after having this wine." He set his spoon down. "I should just leave the car where it is—it'll be safe there—get a room, and stay over."

"Don't be ridiculous," Pamela said without skipping a beat. "Relax and eat your custard. I've got four extra bedrooms. You take your pick. Or you can sleep in the solarium upstairs." She took another scoop of custard and licked the maple syrup off the spoon. "I'm not very far from here. It's right on the East River."

Chapter Nine

It was nine o'clock. Sean was already an hour late for his meeting with Monique Gerard. Upset with himself for getting lost, he hit the brakes and skidded to a stop along the side of the narrow country road. Feeling hot and stuffy, he unlatched the ragtop, pulled it back over his head, and slapped it down flat behind him.

He slumped back and sat staring up into the night sky, a mottled blanket of gray and indigo blue, stained with a warm yellow glow from the early-rising moon.

"It's got to be there," he argued. "You probably drove right past it." Downshifting, he hung a sharp U-turn and raced back up the hill behind him.

At the top, he pulled over and rolled to a stop on the gravel shoulder. With a poke of his finger, he killed the lights, leaned over the wood-rimmed steering wheel, and sat staring down into the valley, a patchwork quilt of fenced-in pastures, braided rows of just-tilled earth, and shallow waves of winter wheat, all kept from drowning in a pool of black by the light of the full moon. His gaze moved from one cluster of buildings to another as he searched for the barn George had described to him—"huge and gray, not red, with a brand-new cedar shake roof." But every single roof he found was black or weathered to a dark gray. "It's also got a strange weather vane on the cupola," George had told him. "I think it's a gargoyle. But you can't see the barn from the road—look for a dense cluster of old oak trees about a half mile off the road."

Sean sat up. "That must be it." He laughed, pointing at a small patch of blond cedar shingles buried amid an oasis of overgrown trees. "It's just past that abandoned fieldstone silo you almost drove off the road gawking at."

He tapped the accelerator. The engine growled back to life and he started down the steep, winding road. The nose-down pitch of the car caught the reflection of the rising moon, turning its round yellow face into a shimmering puddle of amber green on the shiny hood of his roadster.

Halfway down the hill, Sean stuck his hand into the white canvas tote bag lying on the passenger seat beside him to check if the bottle of wine was still cold. It was barely cool. Adding to his disappointment was the fact that the small round of brie that he'd picked up the morning before on his way out of the City still wasn't ripe. He checked again with a firm squeeze. It felt more like a wheel of soggy cardboard, not soft and creamy, waiting to ooze out with the first cut of the knife. To make things worse, when he fingered the baguette he'd driven over to Woodstock for, it was almost as hard as the brie.

The car leveled off with a thump, giving up the moon's eerie reflection. Sean dropped it into first and accelerated down the dirt-and-gravel road, kicking up a tunnel of dust behind him, scattering the moonlight.

When Sean slowed and pulled off the road, the car sank into the tall grass up to the door handles. The submerged headlights dimmed to a murky splash of incandescent yellow and chlorophyll green as the exhaust quieted down to a watery gurgle in the dense grass choking the overgrown entrance road. He stopped dead and flicked his high beams on. They were no better, so he killed the lights and waited for his eyes to adjust to the moonlight.

The moment he could see, he searched for signs of someone having driven down the overgrown road recently. Not a
single blade of bent grass was to be found. He inched forward, wincing at the sound of the sharp blades of corn grass
scratching over the sides of the car. He pulled the lights on,
but just as quickly pushed them back off.

With a shrug of his shoulders, he accepted the soft light
of the moon, a buttery yellow hole punched through the night
sky directly in front of him, and slowly made his way down
between the weathered split-rail fences. As he drew steadily
closer to a cluster of towering trees up ahead, he realized
they were maple, not oak as George had said. This only
added to his growing fear that he'd pulled off the road between the wrong pair of fences and was now driving to nowhere. When he flicked on the dash lights to check his
odometer, he saw that he'd already gone two-tenths of a mile
past George's explicit instructions that "the barn is exactly
half a mile off the road."

"You're lost, admit it," Sean growled, and hit the brakes,
stopping dead. He spread his arms over his head and shut
his eyes, trying to stretch the tension out of his back. When
he opened his eyes, he was taken aback for a moment by the
sight of a figure on the face of the moon. "What the hell—"

He laughed at himself when he saw the delicate silhouette
of a cupola, then the roofline of a barn, and realized he was
looking at the weather vane George had told him about.

"You're right, it does look like a gargoyle," he muttered
as he held the face of his watch close to the dashboard again.
"Not bad, MacDonald, you're only an hour and a half late."

Chapter Ten

With tote bag in hand, Sean walked up and stopped just short of the barn's moonlit shadow. Thin lines of orange light leaked out around the edges of the loft door overhead, but not a single thread of light could be seen around the top, sides, or down the center seam of the heavy sliding doors directly below the loft. Knowing all too well what old barns were like—aging skeletons of weathered wood miraculously resisting the winds of time—Sean stood gazing at the old building, searching for the tiniest sliver of light knifing through cracks in the siding, which he knew had to be there. There was nothing, not even a leaky knothole winking back at him.

He couldn't help wondering, *What if she's already gone to bed?* He looked up into the face of the moon, as if she—for Sean the moon had never been male—could somehow tell him whether he should stay or leave, and call Monique in the morning. *Just tell her you got lost, and reschedule the interview,* he thought. "Don't be ridiculous," he snarled under his breath, and took aim at the shadowy outline of a Dutch door etched into the side of the barn. A dozen steps later, about to knock, he paused, the thought of disturbing her at this late hour nibbling at the back of his mind.

"What are you afraid of?" His question, sounding more like a dare, sparked a hard, almost defiant knock. His knuckles scraped on the rough, splintered wood of the old door, which didn't budge in its jamb.

He raised his fist to knock again, but stopped in midstrike when he heard a distant voice say, "It's not locked." He groped for the latch in the dark, a small hook of rusty wrought iron, lifted it, and pushed the door open with his shoulder. He stumbled inside, his gaze cast down to adjust to the light, although soft and muted. When he turned to shut the door, he saw why no light had leaked out of the barn on the ground floor: The interior walls were paneled over with unstained oak planks. The door had been given the same treatment, the seams all around sealed up with overlapping strips of matching oak trim. The opening for the sliding barn doors had been completely walled up, rendering them useless decorations from the outside. The hardwood planking, its tight blond grain streaked with red and brown, was softened by the warm amber light coming from deep inside the cavernous belly of the huge barn.

Sean turned around, expecting to find Monique standing behind him, angry with him. But she wasn't there. Instead, he saw a small, shadowy figure standing in front of a man-size mound of clay in the far corner of the dimly lit barn-turned-studio. Sections of rusted angle iron, the welded skeleton supporting the earthen flesh, were protruding from the torso where the arms and head should be.

The room was the size of a huge banquet hall, and paneled all around, as was the floor. Running lengthwise down the center was a row of boxed-in columns rising to the ceiling, finished with the skill of a cabinetmaker, supporting hand-hewn beams. These held up the rough-sawn planks covering the loft floor overhead, the coarse seams as wide as a man's finger, and dripping with hay. When Sean glanced around the room, he noticed that new walls had been raised to the headers down one side, closing off all of the old stalls. Those on the other side had been torn out, the walls paneled with oak from floor to ceiling.

Dozens of sculptures, mostly bronze, with a handful of white plaster statues, were scattered about the darkened studio. Nearly all of them were complete figures, life-size or larger, and of men. A few truncated torsos were sitting upright or reclining on the floor. The bronze bust of a man, easily the size of a gorilla, and just as ugly, was set atop a polished alabaster base and pushed up against one wall.

Sean started toward Monique, who hadn't said a word, or even looked up—at least not that he'd noticed—since he'd walked in. "I'm sorry I'm late. I must have misunderstood—"

Monique raised her hand. "George told me the directions he gave you. I'm surprised you found me at all, especially at night." She waved for him to come closer. "I hope you don't mind if I work while we talk." She poked at the headless clay figure as if it were alive, almost affectionately, like a friend. "I started this yesterday morning, and haven't been able to walk away from it since." She laughed, a quiet, relaxed laugh that invited Sean to feel the same way.

Sean raised the tote bag. "I've brought a bottle of wine," he announced. "It's sorely in need of ice."

As if she hadn't heard him, Monique stepped back from the sculpture and put her hands on her hips, eyeing her work. The sleeves of her black silk smock were rolled up past her elbows, snugged around the base of her biceps, exposing her thick forearms, muscles and veins bulging beneath her skin. Her hands and arms were covered with a slimy film, pewter gray, with a hint of olive green. Three small spotlights were mounted to the beams, almost directly overhead, lighting the work. The sculpture, and Monique's face, were cut into shadowy ribbons by the harsh raking light.

Sean reached into the sack and withdrew the bottle of white burgundy. "Any ice?" he asked.

Without looking, Monique pointed to the opposite side of the studio. "You'll find a small kitchen in that double stall on the end, to the left. There's ice in the freezer. You'll find whatever else you might need in the cupboards. Help yourself.''

As Sean crossed the studio, he struggled to reconcile within himself the visual impressions he had of Monique—strong, brutish, more masculine than feminine—with the soft, womanly, almost sensuous way about her: She looked every inch the malformed hunchback she was, yet acted and sounded, and made him feel, that she was every bit a normal woman. *Whatever normal is,* he thought.

The small kitchen was windowless. Oak cabinets, butcher block countertops—and a finely detailed trestle table surrounded by four straight-backed chairs—raised the craft of woodworking to an art. The counters were free of clutter, not a single canister in sight. On the table was a brown-and-white ceramic cylinder, hollow inside. It took Sean a moment to realize it was an ice bucket, but only a second to ask himself, *How did she know I would bring wine?* Finding the refrigerator was a little more difficult, since it was hidden inside a floor-to-ceiling cabinet without handles, as were the stove and overhead oven, both of which looked new and never used.

As he emptied the ice cubes into the cooler and tamped them down around the bottle of wine, Sean tried but couldn't detect the scent of food in the kitchen. The only smells were of raw wood, old hay, and the unmistakable sweet and sour odor of wet clay. This prompted him to peek into the refrigerator, which, to his surprise, was empty.

After a quick squeeze, he decided to give up on the underripe cheese and stale bread. He riffled through the kitchen drawers for a corkscrew. Everything he saw appeared never to have been used, which only added to his curiosity about the empty refrigerator.

What does she do for food? he wondered as he walked back out into the studio, the heavy stone ice bucket cradled in one arm, a pair of long-stemmed glasses slipped between the fingers of his other hand. He tried not to be distracted by the sculptures surrounding him, an army of silent sentinels, as he walked across the studio toward Monique.

She gestured to a table-size cube of black and silver marble pushed up against the wall a dozen or so steps behind her. "Set it down there," she instructed. "Then come tell me what you think of my new work." She knelt down and began kneading the clay at the base of the unfinished figure.

Sean did what he was told, and walked up behind her. To Monique's left was a small aluminum stepladder, three steps high. Beside it was a pedestal, no doubt secreted away from the academy, topped with a large round object the size of a head and covered with a piece of wetted cloth. To her right was another pedestal, holding an assortment of clay-encrusted wood-handled tools. Nearby, on the floor, a sturdy wooden palette with four dolly wheels was loaded with a wheelbarrow-size mound of shiny wet clay that looked like it had been chewed, swallowed, then regurgitated by some huge beast.

Sean watched in awe as Monique made something out of nothing with her gnarled fingers, giving form to the amorphous lumps of clay she dug out of the pile beside her. When she didn't stop, but kept working, fingering the clay, he inched closer until he was directly over her so he could see better. The heat rising up from her body warmed his face. Her earthy scent, the pungent odor of sweat, oily clay, and something he couldn't place filled his head.

Monique suddenly stood up and dug her thick fingers into the chest of the figure, startling Sean with her powerful jab. He noticed that her hair was matted to her skin. He breathed in, trying to place the strange, almost foreign, bittersweet smell, which he could now taste in the back of his throat. It made him want more. He leaned as close as he dared and quietly breathed in.

"I don't think that's wise, Dr. MacDonald."

Startled, as if caught stealing, Sean stepped back. "I—I shouldn't have—"

Monique shook her head, freeing the hair stuck to her neck. She then shrugged her shoulders and slowly rolled her head around, as if to blot the sweat off her skin.

"What did you think of *Man's Fate*?" she asked.

How did you know I saw that piece? The question rang inside Sean's head like an alarm. Still unsettled from being found out, Sean said without thinking, "I'm sure Malraux would approve wholeheartedly."

Monique snorted. "André is dead. I want to know if *you* liked it?"

André? Sean wondered. "Yes I did, very much, as a matter of fact." Though thoughtful, Sean's response was tempered by the way Monique had spoken about André Malraux. He decided, *This conversation doesn't make any sense,* and asked, "Did you know Malraux personally?"

Without answering, Monique continued working the clay in silence, creating the crude form of a man's chest, the muscles thick and well developed but yet to be finely detailed. Sean thought if he looked away, even for a moment, he would miss something. So he stood there in silence, the smell of raw clay, and of Monique—who was beginning to sweat even more—filling his lungs, his head. His thoughts were slowly escaping him, becoming elusive, replaced by feelings.

Suddenly dizzy, Sean backed away, his fuzzy gaze locked onto Monique's mesmerizing hands as she miraculously worked the clay. As he watched her, he realized he was growing aroused. Confused, and at the same time frightened by his uncontrolled reaction, Sean turned away and walked over to the massive cube of stone. "Care for a glass of wine?" he asked, waiting for his head to clear.

Monique simply nodded.

The cork came out with ease, giving rise to a fear in Sean's mind that the wine might have turned. He sniffed, then held the bottle up to the light to check for color and sediment. That's when he saw something out of the corner of his eye he hadn't noticed before. Peering across the studio, he saw what looked like the life-size figure of a woman, partially clad, flanked by what appeared to be a pair of winged creatures suspended in midflight. *It's your imagination,* he thought, refusing to believe what he saw.

Turning away, he poured each glass half full and stepped beside Monique. "Would you mind telling me what the inspiration was for those sculptures I saw at the academy in George's studio, the seven deadly sins?" Sean was trying his best not to let his curiosity about what he'd just seen—*what you think you saw!*—on the other side of the studio distract him any more than it had.

Monique wiped her hand on the leg of her matching black silk slacks, staining the fabric. Even this simple gesture carried with it a spark of sensuality, warming Sean's feeling of arousal that much more. She accepted the glass, pinching the delicate stem between her manly thumb and forefinger. The crystal goblet looked like a toy in the hand of a giant. She drained the glass in a single breathless sip and handed it back to Sean. He promptly refilled the glass and slipped it into her waiting grasp.

"My sins?" Monique asked. "No one was supposed to see them," she said, making it sound like a reprimand.

Sean put on his best altar-boy face. "I had no idea they weren't to be seen," he said with childlike innocence.

Monique laughed, a warm, robust laugh that sounded like she didn't believe a word he'd said but at the same time liked what she'd heard. She then tipped her head back, downed the wine in a single swallow, and handed the glass back to Sean without looking. He refilled it yet again, this time close to the rim.

"And *The Seven Cardinal Sins*?" Sean asked, prodding her.

Monique hesitated. "They were for an old client of mine," she said somberly, making it sound like she had nothing more to say.

Sean didn't want to go down that path, *a certain dead end*, he thought, and asked quickly, "Where do you find the inspiration for your work?"

Monique cocked her head to one side and turned around to look at him. The converging beams of overhead light cut deep into her face, exposing every cruel twist and turn of her pallid flesh. Her eyes devoured the light, taking away the glare, then settled on Sean. He thought he could feel her slipping inside, stealing his thoughts, and anything else she touched. He wanted to shut his eyes, keep her out, but couldn't even blink when he tried.

She struggled to take a deep breath. "I don't have to find them—they find me. They rip me from my sleep," she said with an angry growl. She drained the glass again, set it on the floor, then grabbed a handful of clay off the palette and slammed it into the gut of the figure with such force that the massive clay form appeared to rock backward. "They're there, every night, waiting for me. I feel like I haven't slept in ages." She punched the clay with her fist.

The wine appeared to be catching up with Monique. She was now flushed and sweating profusely. Her silk smock dissolved into her moist skin, clinging to her grotesque form, revealing the sharp ridge of her hunch and the beaded line of her crooked spine. Sean was overcome with feelings of repulsion mixed with compassion, stirred by a steadily rising attraction to her, which he fought, but to no avail. Leaning against the wall, watching her, he asked, "How long does it take you to complete a piece? Start to finish."

Monique was working the clay with a passion, giving manhood to the figure's powerful loins with such skill, it raised the flame of Sean's imagination that much more. "A lifetime. Ten lifetimes," she said with a heavy-hearted sigh. She then added with disgust, "But I suppose that's not what *Mister* Johnson's readers want to hear, is it?" She forced a laugh, sounding more masculine than feminine to Sean's ear. "Perhaps I should quote Malraux." Closing her eyes, she shook her head. "No, poor, dear Albert would be a far better man to steal from, since he possessed a deeper sense of pathos than André ever did. Wouldn't you agree, Dr. MacDonald?"

"Poor, dear Albert"? Sean asked himself in disbelief. *Camus died well over thirty years ago. You're too young to have known him.* He searched for something—anything—Monique had said to him that would reveal her age, since her body and her face masked time so well. Monique arched her crooked back into a grotesque stretch, let out a soft groan laced with pain, and returned to working the clay, carving sinewy muscles into the massive thighs.

"Sometimes it moves quickly," she said. "Like this one. But this isn't one of *them*." She gestured blindly with her hand.

Sean turned to look until he realized she was referring to

91

the works that came out of her nightmares. As he turned back, the mysterious figure in the far corner of the studio caught his eye again. Hard as he tried, he still couldn't see it clearly enough to be certain what it was.

Monique plucked a small, knifelike trowel off the pedestal to her right and began carving out the lines of the shoulders and neck of her creation, giving the muscles definition. "I never know what I'll find buried in the clay," she said somewhat whimsically. "Until I stick my hands into it and feel a heartbeat, a soul." Without warning, she drove the trowel deep into the chest of the figure.

"No!" Sean gasped without thinking, and covered his chest with his hand.

Monique laughed. She'd known what she was doing, and gotten the reaction she wanted. She then stood perfectly still, arms at her sides, head back, staring up at the ceiling as if in a trance. Her shoulders rose and fell with each labored breath, inviting Sean to listen to see if she was all right. When it was apparent she was—and wasn't about to say anything—Sean pushed himself off the wall, walked over beside her, and knelt down to pick up her empty glass, intent on refilling it for her without bothering to ask. He felt Monique's open hand on his neck. It was warm, almost hot. He hesitated, letting her soothing touch seep into his body.

When he tried standing, she kept him on bended knee, the weight of her hand like a cast-iron yoke. Sean was suddenly scared. In an effort to hide his fear, he bowed his head in mock supplication. There was an interminable pause before Monique patted him affectionately, her touch once again light as a feather. She then helped him to his feet with the ease and strength of a man, and not just any man. Aware of his growing uneasiness, fearing for his own safety, but not to be daunted, Sean asked, "By the way, what was the title of the piece I saw at the academy the first time we met?"

Monique turned away from Sean's inquiring gaze and began reworking the clay around the wound she'd just made in the chest, healing it, deftly turning it back into muscle and flesh. Sean was about to ask another question, when Monique began to strip youth away from the clay and replace it with age, withering the muscles with the tips of her fingers, wrinkling the skin with her nails. He was speechless.

"It's untitled," she finally said. "For now, at least."

"Is that because of what happened with Anderson Galleries?"

Monique spun around, her eyes ablaze, melting away Sean's every thought. "No," she said through her teeth, and returned to working the clay. Unlike her sudden response, her moves now were slow, selective, her thick-fingered touch even more delicate than before. In silence, she worked and reworked the shiny gray surface, giving, then taking away life. Sean watched her move about, bend and reach and turn. The thin silk clung to her wet skin, let go, then grabbed hold somewhere else. Her moves were no longer awkward, clumsy, but graceful, sensuous. He found himself growing even more aroused. He tried shaking the thoughts loose but couldn't free himself of them—or the visceral feelings growing in his loins, warming his gut—as they lured him deeper and deeper into a dizzying and bizarre world of sexual fantasy.

Unable to resist any longer, Sean finally gave in and in his mind removed Monique's sweat-soaked clothes with an imaginary brush of his hands, then began groping, feeling every twist and turn of her deformed body. He grew more aroused with every imagined touch. His face, his mouth, his tongue, hungrily covered every inch of her body—her womanly breasts, her large brown nipples, her loins—tasting the bittersweet fragrance he couldn't get out of his head.

His throat dry, his heart pounding, Sean finally slipped inside her. He imagined her powerful arms and legs wrapped around him, taking his breath away, her fingers digging into his back as he thrust again and again and again, out of control. It took every ounce of resolve he could find to keep from actually reaching out for Monique, fulfilling his fantasy. He shut his eyes as tight as he could, but the dream played on, driven by rampant lust.

He finally broke free, but only until Monique bent over stiff-legged and the sheer silk pants were drawn tightly around her hips, her buttocks, down between her thighs—

revealing that she was wearing nothing underneath—exposing the fully developed body of a woman, not a dwarf, and a woman aroused.

Sean turned away, but it was too late. He saw himself inside her again, she on her hands and knees this time. Certain he was about to explode, he pushed himself off the wall and started around the studio. He went from sculpture to sculpture, trying to think about anything but her. The harder he tried, the more vivid were the images—every one of them in black and white, crisp and clear, not a single drop of distracting color staining his perverse pleasure.

In a desperate attempt to free himself, Sean stood in front of a life-size nude male figure cast in white plaster. He lowered his gaze, expecting to be set free by the sight of a man, only to realize he was no longer in control of his own fantasy.

He spun around, searching for Monique. He found her, feverishly working the clay as if she, too, was caught in the same bizarre trance. Nearly out of control, he started back toward her, but stopped when he heard the irritating sound of metal grating against metal—more like tin than iron or steel, and hollow.

When the noise repeated itself, he turned. Without realizing it, he'd made his way around the studio and was now only a dozen steps from the statue he'd noticed earlier but hadn't been able to make out clearly. He could now see that it was a painted bronze statue of a woman, as tall as a man. Taller. She was standing upright, arms held out like the Madonna, as if inviting him to her. Her skin was olive brown, her hair auburn. A sari, the color of heaven on a warm summer's day, was draped over her shoulder, covering only one breast, and wrapped loosely around her waist. It fell gracefully to the top of her bare feet. Her toenails were painted a rainbow of precious colors. She had the look of a warrior, yet at the same time was soft and feminine. Ageless.

Flanking her, miraculously suspended in midair, was a pair of grotesque angels, half woman, half beast. Their wings were tough and leathery. Their sharp canine teeth were bared, ready to rip flesh off bones at her command.

Sean inched forward like a man walking on thin ice. Her eyes, painted sea green—and just as deep—appeared to grow brighter as he drew nearer. Suddenly, a bitter cold knifed into his chest, deep into his bones, taking his breath away. He winced, shrugged it off, and risked another step.

"No!" Monique called out in a shrill voice.

Startled, Sean stepped back, his breathing now labored.

"You must go now," she ordered.

Sean took one last lingering look at the striking bronze, capturing her image forever, and started back across the studio. He quickly realized that he, like Monique, was soaking wet; His short-sleeve madras shirt clung to his back and chest: his tan cotton slacks were stained from perspiration, and spotted two shades darker in his loins. He brushed at the spots as if they could somehow be made to disappear, only to be surprised by their all-too-familiar soapy feel. He brought his fingers to his nose, his nostrils filling with the acrid scent of his own fluid.

Confused—and embarrassed at the realization of what had happened—Sean looked up to see Monique slipping the shroud off the object on the pedestal to the left of the bronze, revealing the faceless head of a man. Tossing the fabric aside, Monique grasped the partially finished head, lifted it off the pedestal, and slowly climbed the small ladder. She moved as if she was dead tired, drained of every last ounce of strength. At each step, she paused to catch her breath.

Hurrying to her side, Sean braced his leg against the ladder and held his hands out, ready to help should she need it. Glancing down, Monique smiled warmly, a gesture that surprised him. She mounted the top step. Unsure if he should, Sean placed his hands on her hips and held her steady, fully expecting her to pull away. But she didn't; she actually braced herself against his touch as she raised the heavy clay head and jammed it down onto the steel spine jutting up out of the neck of the figure. There was a dull thump, followed by a soft sucking sound as Monique twisted the head into place, her thumbs and fingertips digging into the soft clay, scarring the head and face.

Her job done, she slumped back, falling into Sean's arms.

His legs buckled under her weight. He dropped to his knees, but managed to keep Monique from hitting the floor by guiding her on top of him. He thought his chest would be crushed. Had she not gotten to her feet, he would not have been able to lift her off him. He was embarrassed at what he'd done—at what he hadn't been able to do—and was unable to accept the fact that he couldn't hold her.

Monique offered Sean her hand. He took it, only to feel his embarrassment deepen when she pulled him to his feet like he was an empty sack. "Monique, I'm sorry, I don't know—"

She gestured toward the door Sean had entered through. "Let me see you out," she said quietly. Her hand came to rest on his arm. She gave him a gentle, almost affectionate squeeze.

Sean said, "But we haven't even—"

Monique labored to raise her hand. "There will be other times," she whispered reassuringly.

"May I call and—"

"I have no phone. I will have George let you know when next to come."

All Sean could think was, *This isn't going to work. I'll be chasing you all over the place to try and pin you down to another meeting, I just know it.* Speaking as calmly as he possibly could, Sean suggested, "Why don't we just agree to meet once a week until I've gotten what I feel is enough background. Your studio is as good a place as any, if it's all right with you. Sound okay?"

Monique hesitated for what seemed like an eternity to Sean. "That's fine," she finally said quietly. "If there's any need to change it, I'll have George call you."

"Why does George have to—"

"Because that's the way I want it," Monique said impatiently.

Having gotten what he really wanted, Sean told himself, *Quit while you're ahead, MacDonald,* and simply nodded in agreement.

A few steps outside, Monique began shivering. Out of habit, but fostered by what he suddenly realized was his caring for her, Sean reached out to put his arm around her. She stood perfectly still, as if welcoming his touch—actually leaned into it—then turned and slowly limped back into the barn, locking the door behind her.

Sean was left standing alone in the tall willowy grass, glistening with dew all around him. A light breeze stirred the air, chilling him with its cool night breath. The creak of metal gave him a start. Anxious, his heart jumping ahead of him, Sean looked up to find the weather vane turning slowly, seeming to search for the moon. With a shake of his head, he started for his car, tired, his body sore, trying to sort out what he'd seen—but most of all what he'd felt, experiences he knew he wasn't about to forget.

Chapter Eleven

Every time Sean had set foot on campus since resigning he'd felt a strange sense of sadness, yet at the same time he wanted to shout "I'm free!" at the top of his lungs. Those mixed feelings had replaced equally conflicting thoughts he'd struggled with over the months leading up to his departure from Hart College: feelings of unbridled excitement and enthusiasm about what lay ahead for him, which could be reined in without warning by panic, sparked by the nagging fear that he was doing something terribly wrong.

Today, as he circled the Common, Sean was chased by all of those same feelings when he saw the familiar sight of row upon row of folding chairs, the wooden kind with loose-fitting slats on the seat, still waiting to be collected from the previous day's commencement exercises. Floating in a sea of discarded programs and tear-soaked tissues, the chairs rose and fell over the invisible undulations of the ground as they drifted away from the abandoned podium. With a determined nod, Sean put thoughts of another missed graduation—always a bittersweet day for him—out of his mind as he pulled down Merrywood Lane on his way to Merrywood Hall.

Gifted to the school in the fifties, along with two hundred acres of rolling, wooded land bordering the Hudson River, Merrywood Hall was an American version of a stately English manor house left over from this country's gilded age. Christened Merrywood by its wealthy owner when he built this elegant summer home at the turn of the century, it was ceremoniously renamed Merrywood Hall, then unceremoniously—but respectfully—gutted and renovated into offices for the history, English, and art departments: "The Holy Trinity," according to Dr. Oliver Shore, professor of ancient religion and a leading expert on mythology, the man whom Sean was on his way to see. With its limestone face stained brown with age, its gray slate roof missing tiles, and its sagging crown of fat copper gutters, Merrywood Hall stood proudly on a ridge overlooking the Hudson across from the eastern foothills of the Catskills.

Two steps inside the building, with Monique's portfolio tucked securely under his arm, Sean was stopped by a familiar wall of hot, stuffy air. It was a blunt reminder of his self-imposed sentence, imprisoned as he was for two decades within these very same stone walls. He slowly walked down the corridor, trying his best not to make a sound. But the crack of his leather heels on the marble floor succeeded in echoing down the hallway ahead of him, announcing his arrival as he made his way to Oliver Shore's office.

Short, stocky, with a solid barrel chest, Oliver was standing in front of a rolltop oak desk. His Irish-red hair was slicked down, his usually bushy red beard neatly trimmed. He looked like a little boy just back from the barbershop on a Saturday morning, playing grown-up with an actor's clip-on beard. His Ben Franklin glasses were slid halfway down his nose, giving rise to the fear they would fall off the first time he bent over. They never did, of course, since they were wired securely to his oversized ears.

Oliver's office was floor-to-ceiling books. The solitary leaded-glass window was covered with a smoky film. An unsightly mess to some, an orderly clutter according to Oliver, the room was filled with the smells of leather, stale tea, the musty bite of old books, and the unmistakable scent of charred tobacco from a hidden pipe, the whereabouts of which only Sean knew.

As Sean stood in the doorway, unnoticed, watching his friend, the squeak of plastic against plastic broke the silence. Sean took a step inside. Oliver turned around, a steaming-hot white Styrofoam cup in one hand, a scone in the other. With a courteous nod, he walked over to Sean. "Eat," he said, offering Sean the coffee and scone. Oliver was known for his single-word greetings, which sounded brusque to some.

Sean wanted to give his old friend a bear hug, tell him how much he'd missed him, but didn't. He convinced himself it was because he didn't want to push his luck, having gotten Oliver to see him at a time Oliver considered the middle of the night. And for him, it probably was, since he often worked through the night, and could be found trundling out of Merrywood Hall, his arms filled with books, as Sean was walking in. "The changing of the guard at sunrise," Bruce Fanning had dubbed it some years before.

Sean glanced around for a place to put the binder. He chose the ottoman in front of Oliver's threadbare armchair, the headrest and arms draped with oil-stained lace antimacassars. On either side of the old wing chair, stacked on the floor, was a pile of newspapers, *The London Times,* obviously well-read. The heavy binder made a muffled thwack when it landed on the withered leather cushion of the ottoman.

Oliver handed Sean his coffee and scone. "Sit," he said, and gestured to his armchair.

Sean took one look at the dirty lace antimacassar on the back of the chair, recalled Oliver's protectiveness about anyone sitting in his chair, and said with a polite bow, "Thanks, but I'll take the windowsill." Before Oliver could protest, Sean walked over to the deep-set stone alcove framing the window and put the coffee on the sill. He then pushed the leaded-glass window open all the way, snatched his coffee back up, and sat down. Raising the cup to his nose, sniffing, Sean asked, "Irish coffee?"

Looking a bit insulted, Oliver shook his head. "It's too

early—even for me." He retrieved a cup off the desk. A tail dangling over the lip revealed it was tea. He grabbed the other scone, nudged his old wing chair around to face Sean, and sat down, sinking deep into the cushion. "How's the second book coming?" he asked, noisily sipping his tea.

Sean eyed his friend for a moment, the thought of giving him that bear hug still alive. "Signed, sealed, and delivered to my editor almost a month ago," he finally said, and offered a toast. "The only thing I have left to do is edit the galleys when they come back, which takes all of a week—maybe ten days, tops."

Oliver alternated between nibbling on the scone and nursing his steaming-hot tea. These extended periods of silence, during which Sean was convinced Oliver concentrated on composing the shortest possible questions, were another side of this curious man Sean loved like a brother.

"And *The Strawberry Moon*?" he asked. "How's it doing?"

Sean beamed. "It's going into a second printing."

Oliver pursed his ruddy Celtic face into a made-up pout. "So I guess there's no hope of ever getting you back here, is there?"

Sean growled playfully, "Not if I can help it," and took a hearty bite out of the crusty scone. He sat chewing it, his cheeks deliberately puffed out, as he twisted his head side to side as if to reaffirm his answer.

Oliver reached around and picked the portfolio up off the ottoman. He handled the thick binder like it was a notepad. "Is this what you wanted me to look at?" He dropped the bulky binder into his lap.

Sean put the cup to his lips and nodded. His hazel eyes wrinkled into a smile over the rim of the cup. Oliver flipped the cover open, blinked as if surprised, and looked up at Sean. He eyed him suspiciously for a moment, then returned to staring at the pair of full-page black-and-white photographs, a front and back view of *Man's Fate*. "Interesting," he muttered into his cup.

After a moment, he turned to the next two pages, both of them covered with a collage of photographs, some full figure, others close-up details. He sat scrutinizing them, motionless, his gaze shifting from one detail to the next. Then started over. His lips moved, but he said nothing.

Sean had finished his scone and drained his cup dry before Oliver had gotten halfway through Monique's portfolio. Oliver's scone, precariously perched on the arm of the chair, in the very center of an antimacassar, was half eaten. His cup of tea, buried in his burly hand, had given up its puff of steam, and was no doubt cold by now. "What do you think?" Sean asked. "Any good?"

Oliver shrugged his shoulders, wrinkling his beard, and continued paging through the portfolio. Now and then he paused and nodded. A few times he frowned, his bushy eyebrows almost covering his eyes, and shook his head. Once, he closed his eyes and tipped his head back, apparently thinking about something. The last few pages, which were all photographs of Monique's early work, he skimmed over as if they were blank.

He finally looked up at Sean. "Any good?" he asked, repeating Sean's question. "I think they're fantastic. I'm no expert, but as far as I'm concerned, these are masterpieces. Whoever did them was a bloody genius." He closed the portfolio. "And probably insane at the same time." Oliver shook his head. "But then, from what I know historically about artists, sculptors in particular, he might have appeared—artistically speaking, that is—to be as normal as you and me on the outside."

Sean smiled. "Speak for yourself." Oliver laughed. The moment Sean had Oliver's undivided attention, he pointed to the portfolio and said, "He is a she."

Oliver turned his head to one side, eyebrow raised in doubt. He reopened the binder, turned a page, then another, and stuck his finger on one of the photos. "Have you ever seen this one?" he asked. "The one with the woman holding the man's head."

Sean set the plastic cup down on the stone sill. "Yes." He feigned a shiver, which got out of hand. "It may have been bronze, but it was alive—flesh and blood—as far as I was concerned. I couldn't get it out of my head for days. I still can't.''

"And the others?'' Oliver asked. "Have you seen any of them?''

Sean nodded. "A few.''

Oliver began flipping through the photographs of Monique's work all over again. He stopped and lingered on certain pieces. Finally, he laughed, but more to himself. "I can't help thinking Michelangelo when I look at these, but a Michelangelo possessed by the Devil, not touched by the hand of God.''

"You're not alone in that feeling, I'm afraid.''

Oliver waved his hand, correcting himself. "No," he said quietly, "he—" Oliver peered over his glasses. "*She* is actually better.'' He looked down and mumbled, "And I know Michelangelo's work better than most art historians do.''

This was not an idle boast, and Sean knew it. Oliver's expertise came from the years he'd spent in Rome, working in the Vatican. That's until the Church discovered what he was writing about, and banned him from their private libraries and galleries.

"So," Oliver asked, shutting the binder, this time not so gently. "Exactly what was it you thought was so bloody important that you had to keep me from going home and going to bed?'' He patted the binder, almost affectionately. "Besides to show me photographs of work by some mad genius who's been dead for a few hundred years.''

Smiling, Sean wandered over to the rolltop desk and picked at the crumbs left from the two scones Oliver had brought in for their breakfast. "I've got a hunch—and don't laugh—and need your help to see if I'm on track. Or, as you always told me, I've lost my marbles.'' He paused and took a breath. "If it's not too much trouble, I'd like you to go through all of the photographs and see how many of the images you can match up with mythical deities, or events in mythology. Even events in biblical lore.''

Oliver sat up. "Are you serious?''

Wandering back to the window, Sean stood staring outside. "I'd also like you to put them in some sort of chronological order, too,'' he said, as if he hadn't heard Oliver.

"You are serious, aren't you?''

Sean turned to face Oliver. "But if you've got other, more important things to do, or don't want to do it, I'll understand.''

Oliver appeared irritated. "That's not what I meant.'' Smiling, he suddenly lightened up. "Does this have something to do with your next book?''

Sean stood looking into Oliver's expectant gaze. Oliver's question gave rise to a thought that hadn't crossed his mind, and he took a moment to give it some consideration. "No,'' he finally said, but unconvincingly. "At least I don't think so. I took over a project—a series of articles—Bruce had been working on for a magazine called *Entasis*. Brad Johnson, who owns the magazine—and a number of others, it seems—contacted me and—''

"*Bradley* Johnson?'' Oliver asked, clearly surprised. "Since when are you on speaking terms with that man?'' Oliver sat glowering at Sean in disapproval. The wiry whiskers of his red beard bristled in concert with his bushy eyebrows. "Well?''

Trying his best to sound convincing, Sean said in Brad's defense—or perhaps it was his own, "I don't think he's like that anymore.'' The moment he said it, Sean knew he didn't believe it himself, but decided to leave well enough alone.

Oliver grabbed the portfolio and stood up, his doubtful gaze fixed on Sean. "Snakes shed their skin, but they're still snakes, my naive friend. Are you *ever* going to learn that about people?''

Sounding like a child who'd been caught with his hand in the cookie jar, Sean said, "I only agreed to do it because of Bruce.'' His boyish smile began working its way onto his face.

Oliver appeared to recognize it the moment he saw it. "Bullshit,'' he replied.

Sean was amused at hearing Oliver use an expression he'd never heard him use before. "Okay, I was bored, I needed a break.''

Oliver shook his head. "Try again.''

Sean stepped over and took hold of the lapels of Oliver's bulky tweed blazer and shook him affectionately. "I really did need a break," he said quietly and firmly. "I had a bad case of cabin fever. For the last year and a half, I've been doing nothing but writing and running, six days a week. The seventh day I'm in the friggin' library, doing research. The only human voice I hear most days is my own, and that's when I'm talking with one of my characters. It's not normal."

Sean patted, then smoothed Oliver's lapels flat. "You like the sculpture, don't you?" Oliver smiled. "It's good, isn't it?"

"Very good," Oliver admitted. "And also very disturbing." Turning away, he set the binder down. "Normal people don't—"

"Artists aren't normal people," Sean interrupted. "Trust me, I know."

Oliver slipped his arm through Sean's and led him out into the hall. "Are you trying to tell me you're not normal? Do you think I don't already know that?"

"Then you'll do it?" Sean asked excitedly.

Oliver turned Sean around. "Go," he said, giving him a playful shove. "Get out of here before I change my mind."

Sean started down the hall, walking backward, a wry smile on his face. "One other thing," he said. "Remember that mad genius you said had been dead for a few hundred years?" Oliver nodded. "Well, she's alive, and has a studio not fifty miles from here."

Oliver stood at attention. "What?"

Sean waved. "I'll track you down sometime next week. Will that give you enough time?"

Oliver reached out. "Sean. Wait. Come back here."

Sean shook his head. "Can't. I've got to get into the City. I've got a stop to make at a gallery in SoHo, then I've got a class to get to."

"Class?" Oliver began to follow him. "Have you taken a—"

Sean flagged Oliver to a stop. "Relax, I'm not teaching anywhere. I'm posing," he said, stifling a laugh as he disappeared around the corner at the end of the hall.

"Posing?" Oliver muttered to himself as he walked back into his office. "What the bloody hell are you up to now, my friend?"

Chapter Twelve

Vanderbilt Galleries had fielded a new show over the weekend, a collection of abstract sculpture cast in chrome and stainless steel. According to the copy in the quarter-page ad in Friday's *New York Times* announcing the Saturday opening of the show, Ilya Protochenko was an "exciting new discovery." In gallery-speak this meant Skip Vanderbilt owned the man. An indenture, however, that would last only for as long as it took Protochenko's work to start selling, Skip to raise the prices, and Protochenko to learn what the word *lawyer* meant in English.

When a show opens to the public on a Saturday, rest assured the insiders—existing clients, the hooked-but-not-yet-landed, friendly critics, and the usual band of wanna-bes with more clout than money—have already met and fallen in love with the artist's rough manners and broken English at a lavish, invitation-only catered reception a few nights earlier. It's there, with Skip Vanderbilt preying upon their fragile egos and surprising lack of self-confidence—working the crowd like a pusher at a trendy East Side cocktail party—that the real addicts snatch up the best of the best, leaving the recreational users to scramble for seconds.

Skip had managed to carve a well-dressed, middle-aged couple out of the lunch-hour crowd milling about in his gallery. He had them cornered near one of the smaller polished-chrome creations, which appeared to have erupted out of its chest-high marble base like sterling-silver lava, before cooling in midair. Skip's back was to the wall, forcing the well-tanned man and his forever-young companion to look at Skip and the shiny metal sculpture, which was no more than inches away from them.

Keeping an eye on them so Skip couldn't slip away from him again, Sean took up a position in front of another one of the cast metallic illusions perched atop its own neutered marble column, stripped of fluting, base, and capital. He glanced at the plaque, which read ''Flight of Fancy,'' and noted the price tag of $25,000.

Twenty-five thousand! he thought, and stepped back, trying to figure out whether the convoluted casting was a bird or a man. *Or an expensive joke,* he wondered, smiling to himself.

''Exquisite, isn't it?'' a man behind him purred. ''Can't you just see our imprisoned subconscious. Our suppressed female side. The salvation of our very soul.''

Give me a break. Sean turned around to find a wiry man hovering behind him. His small charcoal-gray eyes were sunken deep into his hollowed-out face. When he smiled, he revealed a jagged row of coffee-stained teeth. In his birdlike hand, held by the very tips of his bony fingers, was a clear plastic cup filled with a liquid possessing the color of something that had already been drunk. The rim of the glass was covered with smudged lip prints.

''Interesting interpretation,'' Sean said as he eyed the explosion of stainless steel, appearing more liquid than solid. He turned back to the gentlemen, whose gaze was riveted to the sculpture. ''I take it you like it.''

''It's mine,'' the man said in a throaty whisper.

Sean glanced at the man's hands. *Too small,* he decided. *He must have bought it.* He tried his best to sound impressed when he said, ''Congratulations.''

The man glowered at Sean in silence, then stepped past

him and slowly circled the sculpture, devouring it with his vacuous gaze.

Amused, Sean gave up on the art junkie and looked into the far corner of the showroom, expecting to find Skip Vanderbilt and the hapless couple he'd dug his claws into. But they were gone, all three of them. Upset with himself, Sean panned the showroom, but they were nowhere to be found. To be sure he hadn't missed them in the crowd, which was now twice the size it was when Sean had arrived an hour earlier—shortly before noon—he canvassed the serious faces one by one, but came up empty-handed.

"Mr. Peters?" a woman asked. It was that electronic voice Sean had heard over the intercom the last time he was here. *Peters?* Sean asked himself. *Oh, right, that's me.* He turned around and instantly revised the mental image he'd formed from the static-filled voice, when a woman, not a girl, nailed him with her grown-up gaze. She was art-gallery anorexic, her salt-and-pepper hair pulled back and tied into a hard knot. She was wearing a tailored black, knee-length dress. A broach, a cluster of tiny diamonds circled by a ring of rubies, sapphires, and finally emeralds—a target of jewels—was pinned over her nonexistent left breast. Her ashen cheeks were covered with blush, her eyes outlined in black, lipstick more purple than red.

"May I help you?" Sean asked, smiling.

"Lydia Thompson," she said, extending her hand. "I'm Seymour's partner."

Sean accepted her brisk handshake. "My pleasure, Ms. Thompson."

Holding on to his hand, Lydia Thompson led Sean away, beyond earshot of the man circling the sculpture. Before Sean knew it, he, too, was standing with his back to the gallery, facing Lydia and a twisted piece of metal. She said in a hushed but firm voice, "I'm afraid Seymour will be tied up for some time with clients."

"*Tied* up?" Sean asked, smiling. "Sounds a little kinky."

Lydia paused just long enough to be polite, her face blank, then asked, "Is there something I can help you with, Mr. Peters?"

Sean wanted to say, "Yes, you can try lightening up a little," and almost did, but stopped himself. "I was in last week. Skip showed me the Gerard bronze in the back room. I wanted to talk with him about making—"

Lydia's painted ceramic face softened. "I'm really very sorry, Mr. Peters, but I'm afraid it's gone," she said, sounding anything but sorry.

On a hunch, figuring he had nothing to lose—*unless you get caught in a lie*, he thought—Sean said with a disappointed sigh, "Don't tell me Richard beat me to it again."

Lydia turned her head ever so subtly to one side. Her eyes, the only part of her Sean liked, showed signs of life. "You know Mr. Hunt?" she asked cautiously.

Sean told himself, *Don't stop now.* "When I had lunch with Brad last week, he mentioned that Richard—"

Lydia put her hand on Sean's arm, her face cracking with a smile. "I'm afraid you just missed the two of them," she said warmly, and stepped closer. "But Mr. White is still here." She gestured toward the rear of the gallery with a discreet nod of her head. "He's helping the shipper wrap the Gerard piece. Do you want me to tell him you're here?"

All Sean could think was *Brad and Richard Hunt with George? What the hell are those three up to?* He shook his head. "No, it's all right, don't disturb him. I'll probably see him at the academy later this afternoon." Sean halved the distance between them, which seemed to draw Lydia even closer. "I'd appreciate it if you didn't mention to George I was here. He can get a little . . . well—you what I mean."

Lydia growled, "Don't I know it," revealing her true feline nature. She suddenly looked past Sean, stepped to one side, and said in a syrupy sweet voice, "Yes, Stuart, what may I do for you?"

Sean turned to find that withered fence post of a man leering at Lydia Thompson. He set his plastic cup, now empty, on one of the columns. "I want my bronze," he said, making it sound like a threat. "I don't want to wait until the show closes." He reached into his coat pocket and retrieved a palm-size cellular phone. Flicking it open, he tapped in three numbers. It beeped back a rapid-fire tune. He clapped the phone shut and pocketed it. "My car will be here shortly."

Raising her hand, Lydia asked sweetly, "Can we talk about this, Stuart? I think it's unreasonable to—"

She was silenced with an angry "There's nothing to talk about."

Bristling—if she'd had claws, they would have been extended—Lydia turned to Sean. "Will you please excuse me, Mr. Peters?"

Sean nodded. "Certainly."

Looking anything but pleased, Lydia started for the rear of the gallery with the Stuart person stuck to her side like an unwanted Siamese twin. With a perverse pleasure, Sean watched as Lydia weaved her way through the dwindling crowd toward the stairs in the far corner.

The moment the pair disappeared from view, Sean headed for the front door. He was pleased with himself for having gotten Lydia to slip up and say what she did, though he was concerned about the unholy marriage of Brad Johnson and George White. "And this Richard Hunt," he mumbled. Before he could sort it out, Brad Johnson's alcohol-worn face appeared in his thoughts. *What else aren't you telling me, old friend?* Sean wondered. *And you, Mr. White, are you doing Monique's bidding, or serving Caesar?*

Sean's rational, arm's-length curiosity suddenly turned to anger as the reality of having been deceived by both of these men finally sank in. "You son of a bitch," Sean growled as he pushed his way past a group of blue-jeaned young men entering the gallery wearing crisp new T-shirts emblazoned with the slogan "We're Queer and We're Here."

"You fucked me once, Johnson, you're not going to get another chance, not if I can help it," Sean grumbled, turning the men's heads as he charged out onto West Broadway.

Chapter Thirteen

Sean stepped out of his briefs, folded them over, then again, and tucked them into the pocket of his slacks, which were hanging on the door on a hook beside his shirt, sweater, and sports coat. When he turned to reach for the terry-cloth robe he'd taken off another hook and tossed onto the desk, he paused to look at himself, naked, in the full-length mirror on the wall beside George's desk.

He laughed to himself. "Two legs, two arms, and a hairy chest—most of it black. What else do they need?" he asked, still refusing to face the reality of what he'd gotten himself into. "Remember," he said, trying to reassure himself, "you're not a person, you're just a thing to them." But it didn't help one bit.

A knock on the door startled him into snatching up the robe, a move that made him smile at himself for doing it. "Yes?"

"We're ready for you," David Rosenberg announced briskly.

As Sean slipped the robe on, Latitia Morrison's words popped into his head: "Don't forget to tell Dr. MacDonald what happens to the male models.'' He checked the mirror again, chuckled at his own vanity, and walked out into the studio, asking himself all over again how he'd gotten himself into this. *Stupidity*, he decided.

The students, what looked to Sean like twice as many as had been in George's class, were clustered much closer to the small stage; at least it seemed that way. As he made his way through the studio, Sean's attention was on the marble bench, his thoughts filled with just how cold it was going to be to sit on.

The moment he stepped onto the stage, David Rosenberg was at his side, his hands held out. Sean looked at him, perplexed. ''The robe?'' David said. Secretly gritting his teeth, trying his best to look relaxed, confident—even though all of a sudden he felt like a fool—Sean slipped the robe off and handed it to David.

David draped it over his arm, then patted the bench. ''We'd like a semireclining pose. Try leaning back and bracing yourself on one arm, while facing the class. And I want you to prop one leg up. Once you're comfortable, pick something to look at—a chair, a pedestal, something on the wall—and hold that pose for fifteen minutes, longer if you can. Okay?'' he asked, walking off the stage and taking up a position behind one of the clay-topped pedestals.

Sean nodded and sat down, and almost stood right back up from the bite of the cold stone on his bare skin. Latitia's words raced in and out of his head again. He had all he could do to keep from looking down—checking—not that he could have done anything about it anyway. He forced himself to look around the studio.

Oh, shit, he thought, and almost blurted out, *What are you doing here?* when he saw an all-too-familiar splash of orange color in the last row. His anxious gaze settled on Pamela Eagleston's face, her gaze cast down, her attention focused on a large white pad lying open in her lap. She was casually sketching, while toying with an ever-so-subtle smile, as if she'd read his thoughts.

*   *   *

Sean pressed his forehead against the rain-streaked sliding glass door in the living room of Pamela's apartment on Sutton Place, overlooking the East River. His breath fogged the glass as he peered out into the dreary night. At the sight of Pamela's reflection, he stood back and tapped a fingernail on the glass door. "What's that flashing light off in the distance?" he asked, and took a sip of red wine from the goblet he was holding.

"It's the lighthouse at Execution Rocks, right at the mouth of Long Island Sound, between New Rochelle on the Westchester side and Sands Point on Long Island."

"Execution?" Sean repeated. "What a foreboding name. I wonder where it came from?"

Stepping alongside him, Pamela held out a small sterling-silver tray covered with thick round crackers topped with chunks of blue cheese. "There's a chart in the Raynham Hall Museum, in Oyster Bay. It was published in London in the late 1780s for His Majesty's Ships of War, according to the legend on the chart. It refers to the rocky hazard as the 'executioners,' a name well-earned by those jagged shoals—especially during low tide—before, during, and long after the Revolutionary War. They were first lighted in 1850, and finally automated in 1979. The light flashes every ten seconds. It's visible for roughly thirteen miles out into Long Island Sound. It also emits a foghorn blast every fifteen seconds in really thick weather, along with a radio signal every six minutes."

Looking duly impressed, Sean took a cheese-laden cracker, popped it into his mouth, and palmed another. He then leaned forward to take a closer look at the broach pinned to Pamela's black crew neck sweater just over her right breast. It was a life-size copy of a butterfly. The colorful wings were filled with rubies, sapphires, diamonds, and emeralds, the body made up of a cluster of shiny opals. The eyes were small black pearls.

"Do you sail much?" he asked, still examining the fanciful broach.

"Did—and still do," Pamela said quietly as she turned away from Sean and set the tray on the coffee table behind them, a sun-bleached skeleton of driftwood holding up a large, amoeba-shaped piece of tinted glass easily an inch thick. "I literally lived on Daddy's boat during the summer when I was growing up. In the spring and fall, I spent my weekends on it. Daddy kept it at City Island, at the private dock outside the summer house we had there."

She turned back to face Sean, her eyes moist. "How did you know it was a sailboat?" she asked suspiciously, yet with a smile.

Sean put his hand on her shoulder. "For some reason, Miss Eagleston, you didn't strike me as a stink-boater," he said, and turned away, taking aim at the bottle of red wine sitting on the parson's table behind the huge brown suede sofa. Circling the sofa, he refilled his glass, and Pamela's, too, which she'd set beside the bottle on her way back from the kitchen, having already drained it for the second time.

Pamela leaned back against the glass door. "And exactly what does a stink-boater look like, in your opinion?" Her look of suspicion had been replaced by one of healthy skepticism.

Out of nowhere, Sean asked, "Why did you come to the class tonight?"

Pamela turned on her heel and looked out into the rainy night. After a moment of silence, she said somewhat whimsically, "I don't know—curiosity, I guess." She turned back to find Sean looking at her, still waiting for an answer to his question. "Are you upset with me because I was there? Because I sketched you? Or because you were naked?"

Unprepared for her questions, Sean hesitated. "Upset?" he wondered aloud. "With you?" He shook his head. "No. If anything, I'm upset with myself. I had no business whatsoever doing what I did tonight. It was an ego thing, pure and simple. I don't have the experience—or the body—to be—"

Pamela scowled. "You were fine," she said unequivocally, and walked over to pick up her glass of wine off the table. "Quite honestly, you were better than most of the models we get—paid or volunteer. No, you're not some twenty-year-old Adonis." She smiled, but more to herself.

"But you are certainly worthy of being sculpted or painted, trust me. Besides, there was a sense of modesty about your poses, something most of the experienced models have lost. Except for the real pros, like—"

"Latitia Morrison?" Sean interjected.

Pamela smiled. "Yes, like Latitia. Even though she's been modeling for nearly twenty years now, she still makes it look like she's slightly embarrassed about what she's doing. And in spite of her age, she can look young, almost virginal. She can also look luscious"—Pamela grinned—"which I understand is exactly what you thought after seeing her."

Caught, embarrassed, Sean started back to the window, which was now being pelted by raindrops. "George has a big mouth," he said in a disdainful tone of voice.

Pamela flopped onto the couch, sinking deep into the plush suede cushions. She held her finger up. "Rule number one when it comes to Mr. White," she announced. "Do not say anything to the man you don't want repeated." Pitching forward, she peered at Sean's reflection in the window like she was half blind. "The man is a real Molly Goldberg."

Sean smiled broadly, unabashedly. "Even I'm too young to know about Molly Goldberg firsthand." Looking into the glass, he returned Pamela's made-up squint.

She gestured to one wall covered with a series of translucent smoke-gray acrylic cabinet doors hiding an assortment of stereo components. "I've got my father's collection of tapes with hundreds of radio broadcasts from the thirties and forties. I started listening to them when I was a child. Still do. My favorite program is 'The Shadow.' I know every episode by heart."

Pamela lowered her voice to a mysterious whisper. "Only the Shadow knows."

Sean was tracking the reflection of her animated gestures in the window. "Ever wonder what Lamont Cranston looked like?"

Pamela shook her head playfully, petulantly, sending her long orange hair flying out like a candy-colored mop. "I already know what he looks like. I knew the first time I heard his voice.'' She laughed. ''It's a girl thing—you wouldn't understand.''

Sean turned, trading the reflection in the window for the real thing. ''And I suppose you still believe in the tooth fairy, too?''

Pamela mimicked Sean's doubtful frown. It was something she did—an irreverent little gesture—that Sean now realized he found endearing. Refreshing. Lovable. She sat up. ''We girls can tell what a man's like by the sound of his voice. Didn't you know that?'' Pamela drained her glass, kicked her shoes off, and buried her bare feet under one of the cushions.

''Tired?'' Sean asked. ''Should I be heading home?''

Pamela set her glass on the table behind the sofa and lazily stretched her arms over her head, exposing her snow-white midriff, made even whiter against the velvety black of her sweater and black wool slacks. ''No on the first count,'' she said, stifling a yawn. ''I'm just wonderfully relaxed, no doubt from the wine. As for the second part of your question, Dr. MacDonald, the choice is yours.''

She motioned for Sean to turn around and look outside. ''But before you decide to drive home, you better ask yourself if you have oars for that little Healy of yours.''

Sean didn't have to look. He could hear the rain pounding on the glass behind him, and knew there was nothing English cars hated more than rain, in spite of where they'd grown up. He watched as Pamela snuggled down into the corner of the sumptuous sofa and kicked her long legs out straight. Smiling at the sight of iridescent-red polish on her toenails, he gestured to her colorful toes and said, ''I suppose the only thing missing is a tattoo.''

A broad pixieish smile spread across Pamela's face, melting years away. ''And what makes you think there isn't one?''

Sean ambled over to the sofa and sat down on the opposite end. ''Does that mean the mysterious lady with the orange hair is not only pierced *and* painted, she's also tattooed?'' Pamela nodded but said nothing. ''I wonder what it is,'' Sean said, smiling.

She jammed her bare feet into his thigh. "You get one guess, so make it good."

"Do I get to see it if I guess right?"

Pamela said with a throaty growl, just beyond a purr, "Don't get your hopes up."

Sean absentmindedly patted, then affectionately rubbed Pamela's foot. He withdrew his hand when he realized what he'd done. Pamela glanced at her foot, then Sean's idle hand, and pursed her face into a disappointed frown. Sean's gaze moved up and down Pamela's long, lanky frame. He lingered for a moment at her thighs, her hips, then tummy. He glanced right over her breasts. She lay there, relaxed, expressionless, her eyes wide open but closed to him for the first time, revealing a competitive side to her Sean had not seen this clearly before now.

"*Papillon, mademoiselle?*" he asked with a wink of his eye.

Pamela sat up with a start. "How the hell did you know?"

Sean allowed himself the pleasure of a victorious smile. "The butterfly broach," he said. "I figured it had to have been custom made. Besides," he said with a sly twist to his words, "you, Miss Eagleston, are a butterfly, metaphorically speaking, that is."

Pamela looked indignant. "If you're so smart, where is it?" She folded her arms over her chest, as if daring him to guess.

Sean knew he shouldn't even try guessing, given Pamela's nature. And his own. *If you're right,* he reasoned, *you'll force her into a corner. She'll have no alternative.* He eyed her thigh again, the hollow of her hip, then looked away, out the window, avoiding her breasts. "It was just a lucky guess," he said with a shrug. "There's no point in going any further."

Pamela jabbed him in the leg with her foot. "*Who* told you?" she asked, and poked him again. "George? One of the students?"

Sean pulled his leg away. "I don't know any students, except for that little cretin, Rosenberg. And unlike what you said about dear George, it was like pulling teeth to get the man to tell me much of anything." The mention of George's name again brought to mind what Sean had learned about him—or what he thought he'd learned—while he was at Vanderbilt Galleries. "As it is," he continued, "I don't believe much of what he told me anyway."

"Then guess," Pamela ordered, taking another shot at him but missing. "A deal is a deal. You lose, you owe me a back rub."

"And if I win?" Sean asked slyly. "Do I get—"

"You're stalling," Pamela charged. "And you're embarrassed, just like you were this evening when you were posing. I don't believe it! A man with your—"

"It's on your right breast," Sean said, silencing her.

Pamela clapped both hands over her breast as if to cover herself up. "How did you know?" she demanded.

"Because the other breast has a nipple ring, Miss Eagleston, and I just figured that you'd balance things off. That's how."

Pamela was speechless. Sean stood up, telling himself it was best to put some distance between himself and Pamela in case she kept her word and showed him the tattoo of the butterfly. The other reason he got up and walked over to the window was the realization he would be hard-pressed to keep from touching her if she did something like that, which was now all he could think about.

"A bet's a bet," he heard her say. He glanced into the reflection in the window and saw her raising her sweater. "See?" she said.

Sean slipped his hands into his pockets and stepped to the window, looking for the lighthouse in the pouring rain. "I'll take your word for it," he said softly. But taking Pamela's word was not what he wanted to do—far from it. Even worse, he now realized his hunger for her, which he'd sensed those first few moments after they'd met, but ignored—forced himself not to think about—was strong enough to break any resolve he might have not to reach out and touch her. "I'm sure it's as beautiful as you are."

There was the muted scuff of wool over suede. Before Sean could turn around, Pamela was standing behind him, her hands on his waist, holding on to the one soft spot on his body he was self-conscious about. The wind was now hurling raindrops at the window like lead shot. The air inside was warm and close. Sean could feel the heat of Pamela's body bleeding into him, the fragrance of her perfume swirling around his head. His last ounce of resolve melted away when he felt her warm breath on the back of his neck.

Ignoring his own advice, Sean turned around and wrapped his arms around her. His mouth found hers. He hungrily drank her in, taking her breath away, losing his own. He felt her breasts against his chest, the faint outline of a small, hard ring pressing into him. The thought of it made him want to rip her sweater off and suck her nipple. That image unleashed a hundred more, each demanding to be satisfied. Before he could answer even one of their calls, he felt Pamela's hands slip inside his shirt. He held his breath, waiting for her touch. Her hands were cold, her fingers eager as they gently rubbed his nipples. *This is insane,* he thought when he realized he was suddenly close to losing it.

He pulled back, unable to look at her. "It's been a long time," he said. "I—I don't know if I can—"

Pamela silenced him with a tender kiss. "I know," she whispered, and slipped his shirt off, tossing it onto the sofa. "Don't worry, we have the whole night ahead of us." She smiled. "That's if you're staying."

Sean reached down and pulled Pamela's sweater up over her head, exposing her gently sloping breasts. His gaze moved back and forth between the colorful butterfly on the side of her right breast and the solid gold ring piercing the center of the dark brown nipple of her left breast. Bending down, he tenderly kissed the butterfly, then gently tongued the stippled brown flesh around the golden ring, tasting her skin.

Pamela eased Sean away, unzipped her slacks, gracefully stepped out of them, and dropped them on top of her sweater on the floor. Her red silk panties followed. She stood naked before him, her skin untouched by the sun. Sean smiled at what he saw: a woman, not a girl, her body firm but delightfully soft with age. In the time it took her to comb her fingers through her long orange hair, then shake it free, Sean was out of his pants and briefs, standing naked before her, aroused, full, but not yet erect.

He reached for her. Holding him off, Pamela stepped over to the wall, turned the lights down to a warm incandescent glow, and walked back. She was a sensuous silhouette of pink and white against the glistening black skyline outside. Sean knelt down in front of the window, inviting Pamela to kneel across from him.

Smiling, she followed his lead.

At the sound of Pamela's footsteps in the hallway leading from the master bedroom to the living room, Sean marked his place with his pen and closed the journal he was writing in. "Sleep well?" he asked as Pamela shuffled sleepily over to the window and stood in the bright morning sunlight, her back to him, wearing only the bottom half of a man's blue cotton pajamas. Wondering, *Where did those come from?* Sean sat enjoying Pamela all over again as she spread her long arms over her head into a lazy stretch.

"I slept like the proverbial log," she said through a yawn.

"Coffee?" Sean asked, topping up his mug.

"Coffee!" Pamela turned around, her face cast in a shadow from the sunlight streaming in through the wall of windows behind her. "Are those corn muffins?" she asked, pointing to the pile of muffins in the napkin-lined wicker basket sitting in the center of the glass-topped coffee table. "Where did you get everything?"

"From that little bakery around the corner, on York Avenue. They're pretty good. Want one?"

Pamela walked up to the table and knelt down. She appeared completely at ease, sitting on her heels, naked from the waist up. Sean couldn't help noticing that the nipple ring was missing. "Lose something in the sheets?" he asked, glancing at her breast, then up into her eyes, still half-filled with sleep.

She tenderly cupped her hand over her breast. "No," she said, sounding wounded. "I did not lose anything in the sheets. I had to take it out before you bit it off. What got into you?'' she asked, snatching up a muffin and taking a playful bite out of it, sending crumbs all over the table.

"Abstinence," Sean muttered into his Styrofoam cup. "It's a very serious disease, with only one known cure. But it takes more than just one treatment," he said, toying with a mischievous smile.

Pamela tore open and sprinkled a packet of sugar into her coffee, then lazily stirred it in with her finger. "I couldn't believe it, you were practically insatiable."

"I don't recall hearing you complaining," Sean said.

Pamela drew serious. "I was only kidding," she said caringly. "To be perfectly honest, it's been—" She stopped herself for a moment. "It's been a while for me, too," she said quietly, and started sipping her coffee, avoiding Sean's gaze.

"You're beautiful," he said in a whisper.

Pamela nodded graciously. "Why, thank you, sir."

Sean sat back, his arms spread out, resting on the sofa. He chewed on his lip for a moment, head cocked to one side, then asked hesitantly, "Exactly how long ago did your father disappear?"

Pamela's eyes were suddenly more gray than blue, like steel, face blank, body stiff. Lowering her coffee cup to the table, she wrapped her hands around it as she took Sean on. "Why do you ask?"

Sensing he'd made a mistake, Sean reached out and rubbed Pamela's hands with the tips of his fingers. "You talk about him as if he's still alive, that's why. But if you don't want—"

Pamela shook her head. "No, it's okay." Settling back, she took a deep breath. "Daddy disappeared three years ago this past March. March twelfth, to be exact." She stood up. "I'll be right back." She hurried down the long hallway to her bedroom, then returned a moment later, wearing the top half of the pajamas. She picked up her coffee and stepped to the window. "Now, before we go any further, I want to know who I'm talking to. The man I made love with last night? Or a freelance writer working for *Entasis*. Or is it that other writer, the one who penned a story that left me thinking he hated women?''

Pamela leaned up against the wall of glass, dead serious. ''Which is it?'' she asked in a suddenly cold and distant voice.

Your timing sucks, MacDonald, Sean told himself as he pushed himself up off the floor and walked over to Pamela. He reached out for her. She leaned away, not beyond his reach, just far enough to let him know to keep his distance. A few years before, Sean would have heeded the unspoken request and recoiled from the rejection. He might even have left, offering some half-baked excuse why he suddenly had to go—something forgotten and just remembered. But he knew now that it was him, his problem—his inability to let anyone get close to him—not anything Pamela had said or done.

Risking her anger, Sean slipped his arm around Pamela and drew her close to him. He could feel her stiffen as he held her close, waiting for her to look at him.

''I'm really sorry,'' he whispered, and gave her a kiss on the side of her head. ''It was thoughtless and insensitive of me. I won't—''

''Yes, you will. You can't help yourself. It's your nature.'' She gave him a peck on the lips. ''It's who you are.''

''Thoughtless and insensitive?''

''No, not you—not knowingly. I meant the questioning part. You're like a Jekyll and Hyde.''

Sean tipped back, a puzzled look on his face. ''I don't understand.''

Pamela slipped his grasp and stood back at arm's length. Her eyes were now as blue as the cloudless sky outside. ''Hiding inside that delicious body of a man, Sean, is the precocious mind of an inquisitive young boy. You're like a voyeur, searching for every morsel of information with your hungry eyes.'' She pressed her finger to his lips when he started to say something. ''Don't get me wrong, I don't see you as evil in any way, just compulsive.''

She held her hand up, pinched her thumb and finger together, then opened them back up a fraction of an inch. "You're this short of being obsessive about it. Painter, poet, composer, sculptor, writer—all artists are the same. I know only too well, because I lack that special quality that sets the gifted apart from the average—the mediocre, if you will. I'm good, mind you, but not driven like you are, which is why I'll never make it as a painter. I'm not obsessed with my art the way you are with your writing."

Pamela collared Sean, pulled him to her, and kissed him. "On the one hand, I envy you, Sean. On the other, I pity you—all of you." She gave him another kiss. "Am I making any sense?"

Before Sean could answer, Pamela walked over and threw herself into one corner of the sofa. Then she leaned forward and snatched up another corn muffin. "Go ahead," she said, hungrily eyeing the muffin. "Ask me what you want to know. Just remember, this will be your only shot at me, so make each question count. When you're finished, the only man I want to be with is the one I spent the night with—the real Sean MacDonald—not the one everyone else sees. I want that writer who makes love like a man possessed."

Pamela turned to look at the antique grandfather clock standing against the wall beside the entrance to the kitchen, bracketed by a pair of nineteenth-century landscape paintings. She zeroed in on Sean. "You've got until noon, a little more than an hour. Then I'm taking a shower and going over to the Met for a trustees meeting at one o'clock, which will take all afternoon."

She settled back, appearing at ease once again. "You're welcome to stay here and write if you like. You can even use the computer in my study. I'll make up some excuse to get out of having dinner with the other board members, and meet you back here, hopefully by five. Six at the very latest. My treat for dinner. And my choice of restaurant this time. Interested?"

Sean circled the sofa, braced himself on the parson's table, and bent down to kiss Pamela on the top of her head.

"Sounds delightful to me. Is there anything I can do while you're gone?"

"Yes." She laughed. "Rest up."

She patted the cushion beside her. "Now, sit down. Let's get this damn thing over with."

Chapter Fourteen

The moment the elevator door slid shut, swallowing up Pamela, Sean ran his tongue over his lips for another taste of her parting kiss. The creamy sweet flavor of her lipstick was a perfect match for the delicate fragrance left behind on his face from the herbal shampoo in her silky clean hair. Holding on to the delicious images cued up by these tastes and smells, Sean glanced around the small private lobby outside Pamela's Sutton Place apartment.

The walls were upholstered with a dove-gray silk brocade fabric, the same shade as the interior of her Maserati, and hung with curio-size paintings mounted in fancy French frames: summery beach scenes filled with cabanas, umbrellas, and children playing in the sand, building dreams. Stained-glass panels had been fitted over the pair of narrow, floor-to-ceiling windows; one scene depicted a cascading waterfall with a kaleidoscope of woodland colors, the other a bubbling brook. Standing between them was a life-size black marble sculpture of a nude woman. "She was an internationally known modern dancer," Pamela had said, acting reluctant about revealing her neighbor's name. "Now she's the director of the company."

Upon close examination, the unmistakable Nubian face left no doubt whatsoever in Sean's mind who it was. "Dame Judith," he said with a confident nod, and walked back into the apartment.

As he looked around the sprawling penthouse, alive with sunlit colors, the walls plastered with paintings, Oriental rugs scattered over the hardwood floors, Sean was struck with the realization that this was the real Pamela Eagleston: the daughter of John T. Eagleston, and the woman he'd made love with the night before, not the wanna-be hippie he'd met a few weeks before, who was hiding behind orange hair and a recently pierced body for some as yet unknown reason. *But the tattoo is her,* he thought.

Filling one wall was an ensemble of pen-and-ink drawings of the nude male figure by an artist who'd signed the works "PE" with a stylish flair. They brought a smile to Sean's face the moment he realized Pamela had drawn them. His smile broadened when he saw that every drawing was of a different man. "A trophy wall," he whispered, and laughed away his fleeting feelings of jealousy, or so he thought.

Sean started down the double-width hallway leading to the other rooms in the apartment. The walls on both sides were covered with what seemed like an endless collection of small oil paintings, cheerful watercolors, and intimate pastels. He paused to look at ones that caught his eye, which he realized he had once seen in Bruce Fanning's office. As he moved down the long hallway, enjoying the quality of the paintings—impressed by the signatures on them—Sean was filled with a steadily growing curiosity about this complex, and equally mysterious, woman, a woman who was now a part of him, like it or not.

I like it, he decided, and stopped when he got to Pamela's bedroom, the air still damp from her shower. She'd taken it with the shower door left open so she could talk with Sean as he sat on the edge of her bed, watching her, of course. With his train of thought momentarily derailed, Sean backed up and slipped into Pamela's study. He sat down at her desk, where he'd left his journal lying open to the last page of thoughts he'd written earlier this morning, while working on his next book. He toyed with the idea of jotting down notes of the things Pamela had said, just in case he had to back up what he wrote should Brad Johnson ask him to.

He began doing that but tossed his pencil down, having decided that very moment, *I don't want to write that kind of article.* He made a quick calculation, multiplying the number of words Brad said he wanted for each article—"try and keep it under five thousand"—by seven, the number of articles he wanted. *Just right for a long short story,* he thought. *Or a novella.*

Sean rubbed his hands together, ending with a clap. "That's it! Make it narrative rather than reportorial. Write what you know, MacDonald. Tell a story. Serialize it. His readers will love it, even if he might not." As if arguing his own defense, Sean announced, "If Bruce could do whatever he wanted, so can I."

Although Sean's decision was prompted by his desire to give the series of articles for *Entasis* his own stylistic signature, it was no doubt equally motivated by the condition Pamela had set down for the interview: She'd made it crystal clear that she was not to be quoted, or even cited as a source, regardless of how hard Sean had tried convincing her otherwise.

Determined to at least sort things out from the interview—separating what she'd actually said from what Sean thought she meant—Sean kicked his loafers off and propped his feet up on Pamela's desk, his hands behind his head. As hard as he'd tried, he'd been unable to keep their conversation from turning into a formal interview, a back-and-forth exchange of answer for question. Pamela had seen to that, volunteering nothing, forcing him to ask exactly what he wanted to know, then giving him no more than what he asked for—what she thought he needed.

She was, in fairness, however, forthright in her answers, though painfully thrifty, leaving Sean unsatisfied at every turn. Unlike last night. Two things, however, had become crystal clear to him as they spoke: Pamela did not like Monique Gerard's work, or Monique, which surprised him. When he finally came right out and asked her why, she told him point blank, "Don't get me wrong, I respect the woman's talent—she's a genius—I just don't like the subject matter. It's violent, unnecessarily graphic and cruel."

Sean was surprised to learn that Pamela's father had felt the same way, at least Pamela thought he had, yet still acquired a number of Monique's sculptures, ensuring that her work was well represented in both his personal collection and the foundation's. "He chose the best," Pamela had said with an obvious note of pride. "While he acquired recent works—the more violent ones—he also purchased a number of her earlier bronzes, created before anyone knew much about her. And before that critic, Allan Stern, put her on the map with his reviews of her work."

When Sean had asked Pamela what she meant by that comment, she mentioned reading the review of a one-woman show, which was held while she was still in Europe. "From what I could see, after looking at the exhibition catalogue Daddy had in his reference library, I could understand why the man said what he did. Her work was awesome, though I felt at the time he went overboard. Daddy's journal entries at the time indicated he thought the man was trying to make a mark for himself by coming out as a champion of Monique's work, making it appear as if he'd discovered her. Riding on her coattails, so to speak. It apparently worked, given his publishing credits after that. But he seems to have dropped off the face of the earth in the last year, perhaps because he changed his tune a year or so ago, viciously attacking her work, which I thought went overboard in the opposite direction. I guess no one wanted to have anything to do with him after that. The irony is that it worked to Monique's advantage—backfired in a way—since it drew her back into the limelight, fanning a renewed collector interest, while driving her prices up. I'm sure it made a lot of collectors angry, since they now had to pay much higher prices for her work."

What was particularly interesting to Sean, however, was the fact that Pamela was certain she'd read those negative reviews of Monique's work in *Entasis*. Sean's follow-up questions about Brad Johnson earned him an indifferent shrug of the shoulders. When he jumped to Richard Hunt, Pamela had said, "I don't really know the man," much to Sean's disappointment. His curiosity about George White met with similar results, turning his disappointment into skepticism in light of what Pamela had to say about George when Sean first met her, since it contradicted what she'd said the night before. When he shifted to the subject of her relationship with Monique, Sean was cut off with the terse reply "We have none. Professionally or personally." Finding that hard to believe, Sean had pressed Pamela on it, asking one question after another, but still came up empty-handed. She had simply stonewalled him.

One thing that truly surprised Sean was Pamela's disclosure that she was chairman of the academy's board of trustees, having assumed her father's position as representative of the John T. Eagleston Foundation owing to the fact that the foundation was the academy's single largest benefactor. Apparently, the school had hired her without realizing she was related to John Eagleston. According to Pamela, "They never asked, so I never said anything." Pamela had then grinned and said, "Don't ask, don't tell."

The appointment to the board had proven to be just as much of a surprise to her as it was to the academy when the conditions of her father's will were made public, and she was named chairman of the foundation, which, she explained, "meant that I automatically replaced him on the boards of all nonprofits he was sitting on. Unless, of course, they didn't want me on their board, and in that case they lost their funding, and I had one less dollar-a-year job."

With each disclosure, which progressively revealed Pamela to be far more than what she'd held herself out to be when he first met her—even up to last night—Sean found himself wondering what this intriguing and unquestionably competent woman was doing playing the role of a leftover hippie. *Why the charade?* was one of the questions he'd wanted to ask her. For some reason, he hadn't asked that—implied it maybe, but didn't come right out and ask it—even though it had crossed his mind more than once.

As Pamela talked, she sounded less and less like a painting

instructor at some avante-garde art school, and more and more like a Wall Street investment banker, a millionaire a hundred times over. She was every bit her father's daughter—the daughter of a man, who, Sean soon learned, had retired at the young age of forty to chase his dream of immortality through a legacy of art.

Another unasked question—*Why do you think he disappeared?*—was rhetorical, perhaps even argumentative, and Sean knew it, so it never even came close to being asked. There was one other, a question he'd pursued, but through the way he asked his questions, not what he actually said. That unasked question was *Why are you wasting your time at the academy?* In the absence of an answer from Pamela, Sean tried answering it for her. But no matter what excuse he came up with, nothing made sense, at least not to him.

''Something's keeping you there,'' he decided as he leaned forward and turned the computer on out of habit. Realizing what he'd done, he was about to flip it off when he saw that it was a program unfamiliar to him. Curious, he decided to see if he could figure it out. He stumbled his way through the prompts until he got to the main menu, which took him nearly half an hour. Then he succeeded in calling up the working directory, only to remind himself that he had no business looking into Pamela's private files.

Before Sean could figure out how to exit the program, a number of files, all seemingly clustered together, caught his eye. He scrolled down, reading them aloud, ''Gerard? Hunt? Johnson?'' He stopped himself from retrieving the one labeled \GERARD. Unable to decide whether or not to continue—buying time—he scanned the other headings. Two more stood out: \SEARCH.DAD and \WHITE.

Sean pitched back in his chair, feeling angry. ''I guess I didn't ask you the right questions—phrase it just so—did I?'' he whispered. ''I guess with you, close doesn't count.''

Looking for a reason, an excuse—grasping at straws—to justify doing what he knew he shouldn't do, but at the same time knew he was about to do, Sean recalled Pamela's own words: ''You can't help yourself ... it's your nature ... you're a Jekyll and Hyde.'' As if needing one more push to nudge him over the edge of reason, Sean thought of the one thing Pamela had said that had struck home more than the others: "You're like a voyeur, searching for every morsel of information with your hungry eyes."

He clicked the mouse.

"Hello?" Pamela called out, followed by the sound of the front door closing. "It's me," she said, hurrying down the hall. "Where are you?"

Startled, Sean stood up, deliberately blocking the screen. His face was flushed red with embarrassment. Turning the computer off, he turned around. "I know I shouldn't have—"

Pamela stuck her head around the corner and said, "Hi!"— smiled and waved—and continued down the hall. Sean looked at his watch. *It's only two o'clock?* He was at the door. "How come you're back so soon?"

Pamela called back, "The meeting was postponed. The chairman of the acquisitions committee didn't show up, and his office didn't know where he was. Since that was the only reason for me to be there today—we had to vote on a number of pieces of sculpture the museum was negotiating to buy—I left."

Sean heard the water running. "Are you taking a shower?"

Pamela yelled over the noise of the water, "Yes. I can't stand the smell of their disgusting cigar smoke—it's all over me. I won't be long."

Struggling with his guilt, Sean started down the hall for the bedroom. Pamela's voice was suddenly subdued, inviting. "Care to join me?" she asked, stepping into the doorway, wearing nothing more than a smile and her exquisite monarch butterfly. Caught off guard, Sean came to a dead stop a foot or so from her.

"Well?" she asked, stepping backwards into the bedroom, inviting Sean to follow, a come-hither look in her eyes. "Are we up to it?"

Chapter Fifteen

Sean was determined not to be late for his second meeting with Monique, so much so his resolve brought him down Old Country Road in front of the overgrown entrance leading back to Monique's studio a half hour early. With time to kill, he drove past, looking for something to keep himself busy. Having arrived two hours earlier than he had last time, he had enough light to see what the property around the converted barn was like. As he'd suspected, it had once been a horse farm, abandoned for what appeared to have been ten years—perhaps longer, based upon the height of the saplings, tall as a man, sprouting in the overgrown fields, and the dilapidated state of the split-rail fences.

Curious as to how large the old farm was, Sean followed the roads paralleling the falling-down fences bordering the pastures linked to hers, driving for a distance, turning right, another mile, then right again. He was certain there had to be other buildings for a farm this size, and wanted to see where they were and if they were occupied. When he guessed he was opposite the grass-covered entrance—on the other side of what he figured had to be a one-hundred-acre square, judging from the distance he'd traveled—Sean came upon another abandoned access road with fences guiding it back to a cluster of shade trees well off the road.

There's got be a house back there somewhere, and at least another barn, he thought, staring at the trees, trying to see if he could make out the lines of a house or barn. He wanted to check it out, but he had less than ten minutes to circle back to where he'd started and make sure he was knocking on the door of Monique's studio before eight o'clock, even if only a second before eight. *Next time,* he thought as he pulled his lights on, turned around and started to backtrack, *get here an hour earlier. And wear boots, so you can walk back instead of driving. Don't push your luck; this road doesn't look as smooth as the other one.*

The moment Sean turned off Old Country Road, just before sinking down into the tall grass, he noticed a set of tire tracks leading back to the studio. *Are those mine?* he wondered, and began mentally counting the days back to his first visit. He shook his head; the grass would have popped back up by now. *Even with this dry weather we've had.*

With the moon not yet above the trees and waning, there was less light that night than the week before. Once in the grass, the first thing Sean noticed was that he was driving between the tracks, not over them, which meant they were wider. *A truck?* he wondered, but quickly ruled that out when he saw the grass between the tracks was also bent over, telling him that whatever had been driven down the overgrown road didn't have much more clearance than his Healy. *It's probably a sports car of some sort,* he decided as he steered down the center of the tracks.

Wait a second. He bumped to a stop. *There's only one set of tracks, which means whoever it was who drove in must still be here.* He couldn't help wondering, *Are you sure it's Friday?* He held his watch close to the dash and checked the tiny day and date displays to make sure he hadn't gotten his days mixed up, which was something he'd been doing more and more ever since he left the college to write. It had gotten so bad that unless he actually looked at the calendar in the kitchen of his apartment and saw what day it was, or thought to check his watch, the only thing Sean was certain of these days was what month it was. Even then, he slipped up when it was the last or first few days of the month, and he could be wrong about that, too.

"Friday it is," he assured himself, and continued creeping through the grass. "Maybe she forgot about our meeting."

When he pulled into the clearing in front of the barn, there was no other car to be found. Perplexed, he flicked his high beams on, sat up, and peered over the steering wheel. He could just barely make out a patch of matted-down grass where someone had stopped—appeared to have backed up—then circled around the side of the barn out of sight. He wondered if there had been tracks coming out of the abandoned entrance on the other side of the farm, and tried picturing the road in his mind. But he came up with a blank, realizing he hadn't thought to check. He'd been more focused on what buildings might be back there than the road, and simply couldn't remember if there were or weren't any tracks.

There must have been, he decided as he climbed out of his car and shut the door. *How else could they get out of here?* He hesitated. *Unless they're parked around back and haven't left yet.* Out of a compulsive need to know, if only to satisfy his curiosity about what kind of car it was before he met the driver, Sean started to follow the tracks as best he could in the fading light. As he approached the corner of the barn, he heard the rustle of grass and stopped, peering into the shadows. A small figure, short, stocky, was moving toward him.

"Monique?" he called out tentatively. "Is that you?"

"Yes, of course it is, Sean. Who else would it be?"

Sean? he thought. *Last week it was Dr. MacDonald this and Dr. MacDonald that, and now all of a sudden I'm Sean. What changed your tune?*

"It's nice to see you again," Monique said as she drew closer. It sounded as if she actually meant it, too. Before Sean could say anything, Monique slipped her arm through his, turned him around, and started for the entrance to her studio.

Sean glanced back over his shoulder. "Who's here?" he asked.

"No one," Monique replied, and tugged at his arm, holding him on course. "They left. I was just coming back from showing them how to get out the other side. I didn't want the two of you bumping heads."

Or is it that you didn't want us meeting? Sean thought. *I must have just missed them on the other side when I turned around to come back.* "Were they by any chance driving a sports car?" He gestured toward his Healy. "Like mine, only bigger?"

Without looking, Monique said quietly, "I'm afraid I don't know one car from the next. I can't even drive." She opened the door and waited for Sean to go inside.

Then how do you get here? Sean thought, acknowledging her invitation but urging her to go ahead of him. Smiling, she hurried inside with what could only be characterized as a jaunty skip to her step. "You seem chipper tonight," he said, latching the door behind him. "Spend the night alone?"

Monique slowed but didn't turn back. "I beg your pardon?" she asked, her question laced with caution.

"I was referring to those sleepless nights of yours, remember?" Sean explained. Monique kept walking, her head turned to one side, waiting for Sean to go on. "Inspirations?" he asked anxiously. "Haven't slept in ages. Remember now?"

Monique nodded and resumed her pace, which was free of a limp. As a matter of fact, had Sean not known she limped, it wouldn't have been noticeable. He found himself watching for her limp to return as he walked behind her. "So," she said with an eager clap of her hands. "I'm all yours. There's nothing to distract us tonight. What shall we talk about?"

Sean glanced across the studio to where the sculpture she'd been working on last week had been standing. It was now wrapped in a pristine-white cloth, head to toe, and tied around the base with rope, the same way *The Seven Cardinal*

Sins had been bound and hidden from view in George White's studio. "Do I get to see it?" Sean asked excitedly as he hurried past Monique and planted himself directly in front of the linen-shrouded figure.

Monique said softly, almost affectionately, "No, Sean, you do not get to see it." In spite of her upbeat mood, Monique left no doubt whatsoever she meant no. "I don't like anyone to see my work until after it's been cast and I have personally put the patina on that I want for that particular work. You'll have to wait."

"But I—"

"Care for some wine?" Monique asked as she started across the studio toward the kitchen. "My previous visitor was kind enough to bring me a bottle, but we never got to drink it."

Sean thought, *It's a dead issue, MacDonald, you're not going to get to see it, so drop it before you end up antagonizing her.*

"I'd love a glass of wine," he called back.

The moment Monique was out of sight, Sean reached out and touched the linen, feeling the rise and fall of the folds, trying to imagine what the clay model looked like underneath. He noticed that it seemed taller and bulkier than what he remembered, and decided it was because of the shroud. No sooner had he stepped around the side than he saw a stool in the shadows a half-dozen steps away. A black terry-cloth robe was casually tossed on top. The sight of the robe instantly brought to mind his own modeling experience; however, that thought was pushed aside when it dawned on him that whoever it was who'd been here had undoubtedly been modeling for Monique. *And for this piece.*

Sean picked up the robe to sit on the stool and ponder the clay beneath the shroud. He couldn't help noticing it was damp. Before he could put it down, a sour ammoniated smell turned his head away. Apprehensively, he brought the robe to his nose and quickly threw it to the floor. He wiped his hands on his pants, but when he checked, the acrid smell was still there. *Jesus,* he thought, *whoever it was must have been sweating like a pig.* He glanced around. *And it's not even hot in here.*

Refocusing his attention on Monique's hidden creation, Sean let his gaze slip in and out of every shadowy fold in the shroud as he again tried imagining what the clay now looked like. What had she done to him? Was he young or old? Dressed or naked? Alive or dead? "Or almost dead?" he whispered, and shivered just for the fun of it. He wondered who could possibly have been modeling for her and was left with only one choice, given the fact that he knew only one other person that Monique knew. As the thought of George White sitting on the stool played itself out, Sean found himself intrigued by the idea of posing for Monique himself. He even felt a twinge of jealousy, which he laughed away as he let his imagination loose, but on short rein, all too aware of what happened the last time he was here, something he still couldn't explain.

"You were out of control," he muttered, fishing for an excuse for his behavior.

"Who was out of control?" Monique asked as she stepped beside him and held a glass of wine in front of him. "Here," she said. "Just don't ask me what it is. All I know is that it's red and it tastes good." She walked over, stood squarely in front of the sculpture, and turned to look at Sean, a relaxed smile on her face. "Cat got your tongue?" she asked, and took a hearty sip of wine.

Sean started to sit on the stool, but instead stood behind it, watching Monique as she stared back at him, slowly sipping her wine. Her eyes were surprisingly cool, inviting, no longer pools of molten glass or smoldering coals. For the first time Sean could see beneath the surface, see what he thought was a smile in her heart. *There really is a woman inside you, isn't there?* At that moment, the smell of the robe found him, distracting him, until he moved farther away from the stool, beyond its malodorous reach.

Sean realized he felt relaxed and uneasy at the same time, conflicting feelings that left him confused, since he couldn't think of anything he was uncomfortable about. At least nothing he was conscious of. *It's your imagination,* he decided, and shook his head, as if that might somehow rid him of the disquieting feelings.

"A penny for your thoughts," Monique said.

Sean smiled. "Save your money. I'm afraid they're not worth it." He stepped closer. "Although it's funny you should say that, because the last time I was here, I got the feeling you could read my thoughts. You seemed to know what I was about to say. Or do."

Monique drained her glass. "I've been accused of being a lot of things, Sean, but never telepathic." She raised her glass. "More wine?" she asked, her face softened by a genuine smile.

Sean peered into his half-full glass, still yet to be tasted. "I'm afraid I'm not keeping up with you." He promptly emptied his glass and handed it over to Monique. "There, we're even."

Monique took his glass and headed for the kitchen.

She was back before Sean completed a full circle around the cloaked figure, returning his glass to him, now filled to the rim. He glanced at the wine, Monique, then the sculpture. "How long have you been doing this?" he asked. "Sculpting, that is."

"For as long as I can remember," she said without a second's hesitation. "Sometimes, it feels like I've been doing it forever, from the beginning of time. And when it works, it's a joy."

Sean was surprised to hear her say this, use the word *joy*. At the same time, he sensed that very same feeling in her voice, then inside him, too. Something made him move closer to her.

Monique sighed ever so faintly. "Then there are times when I can't have my way with the clay, and it seems like I don't know what I'm doing. That I'm lost. Then it all miraculously comes together, like someone else is inside me, moving my hands."

Sean was touched by Monique's spontaneous—and revealing—replies. "Does it always come together?" Reaching out, he placed his hand on the shroud where the face of the figure would be, caressing it ever so tenderly, trying to feel the features with the tips of his fingers.

Moving beside him, her body pressing into his, Monique covered his hand with hers. "No," she said softly, leaving Sean wondering if she was answering his question or telling him not to touch the clay. "There have been times—more than I care to remember—that I've ripped the clay down, rebuilt the armature, and started all over again."

Monique wrapped her gnarled fingers around Sean's hand and lifted it off the linen. "I know you think you want to see it, Sean, but you don't, not really," she said solemnly.

Sean's contentious feelings raised their divisive heads again. *How do you know I don't want to see it?* Just as quickly he told himself, *Forget it, move on to something else.* "Any interest in this bronze?"

Monique took a sip of wine. "It's not for sale."

Sean held up his hand. "Let's just say for a moment that it was—what would the price be?"

What appeared to be an amused smile spread across Monique's distorted face, warming her eyes a few degrees. "Are you thinking of buying it?" she asked. There was actually the hint of a playful tease in her voice.

Sean liked that, and laughed. "Me? As much as I love your work, Monique, I'm afraid my budget will keep me at the Animalier bronze level until I have a best-seller. Or sell the film rights to one of my books."

Her smile broadened, her eyes alive with mischief. "You really do like my work, don't you?"

"I love it," he said without reservation. "Even though it frightens me—which I suppose is due to my own inability to deal with the feelings your pieces arouse in me—your work takes my breath away. Everything is so real, so faithful to life, yet at the same time it's surreal. But best of all, they're uncanny when it comes to illustrating man's inhumanity to man." He shivered and took a quick sip of wine.

"No," Monique said sternly. "Man's inhumanity to *woman*." She'd reclaimed a serious tone in her voice. "After all, she is the creature he fears most in this world—and therefore hates the most—because of what she is, what she can do and he can't. His blind fear drives him to control her, dominate her, strip her of her identity. Not only is he driven to ravage her body, but he rapes her very soul." Monique tossed her head back and drained the glass of every last drop of red wine.

Taken aback by what she'd said, but more so by how she'd said it, Sean looked at the linen-draped sculpture, his imagination creating endless variations on the figure that he'd last seen unfinished, in a futile effort to complete some vague metaphor inside his head. As he struggled with what Monique had said, he realized she'd just answered a hundred unasked questions. At that moment, the pages of her portfolio started turning in his mind, one masterful creation after another cast in a new light. Then came the vivid images of the works he'd seen in person, from the first bronze at the academy, which had taken his breath away, hypnotized him, to the foreboding *Seven Cardinal Sins,* then the frightening memory of *Man's Fate,* and now the mysterious figure standing no more than a few feet away from him, faceless and, he realized, just as frightening as the others.

For Sean, every one of Monique's masterpieces now had a driving force—an underlying theme—behind the allegorical scenes she'd portrayed. Emotions were now attached to agonizing faces, offering explanations for the decimated bodies. One piece, however—an image in his mind created by someone else's words—was yet to be seen, touched with his own eyes, not through someone else's, or the eye of a camera. Ignoring Monique's challenging gaze, Sean asked, "Where is the head of Christ you sculpted?"

Monique appeared to stiffen. "You don't want to see it," she said, ice covering her words. She started for the kitchen.

Sean blocked her path. "Why not?" he asked, gently placing his hand on her shoulder, his touch light, caressing her.

She tried stepping around him. He parried her move. She leaned back and said, "You're not ready yet. Perhaps later."

His eyes, his whole body took her on. "Later? As in later tonight? Or when you think I'm ready, whatever *ready* means?"

Monique's granitelike resolve appeared to soften. "You really want to see it, don't you?"

"Yes," he said, trying to reassure her with an affectionate squeeze of her arm. "I really do."

Monique handed Sean her glass, her gaze devouring his before he could turn away. "Get me some more wine. I'll be back in a moment or two."

Sean watched her cross the studio and slip through a door he hadn't noticed before on the opposite wall. Examining the overhead beams cutting through the oak-planked wall, he guessed there was an addition on the back of the barn. *It must be where she stores things,* he thought. *Maybe that's where she lives, too.* He started for the kitchen, his head down, thinking, *What's so special about the head of Christ?*

He stopped and knelt on one knee to get a closer look at the outline of what appeared to be the residue of a dark stain on the floor, shaped like a large puddle. It felt tacky, as if not quite dry. He noticed others, barely visible, spotting the floor all around the wooden stool. *Looks like wine,* he thought. Licking his finger, he dragged it through one of the smaller spots, causing it to smudge. *Nope, too thick.*

He was about to smell it, but for some reason stopped and stood up, his thoughts—his actions—suddenly not his own. As he headed for the kitchen in a daze, he absentmindedly wiped his finger on his tan cotton pants, leaving behind dull red smudges.

Upon his return, having drained the bottle of wine to fill Monique's glass one last time, Sean heard the door behind him creak open. He turned to see Monique entering the studio, carrying a large burlap sack with rope for handles. From the sag of the burlap it was evident that whatever was inside the sack was heavy, though Monique carried it with amazing ease.

Sean slowed his pace, letting her catch up. "This is the last of the wine," he said, holding up the glass. Monique nodded, but did not accept the glass. "Want some help?" he asked, offering his free hand.

Monique shook her head. "I prefer to carry it myself, if you don't mind. It's heavier than you think."

Stepping ahead of her, Sean kicked the foul-smelling robe out of her way and set the glass of wine on the stool. Monique was right behind him. She stopped, turned, and carefully set the sack on the floor.

"I'm ready," Sean said, and drew his hands behind his back, looking bright-eyed and bushy-tailed.

"We'll see," Monique whispered to herself as she reached into the sack. Sean tried peeking over her shoulder but couldn't see anything. With startling speed, she spun around and held her arm up, hand raised high. "Behold," she said reverently. "Christ."

Sean gasped. He couldn't speak, couldn't move. Overcome with grief, he shut his eyes. But it was too late; the image was now burned into his memory forever, deep into his soul.

"I told you that you weren't ready," Monique said quietly, a note of scorn in her voice.

Before she could hide the fired clay head in the sack, Sean snatched it away from her and locked his gaze onto the face of Christ. Monique reached for the sculpture, but Sean refused to let go, his grip suddenly now stronger than hers. Blood suddenly appeared on Sean's forehead, oozing out of the pores of his skin, turning into tiny rivulets as tears filled his eyes.

"Don't!" Monique screamed, and grabbed the head away from him. Sean stumbled backward. Monique buried the head in the folds of cloth and placed it back into the sack. Then she tore off a piece of fabric and turned around. Sean was about to touch his face. She brushed his hand aside and wiped the blood off his forehead, his temples, and down the side of his face.

"What happened?" he asked.

"It must have been the wine," Monique replied as she stuffed the bloodstained cloth into the pocket of her silk smock.

"No," Sean argued. "It wasn't the wine, and you know it." He shook his thoughts clear. "It was the sculpture, wasn't it?"

Monique avoided his demanding gaze. "I told you that

you weren't ready. Next time, listen to me.'' Taking the glass of wine off the stool, Monique circled the shrouded figure, dwarfed by its size but at the same time towering above it. She walked over to the huge cube of black and silver marble pushed against the wall. Climbing up and leaning back against the wall, she brought the glass to her lips and sat quietly sipping the wine, her gaze cast on the floor, empty, expressionless.

Sean felt a sudden surge of anger course through his body at the thought of Monique intentionally doing what she did. He found himself struggling with his feelings, fueled by his sense of inadequacy. Aware of what was happening yet unable to get a grip on himself only made him that much angrier. He started toward Monique, about to say something, but before he could speak or touch her, he was silenced with a stabbing pain in his chest. It took his breath away and nearly dropped him to his knees. Unable to stop himself, Sean spun around, his anger boiling out of control as he started across the studio, blindly drawn to the far corner by a force he couldn't fight.

Anger suddenly turned to fear—fire to ice—when he caught a glimpse of the polychromed bronze, certain that he'd seen it move. He stopped, or was stopped—he couldn't tell which it was. He tried to turn back, but nothing worked—not his legs, not his arms. He couldn't even move his head. When he tried to speak, there was no sound.

Left with no choice, the blood in his veins turning to ice, chilling him to his very marrow, Sean took on the painted goddess. He compared what he saw with what he'd committed to memory the last time he was here. Her arms, while outstretched, were now raised higher, her powerful muscles flexing, not smooth and supple, as if to strike, not embrace. The wings of her grotesque consorts, no longer images of fallen angels, were spread wide, ready to take flight. Feathers were now leather. He was sure he could see hideous claws extended, like a cat about to seize its prey. His gaze fell to the floor amid a spatter of shadowy red spots.

Sean's heart was now pounding him deaf as he tried to think what to do, how to break free. But from what? From whom? Suddenly, something was inside his head, twisting his thoughts into useless knots. *You fool,* he thought. *It's her, it must be. Stop fighting. Look at her. You have nothing to hide. Show her that.* He found her eyes, which were no longer sea green as he remembered them, but crimson, and boiling with hate.

He took her on, his eyes wide open, inviting her into his heart, his soul, hiding nothing from her. He felt a sudden thud in his chest as if his heart had stopped, then restarted. The pain was gone. He felt dizzy, lost his balance, and stumbled backward.

When he looked up, she was just as he first saw her, arms lowered, inviting, not threatening, eyes as clear and green as an emerald sea. The wings of her consorts were raised, as if settling down from flight, and feathery soft. He looked for their claws, but their arms were twisted and turned away, their paws curled up into fists. He refused to believe what he saw, but at the same time he rejected what he'd seen only seconds earlier.

With a bewildered shake of his head, Sean started back across the studio, replaying everything in his mind, over and over again, looking for something, anything that would explain what he'd felt, what he'd seen. "What you think you saw," he muttered to himself as he approached Monique, who was sitting where he'd left her, an empty wineglass in her lap, as if nothing had happened.

"Feel better?" she asked, sounding honestly concerned.

Sean sighed. "I feel like I've just been run over by a truck." He sat on the other side of the marble cube, holding his head, his shoulder touching Monique's. "And to make it worse, I've got a monster headache." He began rubbing his temples with his fingertips in small, tight circles. "Maybe you're right," he whispered. "Maybe it was the wine." Although he'd said it, felt it, he didn't believe it. "I always did have trouble with red wine, something to do with the tannin."

He laughed, but softly, as if it hurt to laugh. "Got any white wine?" he asked, and leaned back, gazing up at the ceiling. "Maybe a glass or two of that will help in some strange way?"

Monique reached out and began to massage Sean's neck. Her move surprised him into sitting perfectly still and shutting his eyes, barely breathing. Now and then she pressed her thumb and fingers into the base of his skull, held them there for a few seconds—melting away his pain—then continued kneading the muscles in his neck. The strength of her hand, the heat of her touch, slowly numbed the throbbing in his head until it was no more than a bad memory.

"What did you think of my new dealer, Mr. Vanderbilt?" Monique asked.

Sean was about to sit up, but opted for Monique's soothing touch and sat still. "He struck me as a very determined man." Sean chuckled to himself. "He reminded me of a vampire, the way he moved in on people. Only, he wants to sink his teeth into their wallets, not their jugular." Sean was certain he could feel Monique smile, sharing his feeble attempt at humor. "Perhaps that's what a dealer has to be like to survive?" he wondered aloud.

"Now that you've met him, Sean, do you think he can sell my work? I wasn't sure when we first set him up, since my bronzes were pricy compared to what he was handling. But George said he thought the man could do a good job for us once he got his feet wet, so I went along with it."

"For *us*?" Sean asked. "Does he represent George, too?"

The smile Sean thought he'd felt bubbled over into the sound of amusement when Monique said, "George is not only my friend, he's my agent. He gets a percentage of everything I sell in exchange for keeping an eye on the dealers to make sure they hold up their end of the bargain." She gave Sean an affectionate pat on the top of his head, then tousled his hair. "As I'm sure you learned from Bruce, dealers are not a particularly trustworthy lot."

"You don't know?" Sean asked.

"Know what?"

"*Man's Fate* was sold. At least that's what Skip's associate told me. I stopped back to have another look at it, and—"

Sean suddenly stopped talking when the frightening pressure of Monique's grip took his breath away. He thought she was going to break his neck, she was squeezing so hard. "Monique, you're hurting me."

She let go and stood up, her back to Sean. "When was this?" she asked, the timbre of her voice that of steel striking steel.

Sean stood up, rubbing his neck. "I was there on Tuesday, around noon. They were just getting it ready for shipment."

"Are you absolutely certain of this?"

With this question tendered—the edge of her words razor sharp—Sean wished he hadn't said anything. "I'm only telling you what I was told."

"Do you know who bought it?"

Sean stood up and stepped beside Monique. She moved away from him. When he tried getting around her, she turned away, refusing to look at him. He gave up. "The woman I spoke with didn't come right out and say who it was in so many words, but when I baited her, she slipped and told me that someone named Richard Hunt had just left." Sean caught and stopped himself from saying that Brad Johnson was with this man Hunt, fearing it would put an end to his working with Monique. "Lydia also told me that George was in the back room helping—"

Monique spun around, fire raging in her eyes. "You must leave," she said in a deadly quiet voice. "Now."

Confused by her reaction, too weak to argue with her—his head still spinning—Sean simply nodded obediently and walked across the studio. Although something told him to, he refused to look in the direction of the polychromed bronze, and slipped outside.

The cool night air washed over him, clearing his thoughts as he dragged his feet through the thick grass to his car, wondering if he'd really seen what he thought he had. "It's not possible," he told himself. "It must be something in the air. It's probably the mold from the hay in the loft. You always did have trouble with sour hay, don't you remember? It always made you sick."

Chapter Sixteen

At the foot of the steep terraced hillside behind Merrywood Library, surrounded by six-foot-high brick walls crawling with ivy, lay Merrywood Garden. Inside the long rectangular garden, white pebbled paths crisscrossed back and forth over the struggling lawn, trapping neatly cut-out circles, squares, and triangles overflowing with flowering herbs such as scented French lavender, sweet pink marjoram, pineapple sage, and silver thyme. Glazed ceramic pots planted with dwarf evergreens stood at attention beside marble benches. At the far end, overlooking the Hudson River, was a sweeping Romanesque portico enclosed with fluted stone columns holding up a weathered cedar trellis dripping with vines.

With his hands stuck in the pockets of his green corduroy slacks, Sean descended the hollowed-out sandstone steps cut into the terraced hillside leading down to the garden. At the bottom, he smiled and nodded, acknowledging the two gardeners—a husband-and-wife team, both former professors now retired—as they slipped out through the arch-topped entrance. Cradled in their arms were bundles of thorny branches from the rosebushes they'd just pruned, the same rosebushes that every year looked like they were going to die, only to burst back to life with swirls of yellow and red.

Opting for the grass instead of the paths, Sean wound his way through the garden, stopping now and then to check out what had died and what had been planted in its place. At the portico, he walked to one end and wedged himself into the corner of the long curving bench. He sat looking out over the river, which was smooth as glass, no sign of movement, not a ripple marring its watery face. *Must be at maximum flood,* he decided. Over the years, with the help of the *Hudson River Almanac*—and Bruce Fanning's constant reminders that "it's not a river, MacDonald, it's a tidal estuary"— Sean had taught himself to read the signs of the ocean's subtle but undaunted excursion hundreds of miles inland.

Soothed by the cool breeze whispering out of the hills across the river, Sean leaned back and shut his eyes. He was dead tired. He hadn't slept more than an hour at a stretch since returning from Monique's studio late Friday night, thoughts of the polychromed bronze and her hideous cohorts waking him in a cold sweat before he could get away from them. *Why?* he wondered. *Why the hell can't you just get in and get out of something like everyone else, without getting involved?* Sean felt himself getting angry, and didn't want to. "You don't have the energy to get angry," he growled, and laughed at himself. But it was no laughing matter, and he knew it only too well. He hadn't even been able to write the last two days, which was something that came naturally to him every morning, as naturally as day followed night. His brain told him one thing, his heart another, as he struggled to make sense out of what he'd seen—"what you thought you saw," he countered—and what he knew could be.

He shook his head. *You never should have taken this project on—you knew it wasn't right before you walked into the academy.* No sooner had he thought this, and resolved to give Brad Johnson his advance back—and tell Monique what he'd decided to do—than his stubborn streak took over. *Don't be a jerk. Your imagination is getting the better of you. She's probably right about the wine—you know how red wine can affect you.*

For a moment it all seemed to make good sense, only it still didn't feel right to him. Sean drew quiet, then asked himself, "If it does affect you that way, then why didn't you have any trouble with the wine at Pamela's?" He slapped his hands down on his thighs and was about to stand up. "That's it, call Brad and—"

"MacDonald!" someone bellowed, Sean's name echoing through the garden.

Sean jumped up and looked toward the library to see Oliver standing on the top of the sandstone steps, his hands stuck on hips. When he appeared to have Sean's attention, Oliver poked his watch with his thick finger and called out, "You're late." Then he turned and marched stiff-legged across the top of the grassy knoll, and disappeared around the side of Merrywood Library.

Sean was suddenly angry with himself for having done something he'd never done with Oliver—not once in the ten years he'd known him—which was to be late. It added one more reason to the list of excuses he now had to call Brad Johnson and beg off.

Lowering his head, Sean raced through the garden, crossing patches of grass and strips of pebbled paths, bolted up the three flights of stone steps, and circled the library on his way to Merrywood Hall and Oliver's office. The grass on the common, sorely in need of cutting, was still covered with the night's heavy dew. His shoes and pants quickly became soaked as he marched across the unkempt lawn. He made it even worse by kicking the dandelions that had gone to seed, one after another, causing them to explode in a puff of white and cling to his pants like a swarm of mosquitoes.

Sean slowed to a tiptoe when he saw Oliver sitting in his overstuffed wing chair—head bowed, hands folded on top of the portfolio lying open in his lap. He appeared to be asleep, as if nothing had happened. Oliver was like that: angry one second, the matter completely forgotten the next. With a mischievous smile, certain that Oliver was faking it,

Sean glanced around the room, searching for the large brass bell he knew Oliver kept in his office. It was the only clue to Oliver's former life as a Jesuit priest, a life only Sean was privy to. Not even Dean Potter knew.

And it wasn't a dinner bell, as Oliver had told everyone who asked about it, but the bell to call the brothers to vespers. Oliver had told Sean, but only after demanding—and getting—a solemn pledge of secrecy, "I borrowed it when I went over the wall. I took it as a reminder. I ring it as hard as I possibly can whenever I have doubts about my secular life."

The thought of Oliver doing just that, his robust little body shaking all over, brought forth a laugh Sean had to stifle as he lifted the heavy brass bell off the bookshelf behind Oliver's chair. He was careful not to let the clapper strike the dome as he raised it over Oliver's head, intent on ringing his friend awake. But his pleasure was denied him when Oliver, in his patented baritone voice, asked, "Now, is that a nice thing to do to an old man like me?"

"You were born old." Sean laughed, and shook the bell anyway.

Dropping the portfolio onto the ottoman, Oliver jumped up, relieved Sean of the bell, and returned it to its rightful spot on the shelf. He made a concerted effort to set it into the circle of dust that had collected around it.

Sean slumped up against the bookshelves, his hands back in his pockets again. "Want to grab a bite to eat—and a cold beer?"

Oliver glanced at the yellowed ivory face of the miniature tall-case clock on the top of his desk. He sighed and shook his head. "Can't," he said. "I've got a meeting with Potter after lunch, and you know how she feels about people drinking."

"I'll buy you a pack of gum," Sean offered. "Juicy Fruit always worked for me," he said with a grin. "It'll cover up just about anything—even garlic."

Oliver stood staring at Sean for a moment, an affectionate smile on his face. "Have you forgotten so soon what that woman is like?" he asked. "Ever since that party we gave you the week before you left, when poor Bruce—God rest his soul—had a little too much to drink, and urinated in her precious ficus plant, she's been a fanatic about anyone drinking during the day. If that woman even *thinks* she smells something on my breath, she'll descend upon me like a bloody harpy and make my life miserable. It's not worth it," Oliver said with a frantic shaking of his head.

Sean couldn't help picturing Sarah Potter, all four foot ten of her, her voice forever scarred from decades of smoking, harping at poor Oliver. But imagining her giving up her own daily dose of martinis—a minimum of two—was a different story altogether. "No one's ever going to take these away from me," she had often said, her nicotine-stained fingers locked around her glass, as if daring anyone to try.

"How is dear Sarah?" Sean asked as he began absentmindedly straightening the books on one of the shelves.

"Still upset as ever that you left—and still taking it out on all of *us* for not stopping you—if that's what you're asking."

Sean gestured toward the portfolio. "Come up with anything interesting?" he asked, sidestepping Oliver's reference to Sarah Potter's grudge against him for having "up and abandoned me," as she'd put it, when he refused to reconsider his resignation.

Oliver's ruddy Irish face came back to life. "Where do you want to start?" he asked. Gathering up the portfolio, he walked over to the window and put it down on the deep-set stone sill.

Stepping beside him, Sean pointed to the open page, fingering the photograph of the bronze he'd seen at the academy the evening he met Monique. "How about right here?"

Oliver chuckled to himself. "It has all the symbolic elements of Medusa," he said authoritatively. "As I'm sure you know. A decapitation, hair that looks like serpents, and a fierce gaze reminiscent of the one Medusa was known to have had, which could turn a man to stone. Only there's a not-so-little difference in this composition as compared with the Greek myth I believe it's derived from: In this composition, a man has been beheaded, not a woman, as was the case with the Gorgon, Medusa.''

Sean nodded, making it clear he knew that already. "And the others?" he asked.

Oliver fanned the pages with a turn of his wrist and flick of his thumb. "From what I can see, all of them are based upon events or characters in ancient mythology, or have been drawn from biblical themes. They're also all sculpted in a similar style, with a strong nineteenth-century academic influence, but then, I'm sure you saw that, too. However, there's one notable point, which appears to be common to all of the pieces.''

"And that is?" Sean asked, folding his arms and leaning up against the side of the bookcase, anxious to hear what Oliver had to say.

Oliver flipped forward a few pages and stopped at the photos of *The Seven Cardinal Sins*. "The faces of the men. Their features are more modern than ancient." He tapped one face after another. "Look at their square jaws and relatively common faces, except, of course, for their hideously ugly expressions. They're totally unlike the women she's depicted, all of whom have a classical look about them.'' He began turning the pages slowly, pausing for a moment at each sculpture, then continuing. "See the wide-set eyes, high cheekbones, and the pronounced noses, just short of what might be considered aquiline?" He turned back to the photo Sean had first pointed out. "All except for this one—the one I call Medusa verso—she's as modern looking as they come.''

Sean was all eyes and ears. "How so?" he asked, scrutinizing the photo as if seeing it for the first time.

Oliver sounded indignant when he said, "Look at her flat nose, wide forehead, broad cheekbones, and the middle European shape of her head. Everything about her says twentieth-century melting pot, while the facial features of the other women are, in my opinion, distinctly classical. A few of them are even older—almost primitive looking. Yet every one of the men, bar none, is as contemporary looking as any man on the street. The only thing missing is a coat and tie.''

Oliver folded his arms and leaned against the end of the bookcase bracketing the other side of the window, unconsciously mimicking Sean's posture. "It's no accident," he said. "And on top of it, each man's physiognomy is distinctly different from any other, telling me that she used different models for each work."

Sean began paging through the portfolio with a whole new perspective. "I see what you mean," he said thoughtfully.

"Here, look at this." Oliver slipped a folded sheet of paper out of his inside blazer pocket. "I prepared this list for you. I matched up the sculptures with the allegorical inspirations I think they've been derived from. Each one is tied into a number that I scribbled in red beside the respective photograph."

Oliver shook the paper to get Sean's attention away from the binder. "Take a look at it and see what you think." He put it into Sean's hand. "One thing's for sure," he said with a note of respect. "This woman knows her mythology—right down to the most minute detail—*and* she also knows her biblical history. The curious thing is that she seems to have only chosen violent events—a rape, decapitation, or some sort of cruel torture—and in nearly every composition has rewritten history. The most obvious example of this is the Medusa composition."

Sean began reading the handwritten list Oliver had prepared. He pictured anew each of the bronzes as he noted the characters or events from ancient mythology that Oliver had identified as the possible inspirations for Monique's provocative—and more often than not frightening—sculptures. At the bottom of the page, he frowned and looked up. "You think she hates men?" he asked, a clear note of cautious skepticism in his voice.

Oliver was waiting for him, his Irish-red eyes twinkling with anticipation, as if he was the student, Sean the teacher. "Yes," he replied unequivocally. "That, or she is out—"

"Are you serious?" Sean interrupted, trying his best not to sound like he was displeased, which he wasn't, not by any means.

Oliver beamed. "That's the same thing your friend asked."

About to pick up the portfolio, Sean hesitated. *"Friend?"*

"Yes." Oliver smiled. "The lady that was here yesterday."

Sean appeared thoughtful for moment, eyed Oliver suspiciously, then asked, "Lady? Here? What did she look like?"

Oliver blinked, then a few more times, as if retrieving a file from a card catalogue in his brain. "Tall," he said smartly, and gestured toward Sean. "About your height. With long silky hair, and a classical face." He patted his face and gestured to the portfolio. "A lot like the women in there. Exquisite. And with eyes as black as any I've ever seen. She was entrancing."

Smiling, Oliver asked in a somewhat envious way, "Where in the world do you find these women, Sean?" He laughed. "Do you think she has a short sister?"

Sean relaxed. "Was her nose pierced?" he asked, tapping the side of his own nose. "With an emerald in it?"

Oliver made a sour face. "My goodness, no."

"Was she on the trim side, with orange hair?"

Oliver smiled devilishly. "Trim? I'd say she was more athletic than trim, but still womanly. And her hair was—" He looked around, as if searching for something. "Her hair was the color of my brass bell, only polished and shiny, not all tarnished." His face lit up. "And she was dark-skinned, but not tanned. I'd guess she was either Mediterranean or Middle Eastern. But whatever her nationality, she was unquestionably exotic in my opinion."

Sean's expression went from curious to concerned as he slowly closed the portfolio. "What makes you think she was my friend? Did she ask for me by name? Did she tell you that she knew me? Had you even seen her with me before?"

Oliver cocked his head to one side. "No on all counts. I just assumed she was your friend, since she knew all about the portfolio you gave me, and about your assignment with *Entasis*. She knew a lot about you, too. So I just thought—"

Sean pushed himself off the wall with a sudden jerking movement. He was upset and it clearly showed. "What was her name?" he asked, making it sound like an order.

Oliver shrugged. "I—I never asked."

Sean threw his hands up. "Some woman walks into your office out of the blue, starts asking you questions—doesn't give you her name—and you tell her anything she wants to know? That's not the Oliver Shore I know," Sean said with a swat of his hand at the air.

As if to redeem himself, Oliver added, "She wasn't alone."

"Oh?" Sean picked up the portfolio. "Who was she with?"

Oliver momentarily appeared befuddled. "Well, I *think* she wasn't alone. Soon after she arrived, I heard the rustle of someone outside my window. But when I looked, no one was there. A few minutes later, I heard someone in the hallway outside my door." Oliver held his hands out. "Sean, I'm sorry if I—"

Sean slipped his arm around Oliver's shoulder and started for the door, the portfolio under his arm. "It's not your fault," he said. "Don't worry about it. Now that I think about it, it sounds like something Brad Johnson might do. He doesn't trust anyone, not even his own mother. Knowing him, he probably sent someone up here to poke around and see what I was doing."

Sean handed the portfolio back to Oliver, then patted his coat pocket. "I'll keep the list, you keep the portfolio. See if you can come up with any other ideas of where these images might have been taken from."

Wrapping his arms around the binder, Oliver asked quizzically, "How do you think Bradley knew to send someone here to see me? Did you by any chance tell—"

Sean didn't hear the rest of Oliver's question. His head was suddenly filled with a hundred questions of his own, all shouting to be answered. And just as many wanted—demanded—to be asked.

"Sean?" Oliver called in a soft, caring voice as Sean walked out of his office and started down the hall, wrapped up in his own thoughts. "Are you all right? Sean? This isn't like you!"

But Sean was deaf to Oliver's pleas. The harder he tried to concentrate, to think about what Oliver had said about Monique's work, what it meant—to try to make some sense out of it all in light of what he now knew—the more confused he became. His head was filling up with unfamiliar and unwanted images. And not because he didn't understand what Oliver was driving at—*This is a no-brainer,* he thought. It was as if something had slipped inside his head, and every time he tried to focus, to make heads or tails out of something, it snatched his thoughts away from him.

What the fuck is happening? He stopped, clenching his fists, forcing himself to concentrate on what Oliver had said—suddenly certain that he saw a link, a theme, a common thread—only to come up with a blank screen, splashed with every possible shade of red, obliterating whatever it was he thought he'd seen.

Each time he was certain he'd grabbed hold of a tiny thread, it slipped away—or was pulled out of his grasp—and was replaced with confusion, frustration, then anger: that infectious, poisonous feeling, the one emotion he'd thought he'd defeated—driven out of his heart—three years before.

Chapter Seventeen

With three precise keystrokes, Sean saved the file he was working on—hit the Print key—and sat back to read the cover letter he'd written to Brad Johnson.

As promised when we spoke on the phone yesterday, I'm sending you drafts of the first two articles for the Gerard series. These will give you a good sense of how I want to approach things, which, as I mentioned, is more narrative as compared with straight reporting. I think the current expression for it is "faction."

I also want to apologize for being a little pushy yesterday on the phone. I was, understandably I think, concerned about someone showing up at Oliver's office and acting like they were my friend. Since they knew about the assignment, and asked a lot of questions about it—and about me—you were the likely candidate who might have sent someone there. Naturally, I had to check it out. Thanks for your understanding. I guess I'll just have to look elsewhere for this mystery woman.

Unless I hear otherwise, I'll continue writing along

the lines of these first articles, and send you drafts of the others as I finish them. I'll also send final rewrites of earlier pieces as I complete them.

Satisfied with it, but still leery of what Brad had to say when Sean had called him the day before—*He was too nice*—Sean pulled the two dozen double-spaced pages out of the laser printer and slipped the drafts of parts one and two of his yet-to-be-titled series on Monique Gerard into the large envelope he'd already hand-addressed. After signing the letter, he added it to the packet, sealed everything up, and sat back. No matter how hard he tried, regardless of what he told himself, Sean knew something was wrong. *If it wasn't someone from Brad's office, then who could it have been? George is the only one who knew I had the portfolio.*

Did you say something to Pamela? Sean wondered, and tried recalling what he'd said to her about his meeting with George White. He laughed. "Maybe Pamela has a half sister? Or perhaps Monique has a daughter!" Recalling that Oliver had said the woman was dark-skinned, Sean thought, *Right, and George White is her father.* This last idea put a disquieting end to Sean's lighthearted humor when he realized it wasn't so far-fetched, given the extended relationship he now knew existed between them.

"Well then, go check it out, Sherlock," he told himself with a sarcastic bite to his words. "You've already ignored your own intuition, which told you to pull out of this fucking mess. Go ahead, just walk in and ask George, 'Hey, buddy, are you fucking Monique?' The worst thing that can happen is he pokes you in the nose." He shook his head. "Now, that's something I'm sure Brad would love to read about."

Not wanting to think about this anymore, Sean exited his working program, turned the computer off, and headed for his bedroom to change and go running. When all else failed, when he couldn't think or see straight, that's what he did; run. It was the only thing that helped clear his head, something he wanted—desperately needed—to do right now. *Before this thing swallows you up.*

"Some vacation between books," he grumbled to himself. He stripped down, threw his clothes onto his bed, and slipped his shorts, T-shirt, and socks on. He grabbed his running shoes off the drying rack he kept them on and darted down the hall to the kitchen. "How about a twin sister? Now, *that* would be interesting." Sean laughed as he slid across the crackly linoleum on the kitchen floor in his stocking feet. Bumping to a stop against the hardwood table pushed to the wall between the windows, he flopped down into one of the sturdy straight-backed chairs to put his shoes on.

The kitchen of his second-floor apartment was like the rest of the country Victorian it was in: oversized and decorated with remnants from the past. The gingerbread on the outside of the house was cracked and faded and dried out, but every delicious morsel was still intact. On the inside, the walls were covered with puffy flower-print wallpaper. The clunky woodwork had been painted over at least a hundred times with thick, glossy enamel. The ceilings were cracked and peeling, except for the one in the kitchen, which was covered with squares of embossed tin, yellowed from age and cooking grease. His study, however—where he spent most of his time—had been scraped and sanded, and painted bone white: walls, ceiling, and trim.

What about a friend of Monique's? A student? he wondered as he raced down the narrow stairway leading from his kitchen to the side porch. *Maybe she's checking up on me?* He pushed the screen door open and stepped outside.

"You're starting to sound paranoid, MacDonald," he told himself as he jumped off the porch and broke into a lazy jog across the threadbare lawn. "Screw it," he grumbled, and sprinted down the quiet country road beside the house without bothering to warm up, as if trying to run away from his thoughts.

When he abruptly slowed to a steady pace, a pair of shadows appeared on the road, drifted ahead of him, then fell behind.

Without breaking stride, Sean looked up to see what was in the sky overhead but was blinded by the glare of the midday sun. *Must be a pair of golden eagles,* he thought. *It's good to see them nesting in the area again.* But something made him stop and look up again, this time shielding his eyes from the sun.

"Jesus!" he said with a disbelieving shake of his head. "I didn't realize they were so goddamn big."

Chapter Eighteen

Sean stood at the bottom of the steep flight of stone steps rising from the sidewalk to the front entrance of the New York Public Library, its granite face blackened with urban soot, its copper roof no longer shiny as a new penny, but green and crusty. The morning sun had finally managed to burn through the smog suffocating the City, warming it back to life. What was left of rush-hour traffic was crawling down Fifth Avenue behind him.

Sean glanced at his watch. It was ten o'clock. It had taken him four hours to drive down from Red Hook, caught up in a caravan of commuting kamikazes, park at the Met, and walk the thirty-seven blocks down Fifth Avenue to the library. This time, however, he'd remembered to wear his running shoes, not the loafers he had worn when he swam his way through the Village to meet Monique at the academy.

He wasn't halfway up the mountain of granite steps and already he hated the thought of doing what he'd come into New York to do. "Let's hope you don't suffer the same fate as Sisyphus," he said, and laughed out loud, startling an elderly woman nearby into scurrying up the steps to get away from him. But Sean knew he had little choice in the matter now that his peace of mind—his orderly world—had been violated by some woman who appeared at Oliver Shore's doorstep, asking all sorts of questions about something she shouldn't even have known about, and about him.

As he stood there, he realized he wasn't just curious anymore, he was angry—still angry—even thought he'd tried his damnedest to keep it from getting the better of him. *But at what? And why?* he wondered.

Grabbing the journal out from under his arm, Sean darted up the steps—taking two at a time—and caught up with the old lady. "Good morning," he said with a polite nod, before slipping sideways through an open door and disappearing into the musty belly of the library, driven by a fierce determination to find out what the hell was going on with Brad and George White—*and that Richard Hunt, whoever the fuck he is.* Maybe then he might find out who that woman was. "Probably some girlfriend of Brad's," he decided.

The first hour was consumed reacquainting himself with the library he hadn't used in twenty years, most of it spent deciphering the foreign language spoken by the electronic terminals. This accomplished, he surfed the periodicals, compiling a list of magazines and journals, each one serving up their own slice of the art market. He found more publications than he'd expected.

Next, he conducted a series of searches using "Gerard" as the keyword. After that, he combined her name with the word "sculpture" or "sculptor." The extent of what he found, and in such a short time, made his research efforts of years ago seem like he'd carried them out in the Dark Ages, skulking about the cloistered halls of medieval monasteries and digging through illuminated manuscripts.

Although he fully expected to find articles and reviews here and there, he wasn't prepared for what surfaced as he poked and prodded the keyboard. Some articles dated back beyond the ten years he'd been led to believe by George White that Monique had been showing her work. *Maybe she really meant what she said when she told you she'd been*

163

doing it forever, Sean told himself half seriously as he plodded on.

Articles popped up everywhere: in monthly slicks, newsprint weeklies, tabloids, and the metropolitan New York–area newspapers. Something, if only a blurb, had been written about Monique, or her work, every few months in publications such as *Art & Antiques, Art & Auction, Art In America, Sculpture, The New Age of Art, The New Criterion,* and even *Entasis.* She was also mentioned in dozens of other equally well-known trade publications and art journals.

The juiciest write-ups, however, and more often than not the most informative, were to be found in the pages of the *Village Voice.* Many of them had been penned by Allan Stern, a name Sean recognized immediately because of what Pamela had told him.

Adding to his surprise about the wealth of media coverage of Monique and her work was the appearance of articles in regional publications, mostly newspapers, in places such as Chicago, Dallas, and Los Angeles. The greatest concentration, however, was in the Philadelphia area. Balanced in their review of her work, many of them included either direct or indirect mention of a young curator at the Philadelphia Museum of Art, Dr. Robert W. Anderson, who appeared to be a champion of Monique's work. "Dr. Anderson is a rising star in the museum world," one critic had written in her glowing review of a show that included one of Monique's bronzes. "Dr. Anderson is a man of vision, possessing the experienced eye of a collector, while guided by the mind of a scholar. He is a man whose lead we should follow," Allan Stern wrote in his review of that very same show. He then added, speaking of Monique's work, "*Treason*—which was selected to receive the show's prestigious $10,000 purchase prize for sculpture—possesses the classical beauty of Michelangelo and the raw, masculine power of Rodin. Mademoiselle Gerard is a genius, towering over her contemporaries."

Robert Anderson had also juried a national competition sponsored by the respected Philadelphia art dealer David Carlton, "whose second-generation gallery is located just off

Rittenhouse Square, in the heart of the city,'' one reviewer noted. It seems Anderson had chosen Monique's entry, *Cybele and Attis*—a piece not illustrated in the portfolio, based on the description of the sculpture in the review—to receive the Erastus Dow Palmer Award. The prize was for sculpture created in a neoclassical manner, a style that E. D. Palmer, a nineteenth-century American master, was himself known for.

What was confusing for Sean, however, was the fact that the award was also a purchase prize, as *Treason* had been, which meant the benefactor funding the award—''an anonymous patron,'' according to the review—would receive the sculpture in exchange for the amount of the cash prize. This made no sense at all to Sean, given what he knew it cost to simply cast Monique's work—*or any bronze of that size,* he told himself—let alone the gallery prices her bronzes were commanding. *Or were they?* he wondered.

Sean soon became overwhelmed with the tedious job of locating all of the publications, leafing through them, then copying those articles worthy of saving. He was about to push himself away from the terminal he'd staked out as his own and call it a day, when he was approached by a woman he'd seen now and then during the course of the day, but always at a distance. Stepping beside him, she put her hand on his shoulder and said quietly, ''I couldn't help noticing your frustration. May I be of any help?'' she asked, and leaned forward, reading the screen, glancing at Sean's notes.

There was something about her—her voice, her touch, which was cool, almost cold, or perhaps the foreign, but at the same time familiar, fragrance of her perfume—that settled Sean down when he was about to stand up and introduce himself. It wasn't long before she'd extracted from him that he was on sabbatical from Hart College—*a tiny twist of the truth,* he told himself—and was quick to point out he could arrange for copies to be made of all of the articles he wanted, and sent to his office at the school.

''It'll take a week, ten days, tops,'' she told him. ''May I show you?'' When Sean stood up, she took his seat and proceeded to scan the work he'd done, as well as to read his

165

notes, beginning to end. Within ten minutes, using a series of repeated commands typed so fast Sean couldn't memorize them, she'd requested copies of all of the articles he'd checked off—stopped to get the address of the college from him—then continued until she was finished. "There," she said, and stood up. "Done."

"I really do appreciate—"

Sean stopped in midsentence, his well-intentioned thought erased from his mind when he came face-to-face with this woman. As tall as he was, her eyes were black as coal, but clear as ice and just as cold. Her shoulder-length auburn hair framed a perfect bronzed face. *It's your imagination,* he told himself when Oliver's words crept into his thoughts.

"Thank you," he finally said, offering his hand.

She took his hand in hers, her skin the same temperature as her penetrating gaze. He felt a chill slice up his arm, cut into his chest. Startled, he blinked away, then turned back. She smiled, as if satisfied about something, and walked away. She moved effortlessly, gracefully, giving the impression her feet had no need for the floor. The moment she was out of sight, Sean went to brush his hair off his forehead, but stopped when he caught the smell on his hand from her touch. He shut his eyes, searching, thinking, then found what he was looking for. "Monique?" he whispered. "Can't be," he said with a disbelieving shake of his head.

Laughing at himself for thinking what he did, Sean sat down and dove back into the keyboard with a vengeance, this time surfing only the New York papers. He'd intentionally left them out of his initial search, having decided earlier that he wanted to read as many of the citations as he could, in spite of the fact most of them were on microfilm. "Besides," he said, glancing at his watch, "you'll miss the rush-hour traffic heading out of the City," thereby giving himself an excuse for staying a little longer.

After making another entry in his journal, one of hundreds of cryptic notes printed, not written in script, Sean spooled the last roll of microfilm into the reader. He scrolled forward to the date noted on the printout from his search, and settled back to read the review of last year's members' show at the New York Academy of Fine Arts, which had appeared in the *Village Voice*.

When he got near the end of the review, Sean sat up like he'd been stuck by a pin and reread in a whisper what Allan Stern had said in his closing comments. "In this reviewer's opinion, Gerard must now be viewed as a modern-day computer copyist—a thief of others' art—hiding inside the hunchback body of a dwarf, begging our compassion."

Sean couldn't believe his eyes as he read the final epithet in Stern's unbridled castigation of Monique and her work: "She's pathetic, and a fraud, like her work."

Confused, he flipped back a few pages in his journal to read what he'd copied from Stern's review of a show in Philadelphia, only a year earlier. *What the hell changed your tune?* He closed his journal and stood up. "Let's find this Stern person and ask him," he decided, answering his own question as he picked his journal up and made his way through the maze of desks and cubicle dividers to the back stairs, on his way out the rear entrance of the library.

Facing Sixth Avenue, about to hail a cab, Sean paused and looked at his watch. *You've got just enough time to get there before he closes.* He raised his arm. *Let's go see if our friend Mr. Vanderbilt can shed some light on the relationship between the honorable Mr. White and Mademoiselle Gerard.*

Chapter Nineteen

"We're closed," Lydia Thompson said brusquely when Sean tried slipping into the showroom as she was about to lock the door.

Sean flashed his most disarming smile. "I just want to see Skip for a moment," he said, gently but firmly blocking the door open and stepping inside.

"Mr. Vanderbilt is busy," she snapped, and gestured with an angry glance of her eyes for Sean to leave as she reached her left hand into the pocket of her skirt.

"Please?" he asked as sweetly as he possibly could.

About to unceremoniously usher him out, Lydia stopped and relaxed against the door. "Mr. Peters?" she asked tentatively. Before Sean could answer, her face relaxed too. "*Bruce* Peters, isn't it?"

Wide-eyed, Sean nodded but didn't dare let go of his smile.

Lydia frowned, as if it hurt her face to think, and pointed at Sean with her raised finger. "You were interested in the Gerard piece, weren't you?"

"I'm impressed," Sean said, hoping he sounded that way,

too. "You've got quite a memory, Ms. Thompson."

Lydia smiled somewhat smugly. "It's my business to remember faces and names." She closed and locked the door. "How may I help you, Mr. Peters?" Lydia turned and walked through the gallery to the rear wall, where she dimmed the showroom lights, then raised a number of individual spots, illuminating the heaps of rusted automotive parts rising off the floor, masquerading as sculpture.

Sean stopped in the middle of the gallery when she raised her hand, indicating not to come any farther.

"Skip?" Sean asked. "Is he here? Please?"

With a sigh, Lydia nodded. "Yes, he's here, but he's in the back with someone. I really can't disturb him."

Sean guessed he had all of two seconds to convince her he meant business, and that it was worth her while to do what he wanted. "Skip had shown me another piece he thought I'd be interested in, and I came back to talk to him about it." Lydia didn't appear convinced, or perhaps it was just Sean's own anxiety that made him feel that way, so he quickly added, "I've narrowed my choices down to two pieces: one at Pace Galleries, and the one you have here, one of those lovely cast-chrome sculptures. Remember?" he asked. "It was the one on the pedestal next to us when we were talking."

Lydia melted into a ball of compliance. "Let me check. I don't think the woman he's with is a serious buyer," she said with a disapproving frown. "Perhaps I can move things along." She smiled. "Now, don't go away," she said with a wag of her finger. "I'll be right back."

Sean watched Lydia disappear down the hallway leading to the private viewing rooms in the rear of the gallery. Pleased with his little charade, he started around the showroom, trying to match the battered hubcaps spot-welded to the piles of junk with the make of car they'd come off of. "That one's easy," he said. "It's a Cadillac." He took aim at another. "And that one's off a—"

Sidetracked at the sound of someone behind him, Sean turned to see Lydia Thompson stumbling out into the showroom, white as a ghost. "Are you all right?" he asked, rushing up to her, keeping her from falling forward. She looked at him—looked right through him—her eyes blank. ''What's wrong?'' he asked, shaking her gently. She opened her mouth to speak, but nothing came out. He raised his voice. ''What is it?''

Turning, she pointed to the hallway, then collapsed.

''Lydia!''

Torn between Lydia and what caused her to react this way, Sean hesitated—but only for second—before racing down the hallway, frantically throwing open door after door as he went from darkened room to darkened room until he barged into one, and stopped dead. ''Jesus Christ!'' he gasped, and threw himself back, slamming up against the wall, hitting his head. He began to retch and heave, his empty stomach only able to regurgitate acid and bile, burning his throat.

Hanging from a rope crudely knotted around his neck, suspended from the painted-over skylight above, which had been smashed open, was Skip Vanderbilt—what was left of him. His clothes had been ripped from his body, leaving him naked, his chest sliced open, his heart chewed to shreds. His arms had been pulled from their sockets, and hung loose. His paunchy gut had been torn open, bowels violently pulled out. The floor was littered with gore and shards of glass, the walls spattered with blood and pieces of raw flesh. His genitals had been mauled beyond recognition, his legs a tangled web of muscle and sinew, barely tethered to pristine white bone. His jaw had been pulled down, snapped from his skull, his tongue ripped out—eyes wide open, as if still able to see.

Chapter Twenty

Detective Michael Marcelli—a tall, pudgy cop in his late thirties, with the doe-eyed face of a choirboy but the booming voice of a monsignor—made a final entry in his pad, slapped it shut, and stuffed the battered notebook back into the pocket of his raincoat. "You've been very helpful, Dr. MacDonald." His brown-eyed gaze locked onto Sean's, taking another look, just in case he'd missed something the first time. "We really appreciate your staying as long as you have. I'm sure this hasn't been easy for you. We'll call if we have any more questions, which I'm sure we will in light of the mess we found here tonight." Marcelli held his hand up. "But before you leave, give me a minute to find my partner. I'd like to double-check and see if he wants to ask you anything more. Do you mind, sir?"

Sean tried coming up with a compliant smile, but it ended up looking more like a weary grimace. "Of course not, Detective. I promise"—he scratched an X over his heart, another one of his childhood things rediscovered—"I won't go near the front door until you tell me it's okay to leave." He slumped into the corner between the front window and the brick wall, and said softly, "Besides, I don't have the energy to walk out of here just yet."

Marcelli flashed a sympathetic smile, nodded, and headed for the hallway leading back to the viewing rooms. Sean glanced at his watch. It was almost eight o'clock. He'd been at the gallery for over two hours now, with nothing more than black coffee and stale donuts—which he'd declined— to stave off his hunger. He could hear his stomach threatening to eat its way out of his body and go get dinner without him. *At least you've got your appetite back,* he thought. No sooner had he begun considering what he wanted to eat than images of Skip Vanderbilt's body smothered whatever thoughts of food he'd managed to scrounge up. *Shit.*

Shutting his eyes, he pitched his head back and stood listening to the murmur of voices milling about in the gallery. The occasional burst of bawdy laughter by what he knew now were the seasoned veterans, like Marcelli, was a refreshing change from the stifled gags and nervous whispers by the officers who were first on the scene after Lydia called 911, and were stunned into silence by the sight of Skip's body hanging from the skylight like bait for a lion hunt gone awry.

Chunks of flesh had even been found snagged on the twisted metal frame and jagged edges of broken glass in the smashed-out skylight, "where whoever killed the poor bastard must have escaped through," according to Marcelli. Every one of the homicide detectives who went up on the roof to inspect the damage, rope off the crime scene, and look for evidence, came back down with the same disbelieving look on their face, and most with the identical comment: "Jesus, I've never seen anything like it, have you?" Oddly enough, or maybe not, none of them expected an answer.

Out of habit—something he did when he was nervous, or really tired—Sean looked at his watch again. *Shit, it's going to be well after one o'clock in the morning by the time you get home. And that's if they let you out of here in the next ten minutes.* "Fuck it," he said with a discouraged shake of his head. "You might as well grab something to eat around here—pray you can keep it down—and stay over in the City tonight. Maybe Pam—''

Sean stopped at the sound of footsteps approaching. Before he could open his eyes, Lydia Thompson asked with a cynical edge to her words, ''Are they finished interviewing, *Doctor* MacDonald?'' Folding her arms, she leaned a shoulder into the rough brick wall alongside Sean, her gaze fixed on him. ''Or do you want to continue playing your little game, and have me call you Bruce Peters?''

Without lifting his head off the wall, Sean turned to face Lydia. ''I'm sorry I misled you,'' he said sincerely. ''I don't know what made me use that name when I first met Skip.'' *Yes you do,* he thought. ''I guess I didn't want anyone—'' He stopped, shrugged his shoulders, and said with a sigh, ''I'm really sorry.''

Lydia began to say something, but instead she simply turned and leaned up against the wall—looking just as weary as Sean—her wiry frame and stark complexion a bizarre complement to the harsh brick and hardened mortar. ''I didn't hear the police ask you why you were here tonight. For that matter, I can't recall the subject being brought up of why you ever came here in the first place. After all, you sure as hell aren't a collector.''

Sean smiled. For the first time tonight it was his smile, not a made-up smile. ''No one ever asked—not directly. They only asked who I was—asked for some identification—wanted to know what I did for a living, and if I collected this 'stuff'.'' He gestured to one of the rusted mounds of junk and shook his head in disgust. ''I gave them exactly what they asked for, even if it wasn't what they really wanted to know.''

Sean suddenly became serious. ''I learned the hard way, following the murder of a friend of mine, not to volunteer anything to the police—*anything*—which is contrary to my instinct to try and help.'' He laughed. ''As for not being a collector, Ms. Thompson, you're wrong on that count. I collect nineteenth-century French Animalier bronzes—the real stuff, not what's piled up on your floor tonight, looking like droppings from an earthmover.'' Sean waited for a response from Lydia, but she didn't tender one. "That same friend of mine who was murdered started me collecting bronzes years ago, and I've been hooked ever since."

Lydia turned and took on Sean again. "So how do you come to know Brad Johnson?" she asked. "And for that matter, George White and Richard Hunt? You don't strike me as their type."

Their type? Sean thought. "Is that a compliment?" he asked, and sat down on the knee-high window ledge with a sigh of relief at getting off his feet.

"You tell me," she quipped. "They're your friends."

" 'Friends'?" Sean asked, sounding just as skeptical as Lydia. "Hardly. For starters, Brad and I were colleagues some years back at Hart College. We parted on not so good—"

Lydia stabbed a finger in the air at Sean. "*That's* where I know you from!" She gave a soft clap of her hands. "I've seen you a dozen times over the years with Bruce Fanning, who also taught at Hart College. I bet he's that friend of yours who was murdered, wasn't he?"

Hoping she wouldn't start asking about Bruce, Sean nodded wearily and went on. "Brad asked me to finish an assignment Bruce had started. At first I thought he asked because I'm a writer, but it now seems that wasn't the reason. The assignment involved writing a long series of articles on Monique Gerard for *Entasis.* I've been on the project for a little over a month now." Sean held his hands out. "And that, Ms. Thompson, is why I was here in the first place, a struggling writer doing his homework, getting some background material."

Lydia tightened the knot her arms were threaded into and stood eyeing Sean, suspicion still clouding her face. "And how did you come to know Richard Hunt? He doesn't let too many people get close to him, especially writer types."

Sean gave a wide-eyed smile. "I don't know Richard Hunt. I wouldn't know the man if he walked through that door over there right now. That, I'm afraid, was a little twist of the truth on my part." Sean smirked. "But you helped with that one by jumping to conclusions.'' He nodded. ''We're even on that account.''

Lydia didn't look like she was about to cut Sean any slack. ''And George White?'' she asked, inching closer, as if to pin Sean into the corner. ''You don't look like the artsy type.''

Thanks. ''I met our mutual acquaintance, Mr. White, at the New York Academy of Fine Arts, when I went there to interview Gerard last month. I met him again when I returned to interview him for background material, since he has some sort of quasi–business relationship with her. Half agent, half friend. Nice fellow.''

''Bullshit,'' Lydia snapped, surprising Sean, not only with her sharp response but with her choice of words. ''George is a royal pain in the ass. And he's as slimy as a snake.'' Lydia tapped the air in front of Sean's face. ''And judging from the look in your eyes, I'd say that you know it. I've never understood what that Gerard woman saw in him. She must be blind *and* ugly.''

Pricked by the word ''ugly,'' Sean sat up straight. Before he could say anything, he found himself agreeing with Lydia about George, but her comment about Monique had upset him. It was the same feeling he'd gotten when Brad had made the comments he did about Monique, when the two of them met for lunch. He tried sorting his feelings out, but couldn't tell if he was taking it personally, and perhaps feeling defensive, or being protective of Monique. *Or worse,* he thought. *You've come to like her.*

Looking like she'd grown tired of waiting for Sean to respond to her, or had simply taken his silence to mean that he agreed with her, Lydia gave a self-assured nod, pushed herself off the wall, and began pacing about, her face wrinkling up into a thoughtful frown.

''You know,'' she said with a nod of her head, ''I've seen her somewhere before. I just can't can't place her face, and that's not like me.''

''Seen who?'' Sean asked, gladly giving up on his struggle with his feelings about Monique, and what Lydia had said.

''That woman who came in to see Skip earlier this evening, and disappeared into thin air.'' Lydia bit her lip. ''Brad

must have known her, even though he told me he didn't.''
She snorted and shook her head. "It sure as hell wasn't the
first time some fashion plate came in here looking for him."
Lydia scowled. "Of course, she could have been one of
Skip's dealers—he had a pretty bad habit. Or maybe she was
just another new lady friend. God knows he had enough of
them, since none of them lasted more than a week or two."
Lydia was pacing back and forth in front of Sean, deep in
her own thoughts. "Now that I think about it, he usually let
them out the back entrance, which we rarely use. I once saw
him slip one of them a key to his apartment, and heard him
promise her money. Which always confused me, since that
man didn't give anything away to anyone, man or woman.
One way or the other, he made you pay. Me included," she
grumbled, barely above a whisper.

Unsure if what he sensed was anger or rejection, Sean
asked in a cautious tone of voice, "Were you and Skip by
any—"

Lydia laughed. "Heavens no. Skip isn't my type. Can't
you tell?" she asked, her hands on her hips, making it sound
like Sean was blind, too. "I'm gay."

Sean couldn't help looking at Lydia as if he'd just met her
for the first time. His gaze fell down her body from head to
toe, as if something was different now that he knew she was
a lesbian. When he looked up, the expression on her face
was somewhere between amusement and condescension.
"No," he finally said, "I didn't know you were gay. I suppose I'm out of touch with these things. I never knew Bruce
was gay, either, and we were close friends."

"You're kidding, right? Everyone knew about Bruce Fanning."

Sean felt himself suddenly wanting to give Lydia a slap
alongside her head—not to hurt her, just to knock some sense
into her. "Not *everyone* knew," he said with a resentful bite
to his words. "I guess some of us *are* blind, like me and
Mademoiselle Gerard." Lydia stepped back ever so slightly,
indicating she'd felt the brunt of Sean's intended jab. Pleased
with himself, he said, "I take it your partnership with Skip
wasn't to your liking."

"Partnership?" Lydia asked with a note of incredulity in her voice. "We weren't *partners*—I own the gallery. I owned Skip, too, lock, stock, and barrel. I was originally a client of his, a very good client. One day, he asked if I wanted to go partners with him on the purchase of an estate, fifty-fifty. I did, and we both made out very well. We did it a few more times, always equal shares. Each time I turned a tidy profit. Then came the big score, as he called it. Of course, I dove in headfirst, only that time it was all my money—over five hundred thousand—not a penny from Skip. He claimed he was temporarily out of funds. When the deal went sour, I ended up owning a lawsuit. Thankfully, my attorney had drawn up a very tight collateral agreement, which I enforced, much to Skip's surprise. I got the gallery, this building we're in, and Skip's condominium, none of which had very much equity in them."

Lydia seemed to perk up. "So, Dr. MacDonald, here I am, your average, run-of-the-mill workingwoman—struggling to make ends meet—when, only six months ago, I didn't have to work if I didn't want to." She suddenly started laughing, almost uncontrollably.

"What is it?" Sean asked, thinking something was wrong.

Lydia took a steadying breath. "I just remembered," she said, grinning ear to ear. "I took out a life insurance policy on poor, dear Skip. And not just *any* policy, either, but one with a double-indemnity clause, thanks again to my attorney." She chortled to herself. "Suddenly, things aren't so bad after all, now, are they?"

Sean's first thought was *You selfish bitch.* But he changed his tune when he looked at things from Lydia's point of view. *She was an unwilling participant,* he told himself. *She's only trying to bail herself out; you can't fault her for that.* Before he'd completely taken her side, Sean recalled Monique's reaction upon learning about the sale of *Man's Fate,* and was quick to ask, "Did many people know that Skip didn't own the gallery?"

Lydia shook her head. "No one knew. It was one of the terms of the contract. It was an ego thing for Skip. So no

177

one would have known, unless he told them—like I just told you—which no longer makes any difference since the son of a bitch is dead now.''

Don't say anything, Sean told himself when he realized he wanted to tell her to stuff it. He took a breath. ''So as far as anyone on the outside is concerned, Skip would have been the only one responsible for collecting and paying the bills, right?''

She nodded. ''We set things up so it looked like he handled everything. He worked with the artists, negotiated all of the representation agreements, set the asking and taking prices, booked the advertising. And, of course, he took care of sales and clients. I simply controlled the cash, right down to his pocket money.''

Questions were popping up in Sean's head like symbols in a two-bit slot machine. ''Why didn't you pay Gerard for the bronze Skip sold to Richard Hunt?''

Lydia stepped back, looking like the wind had been knocked out of her. ''How the hell did you know that?'' she asked, sounding as much angry as she was surprised.

''Lucky guess,'' Sean replied offhandedly. ''Did you?''

Lydia now sounded defensive. ''We haven't been paid in full yet ourselves—that's why Gerard hasn't been paid. But I did tell Skip I wanted to make sure Gerard got her pro rata share of the advance. He said he would take the cash to her personally. He mentioned something about needing directions to her studio, which he said he would get from George.'' Lydia stuck her hands on her narrow hips. ''Now, I want to know how the hell you—''

Sean waved her question off. ''What did *Man's Fate* sell for?'' he asked, wanting to see if what Brad had told him would match up with Lydia's answer.

Looking irritated at being interrupted, Lydia glanced away for a moment, then back, a worried frown on her face. ''Now that you ask, I'm not certain what the final price was. But Skip would have written it in the sales journal upstairs.''

''How much was the advance you got?''

Lydia hesitated for a moment, as if unsure she wanted to tell Sean that. ''Fifty thousand,'' she finally said.

That number rang a familiar note for Sean. "And the split?"

"Seventy-thirty," she said. "The artist gets the seventy percent, so her share of the advance would have been thirty-five thousand dollars, even though it's common practice in the trade to wait until a piece is paid for before settling up."

"And where is the cash?" Sean asked.

"Upstairs in the safe, where it belongs."

"Just your share, or the entire advance?" he asked warily.

"Both," Lydia snapped. "Skip was planning on seeing Gerard tomorrow, right after he got the directions from George."

"Oh? Are you *sure* it's upstairs?"

"Of course. I put—" She frowned. "No," she said, the muscles in her jaw knotting up. "I didn't put it there, Skip did."

Sean stood up and started for the stairway in the far corner leading to the office upstairs. "Shall we go check and see if it's there?" He waved for Lydia to join him. She was at his side before he could take another two steps. He put his arm around her shoulder. "How much was that insurance policy for?" he asked, and let go of her when she pulled away to take the lead.

Lydia called back over her shoulder, "The amount of my initial investment, five hundred thousand. An even million with the double-indemnity clause. Why do you want to know?"

Sean reclaimed Lydia's shoulder—ignoring her stiffening posture—and pulled her close to him. "Because my intuition tells me that you're going to need a good chunk of that money to pay Mademoiselle Gerard for her bronze, that's why, my dear Ms. Thompson."

Lydia tried getting away, but Sean held her close to him, and whispered so no one else could hear, "Unless, of course, you want that bill collector who was here earlier tonight to come looking for you, after the newspapers tell everyone you're the real owner of Vanderbilt Galleries, and that 'poor dear Skip' was just a flunky."

Lydia elbowed herself free of Sean's hold. "What are you

talking about?'' she demanded, sounding and looking anything but ladylike. ''Are you out of your fucking mind?''

Feeling confident, yet at the same time uncomfortable at what he felt—*someone killed that poor son of a bitch, Vanderbilt, and it sure as hell wasn't Brad, or that dirtbag George White, or some broad, regardless of what Marcelli might think*—Sean asked calmly, ''Do you have any idea what Skip did with the other fifty grand he got from Hunt? Or whoever else was party to this scam?'' He also wanted to ask if she thought Brad was in on it, too, but didn't want to deal with that possibility, not yet at least. *Why not?* he thought.

''What other fifty grand?'' Lydia asked as she stomped up the stairs. Sean followed, but at a relaxed pace. When he got to the top step, he saw Lydia kneeling in front of a safe, frantically spinning the dial back and forth. Pulling the door open, she sat back on her heels. ''Damn.'' She spun around, her eyes ablaze. ''How did you know?''

Lydia rose to her feet and charged Sean. ''I asked you a question,'' she said angrily. ''And while you're at it, try telling me what makes you think Skip got another fifty thousand?'' She poked her finger into Sean's chest. ''And what did you mean by that comment about a bill collector coming back for me?''

She gave him another poke. Sean glanced down at her hand, then up into her heated gaze. He just stood there in silence, staring at her, waiting for her to take her hand off him. When she did, begrudgingly, and stepped back, he asked calmly, ''Does the name Anderson Gallery mean anything to you?''

Lydia hesitated, then let out a heavy sigh and flopped down onto the love seat near the safe, her hands folded in her lap. ''Skip was a silent partner with Anderson when the old man disappeared after that fiasco with Gerard's bronze.'' She shook her head. ''I must be blind, too, I never made the connection.''

She patted the cushion beside her. ''Please,'' she asked, ''sit down and explain what you're talking about, before I scream.''

Sean didn't want to be near her and stayed where he was. "You may not like hearing this, but I was winging it when I said those things. I didn't *know* for sure what was happening." He turned to leave. "But I have a pretty good idea now. I just hope I'm wrong."

"Where are you going?"

"To see if a lady with orange hair has had dinner yet," Sean replied as he started down the stairs. "And find out if one of her trustees ever showed up."

"Do you always talk in riddles?" Lydia asked.

Sean laughed. "Only when everything around me is a riddle."

Chapter Twenty-one

When Sean stepped out of the elevator into the lobby, he found Pamela leaning up against the open doorway of her apartment, arms folded, dressed in shiny pink silk pajamas. "This better be good," she said, pursing her mouth into a doubtful frown, shadowing her face.

Sean walked over and came to a stop directly in front of her. He'd rehearsed what he was going to say a hundred times on his drive uptown from SoHo, but suddenly none of it made any sense to him now that he found himself looking into Pamela's eyes, which were not terribly inviting. *It's like spaghetti,* he thought, trying to relax. *Just throw it and see if it sticks to the wall.*

After taking a deep breath, he said quickly, "Skip Vanderbilt is dead—murdered. I found him hanging from a rope in a back room in his gallery." He took another sip of air. "He was torn to shreds, ripped open, like some psychopath had attacked him with razor-sharp claws."

Pamela gave no show of being concerned. "Vanderbilt?" she asked thoughtfully but casually. "Is he that young, smart-assed dealer down on West Broadway, the one who specializes in a lot of new-wave sculpture and European artists?'' Sean nodded. Stepping aside, Pamela invited him inside with a reluctant tick of her head. "How is it that you found him?" she asked, closing and locking the door behind her. "Money burning a hole in your pocket?" She slipped past Sean into the kitchen and hit the lights. "Want something to drink?"

Sean's stomach growled loudly enough for Pamela to hear, as if it had heard the question. "If it's not too much trouble," he said, "I'd really like something to eat—even if it's only a few slices of plain bread. I haven't had anything since early this morning. My stomach's doing cartwheels."

Halfway to the kitchen, Pamela turned and asked, "Does that mean you're planning on staying awhile?" Sean grinned. Pamela just stared at him, her face blank, eyes cold. "Why do I get the feeling I'm not going to like this?" she asked, and ducked into the kitchen without waiting for an answer. She began rustling around, making a racket, as if she didn't want to hear his reply.

Sean began pacing the living room, arranging and rearranging his thoughts as best he could, trying to put everything into a precise order just in case Pamela thought he was crazy, and tried throwing him out before he could tell her everything. He walked over to the sliding glass doors, bowed his head, and braced himself against the glass, still trying to sort out his own thoughts. Hoping that hearing them might somehow help, Sean began talking to himself in a low voice, a notch above a whisper. "George, I can understand; she works with him. But why would she have a file on Bradley in her computer? Where does she know him from? And what about that Richard Hunt, whoever the hell *he* is? Maybe she knows him from—"

"You bastard!" Pamela snarled, and threw the tray of tea sandwiches she was carrying down onto the coffee table, scattering the little triangles and squares all over the glass top. A few flew off onto the floor.

Sean spun around, his hands raised to protect himself from Pamela's oncoming charge. "Wait, you don't understand, I didn't—"

She was in his face. "*That's* what you were doing when I came back early that afternoon you were here, wasn't it?" Pamela shoved him up against the glass. "You prick. I trusted you." Sean reached out, but Pamela slapped his hands away. "Don't touch me," she said with disgust.

Finally Sean said as slowly and deliberately as he possibly could, "I didn't actually read anything, I only saw the file names." He grabbed hold of Pamela's shoulders to keep her from walking away. "I admit I wanted to, and I almost did, too, but I didn't. You've got to believe me."

Pamela easily twisted free of his grip and stepped back. "Why should I?" Her face, her eyes, her whole body had frozen him out.

Sean realized this was a no-win discussion for him, since there was no way he could prove he hadn't read the files. Somehow, he had to get Pamela off the subject long enough for her to calm down so he could explain. He glanced around the room, desperately searching for something, anything, to latch on to and bail himself out, if only for a moment or two. He spotted the little sandwiches she'd brought out—crust trimmed off, bread curling up—which told him Pamela hadn't just made them. He walked over, put a few back together from the mess on the table, and asked calmly, "These left over from a party?" He began hungrily stuffing his face, hoping she'd take pity on him.

Ignoring his question, Pamela stood watching him, curiosity and concern peeking through the angry scowl on her face. "Slow down or you'll choke yourself," she ordered, sounding like an angry mother, and went into the kitchen. She was back in a moment, carrying a glass filled with what appeared to be apple juice, or iced tea without the ice. "Start from the beginning," she said, handing him the glass. She dropped down into one corner of the plush suede sofa and curled up into a ball, her gaze telling him whatever he had to say had damn well better be good.

With his mouth half full, Sean mumbled, "Beginning?"

Pamela pointed to the other end of the couch. "Sit," she ordered. Reaching behind her, Pamela grabbed the lavender afghan thrown over the back of the sofa and wrapped it around herself. "Well?" she asked impatiently. "Are you going to talk or feed your face?"

Well, well—another color for the chameleon, Sean thought. *Little by little we get to see what the little rich girl is like.* Sean gathered up the stray pieces of bread off the table, dropped them onto the tray, and slid it to the other side of the table. Sitting opposite Pamela, as far away from her as he could, he set about putting the pieces back together, matching tops with bottoms. He selected another miniature sandwich, eyed it, and asked again, "Had a party?"

Pamela sat for the longest time just looking at him. "No," she finally said. "I had a trustees meeting yesterday, and we didn't want to take the time to go out for lunch, so we sent out. That's what you get from the Madison Avenue Gourmet Deli on Eighty-third. What you're eating is what was left from two large trays."

"Fancy lunch," Sean said with a smile, and took another bite.

Pamela drew the afghan a little tighter around her and snuggled deeper into the corner of the sofa, making it look like she was armoring herself against what Sean had to say. "I'm waiting," she purred impatiently, sounding much more like a hungry cat than a contented one. "And from the *beginning,*" she said with a subtle but instructive nod of her head.

Sean smiled, his trademark smile, which surfaced without warning whenever he was nervous, whether he knew it or not. "I think I was six. No—wait—I was seven. I remember the—"

"Don't be a smart-ass," Pamela snapped.

Sean gave up on his feeble attempt at levity and asked solemnly, "Where do you want me to start?"

"Don't play games with me, Sean. Start wherever you think what you have to say will explain what's going on. And justify—not that I think you can—your going into my personal files."

Pamela's look, everything about her, was all business. Sean realized he wasn't talking to the easygoing, orange-haired art teacher he'd met by chance a little over a month

185

before, but to the chairman of the John T. Eagleston Foundation—a woman controlling a not-so-small fortune in art and investment capital; a woman who was probably worth as much herself. *Make it good,* he thought, paraphrasing what Pamela had said to him the instant he'd stepped off the elevator.

"I honestly don't know where the beginning is." Seeing Pamela shake her head in disgust and begin to get up, Sean pushed her back with a pat of his hands at the air. "Please, don't leave, I'm *not* stalling. I simply can't put my finger on some arbitrary point in time and say with absolute certainty *that's* where it all began."

When Pamela sat back, albeit reluctantly, Sean did, too, giving up a secret sigh of relief. "From what I've seen— and I know I haven't seen a fraction of what you probably have—I'm convinced someone is trying to corner the market on Monique's work. And it appears they're willing to do it at almost any cost, which, based upon what I saw tonight, I'm afraid involves murdering someone who doesn't play the game according to their rules."

He held his hand up when it looked like Pamela was going to say something. "I don't think Monique has the slightest idea of what's going on. All the poor woman knows is that she keeps coming up on the short end of the stick, so to speak—financially—while her works end up in someone's collection. At first I couldn't, but now I can understand why she's so reluctant to talk to anyone. She probably doesn't trust anyone."

Pamela raised an eyebrow and said in an overly sweet voice, "*Monique? Poor woman?* You talk about her like you're fond of her. Are you?" she asked, a wry smile working its way into the skeptical frown on her face, a look women seem born with and don't have to learn from anyone.

Hearing Pamela say this, especially the way she said it, brought to mind for Sean what had happened the first time he visited Monique's studio. The thought immediately forced him to question what, exactly, were his feelings about Monique. *You did want to fuck her, MacDonald,* he thought. *Why, I still don't know.*

"Fond?" he said rhetorically. "No, I don't think that's how I feel. I'd say it's more a feeling of protectiveness."

Pamela laughed, a knowing, womanly laugh ringing with more irony than humor. "Whatever," she said, adding a sarcastic note as she tipped her head back, staring up at the ceiling. "You were saying?" she asked, sounding like her patience was growing thin.

Determined not to lose her friendship—realizing if he was fond of anyone, it was Pamela, not Monique—Sean settled back and said calmly, "If there's such a thing as a beginning, I suppose for me the questions started cropping up the first time I met George White. It began after I saw that woman come flying out of the academy, onto the sidewalk, looking like she'd been raped." Pamela sat up, her gaze all of a sudden riveted to Sean. "George gave one story to the police about her, then another to me, after the cops had taken the woman away. It was clear—to me, at least—he'd lied to them. Why, I don't know. When I asked, he ignored my questions."

Sean shrugged his shoulders and said thoughtfully, "But then, maybe I wasn't forceful enough? Anyway, from that point on, I never felt I could trust him. The interview he gave me a week later only made things worse, when I got the feeling he was feeding me a line. Then, when I found out he was somehow hooked up with Brad Johnson—and some guy named Richard Hunt—and somehow involved with them buying one of Monique's bronzes, I asked Monique about him. I tried my best not to make it seem like I didn't trust him, since they're very close, even though I really didn't trust him. She told me he was her agent, and didn't seem concerned at first. But when I told her *Man's Fate* had been sold, which I got the distinct feeling she didn't know about, she was not a happy camper. She acted like she wanted to rip *my* heart out, and I'd only told her about it. From my perspective, the whole thing smacked of what I understand happened with Anderson Galleries."

Pamela had been growing steadily more attentive as Sean unwound his tale, and was now coiled like a spring. "Who told you about the Anderson Galleries fiasco?"

"Who else but my 'old friend,' Brad Johnson. He made it sound like it was a lark or something, as if it was all right to steal an artist's work because of what some dealer did." Sean realized that he was upset, and had let it show.

Smiling at his reaction, Pamela gestured for Sean to stay where he was as she threw the afghan off, got up, and slipped into the kitchen. She returned a few moments later with a bottle of red burgundy and two glasses. After filling them, she handed one to Sean, then fell back into the corner of the sofa, curling her feet beneath her. Leaving the afghan untouched, her pink silk pajamas a perfect complement to the brown suede and her orange hair, Pamela offered Sean a silent toast, urging him to go on.

But before he could, she asked, "Is that what got you started on your crusade about Gerard, what Brad Johnson told you about Anderson? Or was it later, when you found out about George White?"

Sean thought for a moment. "Quite honestly, I really don't know," he said. With a shake of his head, he picked up where he'd left off, realizing he no longer felt pressured to vindicate himself, and therefore he was better able to tell Pamela everything that came to mind, even if the thoughts were out of sequence, which was something he'd tried doing but soon gave up on. As he spoke, Pamela sat nursing her glass of wine, her attention focused on his every word, even his gestures, which he caught her following.

Now and then Pamela asked Sean to stop and repeat something, not that she hadn't heard him, but rather because she wanted to be certain she'd understood exactly what he meant by what he'd said. When he wandered, telling a story rather than giving her facts, the way she wanted them told, she nudged him back on track, and not always so gently.

"What did they look like?" Pamela asked after Sean told her about the woman who'd shown up at Oliver's office, and the one who'd helped him at the library, who he thought had been a librarian, but now had his doubts. Especially since the more he'd thought about her, the more he was convinced she was the same woman who had visited Oliver. When he did describe them, in Oliver's words, then his own, and asked why she wanted to know, Pamela only said, "Let's not get sidetracked. I'll explain later."

Sean's face suddenly lit up. "*That's* what crystallized everything for me." Pamela frowned inquisitively, then asked him to explain. "When Oliver told me about that woman showing up at Merrywood Hall, asking all sorts of questions and knowing more than she should, I was really ticked off, probably because I thought Brad was behind it. I'm still not convinced he wasn't. I suppose she's what prompted me to head into the City and spend the day at the library, digging up everything I could about Monique and her work. The reviews were particularly enlightening, especially the ones written by that critic you told me about, Allan Stern. I found out that without any apparent reason, the man did a one-eighty and changed his opinion of Monique's work overnight, as if he had some sort of revelation. Now that I think about it, I guess it was probably Stern's reviews that aroused my curiosity enough to want to talk to Skip Vanderbilt. I thought he might be able to shed some light on who this man is, and what might have contributed to his change of heart."

Pamela nodded but said nothing.

With these revelations of his own, Sean began separating what he felt was important from what wasn't, growing steadily more confident of what he thought and what he wanted to say. He began to randomly, and excitedly, toss out tidbits of information, such as the seven clay figures he'd seen in George's studio, George's rehearsed story about his longtime relationship with Monique, which Sean now doubted completely, his own meetings with Skip Vanderbilt—"that partner of his, Lydia Thompson"—and *Man's Fate,* which Sean described in detail for Pamela at her request. When he did, Sean realized just how much Skip's mutilated body had resembled the bronze, but kept that thought to himself, fearful that Pamela would think he was a little crazy after all.

Here and there Pamela interjected her own thoughts, such as "I'm surprised you trusted him after what he did to you," referring to Sean's decision to work with Brad Johnson. When Sean tried offering an explanation, he realized he didn't have one that held water. "It's one of my many failings," he said humbly, only to have Pamela reject his act of contrition with a poke of her foot in his thigh, telling him she was well on her way to believing him and forgiving him, even if she didn't realize it herself.

Pamela drained her third glass of wine and set the goblet on the edge of the coffee table. "You've pretty much confirmed what I've suspected for over two years now," she said, and stood up, leaving Sean momentarily dumbfounded. "The only thing I wasn't sure of was Gerard—never could get a handle on that woman—but from what you've said, in spite of your personal feelings for her, it would appear she really doesn't know what's going on. I suppose it's that blind side of a savant: She's a genius when it comes to art, yet a fool when it comes to life."

Feeling possessive, Sean was quick to say in Monique's defense, "Perhaps she's just naive." He quickly added when he saw the disdainful look on Pamela's face, "I know, you think I like her." He turned away for a moment, then back. "I guess maybe I do like her, in a strange sort of way. She's actually beautiful when she works—graceful, tender, passionate. Even sexually attractive," he said, and was immediately surprised he'd said that. "When you watch her work, you get caught up in what she's doing, what she's creating, the power of her work—*her* power—and forget about what the woman looks like. You respond to her energy, her spirit, her soul, not her literal form. Before you know it—"

Pamela laughed. "You want to have sex with her," she said, but not with bitterness or acrimony. Or even jealousy. It was more a sense of understanding, laced with subtle hints of compassion and reluctant acceptance.

"Yes," Sean admitted with a sigh of relief. He glanced up at Pamela, anxious. "Do you think that's perverse?"

Pamela avoided Sean's inquiring gaze and said softly, "I don't know if perverse is the right word for it, but I do know I was there once myself, so I have a pretty good idea what it's all about." She walked toward the sliding doors, avoiding looking at Sean's reflection in the glass. "The man I studied with in Paris was anything but good-looking." Smiling, looking embarrassed, she shook her head. "As a matter of fact, by all contemporary social standards, he was downright ugly. A real beast of a man. Yet when he painted, always in silence—as if he was in a trance—he was absolutely beautiful." She turned to face Sean. "I couldn't get enough of him," she whispered. "Until—" She paused and bit her lip.

On the edge of his seat, Sean asked, "Until?"

Pamela smiled. "Until I realized he was only using me, draining every ounce of energy out of me for his own selfish purposes." She crossed the room and started down the hallway. "And began abusing me," she said quietly.

Pamela suddenly perked up, shaking off her own mantle of sorrow. "That's what real artists do, they take whatever they can from anyone they can—willingly or unwillingly—and use that energy to create their art. Like I told you before, only not in so many words, they're vampires, draining the lifeblood out of anyone foolish enough to get close to them."

Pamela was halfway down the hall, her voice fading as she called out somewhat lyrically, "Be careful, Sean, you may *think* you are, but you're no match for that woman. No man is. Trust me."

Hopping off the sofa, Sean was standing in the entrance to the hall as Pamela came to a stop beside the door to her study. "Now," she said, once again sounding all business. "Let me show you the files you almost got to read. Maybe they can be of some help." She waved for Sean to join her as she slipped into her study.

Chapter Twenty-two

Seated at her desk, with Sean standing behind her, his hands on her shoulders gently kneading the muscles in her neck, Pamela called up one directory after another. Selecting certain files for him to read—"Just the important ones," she told him—she served as guide and interpreter, paging through until she found entries she thought were important, waited patiently for him to read them, answered his questions, and moved on. There was little time for anything to be said, other than what she wanted to talk about.

To Sean it seemed like she was in a hurry to get someplace, and he found himself resisting her—until he came to realize that for Pamela, it wasn't some place she wanted to go to, it was someone she wanted to find, and that someone was her father. "And whoever's responsible for his disappearance," she said with a fierce, almost threatening determination, her body rigid as a steel post. "When I find out who they are, they damn well better pray the police get to them before I do." This was said with a chilling ring to her words, leaving no doubt in Sean's mind she meant what she said. He began to step back, a knee-jerk reaction, but forced himself to stay where he was and wait for her to settle down.

"You've known about all of this for some time—the conspiracy, that is—haven't you?" Sean asked. Pamela nodded deliberately but said nothing. "Why didn't you go to the police?"

"I didn't know for sure at first," she said. "I only suspected. When I had what I thought was enough information, I did go to the police." She sounded angry. When Sean started to pull back again without realizing it, she pinned one of his hands in the crook of her neck with a shrug of a shoulder, keeping him from removing his touch. "I'm sorry—forgive me," she said, and sounded like she meant it. "I didn't mean to bite your head off." She slumped back in her chair. "I had my lawyer go to the district attorney over a year ago with what I'd found out, but the man couldn't be bothered. He as much as told Bert it was silk-collar crime. Then he had the nerve to imply that it looked to him like my father was somehow involved in the whole thing." Pamela bit down into her words. "We'll see if that jerk gets reelect—"

Sean tapped Pamela's shoulder. "Hold it right there," he said. "There, two lines from the top, what's that entry with the title *Treason* in it mean? I know that name from somewhere."

Pamela pointed to the heading. "This is a page from a summary I prepared of Daddy's sculpture purchases for the last ten years. The information was taken from the foundation's books of account and my father's personal ledgers. It lists every piece of sculpture, regardless of the medium, my father ever acquired. It sets forth a date-by-date and dollar-by-dollar accounting for every acquisition, whether personally or through the foundation."

She touched the screen with her finger. "That number is the collections code for Monique Gerard, I know it by heart."

Sean gave Pamela a kiss on the top of her head and wrapped his arms around her, his chin resting on her head. "Does that number one-fifty represent what he paid for it?"

She nodded, causing Sean's head to move up and down with hers. "I rounded everything off to shorten the listing."

"Interesting," Sean mumbled. "Does that other three-digit number stand for the dealer he bought it from?" He got a second nod. "Who was it?" he asked.

Pamela hesitated for a moment. "I don't recognize the chart-of-accounts number. Let me check." Hitting two keys, she switched screens, then called up another file. A long summary popped up. Down the left-hand side was a column of three-digit numbers, each one followed by a single-line caption describing what the number stood for. Some listed businesses, others the names of individuals. Pamela ran her finger down the screen. "He bought it from Anderson Galleries." She sat back. "That's funny," she whispered. "He bought it a little more than three months before he disappeared. I never noticed that."

Sean muttered, "A rising star in the museum world." He nodded confidently, then kissed the top of Pamela's head again. "A man of vision," he said, and laughed. "Some vision."

"What are you talking about?"

Sean gave her another kiss, this time on the neck, tickling her into a shiver. "What are the odds that the Mr. Anderson of Anderson Galleries is—or was—related to a Dr. Robert Anderson, a curator down in Philadelphia at one of the museums?"

"I have no idea, but I can check tomorrow and find out."

"Do it," Sean replied, having discarded every ounce of humor.

Pamela leaned back into him. "You still haven't told me what you're thinking."

"Well, unless I misread the newspaper article I found, that piece your father purchased from Anderson Galleries—undoubtedly in good faith for a hundred and fifty thousand dollars—was the subject of a ten-thousand-dollar purchase prize award in a juried competition in Philadelphia, a show for which the *honorable* Dr. Anderson was the juror." Sean gave a throaty and somewhat ominous moan. "How convenient. He selects a work he knows is worth a hell of lot more than the prize—convinces the artist the prestige and publicity are worth more than the cash—then turns around and somehow arranges for it to be sold quietly to, or through, a dealer. And then that dealer resells it to a collector that he knows doesn't make a lot of noise when he buys something, he just tucks it away in his collection. And no one is the wiser.''

Pamela sat up stiffly. ''Do you remember who funded that purchase prize?'' she asked.

Sean tried, but couldn't. ''I don't think it was mentioned in the article, but I could be wrong. Can you have someone at the Met find that out for me?''

''Us,'' Pamela said firmly, correcting him. ''We're partners in this from here on in.''

Sean laughed, and asked, ''Partners? Do I understand you to mean that you want to coauthor my articles for *Entasis*?''

Pamela leaned forward, breaking loose of Sean's affectionate hold on her, turned the computer off, and stood up. ''No,'' she said without a trace of doubt in her voice or on her face. ''All I want is to find out what happened to my father, and see that whoever had anything to do with his—''

Pamela's eyes suddenly welled up with tears. Sean didn't know what to do; it was something he hadn't expected—not from her. All he could think of was to put his arms around her and hold her. When he tried, she pushed him away, walked out of the study without saying a word, and headed down the hall to her bedroom. He followed, but stopped at the doorway when she threw herself onto her bed and buried her face in the pillows. He stood watching her, wondering if he should do what he felt was right or heed her unspoken wishes.

He finally couldn't bear it any longer, and went in and sat beside her, his hand on her shoulder. ''Can I get you anything?'' he asked softly. Pamela shook her head. ''Do you want me to leave?''

She didn't budge; she lay perfectly still.

Taking her silence to mean yes, Sean began to stand. The rustle of sheets was followed by a hand on his leg, holding him back. When he turned, he found himself looking into the anxious eyes of a young girl, not the steady gaze of a woman as worldly and wise as Pamela Eagleston. She slid over and patted the bed beside her. "Please stay," she said. "I don't want to be alone tonight."

For the first time since he'd become involved with this assignment, Sean didn't have a second thought, the slightest doubt, about how he felt and what he wanted to do. Standing up, he turned away, slowly undressed, then slipped between the sheets and drew Pamela to him. "Go to sleep," he said softly, and kissed her tenderly on the forehead.

Pamela closed her eyes and laid her head on Sean's chest, the tears on her cheeks wetting his skin. "Thank you," she whispered.

Chapter Twenty-three

Sean rolled the wet towel into a ball, tossed a three-pointer across the tiled bathroom into the yellow wicker hamper, and slipped back into the bedroom. The smell of fresh-brewed coffee brought an instant smile to his face and a knot of desire to his belly. Wearing nothing more than his curiosity, he followed the alluring scent down the hall and peeked around the corner into the kitchen. "You're all dressed up," he said, sounding surprised and disappointed in the same breath.

Pamela was wearing a fitted two-piece, tan linen suit—the skirt cut fashionably above the knees—lime-green silk blouse, heels, and stockings. Her hair was up, threaded into a perfect knot, and, surprisingly, dark red, not orange. In each earlobe was a single emerald stud the size of a pea. Everything else had been removed, including the stud in her nose.

Holding a mug in one hand, half a buttered hard roll in the other, Pamela nodded and asked cheerfully, "Coffee?" She held up the roll. "And a hard roll smothered in cold butter?" Her blue eyes seemed to twinkle with mischief. "It's one of my many weaknesses." She made a coquettish gesture with her hip. "Does it show?"

"I think I better go get dressed," Sean said. "I'm not what you would call properly attired for the occasion." Wiggling his fingers, he waved good-bye and headed back to the bedroom.

"Better hurry," Pamela called out, "or you might find yourself eating alone. My car will be here in twenty minutes."

"Your *car*?" Sean muttered to himself as he darted into the bedroom.

He was back a few moments later, wearing a blue checked shirt that just barely covered his briefs, making it look like he didn't have anything on underneath. "May I come in now?" he asked, ironing his shirt smooth with his hands, tugging his shirttail straight, then standing at attention.

Pamela circled the island in the center of the kitchen and gave him the once-over. She lifted his shirttail, feigned a disappointed frown, then nodded approvingly. She planted an officious kiss on his cheek. "You pass," she announced, and continued around the island to the coffee machine sitting on the opposite counter beside a wooden tree hung with coffee mugs. "Come get your fix."

Eyeing her suspiciously—wondering what she was up to—Sean circled around the other side and grabbed a mug off the rack. He filled it and leaned up against the counter, his hands cradling the mug to warm them. "Trustees meeting?" he asked, and took a cautious sip of coffee, checking to see how hot it was.

"Nope," Pamela replied, and took a sumptuous bite out of the buttered roll.

Sean tried a different tack. "Something come up at the academy?" He fished a roll out of the paper bag—refusing the butter Pamela offered him—and tore a bite out of the roll.

With her mouth full, Pamela just shook her head, all the while smiling at Sean as if she were playing a game with him—one only she knew the rules for.

"Okay, I give up," he finally said. "Where are you off to?"

Pamela drained her mug and set it in the sink. "Thanks

198

to you, I'm going to Philadelphia this morning.''

Sean thought for a moment, trying to recall what he'd said that would send her to Philadelphia. ''Are you going to see the illustrious Dr. Anderson?'' he asked. She nodded. ''Want company?''

Pamela reached out and put her hand on Sean's arm. ''If it was any other time—any other circumstances—I'd love for you to come with me. But I'm afraid you'll only get in the way.'' Sean pretended a wounded look, which Pamela erased with a kiss. ''I called Bert this morning—got the old coot on his cell phone in some judge's chambers—and asked him to check out both of the Andersons for me. He said it would take two weeks to get what I wanted, maybe longer, so I decided to go find out for myself.''

''Let me guess,'' Sean said, slowly circling the island, nursing his coffee. ''The car you mentioned is your chauffeur, right?''

''Yes,'' she said, stifling an amused smile at Sean's reaction.

Sean found himself caught up in Pamela's playful mood. He stepped beside her and gave her a kiss, which she held on to. ''So, tell me, is the chairman of the Eagleston Foundation going to just walk into the museum where this guy works and ask him if he screwed Monique Gerard out of a hundred and forty thousand dollars?''

Pamela rinsed her hands in the sink, then dried them off on the dish towel. ''That's not my style.'' She winked. ''Not yet, at least. I have an eleven o'clock appointment with the executive director of the Philadelphia Museum of Art, Dr. Jonathan Evergood. Jon and I were classmates at Columbia. He's assured me he will have a file ready when I get there, filled with everything he knows about our friend Dr. Robert Anderson.''

Pamela grinned triumphantly and walked out of the kitchen. Sean followed, a mug in one hand, the remnants of a roll in the other, as he trailed Pamela down the hall, listening to her. ''You name it, we'll get it: his family, his friends, his academic record, jobs held.'' She raised her hand. ''Jon also said he had a file with copies of newspaper clip-

199

pings on anything written about Anderson during his tenure at the museum. A file, it seems, that our friend keeps up to date for the trustees. A little ego thing, polishing his own apple.'' She laughed. "Let's see if we can find a worm or two.''

"And Richard Hunt?'' Sean asked as Pamela slipped into the bedroom.

She stuck her head around the corner. "He's next,'' she said decisively. "But he'll have to wait until tomorrow. I have that postponed acquisitions committee meeting at the Met later this afternoon, and I can't miss it. My vote ensures the Met won't spend money on some useless junk one of my fellow trustees has brought to the attention of the acquisitions committee. Which means I'll have to come right back from Philly after meeting with Jonnie.''

Now it's Jonnie? Sean thought, and just as quickly asked himself, *You're jealous, aren't you?* Refusing to accept that he might be, Sean nodded and slipped past Pamela into the bedroom, suddenly deep in thought, his gaze cast down.

"Stay tonight?'' Pamela asked as she sat down in front of the vanity, primping her hair. "I should be out of the meeting by six-thirty. And since I'll have the car waiting, I can easily be here by seven. Tempted?'' she asked. "I'll make up for last night.''

Still wrapped up in his own thoughts, searching for a common thread—other than Monique—to bind all of these men together, Sean absentmindedly grabbed his pants off the back of the chair beside the bed. Without looking, he stepped into the legs, only to snag his toe on the hem of one leg, lose his balance, and stumble headfirst onto the bed.

Watching the whole episode in the mirror, Pamela smiled, her face filled with affection. Sean sat up, wearing a perplexed frown. "That director?'' he asked, as if talking to himself. "The one who disappeared. What's his name?''

Pamela stood up and straightened her skirt. "Don Beaumont. Donald K. Beaumont, to be exact.''

"What does he do for a living?''

"Did,'' she said with a shake of her head. "He's retired. He made a fortune as an art dealer. Strictly contemporary art, and big-ticket stuff. When he sold out, he had galleries around the country, all in cities with money—Palm Beach, Dallas, Santa Fe, Palm Springs, and Park City, in Utah, just east of Salt Lake City. Although he gives a lot to the museum—in time and money—I wouldn't trust the man as far as I could throw him.'' Pamela shrugged her shoulders. ''It's nothing that he's actually done, just call it woman's intuition. He's the reason I have to be back this afternoon. The purchases we're voting on just happen to be two sculptures from his own private collection, which he's offered to the museum on a fifty-fifty deal. We pay half the appraised value, he gifts the other half, and pockets the tax credit. My vote is no, and he knows it.'' She laughed. ''Maybe that's why he's hiding.''

She turned around, looking at Sean as if she wanted his approval of how she looked. He smiled. ''You look smashing, Madame President.''

The sound of a buzzer down the hall pulled Pamela toward the doorway. She stopped and turned back. ''You don't think there's any link to Don Beaumont and these other men, do you?''

Sean stood up and slipped his pants on. ''Your guess is as good as mine,'' he said, his thoughts now elsewhere. He finally looked at Pamela. ''Let's see what Ms. Eagleston comes up with.''

''And Dr. MacDonald? What is *he* going to do today?''

Sean began tucking his shirt into his pants. ''He's going to go see an old colleague of his on some unfinished business.''

''Oliver Shore?'' Pamela asked.

Sean's head snapped up. ''How did you know?''

Pamela smiled, clearly pleased with Sean's reaction. ''He called the school looking for you yesterday. We had a nice long talk. He really likes you. I forgot to tell you that last night,'' she said, and blew Sean a kiss before dashing down the hall.

''Remember,'' she yelled back. ''Seven o'clock.''

Chapter Twenty-four

As Sean pulled onto the Harlem River Drive at Ninety-sixth Street—heading north out of the City—he smiled, recalling the sight of Pamela climbing into the rear seat of a walnut-brown Rolls Royce, the door held open by a uniformed gray-haired man with a proud smile on his face. *He must have been the family chauffeur*, Sean thought. *He looked at her like she was his granddaughter, not his employer.*

With a shake of his head, Sean let go of this last fragment from the kaleidoscope of images he'd collected over the last two days. Without too much effort, he was even able to bury the sight of Skip Vanderbilt's horribly mutilated body somewhere in the recesses of his mind, hopefully to stay there, at least until the colors faded. Surprisingly, he found himself looking forward to the two-hour drive upstate to Red Hook. *And a decent night's sleep,* he thought. For a moment or two he even toyed with the idea of driving home along the shore of the Hudson instead of taking the Taconic Parkway, until memories of sitting in traffic and crawling through the pretentious little towns with ''-on-the-Hudson'' hyphenated onto their names put an end to that foolish thought. It would take him at least another hour, maybe longer, even at that time of the day.

Sitting up, he slapped the steering wheel and snarled, "The hell with it," as he joined the line of cars shooting up the ramp leading to the George Washington Bridge. *There's a lot less traffic. Besides, the west shore has a better view of the river.*

With his head clear, for the moment at least, Sean picked up where he'd left off in Pamela's bedroom, trying to thread everyone together and make some sense out of what was happening—*assuming, of course, there is any sense to it all.* Unlike Pamela, who knew all of the players, personally or through her museum or foundation work, Sean had only names without personalities or faces. Except for George White and Brad Johnson, his once-again questionable friend, and Skip Vanderbilt, who no longer even had a face, thanks to whoever mutilated his body.

As hard as he tried, however, nothing seemed to fit, which made Pamela's clear-eyed certainty that much more enviable when he remembered how she looked standing in the kitchen this morning, the perfect image of confidence and determination. A part of him couldn't help wondering if she knew more than what she was telling him. After all, she was a totally new woman when he saw her this morning, a woman with a purpose. "A woman dressed to kill," he said with a laugh, recalling how striking she'd looked in her tailored suit, high heels—which she knew how to walk in unlike many women—just the right touch of jewelry, a hint of eye shadow, and her hair put up, hair that was no longer a defiant shade of orange, but red as vintage wine. He realized how beautiful she was without her disguise, then had to ask himself if what he'd seen had simply been just another mask, still hiding who she really was.

Who are you? he wondered, comparing their first night together, a night he wanted always to remember, with last night. He'd held a totally different woman in his arms last night. While he lay wide awake, robbed of sleep, she tossed and turned, refusing to let him get away, pulling him to her every time he tried rolling over. That smile of his was back.

203

"You're hooked this time," he told himself as he down-shifted and accelerated hard off the exit ramp onto the Palisades Parkway, driving as if he was trying to get away from something. Or someone. *It's too late, and you know it,* he thought, easing off the gas, then laughing at himself when he thought of the wall in Pamela's apartment, the one filled with her drawings of undraped men.

You can relax, he assured himself, *it'll never happen. You're just another trophy for her. When she gets what she wants, which is all she really cares about—and you can't really blame her for that—she won't have any use for you anymore.* Sean nodded and sat back, slipping into the flow of traffic. "It would appear that the soon-to-be Dr. Eagleston is every bit her father's daughter. And from what I've seen, Pamela dear, given your training and ability, you'll easily double the fortune your father left you."

The simple mention of John Eagleston brought Sean full circle to where he'd started this morning, trying to make some sense out of what was happening. And most important, at least as he saw it, what it all meant to him and his assignment. *If anything.*

While Pamela seemed to have found a loose thread with the discovery of another player, and appeared determined to pull it as hard as she could to unravel things—or tie everything into knots—Sean wondered if her father could somehow have been involved with all of this, whatever it was. Maybe he had more money than the others, and they couldn't keep up with him, so they quietly eliminated the competition.

Sean immediately asked himself, "But keep up with *what?*"

Frustrated, knowing he was going in circles with this tack, Sean told himself to settle down. *Look at it as if you're writing a story,* he thought. *Create from the neck down. Feel it—make it visceral—don't think it. Then rewrite and edit from the neck up, using the cognitive side.*

He laughed. "The dull side," he said, recalling what his therapist had told him when she was preaching to him about creativity, and his need to free up his own creativity, which she kept telling him was his female side.

Right now he'd take anything he could get just to be back on track. He proceeded to eliminate from his thinking anyone he didn't know personally. Next came anyone who didn't directly affect what it was he was doing. *And that is,* he told himself, hammering his fist down onto the steering wheel, *to write five more articles on Monique Gerard—presuming the first ones are acceptable to dear Bradley—and be done with this woman, Gerard, and this insane art business so you can get on with your life.*

He shook his head in disbelief. "I don't know how you did it all those years," he said as if Bruce Fanning were sitting there beside him as he approached the traffic circle at the Bear Mountain Bridge, wondering if he should keep going or cross the river here.

In keeping with his decision not to think, just act, he stayed on Route 9W, heading north. That small act seemed to spur him along as he discarded one name after another with a slap of his hand, beginning with the current target of Pamela's interest, the illustrious Dr. Robert Anderson.

When he'd finished, Sean had eliminated everyone except for George White, who was stuck in his side like a thorn, festering. Even Brad Johnson fell by the wayside. *And Pamela should track everyone else down—and sort everything out,* he thought. *She's good at it. She's the real hunter anyway, not you.*

"It's *her* dominant male side," Sean said with a smile. "Which is probably why you're attracted to her, MacDonald." He chuckled, but not at what he'd said so much as at the realization that he'd actually meant it, and it didn't bother him in the least. "You're cured," he announced sarcastically, pounding his hand down on the steering wheel like a gavel. "Right."

Free to do what he wanted—brushing aside the nagging guilt that he'd abdicated everything else—Sean focused on George White, and the doubts about him he'd harbored from their very first meeting. Recalling how George had reacted when he returned to the studio and found that Sean had defrocked *The Seven Cardinal Sins* only strengthened the feelings of distrust he had for George, since he'd lied about

205

those, too. His next thought was to tell Monique everything he knew—or at least what he thought he knew—about George. He just as quickly resolved to tell her everything else he and Pamela had talked about.

Sean finally sat back, an amused smile on his face. *Pamela's right, you are fond of her.* No sooner had he admitted this to himself than he growled, paraphrasing Pamela's warning, "Be careful, you're no match for that woman." He made it sound like a challenge, not the warning Pamela had apparently intended it to be when she'd cautioned him about underestimating Monique Gerard.

But he wanted George just now—no one else mattered—so Pamela's words fell on deaf ears once more as Sean replayed his meetings with George White. Looking at him in a new light, Sean didn't get past that first encounter, snagged by the unforgettable images of that well-dressed woman stumbling out of the academy, her face bloodied, clothes torn—her fearless determination—and that fleeting smile of thanks she'd given him. They were images embedded more deeply in Sean's memory than he'd realized, along with the anger that he'd felt then, which suddenly boiled over.

How the hell could you? What were you thinking? That's not like you. If anything, you've always gotten into trouble for sticking your nose into things that weren't any of your business.

Glancing at his watch, Sean abruptly slowed and pulled over without signaling. He ducked as a tractor trailer rumbled past, the driver leaning on his horn and giving Sean the finger. "That was not smart, MacDonald," he mumbled to himself, and sat back, ruminating about what had happened that evening at the academy, and asking himself, *How could you forget about her?* It wasn't like him to forget—his memory was actually a curse—and it started him wondering what else he'd forgotten lately. The harder he pressed it, tried sorting through what he'd seen, the more he found his thoughts slipping away, unable to concentrate for more than a second or two.

What the fuck is happening to you? he wondered as he found himself left with nothing but feelings and vague, undefinable images, off in the distance in the back of his mind, out of focus.

"So go find out who she was," he finally told himself. "You're a goddamn writer, make up some story to get her name from the cops. Tell them you found her watch, and you want to return it to her. Go buy one, for chrissake, and take it with you. Who's to know?"

Sean laughed to himself as he signaled—glanced back over his shoulder—and made a quick U-turn. "Maybe you'll get lucky, maybe you'll meet that mesomorph again. What was his name, Rocky?"

Chapter Twenty-five

As if feeling Sean's pain, Andrea Stern winced each time he did, but she didn't stop dabbing the gash on the side of his head with a ball of cotton soaked in rubbing alcohol. "It's not as deep as I first thought," she said, a studied frown on her small, brown-eyed face. Barely five feet tall, Andrea Stern was all of a hundred pounds, if that, but with the figure of a woman. "I don't think you'll need stitches, not as long as the bleeding doesn't start again."

She dropped the bloodstained wad into the dish on the coffee table along with the others and stepped back, surveying her handiwork. "What in the world ever prompted you to go looking for that man?" she asked, turning her frown into a curious, almost amused smile as she perched on the edge of the sofa across from Sean, her small, delicate hands folded neatly in her lap.

Her penetrating gaze, eyes the color of fired clay tiles, sparked Sean's memory of what he'd witnessed that evening outside the New York Academy of Fine Arts—not that he needed to be reminded of what she looked like. He began gingerly feeling the side of his head with the tips of his fingers, now and then fluffing up his matted-down hair. "I didn't go looking for him," he said in halfhearted defense of what he'd done. "I had just gotten your name from the desk sergeant." Sean reached into his pocket and pulled out a ladies' watch. "I told him I'd found this—that it was yours—and wanted to make sure you got it."

Andrea smiled and nodded. Sean went on. "Anyway, I was on my way out to the parking lot when I met *our* friend, who was just coming off duty with his partner—that kid with the blond hair, who handcuffed you." Sean sat back, toying with a mischievous smile. "Rocky and I just *happened* to bump into each other on the top of the steps outside the station. It was an accident," he said with a wide-eyed innocent grin. "He went flying down the steps, I stumbled backwards in the other direction." Seeing the delight on Andrea's face, Sean laughed. "You should have seen *his* head."

With a nod that said "serves him right," Andrea grabbed the bowl of dirty swabs, the bottle of alcohol, and stood up. Even with her standing and Sean sitting, she was barely a head taller than he. She was even smaller than he remembered, which only served to make Sean that much angrier with George White for what he'd done, then equally upset with himself for not having stopped the police, not that he probably could have—not without getting arrested himself.

"May I get you something to drink?" she asked.

"Yes, thank you. Something very cold, please."

"Scotch and soda?"

He smiled. "You take the scotch and give me the soda. I don't want to make this headache I have any worse than it already is."

The moment Andrea slipped into the kitchen of her apartment, Sean glanced around the busy living room. The walls were plastered with engravings and etchings mounted in simple black-lacquered frames. The bookshelves, tabletops and the glass-enclosed curio cabinet were all cluttered with small bronze and marble sculptures. The larger works were set on marble columns pushed safely against the wall. Some of the sculptures were ancient—Greek, Roman, and Egyptian—but most were modern. The only space without art was the top of a baby grand piano, its polished ebony surface covered with a white lace throw and topped with family photographs locked inside tarnished antique silver frames. Some of the photos were stained sepia brown from age. Others were black-and-white, capturing men in uniforms and women in long print dresses with puffy shoulder pads. One color photo, a snapshot of a couple standing on a beach, caught Sean's eye. It was Andrea Stern, tanned, trim, and smiling, wearing a skimpy bikini, revealing ample breasts and broad hips, neither of which were evident from the way she was now dressed. Beside her was a tall and unusually thin man, with curly black hair and fair, almost parchment-white skin.

Sean stood up, felt dizzy and braced himself against the arm of the sofa for a moment to catch his balance, then walked over to the piano. He stood staring at the photo for the longest time, then hesitantly picked it up to look more closely at the man. He was certain he'd seen him somewhere before, but was unsure where.

"That's Allan and me when we were in Jamaica three years ago," Andrea said proudly as she walked back into the living room. In one hand she was carrying a short fat glass filled with something the same color of her eyes. In the other was a tall, ice-filled glass filled with what looked like club soda drowning a wedge of lime. "It's Montego Bay. It was our first trip back to the island since the racial problems there." She shook her head. "It's not the same anymore. The people smile and say all the right things, as if they've rehearsed them, but they do it all through their teeth. It doesn't take much imagination to guess what they're really thinking. We promised ourselves we'd never go back again."

She offered Sean his glass. "I'm afraid I'm out of soda," she said with a chagrined smile. "This is tonic. I put a squeeze of lime in it. There's also some gin in it, too, but not very much. I grabbed the bottle of Tanqueray out of habit, and began pouring before I realized what I was doing."

She gestured toward the photograph, making it appear like she was offering a toast, and said quietly, "Allan loved gin and tonic." She laughed. "He always said that's why God created summer, so man could have his gin and tonic.''

Wanting to let Andrea's comment fade, along with what he sensed was her sorrow, Sean held his silence as he pressed the cold glass against his temple, then slowly, gingerly, rolled it back over the wound on the side of his head. He held it there until the cold hurt, then took a long, slow sip of tonic, his throat warmed by what was more than just a little slip of the gin bottle.

Andrea walked over and sat on one of the love seats. She pointed for Sean to sit on the matching sofa across from her. ''Now, Dr. MacDonald, why don't you tell me exactly what it is you want from me.'' She took a manly swig of scotch. ''From what you've gone through to find me''—she gestured to the side of Sean's head, and smiled somewhat maternally—''I presume it's rather important to you, or you wouldn't be here.''

Sean reluctantly gave up on the photograph and sat where Andrea had pointed. About to set his glass down, he hesitated, looking for a coaster. Andrea reached underneath the coffee table and came up with a handful of disks hand-painted with colorful Caribbean scenes. She set one out for Sean, then one for herself.

''Why were you at the academy that night?'' he asked.

Andrea slid back and crossed her legs, cradling her glass in her lap. ''I wanted to see that woman, Gerard,'' she replied, her gaze as solid as stone. ''I wanted to ask her a few questions.''

''Why didn't you just wait until the show opened?''

Andrea smiled and took another sip of scotch. ''You don't know her very well, do you?''

''I'm not sure I understand what you mean.''

''Monique Gerard doesn't come to her shows. Allan said it was because she didn't want to hear what people had to say about her work. He also said she made it a point of being there an hour or so before the opening—exactly why, he didn't say—so that's why I was there that evening, hoping to see her and talk with her.''

Sean sat looking at Andrea, wondering if he should ask what George had done to her, afraid he might touch on something that would upset her. *You have to know,* he thought. "What did George do to—" He stopped, suddenly feeling unsure of himself. He took a deep breath and asked quickly, "What *did* he do to you?"

Andrea smiled, causing Sean to feel ill at ease. "The man didn't do anything to me," she said casually. "Except, perhaps, to bruise my ego. I tripped and fell in the dark when I was trying to hide from him in the showroom."

"You mean he didn't—"

Andrea waved for Sean to wait. "I know it looked like someone hit me—or worse—but it was my own doing. All I could think of was seeing that woman. Frankly, I was obsessed with it. I didn't watch where I was going." She smiled, but awkwardly, almost as if it wasn't a natural feeling. "Then I ran into one of those stupid sculptures, which is how I got the black eye and bloody nose. From that point on, things went from bad to worse."

Sean sat back, unwilling to let go of what he felt about George White—refusing to overturn his verdict so easily. "But I distinctly heard you say that it was *him*?"

Andrea looked away, biting her lip. She faced Sean, that same uncomfortable smile on her face. "I was not referring to Dr. White," she said quietly, almost clinically, and stood up.

"Another tonic?" she asked, still not looking at Sean.

Sean handed Andrea his glass and followed her into the kitchen. "If it wasn't George, then what did you mean when you yelled 'It's him'?"

Andrea poured the gin by sight, filling the glass half full. She topped it up with tonic, squeezed a wedge of lime into it, and handed the glass back to Sean. Her drink was easy: She dropped two ice cubes into her glass, drowned them in scotch, then led Sean back into the living room, where she walked over to the piano and picked up the photograph Sean had been looking at. "The person I was referring to was Allan," she said solemnly. Andrea turned and handed Sean the framed photograph. "Take a close look at my husband, Dr. MacDonald," she instructed. "A *very* close look. Then tell me if he reminds you of anyone."

Sean held the photo at arm's length. "I know I've seen him somewhere, I just can't place him." He glanced up to find Andrea's eyes filling with tears. Touched by her sudden show of emotion, Sean returned to examining the picture of Allan and Andrea Stern, afraid of his own feelings.

"Take your time," Andrea said, her voice cracking. "And don't be shy. Take a close look at my husband's body, too. It may help."

Taking her cue, Sean traced the outline of Allan Stern's wiry frame—once, then again. He shut his eyes. When he opened them, he zeroed in on Allan's face and whispered, "I don't believe it." He looked up. "You were referring to the bronze, weren't you? That's your husband, isn't it?"

Shaking like a leaf, tears streaming down her cheeks, Andrea nodded, then downed the rest of her scotch in a single swallow.

Chapter Twenty-six

When Sean glanced down, he saw that he'd crept past eighty again. Backing off on the gas, he slowed to a steady, and painfully slow, fifty-five miles an hour. He turned the radio off, which had become nothing more than background noise, his thoughts everywhere else but on the CBS evening news prattle. *Pompous asses,* he thought. *They talk like everyone listening is a jerk.*

Turning to look back over his shoulder before pulling over into the right lane, Sean caught a whiff of Andrea Stern's perfume, a poignant reminder of when she'd buried her face in his shoulder, sobbing and muttering unintelligibly about her missing husband. By the time he'd succeeded in calming her down, the alcohol had begun to take hold of her, helping things along. And it wasn't just what he'd seen her drink, but the entire third of the bottle of Dewar's she admitted to having opened right after he'd called her from the precinct, explaining who he was, where they'd met—dropping Bruce Fanning's name in a moment of desperation to keep her from hanging up—and asking if he could please see her.

While the scotch had freed Andrea's emotions, it also

loosened her tongue, making Sean's intended task of finding out what really happened that evening at the academy that much easier. It also turned what he'd thought might be an hour-long meeting into three. Added to the time he'd spent at the police station, convincing the wary desk sergeant to help him, plus his run-in with Rocky—which probably would have landed Sean in jail had Rocky's levelheaded young partner not intervened—plus the hour it took him to find Andrea Stern's apartment in Queens, which for Sean was like driving into a foreign country, he'd succeeded in blowing the day.

And for what? he wondered. *George gets off scot-free, and now all you have to show for your effort, Mr. Smartie, is the fact that Allan Stern might have—but you can't be sure—modeled for Monique. And naked, according to Andrea, who says only a wife—or a lover!—could have known about the scar on his penis, which she was convinced she saw on the bronze.* Sean smiled to himself. *I didn't look that close, but I did notice he was circumcised, which was out of style for a work like that.*

"All's fair in love and art," Sean said with a laugh, his amusement fanned by thoughts of the unflattering caricatures Monique could create of him if he ever modeled for her. But his upbeat feeling lasted for only a few seconds before he suddenly recalled what Andrea Stern had told him after he took advantage of his time with her and asked if she knew why her husband had had a sudden change of heart about Monique's work.

"Allan did not write those reviews," she'd said angrily.

Surprised, to say the least, Sean had pressed her on what she meant—referring to the articles he'd read in the *Village Voice* and *Entasis*—only to hear Brad Johnson's name mentioned in the same breath with her description of how shocked her husband had been when he saw his name on those very same reviews. As Andrea told it, when her husband went to see the managing editor at the *Village Voice*—"demanding to know what the hell was going on!"—he was told that he, himself, was the one who'd submitted the review, and was even shown a covering letter to that effect.

Confused, but by no means daunted—"or any less angry,"—Allan Stern had stormed uptown to the offices of *Entasis* on Madison Avenue—with Andrea in tow—only to be told that the whole thing was simply a stupid mistake by some fledgling editorial assistant, who had already been fired. In what Andrea said was an attempt by Brad Johnson to placate her husband, "he offered Allan five thousand dollars and a promise to print a complete retraction, clearing my husband's name. Which he did." However, when Sean asked her about the money—wanting to know if Allan had accepted it—Andrea sheepishly admitted that he had taken it. "He said that it was only fair considering what had happened to him."

Sean was left not knowing what to believe, except that he understandably found himself siding with Allan Stern in light of his own experience with Brad Johnson years before. With an exasperated shake of his head, Sean settled back—not that he was by any stretch of the imagination relaxed after the day he'd had.

Noticing the daylight fading rapidly, he pulled his headlights on and glanced at his watch. "Shit," he growled when he realized he'd completely forgotten about meeting Pamela back at her apartment. *It wasn't a definite thing,* he thought, trying to rationalize the fact that it had slipped his mind. *Or had it?* he wondered when he realized there was a part of him that was actually glad not to be seeing her, knowing he'd struck out, so to speak. *While the rich lady in the Rolls Royce probably hit a home run in Philadelphia—one way or another.*

It had finally happened, and he knew it: He was jealous—of her, not about her—and that jealousy had supplanted his irritation at the loss of George White as a target for his indignation over what he'd thought had been the physical abuse of Andrea Stern. Or perhaps it was the loss of someone to blame for what he knew he hadn't done, but should have, and that was to have confronted George on the spot the very moment he'd contradicted what he'd told the police. What made things even worse for Sean was the fact that he'd jumped to the conclusion that George had lied in an effort to cover up what he, himself, now knew George hadn't done in the first place.

Back to square one, Sean thought. *Which is where you never should have left, MacDonald.* "Stick to what you're getting paid to do, and leave the other shit to everyone else," he told himself as he raced down the exit ramp off the Taconic Parkway.

"Now," he said with a renewed resolve, "forget about Dr. George White and his lies—and that asshole Johnson—and go do what you promised that poor woman you would do for her, before she drowns herself in that scotch of hers, thinking about her husband having an affair with Monique."

Sean turned right onto Pines Ridge Road, thinking, *After you find out whether or not Stern actually modeled for her—and don't be stupid enough to ask Monique if she slept with him, unless you coax it out of her—then go find a telephone somewhere and call Pamela. And tell her the truth—not some fairy tale—that you completely forgot about dinner, you dummy.*

"Wait a second," he muttered, slowing down. "There's no way in hell that cheap son of a bitch Johnson would just hand over five grand like that. It's not his style."

Sean turned onto Old Country Road and began speeding up, his gaze cast off somewhere in the distance as he blindly followed the winding curves of the unpaved road. It was as if he were driving by instinct, not sight. *That review in the* Village Voice *was no mistake by some editorial assistant. Someone deliberately planted it. That, or Stern really did write it—along with the one in* Entasis—*and was just trying make it look like he didn't.*

Sean sat up, the muscles in his jaw suddenly wired into knots. *Which means the retraction was just part of the deal, and the money his payment for intentionally trashing Monique and her work.*

"You fucking bastards," Sean snarled through his teeth.

Chapter Twenty-seven

The grass was taller than he remembered, at least it seemed that way. And it appeared thicker, too. Sean took one look at the overgrown road leading back to Monique's studio, recalled the unnerving sound of the dried grass scratching down the sides of his Healy, and decided to park along the side of the road.

"Walk, it's good for you," he mumbled as he climbed out of his car. He toyed with the idea of putting the top up for security's sake, chose not to, and started back to the barn. He made a point of staying inside a single tire track, placing one foot in front of the other, his arms spread wide for balance, as if walking a tightrope. That lasted for all of twenty paces, when he started jogging, then broke into a sprint. His nerves—wound up as tight as a steel spring—had gotten the better of him.

Reaching the clearing in front of the barn, running balls-out, Sean tripped on something buried in the grass and tumbled head over heels, coming to rest flat on his back, staring up into the evening sky, which was blanketed with clouds. "You needed that," he said, rolled over, and climbed to his feet. Dusting himself off, Sean ambled toward the Dutch door, lazily kicking his feet through the grass. He knocked a half-dozen times and waited, knowing how long it took to walk from one end of the studio to the other. *If she heard me.* That thought prompted him to knock again, only a little harder, then begin mentally tracking Monique through the studio—picturing her working, stopping, listening, slowly wiping her hands on her smock, then making her way to the door. He slowed the rhythmic nod of his head, timing her pace to allow for her stride, which was much shorter than his. *And her limp,* he thought as he mentally brought her to the other side of the door and waited for her to open it.

Nothing. Not a peep. Turning to leave, Sean heard what sounded like a muffled cry inside the barn—deep-throated, almost manly. Spinning around, he pressed his ear to the door and held his breath, his eyes shut, listening with his whole body. If he could have, he would have silenced the whisper of the wind blowing through the trees, rustling the leaves.

Giving up, he stepped back, his gaze raking the side of the barn, unconsciously looking for something. But what? He zeroed in on the loft door overhead, which was locked tight. *There's got to be another one in the back,* he thought, and started around the barn, walking as quietly as he possibly could, his ears tuned to any sound that might escape through the cracks. *Which isn't likely,* he thought, *not with these walls.*

"Unless someone *really* screams."

With that said, Sean started running, keeping his hand against the side of the barn to guide him in the dark, splinters from the cracked and weathered siding breaking off and piercing his fingers. Grabbing the edge of the barn, he swung himself around the corner.

"Yes!" he cheered when he spotted what he was hoping to find: another loft door, and a rope dangling down from a pulley secured to a bridge brace overhead. Rushing up, he yanked the rope, once, then harder, to make certain it was tethered securely to something inside the loft. Without thinking whether or not he could still do what he'd done as kid—sneak up into the hayloft using the baling line, while walking up the side of the barn—he started doing just that, though not as quickly or as gracefully as he once had. The muscles in his arms and shoulders weren't as strong as they once were either, offering an all-too-painful reminder to Sean of his age as his grip weakened and he began to slip, the rope burning his hands.

Just when he thought he couldn't hold on another second longer, afraid he was about to end up flat on his back on the ground, he managed to kick himself away from the barn and swing back into the open loft. Rolling over onto his side, he lay there, his arms, hands, and shoulders quivering from the strain of what he'd just done. "At least you could still do it," he whispered, and struggled to his feet. He stood motionless, waiting for his eyes to adjust to the shadowy dark of the hot and stuffy hayloft as he tried placing himself, then imagining a way down into the studio. *Or at least find a crack in the floor to see what's going on down there,* he thought. That idea immediately brought to mind the hay that he'd noticed falling through the spaces between the floorboards that first night he visited Monique.

Dropping to his hands and knees, Sean peered through the cracks as he crawled along the floor, looking for a sliver of stray light—anything that would tell him where he was. *There!* He stopped, trying to focus on what he saw. He recognized one, then a second sculpture, and knew right where he was—a foot or so beyond the kitchen wall, across the studio from where Monique worked. He shuffled along, his face close to the floor, peering down through a steadily narrowing crack until he saw someone move. He stopped dead. He tried the spaces on either side, then a few others farther away, but came back to the one he'd started with, which was hardly more than a slice of light. Pressing his face flat on the floor helped a little by giving him a wider field of view. He could now see the clay figure of a man, its back to him. Directly beneath him was someone standing beside the wooden stool—a man, naked, hairless, more old than young—frozen in place, as if already cast in bronze, and painted over in flesh tones.

Sean breathed a sigh of relief at not finding someone hurt, and began searching for Monique as a breeze slithered its way into the loft, stirring up the musty barn air. *Jesus, what's that smell?* He raised his head and looked around. He sniffed, trying to place the acrid odor, which seemed to grow stronger with each gust of wind that found its way into the loft.

Something died up here, he decided. *And something big, too, not just a couple of mice or rats.* He held his breath for a moment, listening for the telltale sound of an animal quietly moving about. *Could be an owl,* he thought. *Or bats—they can stink up a place to high hell with that disgusting guano.*

Before he could pin down the smell, the breeze backed its way out of the barn, taking the foul odor with it, leaving behind the faint smell of decay. With a shrug of his shoulders, Sean turned his attention back to the studio beneath him. The moment he had his bearings—the stool, the man, who still hadn't moved, and the sculpture—he searched for Monique.

Suddenly, a figure—a patch of flesh—moved through his plane of sight, startling him. In an effort to get a better look, he inched along the seam, moving steadily closer to the clay figure. "What the fuck—" he whispered, before catching himself and crouching down to keep from being found out.

Standing in front of the sculpture was a woman—naked, tall, full-figured, athletic—her bronzed skin glistening with sweat. She was intently working the clay with both hands, busily moving from one spot to another, as if putting on finishing touches.

Where the hell is Monique? Sean flattened his face against the floor. When he blinked, his eyelash swept dust into his eye. Raising his head, he licked his finger—wiped his eye clean—then blew the dust away from the seam in the floor and peered back down into the studio. Surprise was replaced by curiosity as he watched the statuesque woman work, his gaze uncontrollably, but willingly, sliding over her body: her deliciously full breasts; large, dark brown nipples, which were erect; broad hips; rounded but firm tummy; and the dense tuft of shiny black hair nestled between her thighs. The more she moved about, the more aroused Sean found himself becoming. *Could it be one of her students?* he wondered. *But even if it is, why is she working in the nude? It doesn't make—* A muffled voice stopped his train of thought. Sean tracked the sound to the man beneath him, who appeared to move his head ever so slightly and utter another sound, this one gruff and garbled. A quiet yet snide laugh drew Sean's attention back to the clay figure to see the woman walking toward the man, smiling, kneading a lump of clay with both hands. She stopped directly in front of him, leaned forward, and kissed him on the mouth, a long, lingering kiss. Sean waited for him to respond, to take her in his arms. *Do something!* But he didn't move, he just stood there, a pillar of stone. Holding the kiss, the woman reached down and began fondling him as she pressed the softened nugget of clay between her thighs and worked it, slowly, rhythmically, in small, tight circles.

Entranced by what he saw below him, yet at the same time embarrassed by what he was doing, Sean fell prisoner to his own lust as he watched the woman bring the man to a fully aroused state, his thick, curving erection spreading her hand open as she caressed him, all the while working the clay ever deeper into her loins with her other hand, her gaze fixed on his. The man suddenly groaned, then exploded, spurting everywhere, spotting the floor. Tipping her head back, closing her eyes, the woman held him firm as a shiver passed through her body, followed by another. Then, with a sigh, she pulled away and wiped her hand on the man's belly. Walking back to the sculpture, she knelt down and, with that same ball of clay, began working the area around the figure's thighs as the man's excitement rapidly faded.

Sean couldn't help whispering, "You bitch."

The woman suddenly stopped, her head cocked to one side, as if listening. *Shit.* He lay perfectly still, eyes shut, barely breathing. When he looked again, she'd moved out of his narrow field of view, though he could hear her moving about somewhere in the studio. *You better get out of here,* he thought, and began crabbing his way backward toward the loft door on his hands and knees, trying his best not to make a sound.

When he stood up, about to turn around, a noisy flutter of wind burst into the loft, blowing loose hay and dust all around him. Before he could wipe his eyes, Sean heard a deafening screech. "What the—Jesus Christ!" he cried out as pain ripped across his back, taking his breath away. Instinctively he lunged forward, but was struck again, thrown flat on his face, arms spread out, useless. He rolled over and over—bumped into a hay crib—and jumped to his feet, arms raised, fingers balled up into fists, ready to strike.

Shadows were all around him, the sound of wings flapping, a foul stench gagging him. Ducking down, he darted for the loft door, but was knocked backward into one of the posts holding up the ridge beam, hitting his head, slamming his eyes shut. The pain in his back was now wet and warm, and soaking through his shirt.

Whatever it was suddenly rose up, its wings spread wide, eyes on fire, burning deep into Sean's terrified gaze. "Fuck you," he growled, and charged headfirst into the belly of the beast, driving it back into the wall. It let out a horrifying screech, its wings beating Sean about his head and shoulders, tearing his shirt to shreds. Spinning away, Sean lunged for the rope, intent on swinging free and dropping to the ground. Before he could, pain knifed deep into his shoulder, down his arm, pulling a veil of darkness over him as he sank to his knees, his head bowed, arm raised, the rope wrapped around his wrist and locked in his clenched fist.

"Do it," he told himself, and pitched forward out of the loft, the rope slithering around his wrist and through his hand—burning his fingers and palm—as he plummeted to the ground. Landing feetfirst with a jarring thud, his legs gave way as he collapsed to his knees and fell onto his face.

His body wracked with pain, wanting nothing more than to close his eyes and lie down, Sean forced himself to his feet and stumbled through the grass, circling around the barn. He moved faster and faster until he was running full speed down the overgrown entrance.

Chapter Twenty-eight

Sean tried rolling over, but the pain in his back pinned him to the bed facedown, arms and legs spread out like a prize in an entomologist's display case. When he tried pushing himself up, his left arm folded like a pocketknife from the pain stabbing into his shoulder. "Shit," he groaned, burying his face in the pillow.

"Are you all right?" an anxious voice asked.

Pamela? Sean rolled his head to one side and opened one eye. "What are you doing here?" he asked when he saw Pamela perched on the edge of one of the hardwood maple chairs from the kitchen, leaning forward, arms resting on her knees. She was wearing jeans and a well-worn blue denim shirt, her sleeves neatly rolled up above her wrists. Every last hint of orange had been rinsed out of her burgundy-red hair, which was tied back into a ponytail with a yellow ribbon, exposing streaks of silver shooting back from her temples. A cellular phone was slipped into a leather holster on her belt.

Thinking, *Another step closer to the real Pamela Eagleston, ladies and gentlemen,* Sean slapped the pillow into a puffy ball and propped his chin on top. No sooner had he done that than his right hand began throbbing. When he held it up to his face, he saw that his fingers and palm were blistered and swollen with rope burns. He tried making a fist but couldn't. With a discouraged sigh, he buried his face back into his pillow and mumbled, "I guess it wasn't a dream after all."

"*What* wasn't a dream?" Pamela asked. "You look like you were in a fight and—"

"Got my assed kicked." Sean laughed, then winced and sucked in, waiting for the pain to throb itself away. "Don't do that again," he whispered, taking a shallow breath, then exhaling ever so slowly.

Pamela put her hand on his bare shoulder. Her touch was cool and soothing against his warm, moist skin. "What happened?" she asked, gently kneading the muscles in his neck.

Don't stop, he thought, and shook his head. "I'm not really sure. I went to . . ."

He paused and raised his head off the pillow. "How did you know something happened?" He glanced around his bedroom, out into the hall. "And how did you get in here?" Cocking his head, Sean eyed Pamela suspiciously, all the while smiling, then flopped back down onto the bed and wrapped his arms around the pillow.

Pamela kicked her penny loafers off, braced her bare feet on the bed—the polish on her toenails now a conservative cardinal red—and tipped back in the chair. "From what I understand, one of your runner friends found you early yesterday morning, shortly before dawn. You were slumped over the wheel of your car, which had been driven up onto the lawn, just short of the porch steps. You were covered with blood. So was the seat of your car."

Rocking forward, Pamela gave Sean a kiss on the side of his head. "And the reason *I'm* here, Dr. MacDonald, is that the police found a piece of paper with my phone number on it in your shirt pocket, and called me. I've been here since last evening, I got here a little after eight. You've been out of it for two days." She tickled his ear. "Now, how about telling me what happened?"

Sean muttered, "You don't want to know."

Pamela sat up stiff as a board. "Try me," she said, biting down on her words. "I think my track record for listening—and trusting you—is pretty damn good, wouldn't you agree?" She jostled the bed with a shove of her foot.

Sean nodded as he scrunched the pillow under his chin so he could talk. Slowly, trying his best not to leave anything out, he told Pamela about his meeting with Andrea Stern—brought her up to date about the altercation at the academy—told her about Allan Stern being her husband, and missing now for over a year, and then explained what Allan had done—or hadn't done. "In all honesty, right now I'm not really sure what happened," he said.

When he told Pamela what Andrea Stern had said about the bronze, and how much it looked like her husband, Pamela became as quiet as a mouse. Sean also made a point of telling her about his early relationship with Brad Johnson, what Brad had done, and the fact that he'd been forced to resign. Sean left nothing to the imagination when it came to how he felt about Brad—especially now, after talking with Andrea Stern.

"As far as I'm concerned," Sean said with a wave of his hand, which he instantly regretted, "the man is a pathological liar."

He even managed to slip in as a postscript his run-in with Rocky. "And I got this for my efforts," he said, as if bragging, and twisted his head around to show Pamela the scabbed-over gash, which was now mostly hidden by his hair.

For an instant Pamela appeared concerned, but seemed to hold herself back. "Am I supposed to be impressed?" she asked in a disapproving manner, the way women do when confronted with boyish behavior by men: barely tolerant, with a snide twist to their words.

"No." Sean chuckled. "You're supposed to kiss it and make it better."

Pamela leaned forward and ran the tips of her fingers over Sean's back, skipping from one patch of bare skin to another showing through between the bandages covering his wounds. "Will a kiss make *these* feel better, too?"

Scrunching onto his side, Sean sat up like a jack-in-the-box and kissed Pamela before she could pull back. "It might not make them feel any better, my pretty, but it sure will make *me* feel better." Using Pamela's knee as a brace, he stood up. The sheets fell away, revealing that he was naked. Pamela stifled a laugh when he blushed and reached for the sheets to cover himself up, only to have them slip through his fingers when he couldn't close his hand.

Before he could turn away, Pamela reached up and brushed her fingers through the hair on his chest, tracing the scars slicing back and forth over his heart. "Jilted lover?" she asked with a smile, then let her fingers slide down his chest, over his stomach, and circle around to the knotted scar on his left side, just above his waist. "This one's older than the ones on your chest," she mused, drawing a circle around it.

Then she kissed the two-inch-long ropelike scar and asked with a throaty purr, "Do they *all* try to kill you?"

Sean shivered, chilled through and through by the thought of how he'd gotten those scars, not because he was standing stark naked in front of an open window, a cool breeze wrapping itself around him. He grabbed hold of Pamela's hand and held on to it.

"Isn't that what you all do after you've finished with us?" he asked in a not-so-playful tone of voice.

"Only in *your* books," Pamela quipped, and drew her hand back to take a swat at Sean.

He jumped, but not quickly enough as she grazed him with the tips of her fingernails, scratching him. "See what I mean?" He laughed, rubbing the rising welts on his bare ass as he walked over and pulled one of the dresser drawers open. Rummaging around, he scooped out a pair of briefs and slipped them on. "Now," he said, his hands on his hips, trying to sound serious. "How did I get these bandages on my back and shoulder?" He held his hands up as if to surrender. "Not that I object, mind you." Folding his arms, he leaned against the dresser, only to arch his back and pull away, pain shutting his eyes. "Not smart," he whispered, holding his breath.

Pamela stood up, tapped a series of numbers into the cellular phone, then gestured to the walk-in closet on the opposite wall. "Finish getting dressed. I'll be in the kitchen," she said in a firm, businesslike manner, and walked out of Sean's bedroom.

Not two steps down the hall, Sean heard her say, "Dr. Andrews, please, this is Pamela Eagleston calling." Sean turned his head and leaned toward the door. Pamela called out, "If you need help getting your shirt on, give a yell."

Then she continued down the hall on her way to the kitchen, the words "He's sore, and obviously in pain, but otherwise he seems to be all right, Uncle Edward—" fading with her barefooted steps. Those padded steps were sounds Sean hadn't heard in his apartment in over three years.

"Well?" Pamela asked, propping her elbows on the kitchen table and threading her fingers into a two-handed fist. "Did you?"

"I told you," Sean said with a closed-eye shaking of his head. "I don't know who he was. I was almost directly above him, so I couldn't see his face, only his body. And even then, I was looking almost straight down. As I already told you, my guess is he was in his late fifties, maybe older, in pretty good shape, but kind of soft, six feet or so—but that's hard to say for sure, given the angle—and he had a bald spot on the top his head."

Sean raised his hand. "Oh, and he had long gray hair—sort of like salt and pepper—which covered his ears."

This was the third time Sean had answered this question, each time asked in a slightly different way by Pamela. He felt like he was being interrogated, perhaps even doubted, and didn't like it one bit. It reminded him all too well of what he'd been put through by the Dutchess County Sheriff after Bruce Fanning's murder. But Sean knew it was him, not Pamela. However, knowing it didn't make it any easier, especially coming from Pamela, who at first surprised, then slowly angered Sean by her relentless questioning of him, while at he same time seemingly refusing to talk about her trip to Philadelphia in search of the illustrious Dr. Anderson.

And I'll be goddamned if I'll ask you again, he thought.

When Pamela paused to take a bite out of the lettuce-and-tomato sandwich she'd thrown together for herself, Sean snatched up the half-filled bottle of beer sitting on the table in front of her and drained it in a single chug before she could stop him.

Pamela kicked his chair, turning him sideways. "Dammit, Sean, you know that you're not supposed to drink with the medication my uncle gave you. It's not so bad with the penicillin, but you could get sick from mixing alcohol with the codeine in the painkiller."

"I'll take my chances," Sean replied defiantly, and made a noisy show of sucking every last drop of beer out of the bottle.

Pamela pushed away from the table and went to the fridge to get another bottle of Pabst. When she returned, she dragged her chair around the table, opposite Sean—beyond his reach—and sat down.

"And the woman who was there?" she asked. "Did you—"

"Jesus Christ!" he blurted out. "How many times do I have to tell you? Do you think I'm lying?" He paused, deliberately, and waited for what he'd said to sink in. "No," he finally said with a halfhearted slap of his hand on the kitchen table, more for effect than anything else. "I did not recognize the woman who was there. Even though I would love to have known her," he added out of spite, but failing to get the rise out of Pamela he'd hoped for. "So let's drop it and move on. Okay?" he asked, and stood up, trying to stretch the growing stiffness out of his back and left shoulder, grimacing with every twist and turn of his body.

It had been like this for the last hour and a half—*a goddamn inquisition*—ever since Sean had told Pamela about going to Monique's studio and climbing up into the loft. His mistake, however, was describing everything he'd seen. Well, almost everything: The scene with the clay was the one thing he hadn't told her about, and was now glad he

229

hadn't, thinking, *She'd probably tell you that you were a pervert for watching.*

Bullshit, he immediately argued with himself. *She would have watched, too.* He headed for the refrigerator, intent on getting a beer for himself. *Fuck the codeine, all it'll do—if it does anything—is put you to sleep.*

Sean ignored the creak of Pamela's chair as he reached into the fridge for the last bottle of beer. He felt her hand on his arm. When he turned, she took the bottle from him, which was an easy task given the fact that he'd picked it up with his right hand, and couldn't tighten his grip when he tried holding on to it.

Slipping it back into the refrigerator, Pamela nudged the door closed with a lazy swing of her hip and gently turned Sean around to face her. "I'm sorry," she said, and breathed a sigh of relief. "I don't know what happens to me when it comes to that woman."

Sean frowned, a question on his face. "Which one?" he asked.

Pamela smiled, looking more tired than happy. "I'm talking about Gerard, not your naked lady. There's something about the way she treats me, has ever since the first day we met at the academy, and I can't put my finger on what it is. She stays as far away from me as possible, as if she doesn't want me near her. Or have anything to do with me. She only talks to me when I talk to her, and even then it's a curt hello or good-bye. More often than not, she just nods—yet always makes eye contact with me—and walks right past. I feel like a leper."

Pamela led Sean over to the table and sat him down, then circled around to her own chair. "Don't get me wrong, she's always been very polite with me, unlike the way she treats most everyone else who tries getting near her. Except for George White." She pointed an accusing finger at Sean. "And *you.*"

Sean grinned. "Why do you even bother trying?" he asked. "Just ignore it—ignore her."

"I can't. I don't know why, but for some strange reason,

I want her to like me.'' Pamela shrugged her shoulders and sat back.

Sean was about to ask, ''What's the big deal?'' but stopped himself when he realized that Pamela was serious about this, not just miffed or hurt. ''Perhaps you're jealous?'' he offered.

She pursed her face into a disapproving frown as if to reject Sean's conclusion. ''Jealous? Me? Of her? Don't be ridiculous.''

Sean shook his head, a patient smile, mixed with affection, working its way onto his face. ''Not of her—of George, Bruce Fanning, and of me in particular. My going to her studio, seeing her work, getting to know her. Maybe you're jealous of that and don't realize it. Why else would you want to know every minute detail of what I do with her? Do you realize that for the last hour you've peppered me with questions about us: What did I say? What did she say? What does her studio look like? What is she like when she works? How long was I there? You even asked me whether I'm there at night or during the day, and how late I stayed. You're treating me like a child. Or worse, like I'm cheating on you. If it's not jealousy, what would you call it?''

Pamela leaned forward. ''Are you?'' she asked, her eyes ice blue and just as cold, her body a coiled spring, ready to snap.

''Am I *what*?''

''Cheating.''

This is crazy, Sean thought, and sat back, but caught himself before leaning up against the chair.

From Sean's perspective Sean and Pamela were each jealous of the other, only Pamela seemed unwilling to admit it. But then he reminded himself of his own refusal to acknowledge and accept his feelings during his drive out of the City, just before turning around and tracking down Andrea Stern. *And bumping heads with that jerk cop.* As he thought about it, Sean realized he hadn't fully accepted them—his feelings, that is—not really, as in submitted to them and the consequences. *The big C word, commitment,* he thought. *And the loss of freedom,* he was quick to add. After all, he'd been on

231

his own, footloose and fancy-free, for too long to simply turn on a dime and hand over his freedom to anyone. *And you're no different,* he thought, looking at Pamela while holding on to his silence. *If anything, you're even more independent than I am.* This thought only served to strengthen Sean's respect for her. However, Pamela's feelings about Monique, which he began to think of as being something more than jealousy—*It's almost as if you want her approval*—left him confused.

Pamela stood up. "Do I take your silence to mean yes?" she asked, arms folded, still wired.

Sean stood up and wrapped his arms around Pamela, holding her close to him. "No," he said quietly and with absolute certainty. "I am not involved with Monique Gerard—sexually or in any other way. Nor do I have any intentions of becoming involved with her. I have a job to do, which, quite honestly, has gotten completely out of hand. Right now, all I want to do is wrap it up as soon as possible so I can get back to my writing."

Sean held Pamela at arm's length with his good hand. "I'm afraid you're going to have to follow up on this whole conspiracy thing on your own. I simply don't seem to have the head for it."

He glanced down at his shoulder, the bandages pushing his shirt up. "Or the body," he said, and laughed, ignoring the pain that tried to muffle him. "Okay?" he asked, and gave Pamela a tender kiss on the lips, which is when he noticed that she was no longer wearing her ensemble of earrings. He tried but couldn't remember when he'd last seen her with them in.

That thought drew another out of the back of his mind, and Sean found himself wanting to unbutton her denim shirt and see if she was still wearing her nipple ring. *No, she isn't,* he decided, glancing at the soft, unbroken lines of her breast and the barely visible shadow of her nipple pushing up the fabric. He smiled to himself. *Thank heaven for the butterfly.*

"Do you think you can travel without too much discomfort?" Pamela asked.

"How far?"

"My place."

"Why?"

"You can work in peace and quiet there. And I can mother you. Any objections?"

Smiling, Sean thought for a moment. "*Mother* me?" he asked, suppressing a grin. "Can we agree on a different role? I don't see you as the Madonna type."

"And the ride?" Pamela asked, apparently ignoring the implied meaning of Sean's comment. "Do you think your back can take it?"

"Not in my car," he replied without having to think. "And not in your Ghibli, either, I'm afraid. The bucket seats are too narrow and too hard. And the suspension too stiff. But thanks anyway for the offer," he said, sounding honestly disappointed.

"I don't have the Maserati." Pamela turned and started for the hallway, beckoning with a wave of her hand for Sean to follow. "Come," she said, wriggling her fingers. "I'll help you pack. Do you want anything from your study? Your journal? Files? A backup diskette?"

"How about a laptop for the struggling writer?" Sean said jokingly. "That way I won't get in trouble for *almost* reading someone's personal files."

Without hesitation, her words free of animosity, Pamela said briskly, "We'll pick one up on the way down—my treat. I'm sure there's a computer store somewhere along route nine."

What? "How are we getting there?" Sean asked, stalling for time to think this whole thing through when he realized he didn't want to stay at Pamela's but didn't know quite how to tell her. "Flying?"

Pamela waved her hand, as if to brush aside his concerns. "The Rolls is outside. I'm sure you'll find the ride to your liking. You can even lie down and go to sleep if you like. I'll sit up front with Peter. Now, hurry up." She made it sound like a command.

"Yes, sir!" Sean snapped, and clicked his heels. Then he threw her a salute, which she couldn't see.

"Don't be a smart-ass," Pamela shot back, and laughed.

233

The woman has eyes in the back of her head. "Can we make one stop on the way?" Sean asked as he headed down the hallway to his bedroom just as Pamela slipped into his study.

"Yes—as long as it's not Gerard's studio."

Interesting. "I want to swing by the college and pick up a binder I left with my friend, Oliver Shore. It's filled with photos of Monique's work. I'll need it for reference."

Sean was at his bedroom door when Pamela called out, sounding hesitant, "Is the piece that was in the show at the academy in it, the one the Stern woman thinks was modeled after her husband?"

Sean turned and stuck his head through the doorway of his study. Pamela had already gathered up his journal, copies of what he'd sent to Brad Johnson, and was just slipping the backup diskette out of the computer. "Yes," he said. "Why do you ask?"

Pamela squeezed past Sean, out into the hall, and started for the kitchen. "Just curious," she said blithely. "I never did get a really good look at it." She held her hand up. "I'll take these things down to Peter and come back up to help you pack."

"Then do I get to hear about Philadelphia?"

Pamela stopped and turned around. "Yes—right after you tell me the truth about those wounds on your back." She took a half-step toward Sean. "Large raptors—such as a golden eagle or an osprey, which can have a wingspan of over six feet—have four digits, three front and one opposing. *You've* got four parallel cuts across your back. And just for the record, Dr. MacDonald, birds of prey—ones that hunt and kill live prey—grab with their talons and hold on, which rules out the type of wounds you've got."

Pamela turned and started for the kitchen door leading downstairs. "You're going to have to come up with a more convincing answer than the one you gave me before I believe your story about being attacked by an eagle in that hayloft." She spun around. "And that's another thing—eagles, and even ospreys, don't nest in barns. They build their nests as high up in a tree as they can. Or on a cliff side."

234

Pamela patted the cellular phone on her hip. "While you were sleeping, I called the zoo and spoke with one of their curators."

Bowing respectfully, Sean shooed Pamela away, then slipped into his bedroom. *You wouldn't believe me if I did tell you the truth.*

"I'm not even sure I believe it myself," he snorted as he began pulling things out of the closet and tossing them onto the bed, all the while asking himself why he was going to stay with Pamela when he knew he really didn't want to.

He abruptly stopped what he was doing and sat down on the edge of the bed. *She really doesn't give a shit about you. All she cares about is finding out what happened to her father.* He shook his head, refusing to believe what he'd just thought, if only for the sake of his own vanity. But his nagging doubts wouldn't go away that easily. *There's something between her and Monique she's not telling me.* Sean began absentmindedly folding his shirts, doing a half-assed job of it with only one good hand. He gave up and sat back. *Or is it something between her father and Monique?*

"But what?" he muttered, toying with the possibilities, none of which he could ask Pamela about. Not without risking her anger, which he figured was now close to the surface, based upon the way she'd spoken to him about the wounds on his back.

She wasn't teasing, not this time, he thought, then couldn't help wondering, *Maybe she never was, and it only seemed that way.*

"Or you wanted it that way," Sean said, scolding himself.

"Wanted what that way?" Pamela asked as she glided into the bedroom, pulled one of the dresser drawers open, and began collecting socks and briefs. "Well?" she asked impatiently.

"Nothing." Sean sighed. "Just talking to myself."

Chapter Twenty-nine

The drive from Sean's apartment to the college, Red Hook to Anonville-on-Hudson—a little more than ten miles—was covered without a single word being spoken between Sean and Pamela: silent signatories to an unwritten truce to what Sean sensed was a battle brewing between them. *It's just a matter of time,* he thought.

Sean sat in the rear seat, alone, watching and listening. Pamela was in the front, talking quietly to the man she called Peter, her gaze straight ahead, not once looking at her chauffeur. Now and then she interjected an instruction on which turn to take, making it clear she'd driven the route before, as she guided him to the campus entrance. She then navigated the narrow roads on campus to Merrywood Hall, where Peter pulled to a stop directly in front of the path leading up to the double-doored entrance guarded by a pair of life-size cast-bronze lionesses.

The only question on his mind was *How many times have you been here?*—a thought that, he realized, didn't upset or surprise him. *Nothing you do surprises me anymore,* he thought, reaching for the door, only to stop when Peter said firmly, "I'll get that, Dr. MacDonald." He was out of the car and opening the rear passenger-side door about the same time Sean had folded his hands contritely in his lap. "Sir?" Peter said with a courteous nod. Pamela hadn't stirred, which only added to Sean's unsettling conviction. *What's happening to us?* he thought, remorse having gotten the better of his temperamental resolve. *Is it just me?* he wondered as he stepped out, helped by Peter's gentle but firm grasp.

Pamela still hadn't budged—eyes front and center—and Peter showed no indication of getting the door for her. Sean glanced at him quizzically, at Pamela, then back to Peter, and frowned. Peter shook his head, said nothing, a subtle gesture that spoke volumes.

Fuck these silly games, Sean thought, and opened Pamela's door. "Coming?" he asked.

She turned to face him, expressionless, revealing yet another—but not unexpected—side of her. "I thought you said you just wanted to pick up a binder?" She reached for the door to close it.

Sean caught her hand, ignoring her fainthearted resistance, and drew her out of the car. "I'm not ashamed of you," he said with a wry smile. "Besides, I'd like you to meet Oliver. I know you said you spoke with him, but there's no substitute to meeting the man in person. He's a gem." Letting go of Pamela's hand, Sean started for the arch-topped double-doored entrance of Merrywood Hall. "He's very special to me, I love him like a brother, and I know you'll—"

"We've already met."

Sean stopped dead and turned to look at Pamela, his hazel eyes absent even a hint of green. Pamela tried slipping his steely gaze, but he wouldn't let her get away from him. "I should have guessed," he said politely. "How stupid of me. I suppose you know everything about me—everything the lady's money can buy."

Sean started back to the car. "If you don't mind, please ask Peter to open the trunk. I'd like my bag. I've decided—"

"Sean?" someone called out.

Sean stopped and turned to see Oliver trundling down the well-worn granite steps, waving a sheet of paper over his head as he hurried across the lawn to where Sean was standing, his ruddy round face growing redder with each labored step he took. "There's someone here to see you," he said, coming to a stop in front of Sean and taking a series of much-needed breaths. "His name is Marcelli, he's a detective from New York City." Oliver handed Sean the paper, which was a fuzzy black photocopy of a drawing of a woman's face. "He wants to know if you—either of us—recognize her."

Noticing Pamela, Oliver stepped aside, a chagrined look on his face. "Ms. Eagleston?" he asked, peering at her. "You—you look so different," he muttered, eyeing her as if trying to figure out what was different about her. "Please forgive me, I didn't—"

"Chameleons are like that," Sean said with a sarcastic bent as he examined the photocopied image on the paper. "It's hard to tell what their real color is."

Chapter Thirty

Detective Michael Marcelli was standing in front of a wall of bookshelves in Oliver's office, just to the right of the solitary leaded-glass window. His back was to the door, head tipped to one side as if he was reading something. Although his suit coat and pants were both brown, they were off by a shade or two, begging you to look twice and see they didn't match: The pants were striped, and more charcoal than brown, while the suit coat was solid and lighter. And baggy. Marcelli was mumbling to himself in broken Latin, while fingering the spine of a book on the shelf as if he were blind and the binding embossed in braille. He then repeated the title to himself in English, speaking barely above a whisper.

At the sound of Oliver clearing his throat, sounding like a baritone tuning up, Marcelli spun around, the startled look of a little boy on his face for all of a second, before it evaporated into manhood. He appeared exactly as Sean remembered him—his face wrinkle-free, surprising in light of his job, with soft brown eyes and a warm smile, not the look of a seasoned New York City homicide detective. His chestnut-brown hair was straight, thick, and sorely in need of a trim.

"Dr. MacDonald," he said. He made it sound like they were long-lost friends. Marcelli walked up to Sean, offering him his hand. "My good luck you happened to stop by today. I must have misunderstood you about your still working here." His gaze shifted to Pamela, his eyes darting back and forth, scanning her face, her body, exposing him for what he was. "*Mrs.* MacDonald?" he asked, not quite sure of himself.

Taking the initiative, Pamela stepped forward and shook his hand briskly, surprising him. "Pamela Eagleston, Detective." She glanced at Sean. "Dr. MacDonald and I are good friends."

Dr. MacDonald? Sean mused, then hastily spit out, "Pamela, this is Michael Marcelli. He and I met at Anderson Galleries. I may have mentioned him when I stopped by that night to see you on my way home."

Tapping the air in Pamela's direction with his raised finger, Marcelli squinted and turned his head slightly. "Eagleston?" he asked, narrowing his focus. "Are you by any chance related to a John Eagleston?" He pitched forward ever so slightly, leaning into his anticipated answer.

Pamela smiled and said in what sounded to Sean like a young girl's voice, not that of a woman, "Yes, I am. John is my father."

"Is?" Interesting, Sean thought. *You've convinced yourself he's still alive.*

Standing up straight, Marcelli looked at Sean, Oliver, then back to Pamela. "Small world, isn't it? My old partner in the Sixteenth Precinct is the primary on your father's case. Good man, O'Meara. If anyone can find the man who killed your father, Miss Eagleston, Timothy O'Meara can."

Pamela stiffened. Like dominoes, Sean and Oliver did too. She drew a bead on Marcelli. "Do I take that to mean you think my father is dead, Detective, not missing?" Wired, her whole body like a spring, Pamela asked, "Has there been some development in the case since I spoke with Commissioner Stark yesterday afternoon that leads you to believe that?" she asked, implying that Marcelli damn well better know what he was talking about, or shut up.

240

Although he didn't physically step back, Marcelli appeared to retreat. "Well—no—not exactly. It's just that everyone—"

"What can I help you with, Michael?" Sean asked, having decided he wasn't about to let Pamela toy with the man. *He doesn't deserve it,* he thought. *No more than I do.* Stepping forward, Sean handed Marcelli the paper Oliver had given him, and walked over to the window. Cranking it open, he filled his lungs with fresh air and sat on the sill, his favorite spot in Oliver's office.

Marcelli gladly turned away from Pamela and moved toward Sean. He held the paper up. "Do you by any chance recognize this woman?" he asked, sounding hopeful. "Does she look like anyone you know, or anyone you may have seen the day Mr. Vanderbilt was murdered?"

Sean motioned for Marcelli to come closer, which he did willingly. Taking the paper, Sean examined it, then asked without looking up, "Was this drawing done from what Lydia Thompson said that woman looked like who came to see Skip, and disappeared into thin air?"

Marcelli suddenly sounded serious, almost argumentative. "What difference does that make, Dr. MacDonald? Either you recognize the woman from the composite sketch, or you don't." Marcelli stuffed his hands into his pants pockets and leaned against the edge of the bookcase framing one side of the window.

Sean sat staring at the sketch, not that he needed any more time to know that he'd seen this woman. *Say yes, and he's going to want to know where you saw her, and when. Then he'll want to know what you were doing at the library, when you got there, when you left. From there the floodgates will open, and you'll get swept up in the whole fucking mess.* He looked up to find Marcelli, Oliver, and Pamela looking back at him, all with expectant expressions on their faces.

Sean held the paper at arm's length, glanced at Pamela, eyed the sketch again, then looked back at Pamela. "She kind of looks like Ms. Eagleston, don't you think, Michael?"

Pamela glowered back at Sean, letting him know she didn't appreciate his sense of humor one bit, which at the same time told him that he'd hit his intended mark. However, Marcelli was unscathed, and asked, "Do you recall seeing this woman—or someone resembling her—anywhere near or around the gallery that night?"

With the question repeated, and modified just enough, Sean now had the out he wanted. "No," he said firmly. "I did not see anyone who looked anything like this woman near or around the gallery that night." He handed the photocopy of the sketch back to Marcelli. "I'm sorry. I really wish I could be of more—"

"I've seen her!" Oliver chimed in excitedly. "Let me see that sketch again." He scurried over to the window and snatched the paper away from Sean. Pamela followed, taking up a position directly behind Oliver. More than a head taller than he, she had a clear view of the sketch as Oliver stood motionless, holding it with both hands and looking at it in silence. Marcelli crowded him on the other side, opposite Sean. The four of them blocked the window. "It's her," Oliver finally said. "No doubt about it."

He tapped the paper and looked at Sean. "She's the one I told you about, the one who was here asking about you and the work you're doing for *Entasis*."

Sean didn't respond; he just sat there, expressionless.

"Remember?" Oliver asked, trying to hand Sean the sketch.

Sean didn't want to have anything to do with it. Oliver elbowed him affectionately. "Come on, Mac, where's that total recall of yours? Don't you remember my telling you about her, and your asking me if she had orange hair?"

Cautiously, Pamela eased back from the trio huddled in front of the window, her subtle reaction going unnoticed by everyone except Sean, who kept her in the corner of his field of view and made certain she knew it.

Oliver chuckled to himself. "And if I remember correctly, you also wanted to know if her nose was pierced." Oliver pursed his face into a sour frown, a perfect copy of what he'd looked like when Sean had asked him that very same question.

Smiling—more of a grin—Sean glanced over at Pamela,

whose eyes were wide open, but at the same time barring him entrance. He patted Oliver on the shoulder and stood up. "Orange hair?" he asked. "A pierced nose?" He feigned a distasteful frown. "I was kidding, Ollie."

Sean walked over to Oliver's rolltop desk and picked up the binder he'd come for. "You know me better than that, Ollie. That's not my type."

"But—"

Marcelli lifted the paper out of Oliver's hand and held it up beside Pamela's face, his gaze flitting back and forth between the composite sketch and Pamela as his brow wrinkled into furrows.

Before he could say anything, Pamela looked him square in the eyes, causing him to blink away for a moment. "Don't make your life any more difficult than it already is, Detective," she warned.

Pamela then glanced over at Sean, while speaking to Marcelli. "I don't appreciate Dr. MacDonald's adolescent sense of humor." She turned back to Marcelli. "I hope you won't be misguided by it. Have I made myself clear, Detective? Or would you prefer that I call Bob Stark and ask that he explain the facts of life to you?"

With a wag of his finger, Sean added his two cents' worth. "Careful, Michael, the lady carries a big green stick—and she knows how to use it, too. Don't cross her." Sean started for the doorway, the binder under one arm, and waved for Oliver to join him. "Tip a few and talk?" He held up the binder and shook it at Oliver. "I've got some questions about the list you gave me, and I thought—"

A muted chatter, the purr of a muffled ring, cut Sean off. "What's that?" he asked, glancing around the room.

"Me," Pamela said crisply, and slipped the cellular phone out of the holster on her belt. Flipping it open, she pressed it to her ear. "Eagleston," she said, her gaze cast onto the opposite wall as she listened with her eyes to whoever had called.

She took a slow, deep breath. "Are they absolutely sure?" She hesitated, then fell back against the bookshelves, staring down at the floor. "I see." She began nodding slowly, listening. "Do any of the others know?" She shook her head. "In that case, I'll call them," she said decisively. "It's only right."

Pamela gave up a faint smile. "That's very thoughtful of you, Melissa, but under the circumstances, I really don't think it's appropriate to send anything just yet."

She pushed herself off the bookcase and held her hand up. "Oh, one other thing," she said. "Where is he now?" She blinked, and nodded. "Thank you," she said, clapping the phone shut and holding it hidden in her hands.

Although it was written on everyone's face, Sean was the first to ask, "Problems?"

Pamela holstered the phone, her gaze fixed on Sean. "They found Donald Beaumont," she said quietly. "Or what was left of him." Marcelli snapped to attention. Pamela saw but ignored his inquisitive, almost hungry gaze. "Do you want me to drop you back at your apartment?" she asked Sean, walking across the office and stepping out into the hall. She paused, waiting for an answer.

Sean glanced over at Oliver, who appeared unaffected by what Pamela had just told them. "After I run over to the library and check something out, Ollie, do you want to grab a few beers?" He held the binder up again. "I would really like to tap that fertile brain of yours about some of these photos."

Oliver smiled. "Dinner, too?" he asked, grinning.

Sean mirrored his good humor, as if to flaunt his feelings in front of Pamela. "You're on." He turned to Pamela. "I'll bum a ride off Ollie. You go ahead into the City from here."

Pamela shrugged her shoulders, a look of indifference on her face—tempered by what appeared to be a thin edge of anger—and started down the corridor.

"Come get your things," she said quietly.

Chapter Thirty-one

The low ceiling of the bar in the two-hundred-fifty-year-old Red Hook Inn—once a busy colonial tavern along the well-traveled route from old New Amsterdam to Albany—was held up by sagging, rough-cut beams supported at either end by half-round posts spotted with the knotty stubs of branches axed off long ago. The walls were split logs, the seams chinked with mud and moss—now more for effect than to keep the weather out—and covered with palmed plaster. The squeaky, wide-planked oak floor rose and fell like wooden waves, splitting the old seams and allowing the musty scent of damp earth to seep up and mix with the sour smell of stale beer. Wall-mounted lanterns of hammered tin and blown glass—cotton wicks and whale oil having long before been replaced by tiny lightbulbs flickering like flames—alternated with narrow windows filled with small square panes of thick wavy glass.

Sean and Oliver were seated at a table tucked in a darkened corner of the bar, well away from the other patrons. When Oliver had finished examining Sean's bandaged wounds, Sean gingerly pulled his shirt up over his shoulders, buttoned it closed, and turned around to face Oliver.

"Well?" he asked, taking a sip of beer. "What do you think?"

Oliver slid his gold wire-rimmed glasses up the bridge of his nose and squinted at the pocket ruler he was pinching between his finger and thumb, marking a spot. "They're approximately seven centimeters apart and a bit more than thirty centimeters long. And they're more of a clean slice than the rough tear you would expect from the claw of an animal." Oliver tucked the ruler back into his inside blazer pocket, then drained the mug of dark ale sitting on the table in front of him. "And as you already know, there are four parallel cuts across your back, along with five puncture wounds on your shoulder, which means whatever took a swipe at you—and dug its claw into your shoulder—had five digits."

Raising his hand over his head, Oliver waved the empty mug in the air, signaling the waitress for a replacement—his fourth pint of Whitbread as compared with Sean's second glass of Rolling Rock, which Sean was still nursing.

Sean picked up one of the photocopied pages fanned out on the table in front of him. "Then Pamela was right, it couldn't have been an eagle, since they have three forward and one opposing digit on their talons. Anyway," he said, scanning the blurred lines of text, "from what it says here, an eagle is much too small for what I ran into." He tapped the page. "Their maximum wingspan is only four feet across. And their bodies are too small, too." Sean focused on one short paragraph at the bottom of the page. "And although an osprey's wingspan is even larger—it says that it can get up to six feet across—its body is also too small."

Oliver was slowly flipping through Monique's portfolio again, only now his face was growing steadily darker with every page, with each photograph reexamined. When he spoke, he sounded like his thoughts were somewhere else. "And the fact that neither of those species nests in barns—or anywhere near man—would make it even more unlikely." He looked up, but only for a moment, before turning his attention back to the photographs of Monique's work.

Unlike what Sean had told Pamela—a censored version of what he'd seen, and what had happened to him—he'd set out a detailed account for Oliver of everything he could remember, right down to the smells he noticed in the loft shortly before being attacked, which he still couldn't explain. Not even after he'd noted in the materials he'd collected from the library before coming over to the Inn that ospreys had a strong, often foul-smelling, fishlike odor about them because of their diet of striped bass, carp, and other fish indigenous to the Hudson River and surrounding lakes.

Oliver's reaction to Sean's animated description of the scene with the woman fondling the male model had seemed to fall on deaf ears, leaving Sean confused, until Oliver had said, "You forget, my friend, I lived in a monastery with sixty men. After that, *nothing* you could tell me about sexual behavior would surprise me."

What did, however, pique Oliver's curiosity was Sean's telling of his two earlier visits to Monique's, and his vivid descriptions of the feelings he experienced—"I was out of control, emotionally and physically. Even sexually!"—as he felt himself being drawn to the mysterious polychromed bronze. "She was beautiful, and so lifelike. If only she wasn't flanked by two of the most hideous-looking creatures—a cross between angels and gargoyles—and even worse, I couldn't tell if they were male or female. They made the gargoyles on the Cathedral of Notre Dame look like warm and fuzzy stuffed animals. Every time I think about them, I can't help thinking of the description of the Devil in Dante's *Inferno*, only in miniature, that monstrous beast upon whose back Dante descended into hell. Ollie, in all my research, I've never—"

Oliver closed the binder with an impatient slap of his hand, startling Sean. "If you have any sense, you'll stay away from this woman," he said, the clear sound of a warning in his voice, a look of concern on his face. "Finish what you must in order to meet your obligations to Bradley, only do it without going back to this Gerard woman's studio again."

He gestured toward Sean's back. "Something tells me you're lucky that's *all* that happened to you."

247

Miffed by what Oliver had said, and irritated by his haughty attitude, Sean asked, "What the hell are you talking about?"

Oliver sat back, slowly shaking his head. A middle-aged waitress with bottle-blond hair and a midriff recently out of control set another pint of ale in front of Oliver. Slumping her weight onto one foot, her free hand resting on her over-stuffed hip, she asked, "Would you two gentlemen like something to eat?"

Knowing the menu by heart—after all, there was a time when he practically lived in the Red Hook Inn—Sean looked up and said, "I'll have the pastrami on rye, with horseradish and mustard on the side. And a couple of your fantastic ko-sher dill pickles."

Oliver glanced at the multicolored chalkboard hanging above the bar, peered over his glasses, and read aloud in a single breath, "Sugar-cured Virginia ham with sauerkraut and Russian dressing smothered in melted Swiss cheese on dark pumpernickel bread." Grinning, he looked at Sean. "And I'll have those pickles my friend ordered."

The waitress wasn't two steps away from the table when Sean grabbed Oliver's wrist and asked, "What did you mean when you said I'm lucky that's all that happened to me?"

Oliver pushed the binder at Sean and thumped his meaty hand on top of it. "You taught literature for almost twenty years, and all of sudden you can't recognize a simple alle-gorical theme when it's staring you in the face. Why is that?" he asked, slapping the binder again, his anger rising.

Everything about Oliver—the look on his weathered face, his tone of voice, even his body English as he leaned for-ward, his Irish-red eyes simmering—said he already knew why, and wanted to see if Sean did, too. But worse than that, it was Oliver's way—a sort of code they'd worked out be-tween them over the years—of telling Sean he thought he was acting like a jerk.

Sean was pissed, and it showed by the way he answered. "So the woman doesn't like men. So fucking what!" he snarled, forcing Oliver to sit back as if to get beyond Sean's reach. "If you were fucked over by as many women as it appears she has been by men, you might feel the same way. Everyone wants a piece of her, and it seems they want it without paying for it. And if they can't get it, they're going to make sure no one gets it. So she takes it out in her work, casts her enemies in bronze in a way she sees them. She gets a little poetic justice. We all do it, in one way or another. I know I have in my stories. Vengeance is sweet, even if only served up symbolically. And contrary to what you deists believe from the Bible, vengeance is not limited to the Lord.''

Oliver's face puffed up like a balloon, his neck straining at his button-down collar. ''Listen to yourself, Sean. You haven't heard a word I've said for the last hour. All you can do is defend her. What's happened to the astute, intuitive scholar I know? You're acting like you've got testosterone for brains!''

Oliver threw the portfolio open and slapped at the pages, cracking the plastic sleeves protecting the photographs as he turned the pages. He stuck his finger onto one of the images. ''Here, look in the background of this photograph,'' he ordered, his face now as red as his curly Irish hair. ''Is that your precious painted goddess?'' He waited for Sean to look more closely.

Sean did, appeared thoughtful for a moment, then nodded.

Oliver went on without losing his edge. ''See the winged creature behind her?'' He poked the photo. ''There, in the background?'' Sean looked again, more closely, and nodded. ''Well, as far as I'm concerned, that classical bronze of yours, my friend—in my *humble* opinion—is modeled after the early Greek goddess Cybele, whose victims were only men. And that *thing* behind your pretty painted goddess, if in fact she does symbolize Cybele, is her consort, Attis.''

Oliver sat up, looking indignant, his short stocky arms folded tightly over his portly midsection. ''Need I refresh your memory, *Doctor* MacDonald, about the story of Cybele and her various consorts—most of whom were paired beasts—and how she drove her followers into wild, orgiastic frenzies before—''

''No,'' Sean replied coldly. ''You needn't bother, Dr. Shore.'' Sean stood up, stuck his hand into his pocket, pulled out a fold of bills, and peeled off a twenty. Tossing it onto the table, he said in a forced calm, but nonetheless firmly, "I've got a few things to do," and started to leave.

Oliver turned and held his hand out. "Where are you going?"

"You're so smart," Sean said with a sarcastic twist to his words. "You tell me."

Oliver was at Sean's side before Sean could make it to the door. He unconsciously fell into step with him. "And just how do you propose getting there?" he asked, smiling, the look on his face telling Sean that he knew something Sean didn't. "Walk?"

Nothing was said until they'd made their way out into the parking lot behind the Inn and Sean had stopped. "You don't have a car," Oliver said, an I-told-you-so tone in his voice. "I drove you here, remember?"

Oliver gestured to his little mustard-yellow Morris Minor, which he'd parked in the very last spot, in the far corner of the lot. "Don't want to take any chances," he'd told Sean when Sean asked what he was doing.

Oliver straightened his tattered blazer, tugged it over his belly and buttoned it closed, and said with a British air of authority, "You navigate, old man. I'll drive."

Chapter Thirty-two

In the thirteen years Sean and Oliver had known each other, initially as colleagues, then, as the years passed, close friends, silence had never been part of their relationship. After a few moments of ritualistic warm-up—with Oliver sipping his strong English tea, and Sean mainlining his South American coffee—they could be found caught up in a robust verbal joust: Sean regaling Oliver with some obscure ancient myth or bizarre biblical tale he'd uncovered, demanding an explanation, putting Oliver's scholarship to the test; and Oliver parrying the scholarly blow by taking his own shot at Sean, examining him on some esoteric aspect of nineteenth-century literature, such as an essay he once found that was a scathing criticism of Charles Dickens's *Great Expectations* written by an overzealous left-wing Berkeley feminist.

For the most part, theirs had been a collegial friendship—warm, hearty, and steadfast—yet always at arm's length. This was due more to what Oliver was like than Sean. Except for their bawdy interplay and open exchange of ideas, Sean and Oliver's friendship was unlike Sean's relationship with Bruce Fanning. Sean and Bruce had been closer, like brothers—twins—but still well short of being intimate as so many on the faculty had believed, much to Sean's surprise when he learned of their beliefs after Bruce's death. It was a widely held belief, he was told, that was sparked by Sean and Bruce's increasing closeness after the death of Sean's wife and young son—Sean staying single, almost celibate, by all accounts—and fueled by the fact that Sean was blind to Bruce's persuasion. Even now, more than three years after Bruce's death, Sean still found himself unable to accept what the facts—and what Bruce's many friends, one of whom, coincidentally, was now Sean's publisher—told him had been true.

As Sean and Oliver bounced up and down in Oliver's little roadster—the British version of the Beetle—the only words spoken breaking their unwritten truce since leaving the Red Hook Inn were uttered by Oliver, when he asked, "Where are we going?" followed by Sean offering what for him was a thrifty reply: "Gerard's studio, which is a few miles southeast of Pawling."

Nothing was said even when Oliver drove past the southbound entrance to the Taconic Parkway and began winding his way along the back roads leading to the lower corner of Duchess County, close to the Connecticut border, where Monique's farm was located. Not long after that there was a second, and equally brief, exchange, this one initiated by Sean's sarcastic query, "Can't this damn thing go any faster?" To which Oliver replied pedantically, "I don't take her over fifty. It's not safe."

Caught behind a lumbering hay wagon on a narrow, winding, two-lane road, unable to pass, Oliver turned to Sean and asked, "You recognized the woman in that sketch, didn't you?"

Giving the question a lot of thought, knowing that honesty had always been an essential part of their friendship, Sean nodded and said almost apologetically, "Yes."

"Then why did you lie?"

Bristling, trying not to let it show through but failing, Sean snapped back angrily, "I didn't lie." After a quick breath, he said calmly, "I simply chose to answer the question I

252

wanted to, which may not have been the one Detective Marcelli wanted an answer to. If the man didn't know the difference, that's his problem, not mine. What I said was the truth.''

Oliver reached out and put his hand on Sean's arm, as if to tell him it was all right. "And you weren't kidding about that sketch looking like the Eagleston woman, were you?''

Sean looked askance at Oliver. "How did you know?''

Oliver peered at Sean over his glasses, one eye on the road, the other on Sean. "Do you really think after all these years that I don't know when you're serious and when you're not?'' Oliver turned his full attention back to the road to find that a young boy, clad in threadbare blue denim, had climbed atop the bales of hay and was waving for him to pass, all the while looking back over his shoulder to make sure nothing was coming the other way.

Responding to the invitation, Oliver downshifted and floored it. The little Morris Minor lurched forward for all of a second, chugged, then settled down and busily hummed its way past the hay wagon, not once exceeding fifty miles an hour, thanks to Oliver's steady foot. The moment he was safely past the wagon and had pulled over, Oliver asked, "What, *exactly*, happened to this man—what's his name, Vanderbilt?—that Marcelli was going on and on about before you showed up?''

Sean pulled back from Oliver's question, not wanting to think about Skip Vanderbilt. But at the same time, he felt relieved at being able to talk about it with someone, *someone I can trust*, he thought. Relaxing, he settled back and proceeded to describe what he'd seen when he found Skip Vanderbilt, leaving nothing to the imagination. It was as if he needed to talk about it, having, he realized, harbored a foolish hope of somehow getting it out of his system.

Sean wasn't halfway through his account of that evening, the part where he'd walked into that viewing room and had nearly thrown up at the sight of Skip Vanderbilt's body—no more than shredded muscle and bone—when Oliver interrupted, saying somewhat cynically, yet sounding like he was making a joke, "In light of that bronze the Gerard woman did, it's sort of like life imitating art, wouldn't you agree?''

Sean froze upon hearing this said; it was as if he'd been struck dumb. Finding his voice, he muttered, ''That's it. Only it's art imitating life.'' He turned to look at Oliver, asking apprehensively, making it sound like he didn't want to know the answer, ''What if *Man's Fate* was done from an actual model?''

Oliver scoffed, ''Don't be ridiculous. How could anyone—'' He stopped when he saw the hypnotic expression on Sean's face. ''You're serious, aren't you?'' He let his foot off the gas. ''Do you realize what you're saying?''

Sean said under his breath, his gaze fixed on something off in the distance, eyes hard as glass, unblinking, ''Christ— maybe it really was her husband.'' He could feel his heart beginning to beat faster. He waved for Oliver to speed up. ''Let's go,'' he said, just short of making it sound like an order. ''I want to get there while there's still enough light. There's something I want to see before you and I talk with Monique.''

Sean paused and fell into a deep silence, his eyes shut, head bowed. ''No,'' he said softly. ''You can't come with me.'' He took a long, slow breath. ''It's not safe.''

Oliver eased over to the side of the road, holding his speed just below thirty, allowing the cars behind them to pass. ''This isn't like you, Sean,'' he said, sounding concerned. ''You're not making any sense yourself. It's not the man I know—everything's bottled up inside you. Are you all right?'' Oliver asked. ''Is there something about this Gerard woman you're not telling me?''

''What did you say?'' Sean asked as if he hadn't heard a word Oliver had said.

Chapter Thirty-three

Oliver followed Sean's instructions and drove past the abandoned rear entrance to Monique's farm, which still showed no signs of having been violated—unlike the grass-covered path leading back to Monique's studio, which had appeared overrun with tire tracks when they drove past it a few moments before.

"There," Oliver said with a precise nod of his head after checking the odometer. "Exactly a quarter of a mile." He pulled over smartly, killed the engine, and turned to face Sean, who was still staring out the open window as he had for the last mile or so. "Well?" Oliver asked, grabbing the steering wheel and pulling himself up in his seat in order to see over Sean's shoulder. "Spot anything that looks like a barn yet?"

Sean hopped out. "Let's go," he said, slamming the door. Oliver winced and shut his eyes, a painful grimace on his face.

Seeing, but ignoring, Oliver's reaction, Sean marched across the narrow macadam road in the opposite direction of where he'd told Oliver they were going. On the gravel shoulder, he stopped to wait for Oliver to climb out from behind the wheel—make a show of gently but still firmly closing the driver's-side door—and walk sedately across the road. Sean accepted the mimed reprimand with a tolerant but courteous nod. Then he turned, jumped over the single strand of barbed-wire fencing, and stormed out into the open field as if on a mission.

Oliver, looking out of place dressed in wool pants, white shirt, tartan tie, and his signature Oxford blazer, cautiously eased one leg, then the other, over the ominous-looking strip of rusted wire and followed Sean as he plowed his way through the tall grass, heading for a stone wall that separated the overgrown pasture from a deep row of trees and dense brush.

When Oliver finally caught up with him, he asked, sounding out of breath, "Would you mind telling me what we're doing here?"

Sean darted ahead and stepped up onto the fieldstone wall, turned around, jumped off, and started back. "We're making it look like we've gone into the woods," he replied officiously, and began making a concerted effort to retrace the path they'd cut through the dry grass on their way across the field.

"But I don't—"

Sean stopped, pointed to Oliver's feet, and said impatiently, "Stay in line." He then resumed his determined exit out of the forsaken pasture.

Matching Sean step for step, which wasn't easy for Oliver given his shorter legs, he asked skeptically, "I thought we were looking for an abandoned barn, which you said was on the other side of the road. And which you're not even sure exists, anyway." Oliver stumbled to his knees. "Sean, wait," he called out in a huff as he struggled to his feet. "You're not making any sense. Besides, who's going to know—or care—where we are?"

Sean stuck his arm straight over his head, finger in the air. "They will," he said, hurdling the fence without breaking stride. He stepped to the edge of the road and began gingerly picking clusters of spiny burdocks off his pants and tossing them away.

When Oliver looked up, he promptly tripped and fell forward onto his hands and knees. But instead of getting right back up, he lowered his head and crawled underneath the sagging barbed wire. Once through, Sean offered Oliver his hand. Oliver grabbed hold and pulled himself up, his coat sleeves and pants covered with burrs. He refused to let go of Sean when Sean tried to walk away.

"You're not going anywhere until you tell me what's going on."

Sean yanked himself free. "I told you," he snapped, rubbing his wrist. "I'm looking for a barn. Now, are you coming with me or not?" he asked, starting across the road.

With surprising speed and agility, Oliver circled around Sean and blocked his path. Grabbing hold to keep him from slipping away, Oliver raised his voice and demanded, "What is so bloody important about this barn of yours?" His face was flushed red, his brow furrowed, his beard prickly as if charged with electricity.

Unaccustomed to hearing Oliver yell like that, Sean was startled into standing still. Angered, he began to answer, but stopped when he realized he didn't know what to say, that he hadn't given any thought to what he'd done and said in the first place, he had just reacted to Oliver's question. He didn't have a reason for trying to find the barn—something he'd carefully thought out—he just knew he had to look for it. And he knew it had to be there, never gave it a second thought. He glanced around aimlessly, then looked up, only to shut his eyes and turn away from the sudden glare of the sun when it burst through the clouds, blinding him.

"Sean?" Oliver asked in a much quieter voice. "What did you mean when I asked you who would know—after all, we're out here in the middle of nowhere—and you said *they* would? What did you mean by *they*?"

The clouds shifted, stealing back the sun. Sean looked up again, as if searching for something he'd left behind. He blinked, then again, only to realize the spots he thought he'd seen just before the sun forced him to turn away weren't in the sky but his imagination—something once seen but forgotten. And that's when he knew what he'd meant. Glancing down into Oliver's waiting gaze, Sean said with a sudden calm in his voice, sounding absolutely sure of himself, "Whatever attacked me, that's what."

Oliver's face went pale. "My God, man, think what you're—"

Taking hold of Oliver's shoulders, Sean shook him quiet. "I'm tired of thinking, goddammit. Besides, I don't know why—and I really don't care anymore!—but every time I try to sort things out in some rational way—to make some fucking sense out of what's happening—I can't remember what the hell it was I was thinking about in the first place. I can't seem to concentrate for more than a few seconds. If that!"

Sean bore down on Oliver with a steady gaze. "Like it or not, I'm not going to try thinking anymore. It's useless, anyway. I'm just going to follow my fucking instincts."

He let go of Oliver. "And no, in answer to your question, I don't know—as in have a concrete idea in my head—what the hell I'm looking for. Something just tells me I have to look." Sean grabbed a fistful of his shirt over his stomach. "I feel it. Here. Can you understand that?" he asked. "And I'm going to find out if I'm right or wrong. Or lose my fucking mind. Period. End of discussion," he said with a slice of his hand through the air. "Now, you can come with me—crazy as I may be, having no idea of what I'm getting into—or you can sit in your little car and wait for me. Or you can leave, and I'll find a way back. The choice is yours."

With the hint of a smile on his face, Sean poked his finger into Oliver's chest, pushing him back onto his heels. "But if you decide to come, you have to stop asking me what I think. You're the real scholar, the thinker—not me—you always have been, and you know it. So from now on, *you* do the thinking for us. Okay?"

Not waiting for an answer, Sean turned and started in the direction of the overgrown entrance of the once thriving, but now abandoned horse farm, leaving Oliver behind to pick himself clean of burdocks. He was convinced he would at the very least find the main house. *Unless she had it torn down,* he thought. *And if it's there, or even a foundation, it means this was originally the front entrance.* He also knew that if he found a house, he'd find another barn, though not as large as the one Monique had turned into her studio, since that one was for the horses, and would normally have been set well away from the main house.

"She's probably using it for storage," he muttered to himself, and immediately began trying to think of what might be in it, spurred on by the sudden realization that Monique had to have had her new work cast by now. "At least the one she was working on when I first came here. Even the other one," he decided. "And what about the one that woman—"

The sound of Oliver's hurried footsteps, his out-of-breath call of "What did you say?" was all that was needed to distract Sean. He slowed to wait for Oliver to catch up, happy—and for some reason relieved—that Oliver had chosen to tag along.

They simply nodded to each other, reaffirming their bond, then walked into the field. Sean led the way, staying as close as he possibly could to what was left of the split-rail fence that had once bordered the entrance, now only a ghost in the grass. Each time he came upon a fallen rail, he did a tightrope walk on top of it, arms out for balance, in an effort to mask his tracks even more. Oliver mirrored Sean's moves—now and then slipping off but not once falling—as the two of them, in silence, slowly worked their way toward the oasis of trees and bushes off in the distance.

What was left of the fence abruptly ended, giving the impression that the road did, too. Sean was left well short of his intended goal by the distance of a football field, with nothing but an open field filled with dry grass, saplings, and clumps of brush separating him from the island of trees. Oliver stepped beside Sean and stuck his arm out straight. "I think I see a house," he said tentatively. He tapped the air with his finger. "It's buried in those trees. Can you see it?"

Bending down to match Oliver's height, Sean followed the

line of his outstretched arm to one corner of the dense cluster of trees. "You're right!" he said, and stood up, his hands on his hips. "But how the hell are we going to get there without tracking through this damned grass? Fly?" He immediately shook his head and whispered, "That's not funny, MacDonald."

Oliver tugged at Sean's shirtsleeve. "Here," he said, stepping down into a shallow depression off to their left. He swept his arm out in a wide arc. "See the faint hollow in the grass, snaking around the field to the trees?" Looking, Sean nodded. "My guess is it's a culvert—no doubt for drainage—and probably follows the road." He looked up to Sean, an impish smile on his face. "Perfect cover," he said, grinning proudly. "Coming?"

With Oliver now in the lead, they moved in single file, and much more quickly than they had when they were trying to hide their tracks along the fence leading in from the road. The closer they got, the more they could see of the house—a two-story country Victorian, paint peeling off its white clapboard sides, the windows shuttered closed, the front door boarded over, the wraparound porch smothered by wisteria bushes gone wild. The steps had fallen through. Weeds and waist-high corn grass covered every inch of ground, choking the driveway looping past the house on its way to a weathered gray barn, which was no more than a stone's throw away.

A cool breeze spilled out from the trees as they drew closer. Oliver started for the house. Sean pulled him back with a tug of his coattail. "Forget it," he said, "it's the barn I want to see." Sean followed the vague pattern of the curving driveway, which moved out into a clearing, beyond the shadows of the overhanging trees. There it split in two: One spur veered off to the left, dead-ending at the foot of the sliding barn doors, which appeared to be padlocked; the other spur swung to the right and moved up an incline, before disappearing beneath a curtain of aging weeping willows.

"Wait," Sean said, reaching out and holding Oliver back. He gestured to the top of the small hill, where the drive slipped out of sight, then drew a sweeping curve down and over to the barn. "See the tracks?" he asked. Tipping up on his toes to see better, Oliver leaned over Sean's arm and nodded. "Someone's been here, and not too long ago, either."

Releasing Oliver, Sean walked up and examined the tracks. "And the grass is only bent in one direction." He drew an imaginary line, right to left. "Which means whoever came down here must have put the car, or truck, in the barn and left it there." He glanced around, searching for signs of where someone walked through the grass, but found none. *Or is still in there,* he thought but dared not say.

He waved for Oliver to join him. "Come on, let's find a crack in that old siding and see if we can get a look at what's inside the barn, since it appears that we're not about to open the doors and just walk in."

Side by side, Sean and Oliver walked up to the barn, unaware of the shadows that had suddenly appeared on the ground behind them—crisscrossing back and forth through the grass in the clearing—before disappearing when the sun was swallowed up by another bank of clouds. On a hunch, Sean tugged on the padlock. It popped open. "We can forget the cracks," he said with a laugh, lifting the lock off, then flipping the latch open. He turned to Oliver. "Here, hold on to this, you've got big pockets in your jacket," he said, slapping the lock into Oliver's hand. "Just don't snap it shut by accident, or we're screwed."

The look on Oliver's face made it clear he thought Sean's comment was uncalled for. Instead of pocketing the lock, he reached up and hooked it through the latch, letting it hang there. "Better safe than sorry," he said quietly. There was that subtle, trademark, Oliver Shore *I know what's best* sound in his voice.

Sean smiled, his hazel eyes softened. "You're right," he said, and grabbed one of the rusted handles. He slid the heavy barn door open just enough to slip through. "After you, my—"

"Oh my God!" Oliver whispered, stepping to the opening, as if drawn by some unseen force.

The inside of the old barn was an aging skeleton of sturdy

wooden posts and heavy beams draped with cobwebs. Slivers of daylight sliced through unseen cracks in the roof, cutting away the dark. Dust hung in the air, clinging to the light. Filling the barn was a fortune in luxury cars—one or two driver's-side doors thrown open, a convertible top left down—all pulled in and left abandoned in no particular order. The ones in the back were covered with dirt blown in between the seams in the siding, muting their racy colors, turning red to brown, silver to charcoal gray.

Sean stepped behind Oliver, looking over the top of his head. "Holy shit," he muttered, and nudged Oliver inside with a tap of his hand, then moved past to survey the sight before him.

"What do think?" Oliver asked, inching his way past Sean.

Not answering—knowing there was nothing to think about, not this time—Sean walked up to the car nearest him, a classic Jaguar XKE roadster, lipstick red, the top down, in concours condition. A light blanket of dust covered it bumper to bumper, but not heavy enough to dull the chrome, which seemed to sparkle even in the dim light of the barn. Kneeling, Sean brushed the mud and road dirt off the license plate, revealing the letters DKB.

"Beaumont," he whispered, and stood up, absentmindedly brushing his knee off as his gaze went from car to car, paused for a moment or two at each one, nodded, then moved on, as if taking inventory. Or unconsciously looking for something.

"Who's Beaumont?" Oliver asked, doing the same thing Sean had done, only to the license plate on a car off to his left, a silver Mercedes sedan, windows tinted black all around. It had been pulled in at a crooked angle. A smudge the color of wood ran down one side of the car. Splinters were wedged into the rear bumper. Skid marks could be seen in the dirt behind the tires. It looked as if someone had been in a rush, hit the barn door pulling in, then slid to stop.

"This one says FWA," Oliver called out, as if reporting in.

Sean hesitated, blinked—filing the vaguely familiar acronym away to be decoded later—and started working his way around the cars toward the back of the barn. His curiosity had been aroused by one car, smaller and sleeker than the others, that had been backed into the corner, well away from the others. Sean thought he knew what it was; however, the shadows and the veil of cobwebs blurred his vision. As focused as his attention was, he couldn't help noticing each of the cars as he moved past, adding some distinguishing detail—a gold-plated hood ornament instead of chrome, alloy wheels where wire wheels should have been, spiked antennas for cellular phones growing out of rear windows, and bold stickers announcing membership in some yacht club—to the file he was creating in the back of his mind, hopefully not to be lost with so many other thoughts of late.

Meanwhile, Oliver headed for a classic Rolls Royce Silver Cloud, embassy black, its chrome bumper and majestic grille both crumpled from the stately car's having been driven into one of the posts supporting an overhead beam, backed up, and left there. It appeared to have been sitting forever, the dust so thick it covered the hood, wings, roof, and trunk lid with a crusty old skin. The doors and windows were streaked with brown.

Never without one, Oliver retrieved a pen from his blazer pocket, knocked the dust off the license plate with a tap of his shoe, and wrote down the plate number on the palm of his hand. After looking to see where Sean was, nodding reassuringly like a mother hen, he began weaving his way through the cars, meticulously adding one license-plate number after another as he slowly circled around and made his way back to the front of the barn.

Sean stopped, a smile on his face, when he confirmed his suspicion. *A 1967 Mexico*, he thought. *My all-time favorite Maserati, bar none.* "She's beautiful," he said, and moved closer to wipe the plate off. "It's a shame—"

"Sean!" Oliver screamed. "God almighty, help m—"

An earsplitting screech silenced Oliver's cry of terror. Sean clenched his fists—he knew only too well what it was—and spun around, his heart hammering against his chest. He caught a glimpse of a wing, another, then the sight of Oliver's legs kicking, his arms flailing in front of his face, over his head, frantically trying to protect himself as he was dragged outside like a fated prey in the deadly grip of the hideous winged creature, its eyes on fire, lighting the dark of the barn as if warning Sean not to follow, its teeth bared, waiting to sink them into Oliver's mortal flesh the moment he weakened.

Racing through the maze of cars, careening off the sides, stumbling when he tripped—forcing himself to breathe—Sean flew through the opening in the barn doors, out into the waning daylight. Oliver was hanging limp in the creature's grasp, its silvery claws dug into his sides, blood dripping onto the ground, its powerful wings flapping, lifting Oliver off the ground.

Jesus—it's female, Sean thought as he started for it, only to be driven back by the ear-shattering pain of its deafening screech. "No!" he cried out, and leapt forward, grabbing hold of Oliver's legs, pulling him free. Oliver fell to the ground, lifeless. The air was suddenly filled with a blinding swirl of dust as the creature beat its wings furiously, then dropped down and began batting Sean around the head and shoulders, almost taunting him to attack her.

Knowing he was no match for her, Sean straddled Oliver's body and looked up, his arms at his sides, his hands open, not balled into fists ready to fight. He just stood there, staring defiantly into her hideous face as she hovered above him, teeth bared. He wouldn't look away when he felt her searing gaze piercing his eyes, burning into his brain—his heart—searching for something. She was relentless, unforgiving, reaching deep down into his soul.

Unable to bear it any longer, his eyes filled with tears, burning like acid, his body drained, Sean dropped to his knees. His head slumped down, consciousness slipping away, yet he still refused to give Oliver up. "No," he said, barely above a whisper.

The air suddenly grew calm. He waited, certain he would feel her teeth, her rapier claws, sinking deep into his flesh. Nothing, not even the foul stench of her breath. When he dared to look up, he saw her rising, higher and higher, until she was little more than a harmless bird in the sky: that memory he'd lost, or put out of his mind, he wasn't sure now. She joined her mate, and the pair began circling above him, as if waiting for him to die.

Exhausted, Sean slumped back onto his heels, then rolled over onto the ground, flat on his back—arms outstretched— trying to think of what to do. *Oliver!* When he tried sitting up, he was suddenly struck with the fear that had somehow escaped him in the heat of the moment. He fell back down. Beads of sweat began pearling on his forehead, running down the side of his face. His breathing grew shallow and rapid. By the time he took hold of himself—what felt like an eternity but passed in seconds—and struggled to his knees beside Oliver, Sean was shivering.

Forcing himself to ignore it, his hands shaking, he slipped Oliver's tie off, unbuttoned his bloodstained shirt, and pulled it open. A thought slipped past his lips in a whisper—''Jesus Christ''—when he saw the torn flesh, blood oozing out with every beat of Oliver's heart, the white of his cracked ribs.

Chapter Thirty-four

It was early afternoon, not a cloud in the sky, not even a ripple of gray on the horizon. Pamela was standing in front of the wall of sliding glass doors in her living room, her arms drawn stiffly behind her back, staring out over Long Island Sound. She was wearing a black silk blouse, her jeweled butterfly broach, and fitted black slacks. Her hair, now all red save for the telltale streaks of gray that had been allowed to stay, was pulled back and tied up, more folded than knotted. She hadn't moved or said a word for the last five minutes—hadn't even blinked—and showed no sign of saying or doing anything anytime soon.

Have it your way, Sean thought, and began drifting around the living room again, moving from painting to painting—pausing in front of each one—but more out of habit now than anything else, since he'd already memorized every one of them. It had been like this for the last hour, with Sean endeavoring to explain where he and Oliver had gone, what they'd done, and what had happened, and Pamela repeatedly interrupting, rudely cutting him off to question him—to doubt or ridicule him was more like it—or chastise him for what she'd said was "your selfish and irresponsible actions in jeopardizing that poor man's life."

Her angry attacks were followed by periods of unilateral silence, like now, leaving the air in the room as thick and cold as a winter's fog on a January night. The discordant note he and Pamela had parted on in Oliver's office only a few days earlier seemed to have played through, and was now a discordant refrain.

Needless to say, things hadn't gone as Sean expected, leaving much of what he'd wanted to tell her—not the least of which was about the red Jaguar he'd found, bearing the licence plate DKB—still unsaid. And, of course, the winged she-creature, which he no longer had to wonder about, having actually seen it for himself. *And it was no goddamned eagle, either.*

But there was no way he was going to tell her about that, not now. *Not the way you're carrying on,* he thought. *Just leave it out of the equation, MacDonald. Besides, she won't believe you anyway—I'm not even sure I believe it! Just let her go on thinking Oliver got tangled up in some discarded barbed wire, and leave it at that.*

Sean lingered in front of an antique cherrywood étagère in one corner of the room, a new addition since his last visit. His curiosity with the collection of locket-size photographs filling the triangular shelves had finally gotten the better of him. Each one was mounted in handmade miniature copies of Victorian picture frames, carved, gilded, and burnished to look like the real thing. One photograph in particular caught his eye, that of a tall, handsome, dark-haired man standing in front of a silver sports car. Beside him was a lanky redhead in pigtails and braces, wearing a sailor's outfit, her hand buried in his, trying her best to look all grown up.

Spurning Pamela's earlier request—a warning that bordered on a threat—not to touch them, Sean plucked this one photograph off the top shelf to get an even closer look at it.

"Where exactly is he at Columbia Presbyterian Hospital?" Pamela demanded.

Not wanting to be seen handling one of the pieces and fuel her already heated temper, Sean palmed the tiny photo and

267

turned around. Pamela was still staring outside. And still rigid as a fence post. *A woman of a thousand faces,* he thought. He said as calmly as he possibly could, "He's in Harkness Pavilion. On the seventh floor." What he really wanted to do was to shout it back at her, having already told her a half-dozen times where Oliver was hospitalized.

Seeing a question forming on her lips, anticipating what she was going to ask—*the only thing you haven't asked me!*—Sean added, "He's being attended by Dr. Robert Jeffrey, who's a top-notch surgeon on the faculty at the hospital. Bob did a masterful job of taking care of me a few years ago. As a matter of fact, he saved my life." Sean hesitated for a moment, asking himself if he should tell Pamela that the barely visible scars on his chest were Bob Jeffrey's handiwork, the same scars she had said were from some woman, an ex-lover or something like that. *Don't be a fool,* he thought. *She's already pissed off enough as it is.*

"Oliver's doing fine," he said reassuringly, in an effort to ease Pamela's concern, which he still couldn't understand given the fact she'd met him only once and really didn't even know him.

Or do you? he wondered, and wanted to ask her that. But instead, he said, forcing himself to smile, for her benefit if she bothered to look, "I stopped by to see him before coming here. He's already up and walking around. And trying to bribe the nurses into getting him a bottle of ale." Sean laughed, but alone.

This is nuts, he thought, and donned an unwanted veil of seriousness. "Bob said he'll be released sometime tomorrow afternoon. He told me to call admissions for the exact time. I'm staying over tonight at the Park Lane. I'll call in the morning to make—"

"No!" Pamela snapped angrily, and turned to confront Sean. She tapped herself with a poke of her finger. "*I'll* check to see what time he's being discharged. And I'll have Peter pick him up in the Rolls and drive him home. The poor man doesn't need any more of *your* help."

The first thing that crossed Sean's mind was: *Who the fuck do you think you're talking to—some goddamn stranger?*

Taking a breath, thinking, *Why did you even bother coming over here?* Sean held his hands out, in reconciliation.

"Listen, I really appreciate your—"

Pamela was across the room and in his face before he could finish what he was going to say. "No, *you* listen," she growled, jabbing him with her finger.

Sean stepped back beyond her reach, his startled but equally cautious gaze locked onto hers. *Just walk away,* he told himself, and slipped past her, heading for the open sliding glass door leading out onto the patio. *Maybe some fresh air will help.* He knew he'd better put some distance between them before something was said, or done, that one or both of them might regret.

"Where do you think you're going?" Pamela demanded, and reached out, tearing Sean's shirt with her fingernails when she missed grabbing a fistful of him.

Sean spun around. *Take it easy.* "I think you better calm down before—"

Without warning, Pamela stiff-armed Sean with a two-handed shove, sending him stumbling backward into the screen door. "You slept with her, didn't you?" Her face was the same shade as her hair, her eyes just as hot. "This is all a charade. You don't really give a shit about anything we talked about—except that ugly bitch—do you? You're obsessed with her."

So that's what this is really all about. Sean straightened his shirt as he moved away from the screen door. He stopped a safe distance from her and said with absolute surety, "I've already told you, I did *not* sleep with her. I don't know why—"

"You're lying," Pamela snarled through her teeth, and took a menacing step toward Sean. "I read your book—remember? Your character fucked anything with a skirt—and I'm not sure even that would have stopped him." She slapped the air, a look of utter disgust on her face. "Like father like son."

Sean couldn't believe what he was hearing. But he knew one thing—he wasn't about to let Pamela get any closer to him. He turned to go sit on the sofa.

"Dammit! Stop walking away from me when I'm talking to you," Pamela yelled, and charged forward. She took a swing at Sean, hitting him in the bandaged shoulder with an open-handed slap.

Pain shot down his arm and up his neck, slamming his eyes shut. He sucked a mouthful of air and held on to it. *Don't hit her,* he told himself. He slowly exhaled the pain away as he turned back to Pamela, his eyes watering from the pain still throbbing in his shoulder. He held his hands up and made a show of gingerly patting the air between them. "I think we should continue this discussion some other time, after you've had a—"

"You make me sick," Pamela said, slapping his hands away. She immediately drew back to take another swipe at him, this time with her hand curled into a fist.

Before she could, Sean grabbed her wrist and swept her off her feet into his arms, and in the process dropped the small framed photograph onto the glass-topped coffee table. "You are going to shut up and listen to me if I have to sit on you," he said, laughing, but more out of exasperation than amusement. "Do you understand me?"

Pamela turned to see what had struck the glass. "What were you doing with that?" she demanded, and began squirming to be free of Sean's hold. "Trying to steal it, like you did with the files in my computer? You can't be trusted with anything, can you?"

Sean held Pamela even tighter as he walked over to the sofa and unceremoniously dropped her onto the cushions. Taking advantage of her position, her indignant surprise, he stepped up onto the sofa, straddling her, and sat on top of her. He then grabbed her wrists, pinning her down. With her kicking and trying to get loose, he bent over and said quietly, a triumphant grin on his face, "I know you think you're a big girl. And I'm sure you can take care of yourself physically. And no doubt you've intimidated a lot of men with your size. And your money," he added without thinking, then realized he meant it. "But if you think you can push *this* man around, you've made a serious mistake."

As if he had all the time in the world, Sean sat waiting

for Pamela to look at him. When she finally did, albeit begrudgingly—disdain all over her face—he asked, making it perfectly clear from the tone of his voice he meant what he said, "Do you understand me, young lady?"

"Get off me," she groaned. "You're hurting me."

Sean wasn't about to trust her, not yet. Squeezing her wrists a little tighter—*better safe than sorry*—he slid back off her tummy and settled down over her hips. When she wriggled, testing to see if she could get loose, he smiled at the thought of the position he was now in. *Don't even think it,* he told himself.

After checking to make sure he was beyond her reach, Sean let go of Pamela's hands, only to snap his head back when she half sat up and took a swing at him. "You're in better shape than most men," he told her, and snatched her flailing hands out of midair. "And just for the record, I was not stealing that locket, I—"

Pamela said with a snide twist to her words, "It's not a locket, it's a—"

Sean sighed. "Will you *please* shut up and listen, for chrissake?" He shook her hands, hesitated, then grinned. "If you don't, I'll have to stuff something in your mouth to keep you quiet." He glanced around, then down at his foot. "How about a dirty sock?" he asked, stretching the grin into a nasty smirk.

"Truce?" he asked, his head cocked to one side in a doubtful pose.

Pamela settled down, although she remained stiff as a steel rail, ready to take advantage of the slightest sign of weakness on Sean's part, and he knew it. She nodded, but her eyes didn't say yes. "Go ahead," she said. "Say what you want, then get out of here."

Keep this up, he thought, *and you just might get what's coming to you, you spoiled brat.* Sean relaxed his grip on Pamela's wrists, but not enough to allow her to slip free. "Is that your father in that picture?" he asked. She nodded, refusing to speak, her jaw square. "Is that his car he's standing next to?"

Pamela hesitated. "Why do you ask?"

"I'll take that as a yes." Sean pressed her hands together between his, as if in prayer. He took a shallow breath, hoping the answer to his next question was no. "Do you still own it?"

Pamela bit her lip, her face closing down into half a frown. "What are you trying to say?" Contention had turned to caution.

"Please." He sighed. "Just answer my question, and stop trying to control everything. Okay?" Smiling, he affectionately jostled her hands, but got no response from her. "The car?" he asked one more time, trying not to sound impatient, but afraid that he had.

Pamela lay there, staring up at him, not once blinking away. "Yes," she said, sounding and looking reluctant. "It was Daddy's favorite car. He drove it whenever the weather permitted." A faint smile—one of relaxation, not pleasure— was trying to get hold of her face, but she wouldn't let it. "As a matter of fact, he had it out when he disappeared. It was never found, either."

Struggling not to let his feelings show, which he could feel rising inside his chest, lodging in his throat, Sean asked without an ounce of emotion in his voice, "It was a 1967 Mexico, with the Maserati trident on the grille gold-plated, right?"

He could feel Pamela's body go limp beneath him.

"How did you know that?" she asked softly. "You can't see the grille in that picture." She tried sitting up but couldn't, and flopped back, her mouth slightly ajar. Before Sean could answer her, Pamela asked in a whisper, "You saw his car in that barn, didn't you?"

Sean closed his eyes, lowered his head, and nodded. "Yes," he said, releasing his hold of her, his shoulders dropping. "It was—"

"I'll kill that fucking bitch!" Pamela screamed, kicking Sean off onto the floor.

He scrambled to his feet. "Calm down!" he pleaded as Pamela exploded off the sofa in a furious rage, her hands balled into fists, looking for something to strike. Sean saw it coming and tried to turn away, but got caught with a glancing blow on the side of the face. In a blind fury, she struck again. "Fuck this," he growled, and threw a punch at her, aiming for her shoulder, not wanting to hurt her. She flew backward, hit the arm of the sofa, and fell over onto it. He was there before she could get up, his hands on her shoulders, holding her down.

"Stop this!" he shouted, only to be answered with a knee in the stomach, buckling him over. But he didn't let go, he even tightened his grip, digging his fingers into her, trying to let her know he could hurt her if he wanted to.

Suddenly, without explanation, she stopped fighting and collapsed into the cushions. "Get out," she said in a dead calm voice.

Sean hesitated, saw the look in her eyes—blue the color of venom—and stood up.

Pamela rose to her feet, as if in a trance, and walked to the window. She pressed her open hands onto the glass, bowed her head—her whole body shaking—and said in a faltering voice, rage mixed with tears, "I said get out."

She took a steadying breath. "I don't ever want to see you again."

Chapter Thirty-five

Hospitals no longer smelled like hospitals. Gone was the re-assuring odor of ammonia, the confidence of bleach, the candy-sweet scent of the nurses' starched uniforms, their comforting crinkle at bedside, and the trace of ether in the air that made you think you were going to gag—but glad it wasn't you getting it. They were all replaced by a collection of inbred odors with no identity, no meaning, no memory, just the artificial stink of something we're supposed to believe is antiseptic. Sort of like a giant men's room, complete with visitors of all ages. And door handles you really don't want to touch but have to in order to get in and out.

Sean leaned back against the stainless-steel wall in the elevator, listening to a pair of young doctors in front of him discussing a laparoscopic operation they'd just performed to remove the withered gallbladder of an unnamed female patient who, as one of them had whispered, "was like operating on a beached whale, she was so fat!" Laughing, they made it sound like they'd just played a video game—Mario Brothers and Pac Man Lost in the Body of Doom—their reminiscences complete with twitching hand movements and unconscious body English.

You're showing your age, MacDonald, Sean thought, watching and listening in amazement as the two surgeons grew progressively more animated, albeit subtly. Without warning, the elevator abruptly slowed to a stop, pushing his stomach up into his throat. *I hate these things,* he thought as he followed the two young men out into the hallway on the seventh floor of Harkness Pavilion. They turned left for the nurses' station; he turned right, heading for Oliver's room, which was at the far end of the hall, with a view of the Hudson and the Jersey shoreline. He was looking forward to seeing him, and the drive home together.

Maybe we can sort this whole thing out, he thought as he ambled down the corridor.

The sound of hurried footsteps behind him were followed by an authoritative voice asking, "May I help you, sir?" Sean slid to stop and turned around, ready to point to the orange visitor's pass stuck to his shirt pocket. "Oh, it's you, Dr. MacDonald," the nurse said with a sudden politeness that had not been in her voice a second before. She appeared embarrassed, then perplexed. "Are you here for Dr. Shore?" she asked.

Sean nodded happily. "I'm breaking him out of here."

Frowning, she glanced at her watch and shook her head. "I'm afraid you just missed him. They left about ten minutes ago."

" 'They'?" Sean asked, knowing all too well what the answer was going to be but asking anyway. He held his hand up to the level of his own head. "A woman about my height?" he asked. "With long red hair?"

She nodded. "It was red, but swept up into a bun. And there was a nice-looking gentleman with her—very British— who wouldn't let her push Dr. Shore's wheelchair."

Wheelchair? "Why did Oliver need a wheelchair?" Sean asked, putting aside his irritation with Pamela and what she'd done. "Is he all right?" He glanced down the hall in the direction of the nurses' station near the elevator, where the two surgeons were standing and talking. "Is Bob Jeffrey on the floor?" he asked anxiously. "May I see him?"

The nurse slipped her arm through Sean's and started

walking him toward the elevator. "Dr. Shore is fine," she said with a reassuring patting of Sean's arm. "Dr. Jeffrey saw him first thing this morning and signed his release. The wheelchair is simply hospital policy. Dr. Shore did not need it." She laughed. "Not that mischievous Irishman." Stopping in front of the elevator, she withdrew her arm from Sean's and asked, exhibiting a sincere measure of concern, "I take it you didn't know Ms. Eagleston had made arrangements to meet Dr. Shore and drive him home?"

"You know Pamela?" Sean asked, almost not wanting to hear the nurse's response.

She shook her head. "Not personally—not until today, that is—but her family's name is well-known around the hospital. Her late father—"

Sean held his hand up to stop her. "Contributed a lot of money to the hospital," he said. "Am I right?"

Smiling, she nodded. "Do you know Ms. Eagleston?"

The elevator door slid open, spitting out two more doctors, even younger than the video game combatants. "Only *too* well," Sean growled, trying not to sound upset, and stepped into the elevator.

Chapter Thirty-six

No matter which way Oliver shifted around in the big old wing chair in his office, he couldn't seem to find a position that was comfortable. Every time he tried leaning back, or nestling a shoulder into one corner, the surgical tape holding the dressings in place—which he'd tried telling the nurse were too tight when she taped him up, only to be told, "Hush up"—pinched his skin and pulled at the stitches.

Out of desperation, willing to try just about anything at this point, he reached down and snatched up a handful of newspapers off the pile on the floor beside his chair. It had to be at least a week's worth of *The London Times*—the somewhat thinner foreign edition—and without the Sunday edition, of course, which would have made the wad far too thick and heavy to grab and hold on to with only one hand. Leaning forward, he stuffed them behind him like a cushion, propping himself up and away from the suddenly uninviting chair. As he eased back, a smile of relief smoothed away the lines pressed into his face from lack of sleep, his gaze fixed on Pamela.

"You've misjudged him," he said sternly as he sat watch-

ing Pamela pacing nervously about his office. When she
stopped, it was only long enough to tidy something up on
the bookshelves, or fuss with a stack of papers on the small
oak library table, tamping them neat and square, then moving
along and doing the same with another sheaf of summer-
school exams waiting to be graded.

Oliver felt a growing sense of uneasiness with what she
was doing; it was as if someone was tampering with who he
was, trying to make him into something he wasn't. He stiffened, and said in that same manner, "I'm also surprised you
didn't realize Sean doesn't say a whole lot when something
is bothering him. He sort of climbs into a hole by himself,
like a hibernating bear, to sort things out. He's a loner—has
been as long as I've known the man. It's not terribly hard to
see," he said, pausing to make his point. "Not if you really
care about him." This last comment succeeded in getting
Pamela to stop and look at him, something she had seemed
to be avoiding ever since they'd arrived.

With an indifferent shrug of her shoulders, and a patronizing smile that said, *What difference does it make?* Pamela
went back to poking around Oliver's office. Only now her
gestures were stiff-fingered jabs, undoing what she'd already
done, as if out of spite.

The ride up from the hospital, while it started out on a
perfectly pleasant note with Pamela expressing her concern
for Oliver, had quickly deteriorated into an attack on Sean
by her. At first Oliver was surprised, then angered by what
was being said about his friend, though he held his tongue,
the gentleman that he was. At one point he had to force
himself not to take her to task—correct her outright—when
she described what had happened in her apartment with Sean,
since her account was so drastically different from what Sean
had told Oliver when he visited him at the hospital the evening after the "little altercation," as she called it. Any concern for bias on Oliver's part in regard to Sean's version
because of their friendship was stricken when Pamela made
no mention of her hitting Sean.

How could she? he'd thought, having seen firsthand the
signs of a large welt on one side of his face, and the makings

of a pretty good black eye. His torn shirt and scratched skin would have been another point at issue had Oliver elected to challenge Pamela on what she was saying. Again, he chose not to.

When she ran out of reasons to criticize Sean for what he'd done—making it sound like he'd set out to intentionally harm Oliver—she took aim at Monique Gerard. That's when it quickly became all too clear to Oliver that she—Gerard—was the real source of Pamela's anger. He also no longer felt a need to come to Sean's defense, which he'd decided he would, "and with both barrels," had Pamela made one more unflattering comment about Sean.

As Pamela went on, speaking as if Oliver knew "that woman," he became more curious than concerned, since he couldn't understand how a woman with Pamela's striking good looks, uncommon grace, and obvious wealth could in any way feel threatened by another woman. *It must be her talent she resents*, Oliver had decided, having no idea what Monique looked like. Upon realizing that, however, Oliver was prompted to ask Pamela what Gerard looked like, but found it impossible to get a word in edgewise without interrupting, which, he'd decided early on, just wouldn't be prudent.

Making a mental note to himself to ask again later, Oliver chose to continue holding on to his silence. The only exception was that now and then he slipped in a question in an effort to gently, subtly, guide Pamela in a direction he wanted her to go in: to talk about something he thought might help him better understand why she really felt the way she did about Gerard, beyond what he had concluded was jealousy, sparked by Sean's involvement with the woman. "Which has gone well beyond the bounds of any routine assignment," said Pamela, making it sound like she had personal knowledge of the scope of Sean's assignment for *Entasis*.

Oliver's effort to sidetrack Pamela had worked the first few times he tried it. But Pamela, without saying or showing it openly, had caught on to him, and stayed focused on what she wanted to talk about, which was what " 'that woman' had to do with my father's disappearance.'' Her unbridled anger had surprised Oliver, sounding, he thought, out of character.

Knowing what Sean's thoughts were on the disappearance of Pamela's father, having listened to Sean argue with himself about it the night he visited the hospital after what he characterized as their "knock-down, drag-out fight,'' Oliver risked asking Pamela if she'd considered the possibility that her father might somehow, "in some very small way, but unknowingly, of course," been involved in "what Sean believes is a conspiracy of some sort to manipulate Mademoiselle Gerard's work." That one question, no matter how he'd tried phrasing it so it didn't sound accusatory, Oliver quickly learned, was a mistake: From that point on, he, too, felt himself being drawn into Pamela's sights as a possible adversary, and at times even made to feel like the enemy, just as Sean had been portrayed.

Pamela Eagleston, Oliver came to realize, had had only one objective in picking him up and driving him home, and it wasn't her concern for his comfort and well-being, as she'd told him. It was to find out where Monique Gerard's studio was, something she'd tried getting him to tell her more than once during the drive up to the college, which is where Oliver had asked to be taken. Each of her attempts met with failure, much to her unguarded dismay, when Oliver posed the feeble but still convincing claim, "I can't remember for sure, Sean did all of the navigating. I just drove.''

Out of nowhere, Pamela said angrily, "I just want to talk to the woman. Just the two of us—face-to-face—so I can get the truth out of her. Even if I have to wring it out of her.''

No matter what Oliver had tried to say in an effort to dissuade her—urging her to "please talk with Sean, and find out what he knows"—his well-intentioned initiative only seemed to strengthen Pamela's resolve to find Monique.

Whatever hopes Oliver had harbored in getting Sean and Pamela back together, and somehow help them solve this dilemma they both had with Monique Gerard—though for very different reasons—were shattered when Oliver had begun talking about the cars he and Sean had found in the abandoned barn. While Pamela acknowledged Sean having said something about a car he thought looked like one her father had owned—which, she said, "now that I've had time to think about it, couldn't possibly have been Daddy's Maserati"—it was Oliver's mention of "a fantastic, fire-engine-red Jaguar XKE roadster, with the licence plate DKB" that caused something to snap inside her—her face went blank, eyes ice cold, her whole body frozen stiff—and gave Oliver the tiniest of insights into what Sean must have endured that night he'd tried talking with her.

After that, the closer they drew to Hart College, and the fact that "that woman's studio is somewhere around here, I know it," the more agitated Pamela had become. By the time Peter pulled the Rolls to a stop in front of Merrywood Hall, Pamela was so wound up she practically sprang out of the car when Peter opened the door.

Out of the blue, as if in the middle of an argument with someone, Pamela snapped angrily, "Dammit, Sean should have told me what he was up to." She made it sound like it was his fault for what had happened, that she was blameless. "I would have—"

Unable to contain himself any longer, Oliver was quick to interrupt. "From what you told me on the drive up, it didn't sound to me like you gave the man much of a chance to explain anything."

Oliver's feelings then got the better of him, which rarely, if ever, happened. He peered over his wire-rimmed glasses, meeting Pamela's defiant gaze head-on, and said sternly, "And, my dear, you never should have hit him. That, I'm afraid—knowing Sean as well as I do, and knowing what he's been through with another woman who hit him—was a serious mistake on your part."

Then, refusing to respond to Pamela's unspoken challenge to explain what he'd just said—letting her know with a shake of his head there was no appeal to his decision—Oliver stood up. He suddenly shut his eyes, groaning in a way that said something hurt.

Pamela immediately stepped forward. "Are you all

281

right?'' she asked, cradling his arm in her hand to hold him up, not that he needed to be steadied. "Can I get you something?"

That part of Oliver Shore that never permitted him to hold on to his anger longer than it took him to take another breath got the better of him as an impish smile spread itself onto his face.

"How about a nice cold bottle of ale?" he asked, making it sound like a peace offering. He pointed to a small, wood-paneled cube standing to the right of his desk, then sauntered over to it. He gave the box a well-placed tap with his foot, opening a door, and gingerly bent down to pluck two bottles of Whitbread ale from the front row of an army of dark green bottles standing at the ready in the tiny refrigerator.

Standing up, he stuck his fingers into a mug of sharpened pencils on his desk and came up with a church key. He took aim at a wastebasket on the other side of his desk and flipped the cap off one bottle, then the other. Each found its mark, falling into the empty metal basket with a hollow clank. He handed Pamela one of the bottles, which had already begun to sweat, and gestured to a black three-ring binder sitting on his desk. He then said in a suddenly serious voice, "I think you should have a look at that."

Oliver's instruction registered on Pamela's face in the form of an apprehensive, almost rebellious frown. Cautiously, she grabbed the binder, and nearly dropped it because it was heavier than she anticipated. She glanced around the office for a place to sit, the binder wedged under one arm, a bottle of ale in her other hand. Before Oliver could make a suggestion, though he was already pointing to the leather armchair at his desk behind her, and she saw that, Pamela walked over to the deep-set leaded-glass window and sat on the wide stone sill.

Dropping the portfolio into her lap, she opened it and began slowly turning the pages, stopping every few pages to take a ladylike sip of ale. Oliver watched her intently as her gaze scanned every page. She looked up and cocked her head, as if caught up in a problematic thought, or an uncomfortable one; it was hard for him to tell from the mixed expression on her face. Then she returned to wading through the dozens of photographs of Monique's work, each one now bearing a stick-on label with a caption, penned by Oliver, linking that sculpture to something, or someone—or some mythological event—out of the distant past.

With each successive page turned and new sculpture revealed, Pamela appeared to grow more uneasy, almost irritated, by what she saw. "So what am I supposed to say?" she asked, sounding irritated. "The woman is a genius? That's obvious. So what!" she said, sounding bitter, and snapped her head around to look out the window, staring out across the small common at Merrywood Library.

Oliver felt himself wanting to shake some sense into her— verbally, of course. But when he started to say something, he realized that he shared Pamela's feelings—not about Sean, but about Monique Gerard. Perhaps it was the throbbing pain on either side of his rib cage that shook some sense into him. Or maybe it was the fear in his heart when he recalled what had happened to him—what he'd only heard and felt, hadn't seen himself because he'd passed out. Whatever it was, Oliver felt a sudden swell of empathy for this woman whom he had at first liked after meeting her, then didn't, having come to see her as vain and self-centered, and cruel when it came to the way she treated his one real friend, Sean.

But in reality, Oliver's small epiphany was due to his own belief, which he'd tried convincing Sean of but without much success, that just maybe—"by some bizarre twist of events," he'd told Sean, trying to make light of his idea—"Gerard was somehow duped into participating in the scheme to manipulate her work, convinced by someone close to her she would benefit in some way further down the road. And you're blind to it for some reason, my friend. After all, it wouldn't be the first time this happened to you," Oliver had said without thinking, then regretted it when Sean replied coolly, "It's late. I'm tired. I'll see you tomorrow," and abruptly walked out of Oliver's hospital room.

"Where did you get these titles from?" Pamela asked, tapping one of the photographs in the portfolio, which she'd reopened while Oliver was daydreaming, and had leafed through again. "Like this one, *Medusa*," she said, pointing to the first photo. "Which also happens to be the bronze that Gerard put in the academy's show this past April."

Pamela was waiting for Oliver when he looked at her. "And where did you get this collection of photographs? I thought Gerard didn't let anyone take pictures of her work?"

Oliver walked over and stood beside Pamela, leaning his shoulder against hers as he stood looking at the binder. "Sean gave it to me. He said someone named George White gave it to him, and had told him not to tell anyone he had. Why, I don't know."

"Really?" Pamela said, looking confused but sounding curious. "And the titles?" she asked. "I don't recall this bronze, *Medusa*, ever having been titled." She fanned the pages. "As a matter of fact, none of these titles match up with what I know the titles to have been when the pieces were exhibited." Frowning, she tipped back, resting her head on the rough stone of the alcove. "And one other thing: How does this *Medusa* fit in here, anyway? This is a woman holding up the head of a man. It's the reverse of the myth of the three Gorgons, specifically Medusa, and how she died. What gives?" she asked. "Is this Gerard's doing? Some sort of joke?"

Oliver had the precious hint of a smile on his face. "No, they're my notations," he said proudly. "They represent what I think might have been the inspiration—metaphorically—for each of the sculptures." Timidly, he glanced at Pamela. "Sean asked me to do this. I'm not certain, but I think it was right after he met Miss Gerard in New York, and after he spoke with this George White person. He didn't say why he wanted me to do it. But then, he never has given me a reason for what he asks me to do for him: He just gets a hunch and follows it."

Oliver's eyes were warmed by his mischievous smile. "When I think about it, I suppose it's more like *it* follows him. I've always thought he works on the premise that if it's any good—his hunch, that is—it'll catch him, he doesn't have to chase it."

It was now Pamela's turn to smile, but wryly. "And has it?" she asked, gesturing to the hastily stitched tears on Oliver's blue blazer, the bloodstains clearly visible. When he didn't answer her right away, Pamela asked, patting the binder, "Has Sean seen this yet?"

Oliver shook his head. "I don't think he needs to, not now. I'm afraid he's already unconsciously put all of the pieces together. As I said, that's the way he is. He just may not realize it yet, but he will," Oliver said with a confident nod of his head.

"What are you talking about? I thought—" Pamela shook her head, as if that thought had escaped her, and deliberately flipped to the last plastic-jacketed page in the portfolio, holding a pen-and-ink drawing without a title. "What's this?" she asked. "It looks vaguely familiar—I could swear I've seen it before. But one thing's for sure, that cretin didn't sculpt anything like this."

Cretin? Oliver thought, and was immediately reminded of his unasked question. *Now's as good a time as any.* "Just what does Mademoiselle Gerard look like, if you don't mind my asking? I've never met her, and Sean has never described her to me, other than to—"

He caught himself from saying anything that might further antagonize Pamela. "Other than to talk about her work."

Pamela hesitated, looking at Oliver, the expression on her face telling him she suspected he'd held something back to protect Sean. She returned to staring out the window. "She's short," Pamela began. "I doubt she's over five foot, if that. She's sort of chunky, but still has the figure of a woman. And—" Pamela paused, as if at a loss for words. "This is stupid," she said with a disgruntled shake of her head, and turned back to look at Oliver.

"The woman's a hideous dwarf!" she spit out. "She has the face of a—" Pamela suddenly froze with anger. "She's the ugliest thing I've ever seen—that's what she looks like!"

Startled by Pamela's emotional outburst, his thoughts not his own, Oliver glanced down at the finely detailed sketch he'd done from the description Sean had given him of the polychromed bronze in Monique's studio. The drawing depicted an ancient goddess who, the closer Oliver had gotten to Sean's hunch, or it to him, seemed even more real than the myth it represented.

With a look of whimsy on his face, mottled by confusion, Oliver reached out and traced the outline of the statuesque figure in the center of the drawing standing between two smaller figures, each crudely drawn, not man, not woman, yet not beast either.

"This is a composite sketch of sorts," he said thoughtfully. "It's based upon what Sean told me he saw in Mademoiselle Gerard's studio, descriptions of the goddess Cybele taken from ancient Greek texts, and photographs of a handful of extant artifacts dating back to the third or fourth century B.C.E., which are believed to represent the earliest-known forms of Cybele. Some believe, and I happen to be one of those who do, that Cybele is of Oriental origin, dating back thousands of years. In that form, she was often represented standing or sitting between a pair of lions. Or leopards. Or any form of predator beast. Terra-cotta figures depicting these animal consorts were found in digs around ancient Phrygia, dating back to the sixth millennium B.C.E. In my—"

Pamela raised her hand, signaling a time-out. "What does this all have to do with Gerard? And with you and Sean? And with the deaths of that dealer Vanderbilt, and one of my fellow trustees at the Met? My father! With anything, for that matter?" She began paging forward, slapping at the images with the back of her hand. "I don't see any relationship between these compositions and the one you drew. What's the connection?" she asked, her irritability, and her obvious aggression, having suddenly returned.

When Oliver didn't respond, Pamela sighed impatiently and stood up, pushing him out of her way. Then she dropped the binder onto the windowsill, as if to be done with it.

"You and Sean make a perfect pair," she snarled sarcastically. "Neither one of you makes any sense. At least not to me. Either I'm missing something, or you're not telling me everything." She looked askance at Oliver. "Which is it?'' she asked, threading her arms into a knot over her chest. ''Well?''

The word *dwarf,* said by Pamela but not heard until just now by Oliver, suddenly rang loud and clear in his head, awakening long-forgotten images of ancient gods and setting them free inside his head. A pantheon of gods and goddesses, each more powerful and dreaded than the next, each with an equally deadly purpose when set free to roam the mortal world, if only for the time it takes but a few grains of sand to pass through the hourglass of time.

''Wait,'' Oliver pleaded when Pamela shook her head and started to walk away. She didn't stop, so he grabbed her blouse with a pinch of his fingers, gently pulling her to a stop. ''Don't be so bloody impatient,'' he begged. ''Give a man a *bloody* chance to think.''

Startled by his actions, Pamela flopped down into the old wing chair, crossed her legs—like a man, not a woman—and began tapping her foot impatiently.

Oliver nodded curtly, then began walking around the room, his head bowed, hands behind his back. Coming full circle, he stopped directly in front of Pamela and took a deep breath. ''Sean hasn't come right out and said it in so many words, but I have a sneaking suspicion that he thinks the polychromed bronze in Gerard's studio—the one I made a sketch of—is somehow controlling Gerard. That she's a victim of its powers. Exactly how, I'm not quite sure.''

Oliver held his hands up and shook his head, his eyes shut, asking Pamela not to interrupt when it looked like she was about to say something. Or laugh at him. He couldn't quite tell. ''I know it sounds bizarre, but I think he might be right. *Almost.* Everything he's told me—from what happened to him every time he visited her studio, the way Mr. Vanderbilt was murdered, and the way we were both attacked by that—that—whatever it was!''

Upon hearing this, Pamela exploded out of the chair, her eyes on fire, furious with what Oliver had just said. ''*Attacked? By what?''* she demanded. Oliver shook his head and stepped away, unsure of what to tell her—unsure himself of what he'd seen.

287

"You've been lying to me all along, both of you, haven't you?" Pamela asked, grabbing Oliver by his shoulders and shaking him.

Recalling Sean's description of what it took him to subdue Pamela, and her strength—one of the things he'd had trouble believing Sean about, but not anymore—Oliver's first thought was to get as far away from this woman as he possibly could.

But instead, for reasons not even he knew, he stood firm, refusing to let her intimidate him. "Please," he said in a calming, but by no means submissive, voice. "You *must* let me finish." He motioned for Pamela to sit back down. "You said something about Gerard when you were describing her to me that didn't register at first, but has now. It has to do with that early form of the goddess Cybele, which is in reality derived from an ancient form of Vishnu, the powerful Hindu god of reincarnation. If I'm right, and I hope I'm not, we must get to Sean before he goes to—"

With a look of total disbelief on her face, Pamela pushed Oliver back, startling but not frightening him. "Not only are you both pathological liars, but you're both out of your fucking mind."

She started for the door. "You can both go to hell," she growled without looking back, and stormed out of the office, ignoring Oliver's plea that "you must listen to me."

Moving with a stride twice the length of his, driven by an anger he could not hope to match, Pamela was outside and climbing into the backseat of her Rolls Royce before Oliver was halfway down the steps in front of Merrywood Hall, and out of breath.

"Goddammit, don't argue with me," Pamela snapped into the receiver. "Just do what I said—find the commissioner, and give him the message. And tell him to call me back as soon as he has the information. And make sure he knows not to wait until the morning—he can call anytime. Do you understand?" she asked, making it sound like she was talking to some idiot, not the deputy police commissioner of the City of New York, Roger Peterson.

Pamela slammed the receiver down and slapped the top of the leather-covered armrest shut. "Take me home," she said in a far more subdued, but nonetheless imposing, tone of voice.

She then took a deep breath, leaned back, and closed her eyes. "Peter?" she asked when she'd calmed down.

The chauffeur replied without looking up into the rearview mirror. "Yes, Miss Eagleston?" he said in a soothing manner.

"Is my car back from the garage yet?"

"Yes, ma'am. Antonio delivered it last evening, while you were dining with Dr. MacDonald. It's in the garage."

Pamela muttered, "That wasn't a dinner, it was a disaster," and slumped down, stretching her legs the full length of the sumptuous leather seat and folding her arms behind her head, trying to put Sean—and now Oliver—as far out of her mind as possible.

"First things first," she whispered, her thoughts focused on only one thing: *Find her—and find out for yourself.*

Chapter Thirty-seven

All four walls of the living-room-size lobby were paneled glass, tinted smoke-gray, and held up by shiny chrome columns spaced a few feet apart all around the room. The doors leading in and out were glass, too, but Windex clear. The chrome handles showed signs of having been polished over and over again. The carpeting was carbon black, and plush, with a pattern worn into it from the entrance to the receptionist's desk, which was a three-dimensional reincarnation of the walls. The ceiling was covered with frosted plastic, glowing operating-room white. The chairs were black leather and chrome, the end tables giant cubes of solid Plexiglas with past issues of *Entasis,* the pages fanned out, floating, entombed inside forever.

The receptionist—thin, all eyes and cheekbones, skin bisque white, hair midnight black—smiled as she quietly put the phone down. "Ms. Reedy, our managing editor, is on a long-distance call, Dr. MacDonald. Her secretary said she'll be tied up for a while longer, but to tell you that she *very* much wants to see you, if you wouldn't mind waiting." She began to stand up. "May I get you something to drink?" she asked "Coffee? Something cold?"

Sean sighed and mumbled—not intending to be heard—
"Yes, a martini on the rocks." When the young woman
paused and frowned, looking confused, Sean was quick to
wave his hand, shake his head, and say with an apologetic
smile, "Thank you, but I'm fine."

But he wasn't fine: He was pissed off, and he knew it—
now, at least—only too well. He'd left the hospital thinking
he wasn't that upset with Pamela for what she'd done, telling
himself—trying to be rational about it—*It's best for Oliver.
After all, the Rolls is a hell of lot more comfortable than my
Healy.*

That sanguine feeling lasted for all of about fifteen
minutes, until—after pulling onto the West Side Highway,
heading home—he found himself suddenly overcome with
thoughts of throttling Pamela: not hitting her, but shaking
her just hard enough to make her agree to *stop being so
goddamned pig-headed long enough to listen to me, for
chrissake!* He'd actually come right out and said it, too. And
loud enough for the driver in the car crawling along in stop-
and-go traffic beside him, his windows rolled down, to look
at him as if he was deranged, and start weaving his way
through traffic to get away from him.

Caught up all over again by his newly found feelings about
Pamela, Sean muttered, "Who the hell do you think you are,
anyway?"

"I beg your pardon, Dr. MacDonald?" the receptionist
asked as courteously as she possibly could.

Sean turned around, feeling stupid for saying what he had.
"Just doing a little editing in my head," he said sheepishly.
"Sorry if I bothered you."

She raised an eyebrow above one of her large blue eyes,
made to look even larger by the expert use of mascara.
"Oh," she said, forming a nearly perfect O with her mouth
for a split second, then going back to reading whatever it
was she'd been writing when Sean had first walked into the
lobby of Johnson Publishing and announced, "Sean Mac-
Donald for Brad Johnson. He's expecting me."

When he'd first realized just how angry he was with Pamela, Sean had tried forcing himself to think about some-

thing else, *anything*! grabbing at one meaningless thought after another in a futile effort not to dwell on what she'd done. At first, he gave her the benefit of the doubt, telling himself, "It was just her willfulness. She meant well." But the more it simmered inside him, left unchecked—made even hotter when the still-smoldering fragments of what she'd done the night before were remembered, and heaped on top— and the way she'd been slowly changing into someone, some *thing,* he didn't know, and realized he didn't like—the more it had infected his entire being.

It's your own fault, he thought in an effort to stem his rising anger from getting out of control. *You let her do it— let her think you were someone you weren't.*

"Dr. MacDonald?"

Sean turned to see a woman—blond hair cut boyishly short, forty, maybe forty-five, lightly tanned, and amply endowed—bracing one of the heavy glass doors open with her broad hip. She was clutching papers in one arm, offering him her free hand, smiling.

"Yes," he said, and immediately wondered, *Do I know you?* as he shook her hand and began to erase the age from her face in an effort to match her up with one of the hundreds of young women's faces he'd filed away in the back of his mind during twenty years of teaching.

"Joan Reedy," she said. "I'm the managing editor."

Sean had a match, his face lit up. *"Reedy?"* He wagged a finger, but not at her. "Aren't you the—"

A blush warmed her cheeks. "Yes, I was the one," she said, pressing her finger to her lips and glancing at the receptionist—asking for his silence.

Sean completed the sentence, thinking, *The one who was in my office that night with Brad—our would-be valedictorian that year—who was passed over because of what that prick, Johnson, did.*

Joan Reedy invited Sean in with a gentle nod of her head and gracious wave of her hand. "How may I help you, Dr. MacDonald?" she asked, and started down a wide corridor with offices on either side, the walls filled with colorful paintings, mostly abstract, a pair of towering wood-grained doors at the far end, pulled shut.

Sean moved alongside her. "I must admit, I sort of lied to your receptionist. I really didn't have an appointment with Brad. But since I was in the City, I thought I would stop in and see him. There are some things I want to talk to him about." He hesitated, wondering how best to say why he was there without tendering an outright lie and getting caught in it. *And without telling you the real reason I'm here, and have you think I'm crazy, too.* "It's about the articles Brad retained me to write on Monique Gerard. I never heard back from Brad about the draft of the first piece. Or even the next two," he said, trying to make his mission sound that much more important.

Joan took a quiet breath, as if to steady herself, and said, "I'm afraid Bradley isn't here just now, Dr. MacDonald." At the end of the corridor, Joan turned to face him, her free hand resting on a small numbered keypad mounted to the wall beside the impressive wood doors, looking more like doors to a cathedral. "So I'm afraid you're stuck with me, in a manner of speaking."

Blocking Sean's view of the keypad, Joan tapped in a series of numbers and turned back. "Why don't you have a seat in Bradley's private conference room. I'm sure he won't mind, especially not if it's you—considering how close the two of you are—while I go find the articles you sent us. Then we can talk."

Close? Us? What lies has he been telling now? Sean eyed the keypad suspiciously, then turned to Joan. Noticing the expression on his face, she patted him reassuringly on the arm. "It's not a trap, Dr. MacDonald," she said, laughing to herself. "Bradley keeps various pieces from his collection here in the office." She gestured down the hall. "A few of the paintings, such as these, he hangs in the general offices. He periodically exchanges them with others from his collection. The more important works he hangs in the conference room. However, the bulk of his collection—as I'm sure you already know—is divided between his town house and his home in the Hamptons."

An amused smile warmed her brown eyes to the color of dark chocolate. "I should warn you, however, that there's a bronze inside—one he acquired not too long ago—which might be a bit startling if you're not prepared for it. So consider yourself appropriately forewarned."

No, I don't already know that about Brad, Sean thought as Joan started down the corridor, her back to him. She slowed momentarily and said with a sudden note of authority, "The doors automatically lock behind you—and there's a timer—so please let them close or an alarm will be sounded. Bradley doesn't like the staff going in there. If they see it open, they'll look inside. They can't help themselves," she said, this time sounding somewhat maternal and understanding.

Sean leaned on one of the large brass levers—opening one of the doors a few inches—and paused to watch Joan Reedy walk briskly down the hall. *After what he put you through,* he wondered, *dragging your name through the papers along with his—and mine!—how can you work with him?* That thought wasn't a moment old when Sean chastised himself. "Look who's talking," he whispered as he pushed the heavy door open and stepped into the darkened room.

The only light came from a thin strip of blue neon snaking around the base of the walls, creating the feel of an empty movie theater, only without the familiar smell of popcorn. When Sean turned to look for a light switch, he was startled for an instant when the door eased shut and locked itself with a crisp, electronic click. Laughing at his own nervousness, he leaned up against the wall beside a bank of switches—all aglow in blue—and laid his hand over the first dimmer switch. Tapping it, he dialed it up, watching to see what would come to life first.

Beams of antiseptic light converged in midair, framing a monstrous canvas on the right side of the room. Not a drop of light spilled over onto the wall as a thousand autumn colors exploded off the canvas locked inside a massive gilded frame.

Hudson River School, Sean thought, and hit the next switch, turning it up. On the opposite wall, directly across from the fiery landscape, a vast summer seascape appeared, lit more from inside out than by the soft, overhead light streaming down from the ceiling, falling into the breaking surf, scattering over the beach.

Bruce taught you well, Sean thought, and reached for the next switch, twisting it on. "Jesus Christ!" He stood up straight, back pinned to wall, arms at his sides—breathless— staring at the sculpture in the back of the room. *You son of a bitch,* he thought, and pushed himself away from the wall.

"You lying fucking son of a bitch," Sean snarled, biting down on his words. He began circling the huge conference table and endless line of leather-backed chairs, his gaze riveted to the mesmerizing bronze statue standing before him.

A beep, then another, followed by the sound of a door sweeping over carpeting, brought Sean to a stop well short of his mark. "I see you've found her," Joan said, walking over to Sean, the faint click of a lock barely audible over her steps. "I'm afraid you've done better than I have; however—we can't seem to find those articles you sent in. Even the data files from when they were scanned into the computer by the editorial department seem to be missing."

Joan walked over to the base of the bronze and peered up at it. "For the life of me, I don't know what Bradley sees in this piece. Or, for that matter, any of that woman's other works he has in his collection."

Other works! Sean thought, the anger he'd thought he'd learned to control—do away with—suddenly boiling up inside him.

Joan turned to look at him, her face cast in the same harsh light from the trio of spots recessed in the ceiling above, cascading down over the bronze behind her. "Do you know what he sees in this?" she asked, and smiled, creating an eerie contrast with the face of the severed head a few feet above her, his mouth cast open in that horrifying scream of silence Sean had foolishly thought he'd buried and forgotten.

He took a mechanical, almost robotic step forward, and stopped. "How long ago did you say Brad purchased this?"

Joan frowned, the harsh overhead light adding back the years Sean had erased earlier, and then some. "Quite honestly, I'm not really sure. It was just here one day. It could have been two or three weeks ago. Then again, maybe longer. I don't come in here that often anymore, since the room is rarely used, except by Bradley. And to house these," she said, making a sweeping gesture around the room at the paintings, those lighted, others hanging in the shadows, then to the statue behind her. "Why do you ask?"

You don't want to know, Sean thought. In reality, he didn't want to know, either, but he now had little choice. *You never should have gone into that place,* he thought, recalling all too well his apprehension about getting involved instead of listening to his intuition—*that goddamned female side of yours! It's too late now,* he thought, and was struck by the irony of finding himself in that very same position he'd been in before, standing on the curb, watching the garbage clog the drain in the gutter.

"Does the artist know it's here—and that Brad is the one who owns it?" he asked.

Joan said in a matter-of-fact, businesslike way, "If she didn't, she does now. I wrote her a letter to get some background on the piece—date it was cast, the title, and some idea of the value—since Bradley said he'd misplaced the paperwork, receipt and all, and I had to have something for the insurance company. And the accountants," she added with a mindful nod of her head.

Sean reclaimed the step he'd just taken, then another—backing up—trying to distance himself from Joan Reedy.

"Did Brad know that you wrote Mademoiselle Gerard?"

"No," she said somewhat indignantly. "I don't bother Bradley with piddling details like that." Joan approached Sean and stood before him, looking up at him. "I'm really very sorry about the drafts you sent, Dr. MacDonald. I don't know what could have possibly happened to them," she said with a disappointed shake of her head.

Sean took a slow, deep breath and exhaled. "You may not, but I'm afraid I do," he said, and started to leave, thinking, *And I bet George does, too.*

Joan reached out, gently touching Sean's arm, drawing him back. Her face was filled with apprehension, her eyes ready to tear at the slightest provocation. When she finally spoke, her voice wavered. "I don't know what to do, Dr. MacDonald. I've been telling everyone Bradley's away on business, but he's not. The truth is, I don't where he is. Neither do either one of his housekeepers. He's never done something like this. I—"

She looked away, trying to compose herself. When she finally spoke, it was barely above a whisper. "I should have put my foot down," she sighed. "I'm supposed to be his partner. I tried telling him not to get involved with them—that I didn't trust them, any of them—but he wouldn't listen. He told me I didn't know what I was talking about, and to stay out of his personal life. He laughed at me, said I was a victim of my hormones, or something stupid like that."

"Them?" Sean asked, every hair on his neck, his whole body, standing on end, anticipating—wanting—but fearing her answer.

Joan turned back, her eyes suddenly dry and stone cold. "That creep from the Philadelphia Museum of Art, *Doctor* Robert Anderson, the pompous ass. And his lover, that dealer with all the money, the one who's a trustee at the Met." She frowned. "What's his name? Beaumont?"

Fighting back the urge to scream, Sean grabbed hold of Joan's shoulders—more to steady himself than her—and asked as calmly as he possibly could, "What about George White? Is he involved?"

Looking frightened, Joan winced and shrugged herself free from Sean's grasp. Then she said in a condescending tone of voice, her scowl equally disdainful—a look only a woman could give—"Him? He doesn't have two nickels to rub together. He's just a gofer."

Running up the five flights of stairs from the ground floor to George White's loft studio left Sean winded, much to his surprise. He paused on the landing to catch his breath, all the while struggling to contain his feelings about George: One minute he wanted to smash him in the face for what he'd done to Andrea Stern—*She was lying to cover for you, and for that son of a bitch Johnson*, he decided; the next minute he wanted to rip the man's eyes out for what he'd been doing to Monique all these years. *Not a very masculine thing to do, now is it*? he thought upon picturing himself doing just that.

Sean suddenly realized he wouldn't—didn't want to—hold himself back. That thought felt good; he now wanted George, wanted a piece of him. But that same feeling made him pull back—ask himself if he was sure. Just as he was about to walk into the studio, a noise on the other side of the door told him that someone, and not a class, was poking around inside. *At least you don't have to worry about having any students around,* he told himself, and eased the door open, taking care not to knock the metal coatrack again.

The studio was empty, surprising him since he was sure he'd heard someone moving about. He glanced around. No one was there. Even the pedestals were empty, and showed no sign of having been used in days. "Sean?" a woman asked softly, making him jump.

In the far corner of the studio, standing in the open doorway of George's office, was Latitia Morrison, a clutch of papers in her hands. This was not who he wanted to see right now, not the way he felt. "Hello, Ms. Morrison," he said coolly, not wanting to get caught up in idle conversation.

"Ms. Morrison?" she asked, sounding hurt.

Don't give in, he told himself, and asked in a reserved, distant manner, "Is George here, by chance?"

Latitia's body appeared to lose its delicious shape inside the multicolored African caftan she was wearing. She stepped back into the office, reappeared without the papers, and started across the studio, her gaze bouncing off Sean's, looking away, then back.

I don't think I want to hear this, he thought, and felt himself wanting to leave, but didn't—couldn't—budge. She stopped in front of him, staring back at him, and said in a voice that sounded weary, "No, Sean, I'm afraid that George is not here."

She drew her mouth into a thin line across her face, her nostrils flaring, her lips taut, and surprisingly thin. Her eyes were blacker than anything he'd ever seen, making her skin

298

appear shades lighter than it was. ''I don't know where he is. Neither does anyone here at the school. Not even the police have any idea.'' She sighed. Her breath smelled of having been sick.

She then whispered, her words falling like lead on Sean's ears, ''He's been missing for over two weeks now.''

Chapter Thirty-eight

Pamela stood motionless in the large, ceramic-tiled shower, her head tilted back, face raised—eyes shut as tight as she could possibly squeeze them—the powerful stream of water pelting her taut body. Her long red hair, as dark and thick as blood when it was soaking wet, melted down her neck, her shoulders, over and around her womanly breasts. She'd left the glass door of the shower—etched with the image of Venus rising—wide open so she could hear the phone if it rang, causing the oversized bathroom to fill with a dense cloud of steam, the bright yellow walls and floor-length mirrors fogging over and dripping with condensation.

Determined not to leave anything to chance, Pamela had called the commissioner's office, his private line, the moment she'd walked into her apartment. She wanted to be sure that Roger Peterson knew she was back in the City, and where she could be reached. "I expect to hear from Bob tonight," she'd told Deputy Commissioner Peterson in no uncertain terms. "I really don't think you want to fuck this one up, Peterson." Then she hung up, refusing to listen to his excuses.

Pamela's thoughts were fighting with her feelings, tying her up into knots. It wasn't like her. "I hate you," she mumbled, and promptly got a mouthful of water for her effort.

Coughing and spitting it out, she stood at attention, bracing herself, and turned the hot water off. She instantly sucked in a deep breath, gritted her teeth, and slowly turned full circle. Then she reached out and dialed the cold water off. Smiling, she waited: Seconds passed, then it finally came, an all-over shiver that made her laugh as she stepped out of the shower and snatched up the pink terry-cloth towel she'd tossed onto the white marble bench beside the shower stall. Dripping wet, she ambled out into her bedroom, leaving a trail of water spots behind her on the slate-gray wool carpet as she walked over to the bed—stepped up and sat down cross-legged—and began drying her hair.

"When all else fails, Pamela Jean, wash your hair," she muttered, and fell back, naked and still wet, her hair staining the gray satin sheets. Without warning, a chill snuck up and made her shiver again. This time she didn't laugh. Instead, she frowned and grabbed the edge of the sheets, wrapping herself up in them.

Pamela didn't want to care about Sean, which is what she'd kept telling herself on the ride back to Manhattan, in spite of how she knew she felt about him. *I don't need this— not now*, she thought. But she did, and she knew it, she just resented needing someone. Especially someone like Sean, who she'd come to realize was not like anyone she'd ever known before. "You're so damned sure of yourself," she said, which only made her realize how much she missed being with him. *Maybe that's why you treat him the way you do, woman? You're afraid of how he makes you feel, so you push him away?* Pamela just as quickly rejected that thought, still fighting the idea that she could need anyone.

What tempered her thinking, however, was Sean's intuitive side, an aspect of his nature that revealed a side of a man she'd never seen. He was unlike any of the other men she'd known, even that artist in Paris, Jacques Peltier, whom she once thought she couldn't live without. Only to learn that not only could she live without him and his fits of rage, but that she could—and was determined to—live without any man if it meant sacrificing who she was for them, as she was forced to do with Jacques.

But that was before Sean, who, much to her surprise—and guarded delight—seemed to enjoy who she was and accepted her at face value. He was even unfazed by her money. *Men just aren't like that,* she thought. And if any woman knew what men were like, she did. Pamela smiled. *Men think too much. They think about every goddamned thing.* Her smile broadened. *Which is probably why most of them are such lousy lovers—always thinking about what they're doing, and wondering—"How do I look?" "Was I any good?" "Was it good for you?"*

Those thoughts immediately brought to mind images of her night with Sean—unguarded, uninhibited, his lopsided smile a reflection of his boyishness, yet at the same time revealing an unerring measure of his manly self-confidence. Even more so, he'd waited for her, the only man who had. "Oliver was right," she said, once again serious. "You never should have hit him. He could have decked you if he really wanted to. And you know it." She curled up into a ball from memories of Jacques Peltier in a blind rage, striking her again and again with his fist. This time the shiver was inside her, but nonetheless chilling. Pamela buried herself beneath the comforter, her hair still damp, and whispered, "It doesn't matter anyway, girl. It's finished. Over. So move on."

With her head inches from the nightstand, Pamela awoke with a start, her eyes popping open when the phone rang. She sat up, the sheets twisted all around her waist, her face covered with creases from the folds in the pillow. She grabbed the receiver and snapped, "Yes?"

As if whoever was on the other end of the line could see that she wasn't dressed, she drew the sheets up around her. "Hello, Bob," she said, all business, and spun around to sit on the edge of the bed, her feet squarely on the floor. "Thanks for getting back to me." She nodded compliantly.

"Yes, you're right, I was hard on him." Pamela took a breath only she could hear. "I'll make a point of saying something to him." She perked up. "Would flowers help?" she asked, laughing, and relaxed when Robert Stark, a man not known around City Hall for his sense of humor, laughed with her.

Pamela nodded. "Just a minute," she said, wedging the phone into her shoulder with her chin, and pulling the nightstand drawer open. After fishing around, she came up with a pen, but no paper. "Go ahead," she said, and began writing something on the bottom bed sheet, the dark blue ink a perfect, if unsettling, complement to the shiny gray satin.

"Did you say she paid cash for it?" Suddenly serious, Pamela nodded. "I see. And this old horse farm, how far from midtown Manhattan would you say it is—driving time?" Listening, she glanced at the clock radio on the night table beside her; it was a few minutes past eight. She thought for a moment, wondering if she should go tonight or first thing in the morning.

Pamela shook her head. "No, but thanks for the offer, Bob. I have to handle this one on my own. It's personal. Family business. But do I get a rain check?" she asked, the hint of a suggestive tease in her voice—an overture not meant, but intended to sound that way. She abruptly stood up and discarded the sheet. "You're a sweetheart, Robert. I won't forget this," she said, and set the phone down without looking, missing the cradle, looking, then finding it.

Pamela had what she wanted: the address for Monique's studio, and detailed directions on how to get there. *Interesting,* she thought. *It can't be more than forty-five minutes from Red Hook, an easy drive for you, Dr. MacDonald.*

She sat down, set the alarm for four o'clock the next morning, bounced back up, and marched over to her dresser. The finely detailed cherrywood dresser had to be at least ten feet wide, and with enough drawers to satisfy two women. Opening one of the middle drawers, she pulled out a long-sleeve white turtleneck pullover. Stepping over to the closet, she hit the light, walked in, and surveyed the dozens of shirts and pants hanging up in orderly rows. She grabbed the grungiest

303

of the lot—a well-worn pair of jeans, old denim work shirt, and black hooded windbreaker—and walked back out. Laying each of the items in a line beside the turtleneck, she stepped back and stood staring at herself in the mirror over the dresser for the longest time.

"You're a fool if you don't," she said clear as day, and went over to the nightstand, the one on the other side of the bed, and opened the drawer. She took a deep breath and exhaled slowly, reconsidering her own advice. "It's been a long time," she said with a resolute sigh, and reached down, lifting the leather shoulder-holster out of the drawer. With her other hand, she snatched up one, then a second clip. She pressed her thumb down on the first shell in each clip to make sure they were both full.

Eight and eight, she thought. *More than enough.* She stopped to think. *First—find the barn Sean and Oliver were talking about and see if that car really is Daddy's. If it's not, then come home, and let the police handle things. But if it is, find the studio—and her.*

Pamela hesitated, eyeing the Luger her father had given her. It was one of two he'd brought back from the war and taught her to shoot when she was old enough. Refusing to let those fond memories weaken her resolve, she walked over to the dresser, set one of the clips on top of her jeans, then slipped the gun out of its holster. With the skill of a trained marksman, she double-checked the safety, slipped a clip into the gun, and loaded a shell in the chamber. The Luger fit her hand like a glove as she wrapped her long fingers around the walnut grip of the carbon-steel pistol, took steady aim at herself in the mirror, and said solemnly, "If you did anything to hurt him, so help me God, I'll kill you."

The drizzle had been struggling to become rain for the past hour, and was finally beginning to win the battle. Whatever light there was left over from the day had been snuffed out by the clouds. Sean pulled the collar of his coat up around his neck in an effort to ward off the rising wind. With a shake of his head, tossing the rain off his eyebrows, he stuffed his hands into his pockets and leaned back against the brick exterior of the building across the street from Pamela's apartment. He stood watching a shadow, tall, graceful, appearing and disappearing in the window of her bedroom behind the sheer drapes. *It's a shame,* he thought, and shook his head. *We're a good match, Pamela, as different as two people can be.* He smiled. *Oliver's right—as usual—opposites attract.*

Just as he pushed himself off the side of the building, having decided to go see her—telling himself she had to know—the light in the room went out, putting an end to whatever thoughts he had of seeing her. Unless he wanted to get her out of bed.

You'd probably be wasting your time, he thought, and started down the sidewalk to his car, which was parked two blocks away. *Besides,* he decided, making excuses, *it can wait until tomorrow.*

Sean was in no particular hurry. He walked slowly, bumping into one parking meter after another just to hear the coins rattle, even though there was now a steady drizzle and he was getting wetter by the second. He was disappointed about not seeing Pamela, and to his surprise wasn't upset about feeling that way.

She's hard to stay angry with, he thought.

Suddenly, with a shuddering clap of thunder directly overhead that made him duck, the skies opened up, soaking him through to the bone before he could make it to his car.

Chapter Thirty-nine

This was one of the rare times Sean found himself wishing he had fabric seats in his car instead of leather. *Anything that could absorb this goddamn water,* he thought. He was drenched, not a single square inch of him dry, and every time he moved Sean felt like he was sitting on a sponge. And thanks to the relentless head wind he'd picked up after leaving the City, winding his way onto the Saw Mill River Parkway heading home, the ragtop had sprung a leak. It was right where the frame latched to the top of the windshield, directly above him, giving rise to a steady spatter of water that ensured he stayed wet.

Soaked through, head to toe, and now cold—fighting a shiver that kept winning—he mumbled, "This isn't really happening, it's just a bad dream." With that said, and realizing how silly it sounded, Sean started laughing, but awkwardly—falteringly—which is when he knew that his nerves were driving his emotions, not the comic coincidence of the events he'd gotten caught up in.

Because of your own stubbornness, he thought.

Slowly, no matter how hard he tried stopping them, every-

306

thing from the last few days began to play back inside his head, one frame after another, and without sound. The fuzzy images became steadily clearer—and flashed faster—with each event remembered. Some were brighter than others, and filled with color. Others, thankfully, remained a black-and-white blur. Like the night he was attacked in the hayloft. *And we know it wasn't an eagle, now, don't we,* he thought, chiding himself. Then there was the growing tension between him and Pamela, a rift that had left him upset and at the same time feeling somehow responsible. *But how? And why?* he wondered. Every image of that night was spattered with color—colors that looked nothing at all like Pamela's apartment.

And you were a real shit with Oliver, he thought. *He doesn't deserve being treated that way.* And there were the cars they'd found in the barn, confirming his intuition, which he still couldn't make heads or tails out of, and asked himself yet again, *How did you know?* Only to come up empty-handed, clueless, one more time. *And that hideous creature—whatever the hell she is—that attacked poor Oliver!*

A swirl of dust suddenly clouded his thoughts—gray on black and white. Sean couldn't help asking himself, "Why didn't she attack you too?" but came up blank.

Not to be ignored, though he sorely wanted to forget it, was his confrontation—*no, it was a goddamn brawl*—with Pamela. "And for what?" he asked, still trying to understand what had set her off. *And why did she take it out on me?* Even more difficult to accept was his own inability to just come out and tell Pamela what he really thought. That still left him confused, even now. "After all, she's a big girl—she can take care of herself."

And there was the shock—*But I guess I really shouldn't have been surprised*, he thought—of seeing Monique's bronze in Brad Johnson's office. "Somehow, you knew all along Bradley would show his true colors, you just didn't want to believe it." That thought—a conscious realization, not a visceral response—surprised Sean. But when he tried grabbing hold of it, to open it up and examine it more closely, it slipped away from him.

Perhaps the most touching, in spite of how he felt about George White, even now, was the heart-wrenching look on Latitia Morrison's face. *And you knew goddamn well the moment she told you he was missing that she wasn't ever going to see him again.*

But how did you know? he wondered, only to have that thought evaporate, too.

And finally, the painful realization of his own lack of conviction—"which is the exact opposite of what's always gotten you into trouble, for chrissake, MacDonald!"

When Sean tried piecing it all together—to make some sense of it all—and couldn't, no matter how hard he tried to concentrate, a wave of anger rose up and washed over him, taking his breath away. For an all-too-memorable moment, filled with panic, he thought he would drown in the rage that had suddenly boiled up inside him. "Jesus Christ," he whispered, fighting for his next breath. It was a feeling he hadn't experienced in years; he had once thought he'd cured himself of it—had been told he had—*and all that other shit you'd been carrying around half your life!*

With his fingers locked tightly around the steering wheel, *just in case,* he thought, Sean sat back, his anxious gaze searching in the dark, blunted by the solid wall of rain washing away the concrete road ahead of him. He waited, anticipating the aftershock he knew so well. He counted the rising beats of his heart, which he could feel in his throat, expecting to explode any moment and strike out at something—*anything!*—hurting himself in the process, and destroying whatever he touched. "Déjà vu," he said with a sigh, and waited.

But nothing happened. Instead, he felt a calm settle over him: a soft, diaphanous veil of soft white cotton that slowly, deliciously, dissolved into his skin, wrapping itself around his heart, quieting his soul. He actually felt good. Refreshed. Cleansed. He wanted another hit of whatever it was that had melted away every jagged edge he'd felt scraping around inside him—and not just now, but for weeks—trying to rip him apart.

Giving in to it, he smiled quixotically and sat back, but gingerly. "Don't be fooled," he cautioned himself. "The more things appear to change, the more they remain the same.''

Sean was speaking to that part of him that he knew didn't trust what had just happened, and for good reason. But to his surprise there was no reply, though he fully expected one, and in an all-too-familiar voice. There was only the vague feeling of a warm breeze, delightfully dry, desertlike, moving through him, as if drawn in and out by the rise and fall of his own breath, blowing away a lingering cloud of confusion that had filled his head. *For how long?* he wondered the moment his thoughts were once again his own, and he could see them—words and images—not just feel them. And not lose them in the blink of an eye when he reached out for them. *And when did it start?* was his next thought.

Cautiously, still skeptical, Sean took one hand off the wood-rimmed steering wheel and sat waiting. Nothing, not even a twitch, had found its way into a single muscle in his body. Or the hint of his fingers curling into a fist, preparing, uncontrollably, to strike out. Without looking, not needing to—after all, he knew his car as well as he knew his own body—Sean reached up and began fidgeting with the chrome-plated latch on the windshield overhead, patiently trying to unlatch, then latch it closed. After a moment or two—every microsecond filled with the apprehension that he was somehow being tricked—he succeeded in relatching and dogging down the soft top, cutting off the persistent drip that was soaking his shirt and pants and running down his legs into his shoes.

Without warning, pairs of red lights suddenly began blinking up ahead as the line of cars slowed, then shifted into slow motion. The flash of red and orange bouncing off the trees and galvanized guardrails all around him—illuminating the drops of water on the windshield like a Christmas Eve display in Florida—brought back for an instant vibrant thoughts of his first visit to the academy.

He waited for the vignettes of color and memorable forms to be snatched away from him as everything else had been for what now seemed like forever. But instead, they burned crystal clear, lines thin and precise, faces barely inches from his own, voices clear—more clear than first heard—until he willed them away.

The road ahead was blocked by a pair of police cruisers, one crosswise in each lane, nose to nose, their lights flashing wildly out of synch. *I should have known,* Sean thought. *This damn parkway always floods when it rains like this.* He inched along, trapped in the single-file line of cars creeping through puddle after puddle of unknown depth as they eased their way down the exit ramp at a snail's pace to the next hurdle of flashing lights.

It seemed to take each driver an eternity to decide whether to turn right or left at the bottom of the ramp, where a trooper stood waving a flashlight side to side like a pendulum while talking to another officer directing traffic away from the ramp. Now and then a car slowed, window rolled down, as if to plead their case. "Or bitch about something," Sean muttered with a laugh. "As if it makes any difference. Just give in and relax."

Taking his own advice, Sean settled back, relishing the change of pace, while at the same time savoring the thoughts that had eluded him for so long. Without having to think, he turned right, having no idea where he was going. "Follow your nose," he told himself. "You used to know Westchester like the back of your hand. Let's see how good that total recall of yours is, old man."

And he did just that, taking one turn after another purely on instinct as he wound his way through and around one upscale little village after another until he found himself entering a huge traffic circle, and staring at a sign pointing the way to the northbound Taconic State Parkway. "See what happens when you just submit to your animal instincts," he muttered, and downshifted, speeding up as he pulled onto the darkened two-lane road, no longer having to worry about the rain, which had stopped. He cranked the window halfway down, enjoying the feel of the rainwashed air blowing through the car.

Though it was no longer raining, the wind had grown even stronger, buffeting his little Healy like it was a toy car made out of papier-mâché. The black macadam road was pockmarked with hollows, each one overflowing with water. *Summer ice,* Sean thought as he dropped it into fifth gear and settled down to what for him was a snail's pace: fifty-five. Before he'd gone a quarter mile, he was deep in thought, gorging himself after weeks of unwilling abstinence.

It wasn't long before Sean found himself alone, the only car on the road. He had a single train of thought: Oliver's theories about the metaphorical meanings of Monique's work, a line of reasoning Sean hadn't been able to shake for the last twenty miles. *Either accept it or reject it!* he thought.

As if Oliver were there, sitting beside him, Sean started talking. "But none of what you said explains what happened to me when I was in her studio, let alone what happened to the both of us! It only offers a hypothesis to explain the creative motives behind her work."

Sean shook his head. "Besides, before you get into the analytical academic shit, I think you've got to realize that you have trouble with her work, my friend. It frightens you, as I think it does—and perhaps rightly so—most men. It could be why people such as Bradley, and probably many other collectors—all men, by the way—are so attracted to her bronzes."

Sean chuckled to himself. "I know now her work sure scared the hell out me at first—even though I thought it didn't—until I came to see it for what it was, not simply react to the obvious. It's all about what Monique is trying to say about the essential relationship between man and woman. It's a matter of trust. But even more important, it's the violation of that thin, delicate line of trust between the sexes. It's a dilemma as old as mankind."

Sean abruptly sat up and cocked his head to one side, appearing studious. "You have to look beneath the surface—the frightening appearance of the subjects, and the somewhat uncommon compositions—before you can see, and feel, what she's telling us," Sean said firmly, urging his absent listener to embrace what he was saying.

He paused when he realized he was rehearsing what amounted to a lecture for Oliver—a rebuttal of sorts, an essential part of what made their relationship what it was. Sean smiled to himself as he softened his demeanor a bit, but didn't lose sight of his objective. He raised his hand, pointing at the windshield as if to drive home his point. "One of the things I asked Monique, that first time I was at her studio, was 'Where do you find the inspiration for your work?' "

He hesitated, gathering his thoughts. He actually found himself feeling self-indulgent about being able to see them, and so clearly. "Well, old friend, her answer surprised me, as I know it will you. She told me, and in what I can only say was an unnerving manner—as if she was frightened by her own talent—'I don't have to find them, Dr. MacDonald, they find me. They rip me from my sleep.' She then slammed her fist into the gut of the life-size figure she was working on—with such force that it actually rocked backwards!—and said in an eerie sort of way, 'They're there, every night, waiting for me. I feel like I haven't slept in ages.' I'll never forget that. I thought—"

Sean suddenly felt a stabbing pain in his chest, his breath being choked off, feelings—blind, unclear—fighting for control of his thoughts. Confused, then frightened, he shook his head. *What the fuck is happening?* he wondered, feeling anxious, uncomfortable, then angry. Without thinking, not knowing why, he glanced outside to see where he was. The roadside sign, its white reflective letters jumping off the iridescent green background, spelled out "Old Country Road— ½ mile."

Almost in a panic, Sean looked at his watch, only to see a black circle in the dark. He held his hand to the dash, accidentally scraping his knuckles against one of the chrome-plated spokes of the wood-rimmed steering wheel, drawing blood.

Eleven-fifteen, he thought, placing his fist to his lips, licking the blood off his knuckles. *It's later than I realized.*

"Wait a second," he argued. "What the hell difference does it make what time it is?" But for some reason it did matter, and he wanted to know why. When he asked himself why, tried to think about it, everything went out of focus. "Fuck this," he growled, and slammed his foot on the brakes, throwing the car into a spin on the rain-slick road.

Sean began pumping the brakes and fighting with the wheel as he brought his Healy under control, just short of sliding off the road and hitting the guardrail. After checking to make sure no one was behind him, he breathed a sigh of relief and pulled off onto the grass-covered shoulder, not fifty yards from the exit for Old Country Road. *It's her—them!— it has to be,* he thought, just before blacking out from the pain in his chest, which felt like it was trying to tear his heart out.

Chapter Forty

Pamela's eyes bolted open. She had been startled out of a deep but fitful sleep by the sound of glass shattering. She lay perfectly still in the black of her bedroom, listening with her whole body, thinking, *Don't move. Don't even breathe. Let them move first.*

Her next thought was of the pistol on the dresser. She pictured where it was, how she'd set it out, what side it was lying on, and which direction the muzzle was pointing. With the tips of her fingers, she pinched the sheet and slowly, silently, slid it off her—only to be reminded by the damp chill in the air that she'd fallen asleep without a stitch of clothes on. *Great! Bare-assed white—one big moving target,* she thought.

Stupid bitch! raced through her head as she jumped out of bed and lunged for the revolver. She had it in a heartbeat, and was on one knee—both hands wrapped around the grip—panning the darkened room. She jerked and swung around at the flicker of shadows near the window, ready to shoot, only to realize what she'd seen were the curtains being tossed about by the wind. *Blowing through the goddamn window that* you *left open,* she thought.

A second look around the room told Pamela what the noise had been: She noticed that the vanity was tipped over. Even in the dark, she could see that one of the three arch-topped mirrors had struck the corner of the settee, shattering into hundreds of shards of silver and black, glistening menacingly on the carpet.

Breathing a sigh of relief, she lowered the gun and slumped up against the heavy wooden dresser behind her, only to arch her back and pitch forward to get away from the unexpected bite of the cold metal drawer handles nipping her bare skin. Pamela stood up and set the gun back down on the dresser. She took special care to put it in the exact same position she'd found it. Out of nervous habit—a girl thing—she shook her head, then combed her fingers through her hair, and was immediately reminded it was still wet. "Not smart," she muttered, and started for the bathroom. *Go dry it, and get back to bed,* she thought. *You've got an early day ahead of you, and you'll need every bit of sleep you can get.*

A sudden blast of damp air turned her away from the bathroom and started her toward the open window. With the window closed and latched, the curtains straightened, Pamela told herself, "Make sure you leave a note for Katie about the vanity, so she doesn't worry" as she tiptoed around the broken glass on the floor, her attention now refocused on drying her hair.

It took all of five minutes to blow her hair dry and brush it out. Still naked, but no longer cold, she started across the room for the bed, but stopped when she realized that she was now wide awake. *And there's no way in hell you're going to be able to get back to sleep—not for a while, at least.* A quick glance at the clock radio on the nightstand beside the bed—"Shit, it's only eleven-thirty"—started her thinking, a process that lasted two seconds, tops. *By the time you get dressed, grab something to eat, have them bring the car around, and drive for two or more hours to find this place, it'll be light out.* "Or damn close to it."

Pamela stood with her hands on her hips, looking around

the room, as if the answer she wanted was hiding somewhere in the dark.

"Go now," she said with a determined nod. "And get this damn thing over with—one way or another."

Chapter Forty-one

A crescent moon slipped in and out of the billowing black clouds tumbling across the midnight sky, its crooked smile casting a jaundiced glow over everything it touched. The tall wet grass blanketing the fields and entrance to Monique's studio had been blown onto its side and was slithering over the ground, driven by the relentless wind. Every sign of tire tracks leading into and out of the abandoned farm had been erased.

Sean pulled off Old County Road, quickly and without hesitation. There wasn't the slightest hint of reservation to be found in his determination to see Monique and get everything out in the open, once and for all. "You've been holding back, MacDonald—why, I don't know," he admonished himself.

Though clouded not a half hour earlier, his thoughts were now clear, and growing clearer by the moment, not unlike the skies overhead. *Just relax,* he thought, feeling uncomfortable about coming here at this hour of the night unannounced. In an effort to add another dose of reassurance, he told himself, "Odds are she's working on something right now, and is wide awake,'' as he pulled to a stop no more than a car's length from the barn. Flicking the lights off, he killed the engine and sat back to organize his thoughts, which were once again his own. *But for how long?* he wondered when an uneasy feeling rippled through his chest.

He shook his head and frowned. ''Don't even bother,'' he said, bolstering himself up another notch. ''This is a no-brainer. You already know what you want to ask her. Either she knows about it all, or she doesn't. And if she does, either she cares or she doesn't. At any rate, it's her call no matter how you look at it.''

Then why are you even here? he thought. *There's nothing you can do about it—other than to make sure she knows. Or is it for your own satisfaction?* He stayed with these thoughts until he came up with the same answer he'd faced every time he'd asked those very same questions since pulling off the parkway, and realized he still wasn't ready to deal with it. *Maybe you don't have any choice.*

''Says who?'' he argued, and grabbed hold of the car door securely to keep the wind from ripping it out of his hand as he climbed out of the Healy, still soaking wet. His feet squished down into the soggy ground, kept from getting muddy by the thick mat of grass, fattened by the water sucked out of the rain-soaked earth.

The moment he stood up straight, he was blown back a step or two and had to fight to catch his balance. And his breath, too, because of the wind slapping at his face. To his surprise, the air was warm, almost hot. And thick. More liquid than vapor. When he took a deep breath out of habit, it felt like he was under water. He turned away from the irritating slap of the wind and took a secretive breath, but was still left with the feeling of not getting enough air into his lungs. ''So don't breathe,'' he told himself, laughing, as he started for the door, his determination growing stronger with each step taken, until he found himself thinking, *You're actually looking forward to this, aren't you?* That question, which he didn't think needed an answer, brought him to an abrupt stop. *Why?* he wondered as he raised his fist to knock.

Something held him back. *You want to see her, don't you? That's why, isn't it?*

Before that thought could play itself out, and draw others with it, Sean's feelings got the better of him. *Go ahead, admit it, MacDonald. You miss her, don't you?* Smiling, he nodded and whispered, "Perhaps because she's real." He laughed quietly to himself. "That curious woman is more real than any woman you've ever known." He shivered. "And more frightening, which is probably what you're attracted to," he said without reservation. "It's that double edge you like—always have."

Sean's resolve to confront Monique about everything he'd found out was suddenly weakened by the excitement of seeing her. And his thoughts were no longer as clear as they had been a while before, or solely his own. He felt himself growing uncertain with each hesitant, almost labored thought. Yet one flickering point of light inside his head was not to be snuffed out, and he found himself asking, though in a tentative voice, "How could she not know? It doesn't make—"

"Talking to ourselves again, Sean?"

Startled at the sound of Monique's voice directly behind him, and so close, Sean spun around to find her only a step away. *Where the hell did you come from!* he thought, and was about to ask her just that when he was enchanted by the sight of her long auburn hair swirling wildly about in the wind. And her eyes, white-hot, burning away the dark, but cool, soothing, at the same time. She was wearing a loose-fitting caftan splashed with a rainbow of ancient Oriental colors. Wide open at the neck, unbuttoned partway down, the ivory white of her neck and shoulders was exposed to the faint light of the moon, which was no longer a prisoner of the clouds. The steady wind was pressing the silken fabric over and around every rise and fall of her body, then whisking it away before the mind could turn fantasy into form.

"What are you doing outside?" he asked, the dark offering him the cover he needed to look at her body as he never had before.

Monique seemed to discard his question with a casual toss

319

of her head. "Beautiful out, isn't it?" she asked, and looked up into the broken face of the moon. When she did, her hair fell off her shoulders and down her back, blending into the mysterious print of her caftan. She nodded, seeming to agree with herself, and stepped beside Sean. The delicate fragrance of her damp hair, her warm body—whatever was splashed on her skin—wrapped themselves around him and seeped through his pores. Taking hold of the door latch, Monique placed her other hand on Sean's arm. She quickly pulled it back, hesitated for a moment, then gently patted his shoulder, chest, and stomach, as if searching him.

"You're soaking wet," she said with real concern. She reached up and placed the back of her hand on the side of his neck, then held it against his cheek. "And you're cold as ice." She pulled the door open and motioned for him to go inside. "Let's get you dried out." She drew quiet. "Perhaps you'd like to st—"

There was an unexpected pause, as if her words had been stolen from her in midsentence. She sighed, but more to herself, and knowingly. "Tell me what brings you here in the middle of the night?" This was asked in a way that sounded to Sean like she already knew why he was here and simply wanted to see if he would tell the truth. "But only after we get you dried out. *And* have something to drink. Agreed?"

There was no offer of compromise to be found in Monique's question. Nodding, Sean walked into the pitch-black studio, slowly, his arms out in front of him, feeling his way in the dark. The air inside was warm and dry, not damp and cool as he expected it to be. And it was free of the smell of sour hay, which surprised him. That musty odor had been replaced with a vaguely familiar scent he immediately tried placing—and almost had, when the delicate threads slipped away. The thought that followed—asking, *What were you thinking?*—was lost too.

A few paces inside, Sean stopped and waited for his eyes to adjust to the dark. As they did, he could just barely make out a faint beam of light, a sliver of night, in the far corner of the studio where Monique worked. It was as if a single moonbeam had fallen through a crack in the roof onto the life-size clay head of a man. The bust was set squarely on one of the three-legged pedestals, which had been raised up to working height and moved around in front of what appeared in the darkness of the unlit barn to be a full-size work in progress, though smaller than all the others Sean had sean. The figure was wrapped in a pristine-white shroud and hidden from his suddenly wide-open and hungry eyes.

Monique closed and securely latched the door behind her, turning the studio two shades darker by shutting out the light of the moon. The effect was to brighten the clay bust by contrast. When he saw this, Sean's pace quickened, prodded by images of the only other bust of Monique's he'd seen— the head of Christ—which were now replaying inside his head.

Monique was suddenly alongside, then in front of him, before Sean could make it halfway across the huge room. She held her hand up, stopping him, then reached out. "Clothes," she said, her back to the only light in the room, her face falling into darkness.

"Clothes?" Sean asked, placing his hands on his chest in a protective gesture. "What are you talking about?" Thoughts raced through his head, dark as clouds and out of focus, chased by others with the same stormy look about them.

"Your clothes are soaking wet," she said, a hint of impatience in her voice, tempered by a note of compassion. "I'll dry them." Sean stepped back. Monique laughed. "One minute you want to pose for me, the next you're afraid to take your clothes off." Monique shook her head as she made up the distance Sean had put between them, and began slipping his jacket off. "Sometimes you make no sense whatsoever. You really are half man, half boy."

How did you know I wanted to pose? he thought. *I never told you that. Or did I?* He tried remembering if he had, and had simply forgotten, but couldn't seem to focus. *Shit!* He glanced around the studio to see if *she* was anywhere in sight, only to realize that every one of the works that had once been in Monique's studio was gone. He stood panning the room, peering into the shadows, the corners. It was so dark, he couldn't even see the walls. Even the ceiling eluded him, save for a few golden threads of straw hanging down here and there, piercing the dark.

"Where is everything?" he asked as Monique unbuttoned his shirt, slipped it off his shoulders, and tugged it off his arms and out of his pants.

"Being readied for an exhibition," she said in an off-handed sort of way. "Pants?" she asked a second time, and gave an impatient pull of Sean's belt.

"What exhibition? Where is it being held? And why didn't you say anything about it to me before?" he asked, sounding hurt. He began to comply with Monique's repeated tug of his belt, but stopped. "What am I going to wear while you—"

Monique shoved his jacket and shirt into his bare chest, forcing him to grab hold of them. Then she turned on her heel and marched across the studio toward the far wall. He watched her slip into the shadows—become one herself— and thought he could see her bend over and pick something off the floor, but couldn't be sure. She strode back, walking with a purpose and nearly, but not quite, once again free of her limp. She ceremoniously traded a neatly folded linen sheet for his clump of wet clothes. "Wear *that* if you're uncomfortable." Monique was now close enough to Sean for him to see an amused smile on her face. At that moment, she appeared more relaxed than he remembered ever having seen her.

He suddenly felt silly. "What about my—"

"Everything," she said, and stuck her hands out, holding his wet clothes up in front of him. "Just put them here." She shut her eyes. "I won't look," she said, then opened her eyes halfway and grinned, creating the appearance of a Cheshire cat.

They both began laughing. It was the natural, unguarded, relaxed laugh of a man and a woman enjoying each other, sharing something together. This woman that Sean couldn't explain, and understood even less, was proving more intriguing and attractive by the moment. "I guess I'm acting like a jerk, aren't I?'' he asked, dropping the folded linen bundle onto the floor at his feet. He kicked his shoes off and stepped onto the oasis of dry cloth. Next came his wet socks, which he laid out neatly on top of the clothes Monique was holding. Seizing her gaze, he stepped out of his pants, peeled off his wet briefs, and piled everything on top.

"Where do I wait?" he asked. He let go of Monique's gaze and looked over her shoulder toward the clay bust behind her. "Over there?" When he glanced back, her gaze was waiting for him where he'd left it. Part of him was disappointed. He tried telling himself, *She's seen hundreds of naked men*, but it didn't help any. His next thought made it even worse. *And most, if not all, of them were probably a hell of a lot younger and, no doubt, better-looking.*

"Not necessarily," Monique said with an inviting lilt to her words as she scooped his shoes up off the floor and turned to walk away. "Just don't touch anything while I'm gone. Promise?"

Momentarily confused at hearing Monique answer his unasked question, then passing it off just as quickly without further thought, Sean whispered under his breath, " 'Promise'?"

Monique stopped and turned back, her gaze held at eye level with Sean's, still respecting his modesty. "Yes," she replied, surprising him at having heard what he'd said. "Do you?"

"Yes," he said quickly and convincingly. And he meant it, too. "I will not touch anything." He scratched an X through the hair on his chest, over his heart, with his finger. "I promise."

Monique held her hand out. "Even those?" she asked, turning full circle.

Without bothering to look, acting as if he knew what she was referring to—thinking he'd already seen whatever it was she didn't want him to touch—Sean followed the sweep of her gesture. "I won't even—"

He was silenced the instant he saw what it was Monique had been pointing out to him, as if lighted by the point of her finger. Tucked away in the shadows, banished from sight, he saw one, a second, then a third shrouded figure, the cloth clinging to whatever was inside as if it was wet. Each one was standing on a round palette that gave the impression it could turn. With the fourth figure—the one near the clay bust Sean had noticed and become enamored with—the figures quartered the studio, making Sean feel like he was surrounded. He had the sudden urge to flee, but calmed himself.

Two of the figures were the size of a tall man. Including the height of the palette, they easily stood seven feet from floor to top. The third appeared shorter and bulkier. It was more like the one near the bust, only much larger—the size of a man as compared with a woman. It looked like the figure trapped inside the makeshift cocoon was crouching down, or kneeling, and holding something in its outstretched hands.

Out of nowhere—wanting nothing more than to see what was hiding beneath each of the linen shrouds—Sean called out to Monique just before she was swallowed up by the dark, "Can I see just one?" Her silence left him in the dark to answer his own question. Smiling, he muttered, "At times more boy, I fear, than man." Bending down, he gathered up the bundle off the floor, shook it out—waves of white linen fluttering in the dark—and wrapped it around himself, his arms folded over his chest.

Barefoot, curious that the hardwood floor was more warm than cool, but thankful that it was, Sean started around the perimeter of the studio, the edges of his simple robe trailing on the floor around and behind him. He took aim at the figure closest to him, the one along the left side, opposite the walled-up stalls and invisible hallway leading back to wherever it was Monique had disappeared with his clothes. The bolt of cloth snugged around him had the sweet smell of newness, yet it was deliciously soft against his skin. It felt more like it had been woven from cotton than the coarse threads of flax. And it was warm like wool.

He stopped and stood facing the first shadowy figure, taller than he but only because of the palette it was on. Curious, he tipped up on his toes to check. He then squatted down to examine the palette, which he noticed was finely crafted, unlike the ones he'd seen in George's studio at the academy supporting *The Seven Deadly Sins*. And this one was not sitting flush to the floor, which invited him to slip his fingers underneath and feel a round ball fitted into a metal cup. *There must be four of them,* he decided, and stood up.

The spotless shroud—whiter and thinner than the others he'd seen covering Monique's work, which were more like dirty old canvas—clung to it, creating the illusion of a shoulder, an arm, a face, yet nothing quite real. There was the unmistakable smell of fresh clay in the air. Sean had to force himself to gather up fistfuls of fabric and squeeze tight in order to keep from reaching out and touching. As hard as he tried, as much as he wanted to, hungry for the slightest morsel of earthen flesh—a bittersweet taste of reality, no matter how startling it might be—he couldn't make out the form hidden beneath the opaque veil of white.

He gave up and started toward the undraped bust, but veered away when he thought, *Leave that for last—and the figure beside it. She's not hiding it, so it can't be that important.*

No longer cold, Sean loosened his grip on the linen wrapped around him, letting it fall off his shoulders and chest as he crossed the studio to confront the next figure, the one that appeared to be crouching down. *It's got to be kneeling,* he decided as he moved to within arm's length of the figure, which was chest high and set on a much wider palette than was the first figure. Unable not to, he placed his bare foot against the edge of the palette and pushed. It moved an inch or so, and with relative ease. He did it again, but harder. The dull moan of rubber scuffing and rolling over the wooden floor confirmed that the palettes were all wheeled.

Makes sense, he thought. *These suckers are heavy.*

About to turn and go to the third figure, which was buried deep in the back of the studio where the polychrome bronze had once stood, Sean stopped, glanced around, and reached out. He gently set his hand on the highest point of the shroud, where he expected the head to be. But it was rough, jagged, not round. Curious, he followed the line of the shoulders to the arms, which he realized from the way they were pitched forward were outstretched and converging. He fingered his way down the arm, moving over the biceps, then out along the forearm, only to pull back with a start when he felt the shape of a head. "Jesus," he whispered, and tried laughing his uneasiness away, but with little success. *Who have we decapitated now?* he wondered, and was about to feel the face of the head with the tips of his fingers. "No," he told himself, and spun away. "Once you do, you'll only want to see it—and you know you won't be able to stop yourself—so don't even get started."

He started for the third figure, a vague outline of gray in the far corner of the studio. Partway there, he wondered, *Why bother, there's nothing to see. All you want to do is take these stupid-assed covers off and see what she's created.*

About to turn back, his curiosity about the clay bust having taken over, Sean saw another form in the dark, a dozen paces from the third figure, set deep in the corner. Drawing closer, he realized it was the polychromed bronze he thought had been taken away, along with all of the other works Monique had said were being prepared for some sort of exhibition. Not taking anything for granted, he turned to see if Monique had returned. He even waited and listened for the sound of her step, noticeable even when her limp wasn't obvious. He'd come to memorize it, and found that interesting. *She's getting under your skin more than you realize, MacDonald.* He toyed with an amused laugh that remained an affectionate smile. "Remember what Pamela said," he cautioned himself, but not seriously.

Although he slowed his advance, Sean stayed on course for the bronze in the corner, barely visible in the dark. He waited for something to happen—fully expected it to—but there wasn't the slightest twinge in his chest, dizziness in his head, or shortness of breath. His thoughts were clear, his pulse undetectable. "See, no heart attack," he mumbled, making light of the feelings that once made him think his very life was being squeezed out of him.

Stopping no more than a foot from her, yet still unable to see her green eyes, which were snuffed out by the dark, Sean placed his left hand on her right shoulder. Unlike the air around him, which felt even warmer now than it had before, she was cold. He hadn't expected that, but knew he should have. He reached out with his other hand and placed it on her left arm. When he did that, his veil of vanity fell to the floor around his feet, leaving him naked in front of the bronze that had once lured him to her, set a fire to his loins, yet at the same time had struck fear in his heart.

A perverse desire he'd harbored since childhood, ever since setting eyes on his first nude sculpture of a woman—but had never allowed to develop into reality—suddenly took hold of him. He let his hands, his fingers, the soft flesh of his palms, explore her body: not crudely, sexually, but with curiosity. He slowly traced the lines of her sari, slipping in and out of the delicate folds, refusing to accept their hard metallic cast. He placed his open hands on either side of her long neck and closed his eyes as he felt his way up to her face, exploring every exquisite detail with the tips of his fingers—the line of her jaw, her chin, her full lips, the sensual flair of her nostrils, the curve of her strong nose, her wide-set almond eyes, which for an instant he thought moved when his fingers brushed over them. He just as quickly passed it off as his imagination.

Thinking it all somehow familiar, that it was the face of someone he knew, he started over. Only now her bronze skin was warm, not cold. *Or is it me?* he wondered as he retraced every graceful curve and hollow of her face. This done, his doubts still there, his hands slid down her neck onto her shoulders, as if pulled there. He paused, embarrassed for a moment at what he was thinking and feeling. He reached down, his eyes still shut, barely breathing, and cupped her firm but womanly breasts. His thumbs inadvertently, or perhaps out of lover's habit, brushed lightly over her nipples.

At that very moment, whatever cerebral calm, a distancing between mind and body, which Sean thought had existed, suddenly evaporated. His thoughts were no longer his own, stolen from him as they had been before. He felt a fire ignite in his gut and burn hot, then melt down into his loins like molten lust. It was stronger than anything he'd every experienced. Frightened, feeling himself growing aroused beyond control, he tried opening his eyes to face her, but couldn't. He tried pulling away, but his hands were bound to her, his flesh, her metallic skin, now one. What had been cold to his touch was now warm, what had been hard was soft, sensuous. He felt a breath on his face, taking his own away. It was warm and moist, and smelled bittersweet. Lips touched his, tenderly at first, then hungrily. Fingers began caressing his aroused body, drawing out his passion beyond his wildest imagination. His body was no longer his, but hers—hers to do what she wanted with it.

Thoughts of that night in the hayloft, and what he'd seen below in the studio—that faceless man, frozen in time, unable to move, to speak, and that woman, cold, cruel, yet powerfully sensual—raced though his head, his heart, chilling his soul. And that's when he knew what it was he'd thought was familiar about the face of the statue before him. *It was you,* he thought, then wanted to scream *It's you*! as loud as he could when other faces came to mind.

Sean felt a hand on his shoulder, making him stiffen all over, followed by a quiet voice. "Are you all right?" Monique asked.

Suddenly, inexplicably, freed of his invisible bonds, he blurted out, "It's you!" and opened his eyes to find the painted face of the bronze goddess, but at arm's length, not as close as he'd thought, once again buried deep in the dark.

Monique patted his shoulder, as if to calm him down. "Of course it's me. Who else would it be?" she asked. She sounded bemused, but nonetheless concerned. But more for him than about him.

As if he hadn't heard what she'd said, Sean said quietly, "It *is* you," as he stared into the painted face of the inanimate bronze, looking for signs of life he was now certain were there. *Somewhere!* His thoughts were once again his own, and he knew it. He whispered under his breath, "They were *all* you, weren't they?" His question sounded more like an accusation, an indictment without expectation of a defense.

Sean heard the clank of glass behind him, something being set on the floor. The rustle of cloth was followed by the feel of the linen sheet being slipped over his shoulders, followed by the soft-spoken words, "I told you not to touch anything. Please don't make that mistake again—it could be your last." It wasn't a warning he heard in Monique's voice, but a promise. Yet not one that she was making; it sounded more like she was repeating someone else's.

You know, don't you? Sean thought, his gaze still fixed on the mysterious bronze, certain there was something different about her now, but unsure exactly what it was. *The smile?* he wondered, and began looking for anything else that was not as he remembered it. *Wait?* He stepped back and to one side, stopping when he felt Monique's hand on him—holding him in place—letting him know she was there. *Where are they?* He glanced beyond the bronze, panned the darkened wall behind her, end to end, looking for her consorts.

How could you have missed that? he thought, and turned to face Monique when he felt her hand move but not withdraw. He was aware that every ounce of resolve that had been taken from him against his will was now burning brightly inside him. He wasn't about to let anyone—*or anything!*—extinguish that flame, *at least not until I've found out what I came here for*. He watched as Monique knelt on one knee to pick up a bottle of wine and a pair of glasses off the floor. He was struck at how graceful she appeared, moving with ease, not awkwardly, or with that faltering, hesitant gesture that told you she was living with constant pain.

When she rose and looked up into his face, her eyes cool, calm, Sean asked with determination, but without the slightest connotation of implied guilt, "You know about Brad Johnson and George, don't you?" Uncertain what to expect—remembering her reaction when he'd told her about the sale of *Man's Fate*—Sean held his breath and discreetly braced himself against the unknown.

Monique tilted her head to one side, her face smoothed by a slight, almost impish smile, one that spoke of knowledge but not conceit. Her eyes were alive with color—not just a single color, but every cast of the rainbow—and sparkling. "Yes," she said, turning away from Sean's inquiring gaze and walking slowly across the studio. Her head was cocked to one side, giving the impression that she was listening for Sean to say something more. Or waiting for him to join her. "Is that all you want to know?" she asked, appearing not the least bit bothered by what he'd said.

Sean stood watching her, a shadow moving among shadows. The soft light on the other side of the studio cast a gentle halo around her. A shifting silhouette. It appeared to grow brighter as she moved away from Sean and steadily closer to the faintly lit bust and its cloaked guardian, the last of the four mysterious creations that still held Sean's curiosity.

Gathering the sheet around him, he followed, but at a distance, and deliberately so. *You know about them all—every single one of them—don't you?* he thought, quickening his pace, having decided to ask her about each one of them, and how she felt about what they'd done to her. *Start with Allan Stern, then Anderson—Bradley, the jerk—and that trustee, that friend—*

Without warning, Monique stopped, turned to look back at Sean, nodded her head decisively, then continued walking across the studio, leaving him speechless. It also left him feeling that she wanted him to stop. *But stop what?* he wondered.

Doubtful of what he'd seen, that it meant she'd read his thoughts and had heard enough, he told himself, *It's your imagination.* He stopped, half curious, half concerned, and thought, *Or was it you?* He then intentionally filled his head with images of what Oliver had told him, what he'd seen for himself at the library, and the composite sketch Marcelli had shown him.

A casual but unquestionably slowed pace confirmed his suspicion, reawakened his forgotten fears, and left him thinking, *Maybe she really can.* Something suddenly took hold of him with a heart-stopping thud. *Get the hell out of here!* rang loudly inside his head.

Monique abruptly stopped and turned around, her eyes lighting up her face, which Sean realized was no longer pallid but flushed with color. "Please stay," she asked softly, seductively. There was also a plaintive, almost painful twist to her words, tempered by what to Sean's ears sounded like sadness. Melancholy. She added an inviting wave of her hand, causing the glasses she was holding to strike each other and ring like crystal chimes.

"Please, stay, I don't want to spend my las—"

The muted sound of metal creaking, scraping—sending chills up and down Sean's spine—cut Monique off. "No!" she called out angrily, her single word repeating itself over and over again as it reverberated inside the cavernous studio. Yet as fierce as she sounded—startling him with her outburst—Sean could detect what to him was a discordant note in her voice, which instantly struck a resonant chord in his heart. Ignoring his own advice, the voice not that of his intuition but of his fear—deliberately blinding himself to the images created by the eerie and unsettling sounds he'd just heard behind him—Sean walked up to Monique and took the glasses from her.

Turning them right side up, he held them out, one in each hand, his linen robe falling open. "Shall we?" he asked, gesturing toward the bottle of wine. When Monique hesitated, her gaze elsewhere, beyond him, he asked, making it sound like she didn't have to answer him if she didn't want to, "You really don't care about them, do you?" He tapped the bottle of wine with one of the glasses to get her attention. "And you're not going to do anything about what they've done to you, are you?"

When she didn't answer, he struck the bottle again, but gently, replaying the pleasing note of the crystal goblet. Whether it was the ring of the empty glass striking the bottle, or his telling question—he couldn't be sure which it was, nor did he care, which surprised but didn't bother him— Monique blinked away from her thoughts, which were clearly drawn to the other side of the studio. She looked at him, and only him. Her face was another shade darker, but richer, her skin warmer than it had been only moments before. *It's just because you're closer, and there's more light here,* Sean thought.

Monique filled the glasses. "No," she said, sounding weary, but sure of herself. "You're wrong. I do care." She lowered her voice but didn't soften it. If anything, it was deeper, stronger. "I care more than you can ever know." She drew Sean's gaze into hers, as if to drink in his thoughts. "I have given what few have given to their art to save it. To ensure that it will survive."

She was about to go on, she had more to say, but Sean asked, "What are you talking about?"

Monique took a long sip of wine. "You know," she said, again with certainty. "You just haven't listened to your own heart. You fight it too much. You should—"

"I don't understand," Sean said impatiently.

Monique smiled, a forgiving look on her face. Then she said in a patronizing tone of voice, "You will."

That same voice inside him cried out again, *Get out. Now!*

Before he could answer, or ask Monique yet again what she meant by what she'd just said, she drained her glass and set it on the pedestal beside the clay bust, which Sean suddenly realized he'd somehow forgotten about. In silence, moving with a purpose, Monique walked over to the wall. With a twist of her hand, she turned the solitary spotlight off. The only light, if it could be called light, was the brighter gray of night dripping down through the seams of the rough-hewn planks overhead, thinning the darkness just enough to create shadows—black on black.

Standing perfectly still, his senses on edge, razor sharp, his eyes wide open though useless, Sean could hear Monique moving toward him. Then he felt the air moving over his face from her presence. He blinked, still blind. There was the soft muffled crush and rub of cloth. The smell of wet clay filled his nostrils, coated his throat, settled down into lungs. *She's uncovered that one piece,* he thought, straining to see.

He felt a hand slip into his, sure and on the mark. Her touch was gentle, but still strong. With the veil of darkness came a silence of equal measure. The only sounds were those of cloth brushing over the floor, the soft padding of bare feet on wood, hers and his, and the beating of Sean's heart. *What are you doing?*

"Don't be afraid," Monique said reassuringly.

Sean started to tell her he wasn't afraid, even though he thought he was, when he realized that he actually wasn't frightened, *at least not of you,* he thought.

"I know," Monique said with a subtle note of relief. "But you are afraid of—"

Once again her words were severed from her tongue, her breath still there, but no sound. Sean felt her hand shiver, turn cold, then slip free of his. There was the sound of cloth being shaken out, the feel of a light breeze all around him, the renewed smell of fresh linen and wet clay. He felt the shroud settle to the floor, the edge just covering his feet. His impromptu robe was slipped off his body before he could protest, shaken out like the other bolt of cloth, and left to float to the floor on top of the first layer.

After a breathless pause, there was the gentle, almost inaudible rustle of cloth, sounding more like silk than linen. Sean did not need eyes to know what Monique had just done, or thoughts to expose his feelings. He stepped onto the bed of cloth, cautiously, first one foot, then the next, and moved to where he thought the sounds had come from. He held his arms out, hands open. His fingers grazed her body, her shoulders? then caught in her long hair.

Without hesitating, without thinking, he stepped into her, his naked body pressing against hers. She was not as he expected, not anything like the images he'd created in his mind: Her breasts were large but firm, her waist far more narrow than he thought he'd seen when her clothes had clung to her sweat-soaked body that first time he'd watched her work. Her tummy was gently rounded, yet firm. Her thighs, her loins, a thick, inviting tuft of hair, were warm, asking to be touched, tasted. Entered. The smell of her body, the oily fragrance covering her skin, seeped through his skin, found his veins, and rushed to his brain, bursting into an endless sexual fantasy.

Sean bowed his head. His lips found Monique's forehead, then her eyes, which were closed. He kissed one, then the other. She said nothing, her body calm, but there, responsive, warming his. He found her mouth, tasting her for the first time. Pure and clean. Wanting her closer, he slid his hands

333

down her back, intent on holding her tight and pulling her to him. She stiffened, but it was too late: His hands had found the gnarled rise on her back, her twisted spine, the knotted flesh surrounding it.

Monique took a pitiful breath and began to withdraw from him. "No," he whispered. "I want you. I want *you*," he said as he held her even tighter, refusing to move his hands from where they were, suddenly aware that he wasn't repulsed by her body, nor perversely attracted to it. It was simply hers. "You may be able to read my thoughts," he said, a smile in his voice. "But it seems that you can't read my heart. Or can you?" he asked, making it sound like a playful tease. "And it's you who are afraid, not me."

Softening her stance, Monique wrapped her arms around Sean and grabbed him with her powerful hands, taking his breath away for an instant. After a moment, she slid her fingers down his back to his waist, took hold of him, his flesh in her hands, and drew him to her. "I hear much of what you think," she said. "But not all. I can feel the beat of your heart when it senses fear. I can see what you see, and also what you cannot. I taste what you taste."

With a sigh, Monique rested her head on Sean's chest, her words now gently spoken. "But I cannot—I will not—make you do what you do not want to do," she added, making it sound like she could if she really wanted to.

She suddenly released her hold of Sean and pushed him away. "Go," she said. "You don't have to stay. It's best that—"

Sean took her into his arms and silenced her with a kiss. Though his body was now soft, his desire for her was nonetheless firm. "I want you," he whispered. "I want the woman inside this body that shames you but does not offend me. I want to feel that woman around me. I want to know who she really is. Feel her heartbeat. Touch her soul." His passion was returning, his flesh growing firm to match his ardor, pressing against Monique's thighs.

He knelt down and placed his mouth over the end of her breast, his tongue circling her nipple. With each delicious stroke, the taste of oil mixing with salt, Monique took a quiet sip of air, her whole body quivering inside. When he leaned back to guide her down beside him, Sean's head was filled with the aroma of her body, aroused, warm and moist, and sweet as honey. The fragrance was so thick, he could taste her in it.

Once on her knees before him, Monique reached out and touched him with both of her hands, hesitantly, as if she'd never touched a man before. First his face, memorizing every feature with the tips of her gnarled fingers. His neck. She lingered at his chest, tracing every rib, circling each nipple with the tip of a moistened finger, taking his breath away. She pressed her palm flat over his heart as if to calm him. Then she followed the lines of his manly waist, down, then around and over his stomach. She paused, took a steadying breath, and cautiously, almost timidly, slipped her large hands around his rigid erection.

Inching closer, Sean reached down and cupped Monique's breast in one hand, feeling its delicious weight. With his other hand, he searched for the source of the heat rising up and warming his face. He found it, found her, dripping from her engorged flesh. He brought his hand to his face, smelling, then tasting her. He slid his tongue over his lips, collecting every drop of nectar.

Monique sighed. "There isn't much time. Come in me. Now. Please?" she asked quietly, anxiously, her voice suddenly frail.

"Is it something I've—"

Sean felt a finger on his lips, putting an end to his question. "No," she said. "Hurry. Please?" she asked again, and eased back, ready to take him inside her.

He bent down and kissed her lovingly, her face, her lips, as he moved over her. She was open, ready, a fire rising from her loins, licking at his. She raised her legs and wrapped them around his waist, surprising him once again with her strength. He pressed against her, gently—wanting to make sure—then fell deep inside her, his muffled cry of pleasure, the exquisite pain of passion, matched by her deep-throated moan. For a moment they lay still, motionless, breathless, their bodies one, their hearts entwined.

Sean whispered in the dark, "You're beautiful," and tenderly kissed her, only to feel tears wetting his cheek. "Is there—"

Before he could ask his question—to know what she was feeling, thinking—he was pulled down with a powerful thrust of her legs, her hips rising, her body swallowing him up—wanting still more—as she rolled him over onto his back and sat up, straddling him, all in a single, powerful move. She held him, pinned to the floor, when he tried to move—her liquid flesh, once warm and soft, suddenly hard and cold, and tightening around him.

He tried to speak, to ask what was happening—*Why are you doing this*? he thought—but couldn't utter a single word. When he tried to slip her unwanted embrace, she dug her fingers into his chest, her nails suddenly sharp, piercing his skin. And there was a different odor about her, acrid, more like sulfur. The smell of something charred.

She quickly brought him back up, much to his surprise, and against his will, until he was throbbing inside her and ready to explode. But with pain, not pleasure. *What are you doing?* he thought, and waited, expecting Monique to answer his unspoken question, to respond to his plea. But she remained silent as a spark ignited a fire in his loins that spread through his body—burning, not warming him—his every breath a labor as he fought to keep from passing out.

Chapter Forty-two

With his first waking breath, still blind with sleep, Sean smelled the oily fragrance of her body, felt the touch of silk against his skin, and realized that his face was buried in the caftan Monique had been wearing the night before. From its press against his cheek, he could tell that it had been folded and fluffed into a makeshift pillow. When he ran his tongue over his dry lips, he tasted her—tasted them both—all over again. Suddenly, elusive images, ones painted not from sight but from touch and taste and sound, filled his head. He smiled as he watched infinite shades of gray slowly taking shape, refilling his senses.

Before he could savor them, relive those sensuous moments, others followed, jagged, startling, stained with hideous colors, putting an abrupt end to his thoughts of the previous night. Refusing to look at them—thinking they were fragments left over from a bad dream—he opened his eyes, expecting to find a wall of darkness surrounding him. Instead, the studio was filled with a warm glow, easing an unseen pain that had begun to infect his body. There was just enough light to turn back the night and resurrect what had been buried beneath layers of murky silt hours before.

When Sean raised his head, he saw one of the shrouded figures standing directly across from him—the one he was convinced was the form of someone kneeling—awash in a magical waterfall of opalescent light cascading down from the ceiling. It had been moved out from the wall and turned slightly, offering a profile. He glanced left, then right. Each of the other figures on either side of the studio was also cleansed by a soft white light washing over their linen shrouds and spilling into a random puddle on the floor around them. They, too, had been moved out and away from the wall, more toward the center of the room, along with their mate.

Sean turned his head a little more to the right in search of his nemesis, the polychromed bronze. She was there, at the far end of the studio, barely visible. She was hardly more than an elusive shadow, a patchwork of muted colors painted more from memory than what the faint light begrudgingly gave her. And she was still alone, her hideous guardians nowhere to be found. "I hope someone shot the fuckers," he mumbled, wondered for a moment why he'd said that, then rolled over onto his side, only to become tangled up in the bed of linen.

When he reached down to free himself, he found that the bolt of cloth had been pulled up and laid over him like a blanket, covering him from the waist down. Lying beside him were his clothes, neatly folded and laid out in a line—briefs, pants, shirt, socks, and loafers, in that order—left to right.

A movement caught his eye. He turned and glanced up, and just as quickly shut his eyes and looked away from the harsh glare of a narrow beam of light shooting out of the ceiling overhead.

"Sorry," he heard Monique say in a hoarse voice as a shadow fell over him, telling him she'd stepped between him and the light.

Sean pushed himself up onto his knees. The linen sheet slipped off his back onto the floor. He paused, but not willingly, then slowly rose to his feet, facing away from Monique. He tried stretching the knots out of his back, but gave up when his muscles seemed to grow tighter with every move. He continued to look away from the stern glare of the light as he knelt down, gathered up his briefs and pants, and slowly slipped them on in silence. His movements were awkward, stilted. He was aware of a soreness that had settled into his joints, and wondered what had caused it, only to shove that thought into the back of his mind when he thought he saw at a distance what it was.

With a shiver, he retrieved his shirt. He needed extra time to button it closed when his fingers didn't want to work. Then he grabbed his socks, which proved a chore to put on as he kept losing his balance, this earning him an amused but affectionate laugh from Monique each time he stumbled to his right or left. And finally, his loafers, which had shrunk from being wet, then dried out, and required an extra stomp or two to wedge his feet into them.

About to turn, his gaze cast down in anticipation of the light, Sean noticed that one of the linen sheets had been taken away. *Damn,* he thought, realizing he wouldn't be able to see the sculpture he now knew for sure had been exposed in the dark.

He turned to find Monique standing with her back to him, working on the clay bust, blocking it from his view. The life-size figure beside her had been re-covered, as he suspected. But it had been done in haste, leaving a seam exposed down one side. It was wide enough to reveal what appeared to be an arm, muscular and strong. *Must be a man,* he thought, and he immediately tried to construct the rest of the figure in his mind from this single anatomical clue.

"Come here," Monique said. "I have something for you." She stepped aside, exposing the rear of the clay bust. Gentle swirls of short hair covered the back of the head. With the light now behind her, her face fell into a shadow beyond the reach of Sean's sleepy-eyed gaze. She waved her hand, which glistened in the light from a shiny film of wet clay covering her fingers and palm. "I finished it while you were sleeping," she said proudly. She sounded excited but at the same time subdued. And weary, too.

Suddenly more concerned about Monique than the bust, Sean asked, "Are you all right?" He reached out. "You sound—"

Monique waved him off and said quietly, as if it hurt to talk, "I'm fine." She gestured for him to hurry. "Come see what I've done. There isn't much time."

What is that supposed to mean? Sean wondered as he circled around behind Monique, putting the light to his back so that he could see what she'd created. The moment he set eyes on it, he stopped, motionless, and said apprehensively, "It's *me*." His words were equal parts surprise, question, and disbelief. He moved closer, then stepped back, as if not wanting to get too close. "It is, isn't it?" he asked, still unable to believe what he saw.

Smiling, he shook his head in denial. "You've turned a sow's ear into a silk purse," he laughed, giving in to his embarrassment at seeing himself re-created in clay. "I'm flattered," he said softly. "It's—" He found himself at a loss for words, which only made it worse for him. "It's as if it's someone else, someone who looks like me. Or I look like him! I'm not sure."

"It most certainly is *you*," Monique said emphatically. She grabbed his arm and pulled him down to her, but with difficulty. She appeared to need the weight of her body to do it, not simply the strength of her arm. Sean was quick to notice, renewing his earlier concern. She gave him an affectionate kiss on the cheek. "Few of us are what we appear to be, as I'm sure you know only too well, my dear Sean." She reached out, touching the clay bust. "What you see is what I see when I look into your eyes."

Monique paused, took a slow breath, and sighed. "I'm afraid it's a curse an artist must learn to live with, whether sculptor or painter, if they have any hope of capturing the souls of their subjects. It's a sixth sense, which I've come to hate."

Something's wrong, Sean thought, and turned to face Monique. But she'd already looked away from his inquiring gaze before he could see what it was. Realizing she'd anticipated his move, heard his thought, he said sternly, "Don't hide from me.'' He took hold of her shoulders and turned her around. Her head was bowed. Her hair, which looked dry and lifeless, hid her face from him. He placed his hand under her chin, gently raised her head, then brushed her hair to either side of her face. *Oh my God!*

What had once been soft and smooth, though misshapen, was now hard, and etched with age: flesh turned to stone overnight. Her eyes were cold and gray, and set deep in her face. What little light there was to be seen was far away, beyond his reach. Her lips were thin and cracked. And there was a hint of blood where it appeared she'd bitten herself, and not just once or twice, but repeatedly, as if in pain. Sean cupped Monique's face in his hands, bent down, and kissed her—once, then again—moistening her parched lips with his own.

''You must go,'' she said in a whisper, fatigue weighing down her words.

''Why?'' Sean asked defiantly. He refused to release his hold of her when she tried shrugging his hands off her shoulders and slipping free. ''What's happening?'' he asked, jostling her ever so gently in an effort to get her to look at him. ''And what are these figures here?'' He gestured around the studio, singling out each of the three shrouded figures with a point of his finger, before returning to the one beside him. ''Or should I ask, *who* are they?''

Monique gave Sean what he wanted and looked up, her eyes no longer dry like her lips, but moist, glistening in the glare of the spotlight. She tried to smile but couldn't. ''You know who they are,'' she said, a clear note of contempt ringing in her voice, but with the gentleness of a wind chime in a quiet morning breeze.

Without looking, she pointed to the figure along the left wall and paused, an expectant look in her eyes—the only part of her face that seemed able to reveal her feelings. She cocked her head to one side toward the figure, as if prodding Sean to answer her. ''Just feel it.'' A thin thread of impatience was holding her words together. ''The names are there. Only their faces have changed now that their souls are bared. For all but one, that is, and he—'' She turned away.

Irritated, Sean shook his head. "This is ridiculous. I'm not some psychic. I can't read your—"

"Stop it!" Monique growled angrily, startling him. "You know who they are—and *I* know you do. Just say their names," she ordered, and reached out, grabbing hold of his arm. Her fingers and thumb dug deep into his flesh, pinching the bone. Then she let go. For that brief and frightening moment, Sean was reminded of Monique's strength once more. No sooner had she pulled back than she took hold of him again, and with both hands, but meekly, making it appear as if she was suddenly in need of his help to keep from falling. She took a shallow breath. "Listen to your heart, Sean, like you did that first time we met. Say what you feel, not what you think."

Monique's hand slid off Sean's arm as she drifted backward up against the wall and sat on the edge of the large cube of black and silver marble. With obvious difficulty, she pointed to the cloaked figure across the studio. "Well?" she asked. "Who is *he*?"

Sean was certain he could see a spark in her eye, which warmed his heart. He smiled. "What do I get if I win?" he asked, making his question sound like a dare, and trying to get her to smile.

Monique stood up, as if to accept his challenge, but with reluctance. For a moment it looked like she might collapse. Sean started for her, but was held back when she closed her eyes and shook her head. Moving stiffly, she walked past him and came to a stop beside the covered figure, which was standing just beyond the pedestal holding the bust of Sean's head. As she grabbed a fistful of the soiled linen, Monique looked over at Sean, that spark in her eyes now a fire, burning bright.

Too bright, Sean thought. *Something's wrong—very wrong.*

Monique nodded, her eyes shut, as if to acknowledge what Sean thought he'd seen. Then she raised the back of the shroud up over the top of the figure, held it—eyeing Sean doubtfully—and dropped it onto the outstretched arms of the clay sculpture, exposing its identity, while leaving whatever was cradled in its hands still hidden from view. "Is this prize enough?" she asked sarcastically as the light in her eyes appeared to grow brighter.

Whatever emotions the head of Christ had unwillingly ripped from Sean's heart when his gaze had fallen upon it, they paled in comparison to what he now felt as he stared at the disfigured face and misshapen form before him: He was overcome with more pain than he'd ever thought possible, made bearable only by the love washing over him when he realized how he felt about Monique as he stared back into the face of the sculpture. It was her face, each masterful turn and twist of the clay shaped by the agony of ages. Her eyes were pleading—demanding!—to be set free from a body not chosen but given. Countless souls were imprisoned just beneath the shiny surface of the clay, screaming to be heard above the deafening march of time, advancing to a beat not theirs but His.

Sean suddenly wanted to hold her, to tell her how he felt, not what he thought. He stepped forward but was stopped, breathless, when Monique lifted the linen shroud off the rest of her creation, revealing what her mirrored image was holding. In a heartbeat, confidence turned to confusion, compassion to revulsion, and love to hate when Sean saw the head of the polychromed bronze, reproduced in clay, balanced in one hand, so real, so beautiful, she appeared to be alive and breathing. In the other outstretched hand was a human heart, so lifelike that Sean thought he could see it beating—and in time with his own heart!—and couldn't help covering his chest with his hand.

Monique released her fingertip hold of the shroud and let it fall to the floor at her feet. "Love or hate, Dr. MacDonald?" she asked, her words covered with ice. "Which is it this time?"

Sean forced himself not to think; words no longer seemed necessary between them. Dividing his attention between Monique, who willingly gave up her gaze to him, as if taunting him, and her metaphorical self-portrait, Sean said with an ease that surprised him, "That was cruel of you to play with me that way. To wait until I'd given myself up to her—to you—before showing me the rest of the work.'' Monique appeared to be amused, but said nothing. "Is this your last piece?" he asked bitterly. "Your final statement? Shall we call it *Deception*?"

Monique replied wearily, "No more questions. Only answers."

"Why are you speaking in riddles?"

"Perhaps because we are little more than riddles ourselves."

Defying her baleful gaze, a fiery facade of unspoken threats, Sean took Monique in his arms. "You're angry with me, aren't you? Why? What have I done?"

Monique stiffened, then relaxed and laid her head on Sean's chest. She sighed. "I shouldn't have let you make love to me last night. It was a terrible mistake. Please forgive me."

This was the last thing Sean expected to hear Monique say to him. While still guarding himself against an errant thought that might expose a side of him not even he knew about, he asked, "Why was it a mistake? I don't understand. You didn't force me. I wanted—"

Monique shook her head and pushed herself away from Sean, beyond his immediate reach, and turned her back. "You must go."

No, I'm not going to leave until I know—

"Don't argue with me. Just do it!"

His patience wearing thin, feeling himself growing angry, and not liking how he felt, Sean stepped forward and spun Monique around to face him. "I'm not going anywhere until—"

"Yes—you must!" Monique grabbed Sean, pushing him toward the entrance of her studio. He stumbled and caught his balance, and stood looking at Monique in disbelief. The effort needed to do what she'd done appeared to have drained whatever renewed energy she'd found. She steadied herself and said calmly, her voice strained, "Please, you must go, Sean. I can't stop her anymore, I don't have the strength. You don't understand what's—"

She looked away, unable—or unwilling—to face him.

"I'm truly sorry," she whispered, bowing her head. "I couldn't even stop her last night." Monique looked up, her eyes suddenly filled with tears. "That's why I said I shouldn't have let you make love to me, that it was a terrible mistake." She seemed unable to speak for a moment. "You may not remember now—that's her way—but someday the memories will all return, and you'll know."

Upon hearing Monique say this, one fragment after another spiked up from Sean's unconscious. The less he fought it, the sharper her form became, though unseen, until he could feel her around him, over him, suffocating him. Her lips were hard, her tongue cold, her bite sharp. She burned his skin wherever she touched him. She drained his life away all over again. He let it happen, accepted the pain, choosing, wanting to remember. He cut his fingers on every piece of broken glass he picked up and forced back into place, recreating a hideous reflection in his mind: her cracked face, her sulfurous breath, her cruel, unwanted touch.

As he fitted the final pieces into the shattered mirror of his mind, Sean could see the idyllic polychromed image beside that of Monique's, the antithesis of beauty. At first they appeared as opposite poles. Yet as they came into focus, one over the other, then one beside the other, there was something similar about them.

What is it? he wondered. He searched his thoughts, reclaiming every word spoken, every image seen, every sensation, welcomed or not. Nothing seemed to fit, until he glanced over at Monique, her penetrating gaze telling him that she'd heard his every thought.

That's it! He walked up to her and looked down into her eyes, which were now clear and dry, and once again cold and gray. He shivered at their touch, then stepped around her and over to the sculpture. He stood in front of it, examining the earthen faces before him, comparing every detail, still touched by what he saw.

"She *is* you!" he said with a sense of discovery.

"No," Monique replied solemnly. Sadly. "I am *her*."

Hearing this, Sean smiled, fitting the last piece of the metaphorical puzzle into place. "Must I now choose between them?'' he asked, gesturing to the likeness of Monique, the severed head of the goddess, in clay, and the heart of a man lying in the other outstretched hand. He motioned to the shrouded figures around the studio. "Just as they did?"

"See," Monique said, an undeniable note of conceit in her voice as she gestured around the studio to two of the three shrouded figures. "You do know those men." She walked over and stood beside him. Silent.

"Am I there?" he asked, his gaze lazily moving from figure to figure, before returning to the clay model before him. "Or is *this* me?" He reached out to touch the exquisitely sculpted heart, every layer of muscle finely detailed, every artery pumped full of blood. As his finger drew closer, the heart appeared to begin beating ever so faintly.

With blinding speed, Monique grabbed his wrist and pulled his hand back. "You *must* go," she whispered, her command sounding more like a threat. "You've grown too confident. Too proud."

Sean stopped trying to pull himself free of her hold. "Is it because you're finished with me?" he asked. "*Both* of you?"

Ignoring his questions, Monique started for the door with him in tow. He dug his heels in, straining her already weakened resolve. "Answer me," he demanded angrily.

"Please, don't do this," she begged. "You don't know—"

"No!" he argued, and violently pulled Monique to him. "I'm not leaving until you tell me what—"

Sean was silenced, his anger cooled, when he looked down into Monique's eyes and for the first time thought—knew—he could see her soul, stripped bare. Before he could speak, tell her what he saw, she pulled him down to her and kissed him, tenderly, and whispered, "You were right." She held her breath—her eyes now closed to him, cold, though still wide open—and sighed. "That was to be your heart, but it was not I who—"

A deafening screech, then another, was followed by the furious flapping of wings and the scratching of claws in the loft overhead, muffling Monique's words. She fell against Sean, into his arms, frail and cold, shaking. These all-too-familiar sounds were joined by the nerve-jarring grating of metal scraping against metal, sending needles of fire down Sean's spine, exploding into his loins.

"Come," Monique said secretively, and took Sean by the hand, this time gently, and led him across the dimly lit studio to the locked door. There, she caressed his face with her open hand—her own face suddenly decades older than it was only moments before—and kissed him once more. Then, with the strength he once knew her to have, Monique eased Sean outside, deaf to his protests to stay.

Chapter Forty-three

Naked and dripping wet from the steaming-hot shower he'd just taken, Sean was standing in the open doorway of his bathroom and staring aimlessly down the long, narrow hallway into the kitchen at the far end. A green terry-cloth towel was hanging from his loosely clenched fist and falling onto the white ceramic tiles.

I'm starving, he thought, and started down the hall to the kitchen, the wet towel trailing behind him over the Oriental runner. He paused every few steps to pick up, piece by piece, the clothing he'd discarded on his weary walk from the kitchen to the bathroom less than ten minutes before. The last item, but the first to have been shed—his shoes—he opted to kick into his bedroom as he walked past on his way to the kitchen.

With a bundle of clothes cradled in his arms, the towel thrown over his shoulder, Sean leaned up against the painted wood trim framing the archway to the kitchen and settled back to watch the sunlight as it completed its daily journey down the wall opposite the windows on its way to the shiny linoleum floor of the old Victorian kitchen. Streaks of bright yellow light slipped off the wall onto the floor and crept over the embossed quarry tiles, turning them crimson red, the seams of fake mortar dark gray.

Chased by the heat of the rising sun, a cool breeze blew in through the open windows, sending a piece of paper tumbling off the lacquered maple table. Sean watched as it fluttered through the air—stalled—and fell into a puddle of sunlight on the floor. It was a page torn in haste from a wire-bound notebook, and folded over in half. He could see his name boldly written in dark blue ink on one side, and repeatedly circled. *Oliver?* he thought, wondering who could have left him a note. *It must be,* he decided as he walked over to pick it up. *He's the only one who has a key.*

But the moment Sean was close enough to make out the handwriting, he knew the missive wasn't from Oliver. Tossing his clothes onto the table, he bent down and picked up the mysterious sheet of paper, wondering who it could be as he unfolded it.

"What the hell were *you* doing here?" he muttered when he saw Pamela's signature slashed across the bottom of the page.

He scanned the cryptic note.

Sean—

It's 5:00. Sorry I missed you. On my way to find Gerard and get some answers. Directions I had were off, and I got lost. So much for the police! Thought you might help—after I apologized for being such a shit, of course.

In your absence, I'm going to find Oliver and see if he can set me straight on how to get to Gerard's farm. I think he said he often works in his office at this hour. So I'll try him there first, before dragging him out of bed.

I know, right about now you're thinking I'm a selfish bitch. Well, I suppose you're right.

Hopefully, however, you're wrong about that car you said you saw in a barn on Gerard's farm. If you are, then I won't even bother the woman. The police can sort this whole thing out from here on in, for all I care.

But if you were right—and I find my father's car there—she has some explaining to do. And I don't intend to leave until she does.

God help that woman if she had anything to do with my father's disappearance.

Ciao.

Selfish? Sean thought. "Stupid is more like it," he growled, and spun around, the towel flying off his shoulder as he raced down the hall to his bedroom, trying not to think of what Pamela might do after she found her father's car.

What the hell time is it? he thought, wanting to know how long before Pamela had been here and left. He glanced at his wrist, only to find it bare. He remembered having taken his watch off and set it on the back of the sink before hopping into the shower.

"Shit," he muttered when he saw the face of the clock radio on the nightstand beside his bed and realized she had an hour head start. *Maybe Ollie didn't stay and work last night,* he thought, and began dressing with the speed of a man caught in a married woman's bedroom when her husband has just come home unexpectedly.

But Sean knew his old friend all too well—*He's a creature of habit,* he thought—and was certain Pamela would have found him still working in his office. *The poor bastard.*

Maybe he won't tell her was Sean's next thought as he stuffed his bare feet into his loafers, darted out into the kitchen, double-jumped down the stairs, and threw open the screen door. Stepping out onto the porch, he took aim at his car in the driveway, across the lawn still wet from the night's soaking rain.

"Don't bet on it," he muttered as he ran to the car, his shirttails flying about.

* * *

Oliver squinted through the hazy glare of the sun bouncing off the hood of Sean's Healy and into his eyes as he read the roadside sign up ahead. "The entrance ramp is six-tenths of a mile," he said, and glanced nervously at Sean, the speedometer, which was hovering at sixty, and braced himself. He checked his seat belt, snugged it tightly around his prodigious chest and stomach, grabbed hold of the door handle with one hand, the underside edge of his bucket seat with the other, and jammed his oversized feet up against the floorboard. "Must we go so fast?" he asked for the umpteenth time since leaving Merrywood Hall.

Smiling at Oliver's reaction to his speed—*Five fucking miles over the limit!* he thought—but still ignoring Oliver's request, Sean downshifted and turned into the sweeping right-hand curve. The tires squealed in protest over the recently poured concrete as he accelerated up the ramp onto the Taconic Parkway, heading south. He quickly dropped it into fourth, pushed it to eighty, and slipped into fifth gear before backing off and asking somewhat impatiently, "How do you know she had a gun?" He cocked his head to one side, his gaze fixed on the road ahead of him, waiting for Oliver's reply.

Oliver said indignantly, "Because I saw it!" With his right hand, he reached over and patted the left side of his barrel chest. "She was wearing a shoulder holster. It was right there, out in the open. She wasn't hiding it. Scared the bloody daylights out of me when I saw her standing in the doorway of my office. For a minute, I thought she was going to shoot me!"

Sean said with a shake of his head, "The woman's crazy," and began nervously working the thick wood-rimmed steering wheel with his hands, squeezing, then rubbing the wheel, as if polishing it with his bare hands.

Oliver finally released his stranglehold on the door handle, but kept his hand on his seat and his feet against the floorboard. His reply was soft-spoken, a tempering note of caution in his voice. "I don't think so, Sean. Obsessed, maybe—and more than a bit headstrong, perhaps even egotistical—but not

351

crazy. Quite honestly, I think she simply wants justice to be served in the name of her father. You can't fault her for that.''

Sean wasn't buying in to Oliver's sudden swell of compassion. ''Justice? Try revenge. Or how about jealousy?'' he snarled sarcastically. ''No matter how you cut it, my friend, it's not for her to decide what to do. It's up to the authorities.''

Oliver sat up, bristling. ''I see. So that's what you did after you were attacked. And again, after we found those cars. You went to the police?'' Oliver harrumphed and folded his arms over his portly midsection. ''And I suppose that's also why you told that detective from the City, Marcelli, that you didn't recognize the woman in that composite sketch when, in fact, you really did recognize her.'' Frowning, he turned and looked at Sean. ''Perhaps the gentleman doth protest too much.''

Oliver waited, but Sean didn't say a word in his own defense. He sighed, sounding exasperated. ''Sean, this isn't like you. What's going on? Why are you acting like this?'' He scrunched himself around to look at Sean directly. ''It's her—Gerard—isn't it? You know something you're not telling me, don't you?'' He bit his lip, a gesture not like him. ''Or is this personal?''

Sean suddenly jerked the wheel—left, then right—slipping around the slow-moving VW Beetle in front of him. Oliver was thrown forward into the door, then back, his neck snapping down when the seat belt locked up and kept him from hitting Sean. He glanced at the speedometer, making no effort to be discreet about it. Turning back, he assumed his earlier position, only this time he placed one hand on the dash, his arm locked, instead of grabbing hold of the door handle. Staring straight ahead, he said in his most mannerly British way, ''Isn't a hundred miles an hour a bit fast, even for this car? Aren't we pushing it a bit?''

Sean stiffened, toyed with going faster out of spite—but only for a moment—then eased back with a sigh and let off the gas. Oliver tipped sideways and watched the needle fall to seventy. Now moving only slightly faster than traffic, which was light, even for a Saturday morning, Sean took a deep breath and shook his head. Although he started to, his lips moving, he didn't say anything.

Oliver folded his hands in his lap—his sense of security apparently restored—and held on to his silence too. They sat there, nearly shoulder to shoulder in the small roadster, staring blankly ahead, each stubbornly waiting for the other to say something first. Or perhaps they both simply needed a moment or two to calm down. To take a few minutes to think about what had happened, what each had said to the other in anger those first few minutes after Sean had barged into Oliver's office, still half dressed, and let loose with a fusillade of questions, such as "Was she here?" "When?" "Did you tell her how to get Gerard's?" "How long ago did she leave?" "Why did you let her go!" pinning Oliver into his overstuffed armchair. His only possible reply was a curt nod or shake of his head, even in response to Sean's accusations, castigating him for not "having the fucking balls to tell the woman to go to hell," when Pamela had become incensed over Oliver's evasiveness.

When Oliver had finally succeeded in getting a word in edgewise with Sean, and tried explaining to him exactly what had happened, what he'd told Pamela, and that he'd pleaded with her to "please wait and talk with Sean about this," Sean was too wound up to pay any attention to what he was saying. It wasn't until Oliver had raised his voice and bellowed, "Will you please shut up for one bloody minute!" that Sean stopped pacing nervously about the office and sat down on the windowsill to listen to what Oliver had to say, without interrupting him, which required a patient but firm reminder now and then from Oliver.

Sean was the one who spoke first, a tenuous calm in his voice. "You began to say something back in your office about the sketches I made of the polychromed bronze in Monique's studio, the ones I put in the back of the portfolio I left with you." He glanced over at Oliver, who was already looking at him, a scowl still on his face. "I'm sorry for being such a shit," he said. "I don't know what got into me, it—"

Sean frowned when he saw Oliver's eyes grow wide open, his forehead wrinkle into knotted furrows. But he persisted nonetheless, determined to explain his behavior. "Maybe you're right—no, you *are* right—this thing is personal." He held his hand up when it appeared Oliver was going to say something. "Don't even ask—at least not now—you won't believe it if I tell you." He laughed. "I'm not even sure I do." He turned his attention back to the road. "So, what was it you wanted to tell me?" he asked, and skirted around another car, this time a Volvo station wagon, making him think of that woman at the Met he'd frightened.

When he glanced down to check the gauges, Sean noticed he'd let his speed drop off, and he leaned on the gas, telling Oliver when he stirred, "Relax—this isn't your Morris. This Healy is good for well over a hundred and twenty." He nudged it a few ticks past eighty. "So?" he asked blithely. "What has the scholar found now?"

Oliver became very still, his head bowed, his bushy red beard resting on his chest. "I think I now know for certain what that bronze is supposed to represent," he said solemnly. His deep baritone voice added extra weight to his impending disclosure.

Sean perked up. He'd come to heed Oliver's sudden change of moods. He was all ears, even though his attention was now riveted to the road, which had broken up into a series of sharp S curves tracing the edge of steep, stone-faced cliff. "And?" he asked, and leaned sideways to hear what Oliver was going to say.

Oliver sighed. "After Ms. Eagleston described Mademoiselle Gerard to me this morning—and not in very flattering terms, I might add—I began to think about the metaphor—" He paused.

Get on with it, will you! Sean wanted to say. But he knew that to do so would only slow Oliver down that much more. Perhaps even cause him to shut down if he wasn't sure of himself, something that Sean had learned, and come to use as a weapon in their verbal jousts. "And it is?" he asked patiently when he thought the timing right.

Oliver turned to look at Sean. "Is the woman *really* a hunchbacked dwarf?" he asked, an incredulous look on his face. "And is she as ugly as—"

"No!" Sean snapped, angrily cutting Oliver's question off. "She is *not* ugly. Yes, she *is* deformed, but that's—" Sean abruptly stopped talking and sat thinking for a moment, wondering, *What are you saying? Tell him the truth, for chrissake! What difference does it make what she looks like, it's what she is that counts.* He began to say, "Monique is—" but faltered again, still unsure of what he really wanted to say to Oliver. "Her work is beautiful," he finally spit out. "That's what matters, not what she looks like."

Oliver sat with a startled look on his face, staring at Sean in disbelief. Then he took a deep breath and said, "At any rate, I'm afraid I was terribly wrong about that bronze."

Sean turned, an eyebrow raised, thinking, *You? Wrong!* But he said nothing. However, Oliver had seen his reaction out of the corner of his eye and acknowledged it with an awkward shrug of his shoulders that told Sean he was ashamed of what he'd done, ashamed of his bravado.

Oliver continued. "I now realize that Gerard modeled that work after the ancient Hindu god Vishnu, who, according to Hindu scriptures, was reincarnated in many forms. According to the religious epic *Mahabharata*, specifically the *Bhagavad Gita*, Vishnu took the form of ten creatures—avatars, reborn from age to age to protect the virtuous. The innocents. Interestingly enough, the fifth form of Vishnu was Vamana, a dwarf with extraordinary powers, who, it was believed, returned to earth to recover areas of the mortal world from the demons of evil."

With his speed rising above a hundred again, Sean sat arranging and rearranging his thoughts, slipping in what Oliver had just said alongside what he knew, or thought he did, what he'd seen, each of her allegorical creations, and what he'd felt. And most important, what frightened him. With each association, the word *avatar* appeared—a term he knew all too well from his own research and teaching—juxtapositioned with mirrored images of Monique, the self-portrait she'd created, and the polychromed bronze. As if talking to himself, Sean said quietly, "Monique didn't sculpt that bronze, the one I sketched. Does that mean anything?"

Oliver appeared miffed. "How do you know that?" he asked, challenging Sean to explain himself. "Did she tell you that?"

He didn't see the work, Sean thought. *Go easy on him.*

"Because there's no similarity whatsoever in style. Nothing. That work is as different as night is from day from all of Monique's other pieces." He looked at Oliver and said with an understanding smile on his face, "You didn't see the original bronze, only my half-assed sketches, so it's not really fair."

Oliver peered at Sean over his wire-rimmed glasses. "Well, whatever," he said with a shrug of his shoulders. "It doesn't really matter, anyway. It's all no more than pagan mythology."

"Mythology?" Sean asked disapprovingly.

Oliver nodded confidently and said brashly, "Of course. We all know reincarnation is no more than a myth. A fairy tale."

"I see. Then what would you call that *thing* that nearly ripped your heart out? Tinkerbell?" Sean asked sarcastically, and suddenly began pumping the brakes, hauling the car down to a safe speed when he saw the exit for Old Country Road hurtling toward him. "Hold on!" he told Oliver as they flew down the ramp.

Chapter Forty-four

"See anything?" Sean asked anxiously as he skittered to a stop in the shallow, wet grass just off the gravelly shoulder of the road, directly in front of the abandoned rear entrance to Monique's farm.

Oliver sat up and leaned out the window, his gaze sweeping the field back to the dense cluster of trees hiding the old farmhouse and barn, visible only in his mind's eye because he now knew they were there, not because he could actually see them. "I'm afraid she's already been here." With a wave of his hand, he pointed out into the field. "There's a footpath in the grass leading straight back to the trees, and a second one returning." He pulled himself back into the car and glanced over at Sean, his wire-rimmed glasses buried in the wrinkles of a serious frown. "We're too late."

Sean took a whack at the steering wheel with the heel of his hand. "Shit!" He slammed it into first and made a sharp U-turn, fishtailing down the other side of the road—half on the gravel-covered shoulder, half off—spitting stones everywhere.

A moment later, Oliver gasped and grabbed hold of his

seat when Sean flew into a sharp left turn without slowing down. The tires chattered and growled over the rain-slick macadam as the car drifted sideways, out of control. Sean downshifted, floored it, and turned into the skid, regaining control. Then he raced headlong down the center of the road, straddling the white line.

After a few steadying breaths, Oliver released his hold on the seat and folded his hands into a ball of knuckles in his lap. "What are you going to do if she's there?" he asked apprehensively.

Sean bit his lip, hesitated. "I don't know." He shook his head ever so subtly, as if arguing with someone. "I only hope she doesn't—" He stopped himself from letting his imagination get the better of him, and muttered, "I honestly don't know, Ollie."

Sean wasn't just saying this; he truly didn't know what he would do if—*not if, when!*—he found Pamela in Monique's studio. The thought of those two women facing each other, one a bull in a china shop, the other a pillar of stone, unyielding, left him with little hope and fearing the worst. And it wasn't because he couldn't think clearly, either, since his thoughts were his own, and had been ever since he had awoken earlier that morning, only he hadn't realized it until he read Pamela's note, and could do nothing else but think from that point on, easily and clearly, and without being distracted. He could recall every minute detail of what he'd seen, what he'd felt, inside and out, and every sound he'd heard last night and this morning. Everything was vividly etched into his mind, so deep he couldn't have forgotten even if he wanted to. A sudden chill passed through him, bringing with it those unwanted sensations, and wouldn't leave when he tried shivering them away.

Oh my God! he thought, pushing his Healy even faster. "Something's wrong," he said under his breath, catching Oliver's ear. "Something's terribly wrong, I just know it."

Appearing momentarily curious about what Sean had muttered, yet obviously mired deep in his own thoughts, Oliver paused, then asked tentatively, "Do you think that . . ." He seemed to be struggling with his question. He abruptly sat up straight, threw his shoulders back, and asked quickly, "Do you think she'd actually use that gun?"

Sean replied, "In a second."

Oliver nodded, but reluctantly, and sat staring out the window. He no longer seemed concerned about the way Sean was driving, now buried even deeper in his own thoughts. Now and then he nodded, shook his head, or shrugged his shoulders. Once or twice he mumbled something under his breath.

Sean threw caution to the wind as he raced pell-mell down the narrow country roads bordering the perimeter of Monique's huge old horse farm, ignoring tight bends and rusting stop signs sinking into the summer grass. What had once taken him twenty minutes was covered in less than half that time, and without a single word being spoken by either man, as if each was mustering his thoughts, preparing for the unknown.

"Bloody hell!" Oliver gasped when Sean suddenly stomped on the brakes and spun out into a tight three-sixty, coming to a dead stop facing in the opposite direction. On Oliver's right was the pair of split-rail fences bracketing the overgrown road leading back to Monique's studio. Glancing out the window, he took a deep breath and gestured, his hand still shaking. "Looks like someone drove off the road here not long ago." He glanced at Sean. "Now what?"

Sean whispered somberly, "Pray," as he turned and pulled off the road into the tall, wet grass. Oliver began fidgeting and nervously rubbing his hands on his pant legs, as if trying to iron out the creases in his winter-weight gray wool slacks, as Sean accelerated through the grass, holding it in second gear. The car slithered side to side and thumped up and down as they slipped in and out of ruts and bumped over loose stones hidden in the grass.

"There!" he said, startling Oliver. "That's her car."

With a tap of the gas, Sean sped up for the last fifty yards and slid to a stop alongside Pamela's pearl-white Maserati, the top down, the rear fender spattered with mud and blades of wet grass. Sean was out of the car before Oliver could unsnap his seat belt and stood drumming his hands impa-

359

tiently on the ragtop as his gaze nervously flitted back and forth between Pamela's car, a black windbreaker lying on the passenger seat, and the door of Monique's studio, which was ajar a few inches. Oliver finally freed his chunky frame from the cramped quarters of the small roadster and climbed out with a groan. He turned to Sean, who gave a final slap of the leather top and said, "You wait here, I'll go see if—"

A scream—"No!"—but filled with anger, not fear, severed Sean's words from his thoughts. Before he could take a step, a gunshot shattered what little there was left of the morning calm. One, two, three more shots rang out, followed by an all-too-familiar high-pitched screech—the sound of steel fingernails scratching the face of a blackboard—then an eerie hush.

Sean was halfway to the door when another shot rang out, and a second—that bloodcurdling screech again—and a scream. It was that same woman's voice, only this time it was choked off with pain. *Pamela?* Sean thought as he blocked the door open and burst into the studio, which was riddled with clusters of white-hot spotlights, knifing down from the ceiling and slicing holes in the dark, resurrecting each of the sleeping figures, now stripped bare.

"Jesus Christ!"

Lying in a rapidly expanding pool of blood on the floor in the center of the studio was one of the hideous winged creatures, the center of its chest and half its face blown open, its clawed hands and ugly head twitching, its white canine teeth snapping blindly at the air.

Oliver gasped, "Bloody hell!" echoing Sean's reaction as he stumbled to a stop beside him, struggling to catch his breath.

A muffled cry of pain ripped Sean's gaze from the beast writhing on the floor and drew it into the shadows in the far right corner of the studio. "Pamela!" he yelled, and raced toward the second hideous creature, clinging to Pamela's back, its huge wings—one strong, the other limp, blood dripping from its tip onto the floor—wrapped around her body. Its teeth were sunk deep into her shoulder. One claw was clutching her throat, the other, blood spurting from a wound on its long, sinewy arm, feebly scratching at her chest, her heart, tearing her shirt open.

Sean lunged for the beast, intent on pulling it off Pamela's back, only to be thrown aside by a swipe of the creature's powerful wing, the sharp leathery edge slicing across his chest. He rolled over and over onto his back, then scrambled to his feet—his blue denim shirt torn and stained bloodred—determined to try again.

Before he could, Pamela freed one hand from underneath the cloak of the beast's wing, revealing a pistol in her clenched fist. Reaching back over her shoulder, she jammed the butt of the gun into one eye of the gargoyle and pulled the trigger—once, twice. Tissue exploded out the back of the creature's head. She squeezed again, only to have it click a third time, the magazine empty.

With a deafening screech, the beast raised its grotesque head, blood oozing from the empty socket. It opened its mouth wide, this time to sink its razor-sharp teeth into Pamela's neck.

Out of nowhere came a blur—a human projectile—as Oliver threw himself at the beast, matching its cries with one of his own, bellowing like a wild man. The impact split them apart. Pamela was knocked facedown, her arms and legs spread out, the gun still locked in her fist. The creature, its one good wing flapping furiously, the other useless, bleeding, was thrown back up against the wall. Oliver tumbled head over heels and came to rest at its feet, faceup, gasping for air, his glasses lying on the floor beside him.

Sean was at Pamela's side, helping her to her feet. ''Are you all—''

She angrily knocked him aside, and with lightning speed ejected the clip from her pistol, replacing it with one she pulled from the back pocket of her jeans. In a breath, she was on one knee, arms out straight, both hands locked onto the walnut grip of the Luger. She fired—once, twice—striking the creature in the chest as it was about to pounce on Oliver, pinning it to the wall. It let out a terrifying cry, this time more human than animal.

Unaffected, an oasis of calm, Pamela raised her aim, exhaled slowly, and squeezed off one more shot, erasing the creature's other eye from its blood-spattered face, scattering what was left of its reptilian brain all over the wood-paneled wall. As it fell forward, Oliver rolled out of the way and over his glasses.

Pamela stood up and rushed to Oliver's side, the pistol held in front of her, ready to fire again if needed.

Monique! Sean thought, and spun around, searching for her. As he did, moving cautiously, he was quickly set upon by the clay sculptures surrounding him, watching him, as he started across the cavernous studio. He recognized two of the figures instantly, their bodies and faces twisted into cruel metaphorical poses, instantly recognizable and befitting their respective crimes. A third, unfamiliar to Sean upon first glance, was tall and handsome, the look of a god in man's garb. He stood alone, a eulogy of some sort, untouched by Monique's poetic—though frightening—justice.

Sean's determined advance was slowed to a dead stop when he suddenly placed the face of the man into a photograph mounted in a miniature gilded frame, an adoring young girl with long red pigtails standing at his side, smiling proudly, her hand in his.

Before his emotions could catch up with his thoughts, Sean was distracted by a movement across the studio. He looked up and saw Monique, standing beside the stunning clay portrait of herself, her head bowed, her arms limp at her side. She appeared unable to stand, about to fall. His chest tightened, his thoughts clouded but out of concern for her, not stolen. He broke stride and ran to her, refusing to deal with what he'd just seen, and deaf by unconscious choice to the muted sounds behind him of metal creaking and twisting, as if being bent out of shape.

"Are you all right?" he asked as he gently placed his hand on her shoulder, his anxious gaze blanketing her, looking to see if she'd been harmed in any way. "Did she—"

"No." Monique sighed and looked up. "She did not harm me—she has no cause to."

Oh my God! Sean thought when he saw Monique's face, cracked and looking like it would crumble to dust with the slightest touch. Her dark, deep-set eyes, more black than gray, seemed to come to life as she looked into Sean's eyes. She struggled to breathe, and said through a labored exhalation, "You must go. All of you. I—"

"No," Sean replied in a soft yet firm voice. "I'm not leaving you. I shouldn't have left you this morning. You tricked me," he said with a strained smile. He gestured with a toss of his head, motioning behind him. "I'm not afraid of *her*."

When he slipped his arm around Monique to draw her to him, Sean felt her bones, thin and frail, no longer girdled by her once powerful but deformed body. Confused, trying to make sense of what he saw, what he felt—what was happening—he said, "I don't know why I'm not afraid, and I don't care. It's not important anymore. I'm staying," he said defiantly. "Until—"

He caught himself. "I'm staying—that's all there is to it."

Monique reached up and placed her hand on Sean's face, her withered fingers, no longer twisted and gnarled but long and graceful, slowly tracing his every feature before slipping down and coming to rest over his heart. "Thank you," she said, barely above a whisper. "You gave me what no man would. You saw who I was, not what I appeared to be. And you took nothing from me, unlike all the others I trusted. I—"

Monique abruptly grew quiet, her body bitterly cold, a wall of ice against Sean. He felt his chest tighten, his breath grow short. A sharp pain knifed down his arm, curling his fingers into an unwanted fist. Monique sighed and said, "You must move my hand." She tried doing it, but couldn't. Sean did, gently holding her hand at his side. Monique whispered, "I can no longer stop her, and she knows that. You must go. Please?"

About to argue with her, Sean was distracted by the dull clunk of metal, hollow and tinlike. *No, it can't be,* he thought, his worst fears—thoughts buried deep in his unconscious—taking hold of him as he turned to see Oliver crawling about on his hands and knees, feeling around for his glasses, as the polychromed goddess moved toward him, awkwardly, stiffly, not yet flesh and blood but growing more lifelike, and more beautiful, with each mechanical step she took.

"Ollie!" Sean yelled. "Get out of here. Now!"

Oliver clumsily stumbled to his feet, his hands out in front of him as if trying to find the corridor of daylight pouring into the studio through the open door. Suddenly, Oliver grabbed his chest and stopped, as if frozen in place.

"Monique, do something," Sean pleaded. "Please!"

She pushed him away, waved for him to stay where he was, and took a labored step, then another, as she started across the studio. When she faltered, Sean was at her side, his arm around her waist, his other hand gently but firmly steadying her.

"No," she said, sounding stronger. "You *must* leave."

Glancing nervously, anxiously, over at Oliver, Sean saw Pamela, her shirt ripped half off her body, bleeding, step in front of Oliver, putting herself between him and the polychromed goddess, who hesitated, as if momentarily confused. Pamela slowly drew a two-handed bead on the bronze figure.

Monique suddenly stood up straight, as if the gun had been pointed at her. At that moment, the final piece fell into place for Sean—reality replacing fantasy, the subconscious rising into the conscious brain. "No!" he cried out. "Don't—"

A single shot echoed through the studio, the bullet striking the bronze figure directly over the heart, lodging itself deep in the metal, denting but not penetrating it.

Monique stumbled backward.

"Pamela!" Sean screamed. "Don't sh—"

The noise was deafening as Pamela emptied the magazine, each shot finding its mark, a target no larger than a silver dollar, pounding a crater deep into the bronze chest of the goddess. The last two bullets exploded through the weakened metal and ricocheted around inside the hollow sculpture as it fell backward and struck the floor, shattering into a thousand metallic shards, the shrill of breaking glass splintering the air.

Monique slumped back into Sean's arms, a deadweight. He slipped his hands around her to keep her from falling.

The moment he did, he felt the blood—warm and wet and thick—soaking through her silken caftan. *This isn't happening,* he thought as he gently laid her on the floor near the base of the clay figure, her long hair splayed out, thin and dry and brittle, and bone white.

Pamela was suddenly there, kneeling down on the other side of Monique. She threw the gun away and reached out, her hands shaking, hesitant, unsure. Without taking his gaze off Monique's face, Sean began to brush Pamela's unwanted touch away, but stopped, breathless, when he heard Pamela whisper in a frail and frightened childlike voice, "Mother, forgive me, I didn't—"

Mother! rang loudly inside Sean's head as he snapped around to look at Pamela. Tears were falling from her eyes, her watery gaze caressing Monique. Before he could speak—even before a thought could be found—Sean felt a hand on his arm, pulling him back. When he turned, Monique said softly, "My work is now in your hands." She smiled, faintly, painfully. "Care for it as you cared for me. Help others see it as you saw it, as you saw me. Not as some did, blinded by their own greed."

Monique struggled to raise her other hand. Pamela took it, cradling it to her breast, her face filled with unspeakable agony.

Sean glanced over his shoulder when he heard the shuffling thump of familiar footsteps behind him and saw Oliver approaching, his glasses perched at a crooked angle on the bridge of his nose, the wiry frames twisted and bent, the lenses cracked but intact.

"There's nothing left of her but little bits and pieces of metal," Oliver said in disbelief as he came to a wavering stop directly behind Sean and began trying to readjust his glasses.

"Sean!" Pamela cried.

Sean snapped around to see Monique's arm outstretched, the tip of her finger barely touching the base of the figure standing above them. The clay was glowing red hot, the smell of molten metal filling the air. They watched in awe, speechless, as the clay slowly turned to bronze, Monique's mirror image—her pallid flesh, every knotted muscle, each twisted bone, the cruel hollows of her face, the hypnotic abyss of her gaze, inquisitive, innocent, trusting—forever cast in time.

It was only now that Sean noticed the figure's one empty hand, no longer holding the heart of man—his heart—but instead raised up, held out, as if begging an answer to the ages-old question now posed. Sean smiled, certain he knew what she meant—unaware that his answer had already been given—as he looked down, and into the face of a goddess, a woman more beautiful than any he'd ever seen, yet a reflection of every one. Her emerald-green eyes burned with life's eternal flame—flickering, fading—only to be blown out with a final breath Sean felt pass through him. A frail whisper of three words unheard—forgotten—but always to be remembered.

THE TAKING

DONALD BEMAN

What could Sean McDonald possibly have done to deserve what is happening to him? He was a happy man with a beautiful family, a fine job, good friends and dreams of becoming a writer. Now bit by bit, his life is crumbling. Everything and everyone he values is disappearing. Or is it being taken from him? Someone or something is determined to break Sean, to crush his mind and spirit. A malicious, evil force is driving him to the very brink of insanity. But why him?

_4202-9 $4.99 US/$5.99 CAN